"Six one niner, Flagship. Repeat: We show no flight plan for you. Please activate your transponder immediately."

"They're onto us, Nathan," Sarah said quietly beside him.

Gina, the pilot in the lead interceptor was a Patroller, a flight leader, a top gun.

Nathan banked his fighter around the rocky pinnacle in the center of San Francisco's dry harbor. Gina squeezed off a blast from her pulse cannon.

Nathan barely had time to shout, "Hang on, Sarah," before his right wingtip tagged a traffic light and he lost control completely. The fighter skidded in on its belly along Market Street at nearly a hundred miles an hour.

"Sarah? Sarah, we've gotta go. Come on." He turned back to her. Some sharp piece of flying debris had slashed the side of her face and peeled back the false human skin on her cheek, revealing her true reptilian face.

She squeezed his hand, then she spoke with a hoarse whisper, "I love you, Nathan," and with her final breath she said, ". . . Make me proud . . ."

Nathan took a last look at Sarah, then took off running. The Patrollers were within a block of him when he heard a loud whistle and saw a scruffy kid beckoning urgently. Then the youth ducked back around the corner. Nathan followed, but stopped. He was on a dead end street and the kid was gone.

He was standing there breathing hard when he felt something grasp his ankle. It was the leathery hand of a human-Visitor half-breed, reaching up to him from a sewer.

Nathan dropped quickly into the shadowy, steamy sewer. He turned to see a scaly-faced girl reaching out to shake his hand as, her eyes bright, she grinned at him and said, "Hey, sailor. Welcome to San Francisco."

Praise for V: THE SECOND GENERATION

"Johnson was the creative mastermind behind the popular 1980s miniseries *V*. . . . This novel resumes the conflict via an irresistible plot twist. Johnson's energetic prose should give long-suffering *V* fans some new thrills."
—*Booklist*

"Johnson skillfully updates the '80s classic to the new world order, retaining the flavor of the original but adding fresh characters, twenty-first-century technology, and a heaping portion of environmental awareness." —Kate O'Hare, *Tribune Syndicate*

"A fast-paced action-adventure tale of the powerful and entitled Visitors . . . Johnson creates some surprising new characters and relationships." —*Pittsburgh Post-Gazette*

"Johnson's finale to his rousing sci-fi tale is a big winner . . . a breathlessly paced sci-fi adventure that I found irresistible and impossible to put down. Who doesn't love a thriller that revolves around an underground movement to overthrow brutal oppressors? I salute Kenneth Johnson, a very creative guy."
—*TheColumnists.com*

"Johnson's vision and creativity is unparalleled, and his vision of Earth after twenty years of Visitor reign is horrifying. Through amazingly descriptive and fascinatingly detailed passages, Johnson describes to us a world under fascist control, slowly being robbed of what it holds most dear." —*G-Pop.net*

"The novel is a great read. . . . Johnson doesn't waste a second of plot, and he does manage to create a thrilling story. While the story line has turned much darker than the previous *V* miniseries, fans of the *V* narrative will love this powerful submission.

This exhilarating new novel, *V: The Second Generation,* will keep readers locked in as it soars toward an astonishing finish both fulfilling and totally unanticipated."   —*Einsiders.com*

Praise for Kenneth Johnson's *V* Miniseries

"Right at the top we know that *V* isn't just another fling at science fiction—it is nothing less than a retelling of history—the rise of the Nazis done as a cautionary science fiction fable. For television this is probably a first. It is by politics and ideology that you will know *V*."   —*The New York Times*

"The best kind of science fiction: the kind that makes you think about the meaning of life on Earth. '*V*' is a morality tale, a story of how people react in the face of overwhelming tyranny."
                —*Star Tribune* (Minneapolis)

"*V* makes a mesmerizing nightmare."
                —Tom Shales, *The Washington Post*

"Victorious as sci-fi miniseries . . . Dazzling . . . An intelligent, imaginative, engrossing, sometimes shocking drama."
                —Kay Gardella, *Daily News* (New York)

ALSO BY KENNETH JOHNSON

*V: The Original Miniseries** (with A. C. Crispin)
An Affair of State (with David Welch)

*denotes a Tor book

V

THE SECOND GENERATION

KENNETH JOHNSON

A TOM DOHERTY ASSOCIATES BOOK
NEW YORK

This is a work of fiction. All of the characters, organizations, and events portrayed in this novel are either products of the author's imagination or are used fictitiously.

V: THE SECOND GENERATION

Edited by James Frenkel

A Tor Book
Published by Tom Doherty Associates, LLC
175 Fifth Avenue
New York, NY 10010

www.tor-forge.com

Tor® is a registered trademark of Tom Doherty Associates, LLC.

ISBN-13: 978-0-7653-5932-2
ISBN-10: 0-7653-5932-4

First Edition: February 2008
First Mass Market Edition: December 2008

Printed in the United States of America

0 9 8 7 6 5 4 3 2 1

1

THERE WAS NO MOON IN THE NIGHT SKY OVER THE HIGH SIERRAS and yet the snowcapped mountainscape had a very subtle wash of extremely soft illumination.

It was starlight. In the clear mountain air uncountable pinpoints of light, billions of them, thoroughly populated the infinitely deep black of the sky. And the powdery stardust of the Milky Way seemed airbrushed in a swath across the middle of the vast universe.

The only sound was the frigid night wind stirring the tall Sierra pines. Then came the low rumble of a small truck, which was in need of a new muffler.

A gray, four-door pickup with dusty California plates jostled around a stony hillside, its headlight beams grazing across the badly rutted dirt road. The truck's hard life was evident from its numerous dents and dings. On its front doors was the chipped logo of *Burton Construction.*

Riding in the backseat, Meyer was getting a bit stiff. His lower back ached dully. They had been driving for a very long time. He also felt the effects of the thinner air at the high altitude and their distant remove from civilization. He glanced out at the dark, dense forest, trying not to betray the uneasiness he felt as he spoke, "Boy, the fishing must be really good if you guys come all this way."

"It's worth it, sure as shit," Niblo said. He was riding shotgun in the front and swigging from a longneck beer bottle. Though Meyer couldn't see his face, he felt Niblo's attitude turn darker as the big man grumbled, "One of the few good lakes left ever since . . ." Niblo cut himself off, chewed the inside of his lip, took a long final swallow of beer, and tossed the bottle out the window. Like most everyone, Niblo had learned to be very careful about what he said even among friends, and he didn't know this Meyer guy at all.

From his rear seat, Meyer glanced at the back of Niblo's big head and watched the man's ponytail swing against his thick brown turtleneck. Meyer knew the rest of Niblo's sentence would have been, "Ever since *They* came." Meyer drew a breath and looked out his own side window. Through a momentary gap in the pine trees he could see Orion overhead. Since it was February the constellation was well up over the mountains to the south. Meyer knew that the two lower stars, Rigel and Saiph, which represented Orion's left toe and right knee, pointed east toward the brightest star in the black night sky. Being a part of *Canis Major* it had long been called The Dog Star. But Meyer knew that its ancient name was Sirius. It was the star system from which *They* had come.

The Visitors.

They had been "visiting" for a very long time now, over twenty years. Meyer pondered about how things had changed since they arrived. There had been so many phenomenal advancements. But other changes, too, changes that were more unsettling and enigmatic, changes about which Meyer was much less sanguine.

In the front seat, Niblo straightened his back, loosened the khaki fishing vest around his bulky body, lowered his chin in careful preparation, and then emitted a lengthy, raucous belch.

The driver of the pickup, a lean, rugged outdoorsman named Burton, smirked. "I am sure glad that came out the top."

"Hey, I can give you one of them others easy enough. Here you go"—Niblo reached out a fat pinkie toward Burton—"pull my finger."

Burton grinned. "Yeah, how 'bout you pull this, pal." He indicated the crotch of his own black leather pants.

In the backseat Meyer shook his head and chuckled. "What a couple of classy guys." He turned off the tiny book light he'd been using to look through a paperback mountain guide. Seat belt securely fastened, Meyer was smaller, gentler, nearly bald, and more urbane than the other two. He wore a pale blue button-down dress shirt that had gotten a bit too frayed to wear in to work, and a brown suede vest over it. Since he was not as outdoorsy as his companions, his crisp blue jeans hadn't yet faded. And his wife had ironed creases into them, which made him feel particularly out of keeping with his present company.

Niblo was a rhinoceros of a man who two decades earlier had been a solid high school fullback with dreams of going pro. A lack of self-discipline and far too many longnecks had squelched those plans many years ago, although Niblo always found it easier to blame others for his failure. He harbored a bitterness that could sometimes turn him nasty in an eyeblink. His eyes were narrow, too small for his chubby face, which had gone unshaven for several days. His thinning, stringy brown hair was pulled into a long ponytail.

"Definitely classy," Meyer reiterated good-naturedly.

"Hey, I warned you, man." Burton smiled at Meyer in the rearview mirror. Burton was quite handsome. A suntanned sort with thick dark hair, he had a retro mustache that curved around the corners of his mouth. All three men were dressed for the outdoors, but Burton's lean physique made his worn-in leather pants and gray turtleneck look by far the best. He was the kind of confident, humorous, reliable man's man that other men admired and felt comfortable with. Women were attracted to his understated machismo and his humor.

Meyer had met him when Burton's company did a small repair job on the Meyers' Sacramento kitchen. They'd gotten to talking about fishing, which Meyer had enjoyed as a kid in Northern California. Burton told him about this remote mountain lake and when Meyer volunteered a fuel cell for the journey, Burton gladly invited him along on a little weekend jaunt.

But after three hours in the pickup Meyer was ready to end the trek so he was very happy to hear Burton say, "Okay, the cabin's just around that bend. See? It's right up . . ." Burton stopped speaking and slowed the truck to a stop.

Meyer caught the mood shift and felt a low-grade anxiety stir within him. "What's wrong? Is something wrong?"

Burton whispered to Niblo, "You see that?"

"Damn straight I did."

"What?" Meyer frowned, his voice also low. "See what?"

Burton turned off the pickup's headlights. The darkness crowded in on Meyer, who unfastened his seat belt and leaned forward, his nerves getting more on edge. "See what? What is it? What's wrong?"

Burton pointed off toward the small log cabin that could be seen through the trees. It was an old, weathered place with a porch that had sagged slightly to one side over the years. "There." Burton was reacting to a faint blue glow that flickered within the cabin. They watched as it moved from one room to another.

Niblo shot a questioning glance at Burton, who nodded. Then they both climbed out quietly. Burton slipped into his ancient bomber jacket and pulled a flashlight from a pocket in the door. He handed a second one to Meyer, who was climbing out hesitantly. The icy mountain air added to the chill Meyer already felt. His breath showed as he whispered nervously, "Maybe we should go back down and let somebody know that—"

Niblo blew out a derisive puff in Meyer's direction. "Aw, I reckon we can handle this, big guy." He hefted a double-barreled shotgun from a duffel bag in the back of the truck, cracked it open, and slipped in two shells. Then he stuffed a handful of additional shells into one of the wide pockets of his fisherman's vest.

Meyer looked toward Burton, who was checking the chambers in a handgun. Burton's voice was calm, level, and very confident. "You just stay behind me with that flashlight, okay, pard?" He winked encouragingly at Meyer and then moved through the trees toward the cabin.

The heavy front door of the cabin was blasted inward by Burton's perfectly placed kick. He held the flashlight out at arm's length in front of him, aiming his pistol alongside it. "Let's just hold it right there or . . ." His voice trailed off into astonishment.

In the dark room before him were two women whom he had surprised. One was in the process of going through a chest of drawers. The other was investigating a closet. She held a small orb, slightly larger than a softball, which glowed with the soft blue light that the men had seen through the cabin windows. But what had given Burton pause was the fact that both of the women were completely naked.

The women glanced up sharply at him, definitely wary but not fearful. They both had trim, athletic bodies and appeared to be in their mid-twenties. One woman had the very dark, almost blue-black skin coloring of a pure African. She was fine-featured, with a narrow nose and lips suggesting Ethiopian heritage. The other was very fair, as though her ancestors had come from the Norse countries. She had high cheekbones and a straight nose with slightly flared nostrils that seemed to be carefully and constantly testing the air with unusual sensitivity.

Burton's bright flashlight beam danced from one to the other, panning up and down their lovely bodies as Niblo eased in through the door behind him, his shotgun still at the ready in his meaty hands. He grinned with amazement at what he saw. "Well, hel-lo, ladies."

Niblo's eyes went immediately to the blond woman's breasts, as was his instinctive and consistent practice. He saw that they were in ideal proportion to her slender body and perfectly shaped. Perhaps a bit too perfectly, almost sculpted. Niblo noted that they also seemed to lack the malleable fluidity of natural breasts. Implants, he decided immediately, like the dozens of similarly enhanced and hardened breasts he had watched and many times groped at Hooters and the various strip joints he frequented. But his seasoned eyes enjoyed them nonetheless, particularly as he contemplated the uses he might soon put them to.

During that same moment Meyer had peered in and was also studying the women. Though he was still overcome with surprise, and of course glanced at their breasts as Niblo had, Meyer's keener eyes noted more physiological details about them. He saw that their skin tone was somewhat odd. As an X-ray technician Meyer had frequent close contact with people of varying skin texture, but he'd never seen any like that of these women. Their skin seemed to have a slight sheen to it. Not as though they had been perspiring or rubbed with oil, for they were clearly dry, but rather as though the sheen was a natural component inherent in their skin.

It also looked to Meyer as though their skin was hairless. Except for the close-cropped hair on their heads and the slightest dusting across their eyebrows and pubic areas their skin seemed completely smooth. Though they both appeared to be very vital and physically fit, the black woman was somewhat more muscular and slightly taller.

But definitely the most startling aspect of them was something else. Meyer leaned closer behind Burton. "Their eyes," he whispered tensely, "look at their eyes." Those of the blonde were a striking violet. The dark-skinned woman's were bright pink.

They were unlike any eyes Meyer had ever seen, even on a Visitor. They were very unsettling and gave Meyer a strange and palpable feeling of unease in the pit of his stomach. He instinctively knew that something was wrong here.

No one moved. Then Burton finally said, "What the hell are you doing here?"

The blonde held his gaze steadily, her voice was calm, her words measured like one speaking in a language with which she wasn't entirely familiar. ". . . Searching for garments."

Meyer detected in her voice a hint of some foreign dialect, perhaps Eastern European. He peered over Burton's shoulder, shining his flashlight onto the women as Niblo exhaled a long sigh, then chuckled and lowered his shotgun. Niblo eased closer to the women, speaking in a mock-friendly tone. "Aw, now that'd be a real shame. You don't want to cover nothin' up. What with the party just getting started and all."

Niblo reached out his broad, calloused hand and cupped the back of the blonde's head. His narrow eyes twinkled suggestively as he slowly slid his hand down the back of her neck. Then suddenly he flinched in shock. He let out a loud yelp of severe pain and jerked his hand away as though he'd been badly stung.

Meyer jumped, startled. "W-what's the matter?"

Niblo blinked heavily and stared incredulously down at his hand. "I dunno. I—Jesus Christ!" He and the others saw that the palm of his hand was bleeding badly. Then his hand began to tremble. He looked up angrily at the blonde. "What did you do to me?"

The blonde seemed calm and sincere as she quietly said, "I am sorry."

Niblo realized that his whole arm had begun to tremble. His anger suddenly spiked and he shouted, "What the fuck did you do to me, you—?" The words caught in his thick throat. The big man had suddenly choked. He began gasping for air as though he were being strangled. Then his entire body began to quake.

"Niblo! What is it?" Meyer shouted as Burton stared wide-eyed. "What's wrong?"

But Niblo couldn't answer. He convulsed as though currents of high-voltage electricity were shooting through him. He dropped the shotgun. As Meyer watched, the moment seemed to happen in slow motion. The dark-skinned woman snatched the falling shotgun in midair and swung it like a baseball bat. She hit Burton's head so hard that his neck snapped. Meyer heard Burton's cervical vertebrae rend with a sickening crunch. Burton was dead before he hit the floor.

Meyer turned in breathless terror and dashed back out the open door.

The black woman glanced pointedly at the blonde, their silent exchange confirming a course of action. Then with confident resolve the black woman followed Meyer out into the cold darkness. The blonde stood calmly looking down toward Niblo on the floor. There was faint sadness in her violet eyes. Niblo's body and limbs were grotesquely contorted, every muscle cramped and knotted tightly. His eyes were bulged out, the expression on his broad face one of extreme final agony as he lay on the wooden floor, frozen in death.

The blond woman repeated softly, "I am very sorry."

Meyer was running at breakneck speed down from the cabin toward the truck. He was white with panic, breathing hard, his heart pounding. He slipped on snowy patches and stumbled several times over roots and rocks as he raced through the dark forest, his suede vest flapping in the cold air. Tiny branches whipped at his face but he kept focused on the pickup ahead, praying that Burton had left the keys in the ignition.

He was almost to the road when suddenly a pair of black hands whipped down from above him and grabbed the shoulders of his vest.

"No!" he shouted, swatting at the hands in high alarm as he

might have at hornets swarming onto him. "No! Let me go! Let me go!"

The hands lifted him up off the ground. His feet dangled and kicked, trying to find purchase beneath them, but there was only air. "No, please! Please!" He kept hitting at her hands, to no avail.

The dark-skinned woman was somehow hanging upside down within the tree. She lifted Meyer up farther so that he was staring, terrified, into her stoic, upside-down face. Her fiery pink eyes were focused intently on him. He stopped struggling and pleaded with desperation, "Please . . . please, I have a family. I'll do anything you say. Just don't—"

He was suddenly snatched upward with astonishing speed and disappeared into the foliage.

In the cabin an hour later the dark-skinned woman pulled on the khaki fishing vest that Niblo had been wearing. She also wore his woodsy brown turtleneck and khaki pants, all of which had been somehow altered to fit her lean frame. But she was very uncomfortable wearing them. She shifted within the clothes as though they chafed her skin. Her breathing was slightly labored, adding to her discomfort. She stepped closer to her blond compatriot who had fitted Meyer's blue button-down shirt, suede vest, and jeans to her own use. The darker woman began speaking in a peculiar language filled with clicks and consonants. Though she had the stern, disciplined look of a career soldier, her voice was soft in contrast. The blonde interrupted her, "English, Bryke. We made agreement."

Bryke, for so she was called, was annoyed about that, too. What difference did it make when they were alone? Bryke always preferred the simplest, most straightforward approach to everything. But she respected her companion's considerable skills as a communicator and acquiesced. "You made the clothing too tight, Kayta."

The fair-skinned Kayta did not look up from the blue orb that she was adjusting on the cabin's old rustic table. She responded to Bryke quietly, "We're just unaccustomed. They feel strange against my skin also." Then she paused and added in a lower voice, "You needn't have killed them."

But Bryke knew better. With her finely honed instincts and long experience as a warrior she knew that there had been no choice. Not under these very precarious circumstances.

Kayta and Bryke were bathed in the low radiant blue light from the glowing sphere on the table. Kayta noticed that Bryke's breathing was somewhat difficult. "Is it the altitude?"

Bryke shook her head negatively. "The bad air." Then she indicated the orb. "Can you communicate with him?"

Kayta nodded and with her slender fingertips made a further adjustment to the ball. The blue glow within it began to pulse. As Kayta continued to fine-tune the device, Bryke spotted a fat black beetle crawling up onto a corner of the table. She popped it into her mouth and washed it down with a nearby glass of water.

Kayta raised her eyebrows and cautioned, "I told you: it's not a good idea to drink the water."

Bryke, exuding a quiet confidence, held Kayta's eyes and purposefully took another sip. Kayta smiled at her comrade's quiet bravery and then she focused on an electrostatic image that was forming in midair above the blue sphere. It crackled with energy and flashed with high frequency interference. Then it slowly resolved itself into a holographic image of a man.

He was nude. His skin had the same peculiar sheen as theirs and was as hairless. The very short hair on his head was brushed forward in a style similar to ancient Romans. His nose was also Roman. His face had a sturdy squareness to it with a particularly strong jawline. An old thin scar ran along the right side of his jaw from his ear almost to the tip of his chin. There were several other long-healed scars evident on his torso, including a deep one some twelve inches long on his left thigh that Bryke remembered him receiving. His eyes were amber and had a particularly piercing quality, yet Kayta had many times seen them alight with humor. He was a commander much to be admired.

He was standing in what appeared to be a shadowy, natural cavern. Flashes of strange data could occasionally be seen on illuminated crystalline sections behind him.

Kayta spoke to the ephemeral image, "Ayden? Are you receiving this transmission satisfactorily?"

After a brief pause, suggesting that some time was taken in the message reaching him, the man responded, "Yes, Kayta. I presume you and Bryke have achieved the initial objective?"

"Phase one is accomplished, sir. Although"—she was thinking of the three men—"there was some collateral damage, I'm sorry to report."

"That is sometimes unavoidable, I know," he said in a lower voice but with the resolve necessary in a seasoned military leader. "Are the conditions as we expected?"

"I should say that all the gravitational and biological aspects are nominal. Atmospheric is . . ." Kayta paused and glanced at Bryke questioningly. The pink-eyed woman sniffed and made a slightly sour expression, but nodded that she could live with the circumstances. That prompted Kayta to continue. "We feel that atmospheric is acceptable."

"What about the geopolitical aspects?"

Bryke spoke softly, "Our initial impression is confirmed. If we proceed with utmost stealth this is by far the best opportunity we've ever had."

Ayden said nothing immediately. His amber eyes grew distant and thoughtful. He turned slightly away from them. Bryke and Kayta exchanged a private glance. They both knew well what Ayden was doing. They had often seen him walk away from a strategy session and pace quietly with his head down. Sometimes an hour would pass during his contemplations. They knew that he was considering all aspects of a situation, all the possible permutations and pitfalls, before speaking.

In this case nearly a full minute passed before he looked back toward them and said, "Very well. I'll leave immediately to join you. Find someone who can lead us where we need to go."

2

THE DESERT SUN WAS WARM ON HIS SCALES. IT FELT WONDERFUL, radiating deeply inward to heat his naturally cold blood. With his leathery lids tightly closed he turned his reptilian face directly toward the hot, bright sun and then became motionless. This was paradise.

But after a moment he began to sense something, some extremely faint vibration disturbing the hot air. He opened one of his beady, bulging eyes and rotated it to look out across the flat scrub desert country that was dotted with sagebrush, mesquite, and an occasional cactus. Something was definitely coming and he knew better than to remain lying there in spite of how much he was enjoying the warmth of the sun and the lovely flat rock beneath him. He couldn't take a chance on being that exposed, so the big iguana wiggled off the top of the rock and crawled underneath.

Peering out he saw something streaking toward him very low over the empty desert wasteland. Though he didn't know what to call it, he had certainly seen many of them over the years.

The sleek Visitor fighter was doing well over a thousand miles per hour, about Mach 1.5, so when it flashed past the iguana there was a silent moment before the sonic boom caught up and exploded thunderously over the barren desert.

The interior of the narrow craft, however, was extremely quiet except for the measured breathing of the pilot and the wounded Visitor female, Sarah, who sat behind in the rear seat. She glanced down at the third individual inside the craft, who was lying on the floor and not breathing at all.

A pool of his green blood was coagulating beneath his head. Part of the false human skin had been torn away from his face during the earlier fight and his true reptilian features were exposed beneath. Like all Visitors his real face was thickly scaled, with heavy hairless brows. He had no nose in the human sense, but rather a broad flat lump with wide nostrils. The mouth was also wide and virtually lipless. It had gaped open when he died. Inside the mouth Sarah could see the sharp-pointed teeth and long forked tongue common to the Visitor race, like her own. She also saw that the human-looking contact lenses had been knocked from the creature's eyes revealing yellow vertical irises beneath. They had dilated wide in death and were staring blankly up at her.

A stab of pain from her pulse wound caused Sarah to look away and try again to master her discomfort. It was becoming increasingly difficult. The green bloodstain on her shirt had been slowly growing over the last two hours. She was wearing what had become the primary Visitor garb: dark pants and ivory shirt with subtle rank stripes on the collar. Commandant Diana had decided more than a decade earlier that the Visitors' standard uniforms presented too strong a military image. She had given much thought to the matter and for public relations reasons had adopted this more casual dress, except for the Patrollers, of course. Those troopers remained uniformed as militarily as ever. Their orange jumpsuits with their black, quilted armor vests, broad black utility belts, jackboots, and dark-visored combat helmets emphasized their martial status and made them a feared and forbidding force.

Sarah drew another long breath, but it hurt very badly. She looked around for something to distract her and caught her own reflection in the weapon-ranging screen on the side instrument panel. She looked to be in her late thirties by human standards.

She had seen this face for so long that she almost thought of it as her real face, yet now she remembered the day she had chosen it to be fitted over her own reptilian features. That was so long ago, nearly twenty-five years earlier, during the initial journey of the Visitor Armada from their home planet orbiting Sirius. That was before Sarah had met the humans and grown sympathetic to their cause.

But long before meeting the humans Sarah had begun to lose respect for her own Commandants and particularly the distressing direction in which the Visitor Leader was taking their society. The Leader was a charismatic, who had been swept into power after years of war and corrupt government had left their planet disorganized and vulnerable. The Leader's stirring orations and calls for strict, healthy discipline had struck a chord with the masses, including Sarah at the time, and strengthened the people's confidence. The Leader had reshaped their society into a tightly structured, aggressively militaristic world. Opposition to the Leader was dealt with at first by false diplomacy but then more and more swiftly by disappearance, unfortunate accidents, and finally outright assassination. The Leader had ultimately become the sole and supreme authority, who was determined to conquer other worlds and civilizations and then absorb them.

The Leader had not yet deigned to visit the expedition to Earth. Commandant Diana was in charge of the Earth-side operation and was carrying out her mission in the style dictated by the Leader: with a disarming smile and an iron fist.

There were a number of Sarah's fellow Visitors who secretly felt as she did, that the Leader's totalitarian rule and growing ambitions were ill-conceived and morally wrong. None spoke of their concerns aloud, however, except in extreme secrecy. Retaliation for any whisper of treason was lightning fast, horrifyingly brutal, and ultimately lethal. Yet Sarah knew that in spite of the prospects of prolonged torture and death, there were others like herself who were willing to take the risks. In spite of the fact that

Commandant Diana and her minions had cracked down ever harder over the last few years, in spite of the huge setback known as the Great Purge in 1999, when so many of Sarah's human and Visitor comrades had been betrayed and imprisoned or murdered, Sarah and others were trying equally hard to bring new recruits to the cause of Resistance. The young human piloting the fighter was the newest recruit and Sarah felt he might perhaps turn out to be one of the best.

Sarah gazed at the back of his sandy-blond head in the pilot's seat in front of her and recalled the first time she'd seen Nathan. Eleven years earlier he had been a rather solemn and angry youth of fifteen. He'd been recently orphaned and had eagerly joined the Teammate unit that Sarah helped to oversee on the Big Island.

The Teammates were a quasi-military organization that had been created by Diana shortly after the Visitors' arrival. Originally called *The Visitor Youth* and designed to draw in exactly such disenfranchised young people as Nathan, the Teammate mission had been quickly and considerably expanded by Diana. She now required all physically fit humans to serve at least part-time.

The Teammate unit became a family of sorts for the friendless boy. Sarah had sensed Nathan's particular loneliness. She also divined his keen insights and raw native intelligence. She had taken Nathan under her wing. Over the years Nathan had come to look upon Sarah as more than just his Teammate leader, she was also something of a mother figure. They had grown very close. Sarah was surprised to discover how much genuine love she could feel for someone not of her own species.

Over those same years, Sarah's loyalty to the Visitor mission and its commanders had continued to deteriorate. She kept her dissatisfaction most private, however, and had never shared her growing sentiments with Nathan. Partly she held back out of a desire to protect him from any harm that might come to them if her feelings became known, and partly because she feared that

Nathan himself might reveal her secrets and denounce her. Informing was a common occurrence among passionate Teammates such as Nathan. Many Teammates became informers within their own families, condemning their own relatives, even their own siblings or parents. If a loyal Teammate discovered that relatives had been working against the Visitors or, most damning of all, actively colluding with the Resistance, reporting them was demanded and grandly rewarded.

Sarah knew that Nathan harbored a virulent anger toward the Resistance. She knew his burning reasons for that feeling, the murder of his parents. She knew that his intense personal loathing for the Resistance had driven Nathan to become one of the most ardent soldiers against their cause. He had fought and captured many of them and had risen swiftly within the Teammate organization.

But when the Resistance was weakened by the Great Purge, when Visitors sympathetic to their cause were increasingly discovered and killed, Sarah realized that they needed all the help they could get. She knew that Nathan could become a powerful adjunct to the Resistance Allies—if she could convince him to change his allegiance.

On this day aboard the Honolulu Mothership she had finally been forced to chance it. If he had informed on her it could have meant the abrupt end of her life. But upon seeing what she had shown him, Nathan's astonishment and his comprehension of what it meant had been instant. It was as though he'd been struck by lightning. He told her he likened it to a key story from Hawaiian history.

In 1779 the natives welcomed the English explorer Captain James Cook, believing him to be their returned god Lono. They worshipped Cook as a god, though he and his men sometimes treated them brutally. Then one day during a fracas at Kealakekua Bay an angry native struck Cook and the islanders heard the captain groan. They were astonished. Gods did not groan. As they began to prod him they instantly realized he was as mortal as they. It was a cataclysmic revelation. The whole basis of their deepest beliefs suddenly crashed down around them and in their unbridled fury they literally tore the man to pieces.

That was how Nathan now felt about the Visitors. Sarah's instincts had proven to be exactly right. She had indeed turned him to the Resistance cause and now there could be no turning back.

Though they were skimming only fifty feet over the desert to avoid detection, Sarah had complete confidence in Nathan. He was flying with enormous skill. He had learned to pilot a Visitor fighter during his years working alongside them. Though Nathan had deserted hours ago when he and Sarah stole the fighter, he was still wearing his Teammate uniform of dark blue cords and blue chambray shirt with his three rank stripes on the collar. He had nearly lost his blue uniform baseball cap during his struggle with the Visitor ground crewman who lay dead at Sarah's feet.

Sarah had hoped to win Nathan over by showing him what was hidden aboard the Hawaiian Mothership, but she was unprepared for the vehemence of his reaction to what he saw and his fierce determination to take immediate and violent action. Had he not been quite so impetuous and rash they might have slipped away quietly or at least escaped without her being shot. Still, she was happy to have opened his eyes to the truth.

The radio in the fighter crackled. The voice had the peculiar sonorous resonance common to all Visitors, "Honolulu Six one niner, this is Flagship. We show no flight plan for you."

Sarah drew a concerned breath. "Uh-oh."

Nathan was unfazed. "Stay cool, Sarah." He looked back at her. "How you doing?" She saw that the wound on his left cheek was still damp with blood and the bruise on his jaw had spread, but that his warm brown eyes were as alight and intense as ever. His face had the native Hawaiian roundness, smoothness, and perpetual Polynesian tan of his father while his mother's English-Danish heritage had lightened his hair toward blond and provided him with a thin, straight nose.

"I'm all right," Sarah lied and Nathan knew it. One glance at how the size of the green bloodstain on her shirt had increased told him that he had to get her medical help very quickly. Nathan's feelings for Sarah ran deep and true, flowing as they did from all the mentoring, special attention, and care she had given him over the years. But in the last six hours his admiration and love for her had taken a quantum leap because of the dangers she had undertaken in his behalf. He would save her life or die trying.

The radio voice spoke again, this time more emphatically, "Six one niner, Flagship. Repeat: we show *no* flight plan for you. Please activate your transponder immediately."

"They're onto us, Nathan," Sarah said quietly.

But his confidence unshaken, he grinned tightly back at her. "Hey, we've ducked 'em for two hours. We're almost to the coast."

He looked ahead through the tinted cockpit window, ignoring its numerous transparent superimpositions of flight data and targeting statistics. Brown, scrubby desert vegetation was flashing past beneath him. Ahead some forty or fifty miles he could see a range of low mountains that rose over a thousand feet. Between the two most prominent mountains there was a gap almost two miles wide. Stretching between the two mountains across the deep dry valley was a massive yet graceful suspension bridge.

Nathan smiled. "I can already see the Golden Gate."

His fighter was approaching from the west toward the city of San Francisco. The desert he had been flying over stretched westward behind them to the horizon. The desert had once been part of the Pacific Ocean.

The staticky Visitor voice on the radio was commanding now. "Six one niner, slow to two hundred. Climb and maintain three zero and await escort. You're in violation of regs."

Nathan muttered darkly to himself, "I got your fuckin' regs."

Something over the city had caught Sarah's eye. "Nathan—look there!"

His voice was clipped. "I see 'em, Sarah."

Two Visitor fighters similar to the one Nathan was flying had dropped from one of the myriad landing bays on the bottom of the sixteen-mile-wide Mothership, which was equal in size to the hundreds of others like it around the world. Dish-shaped, with a thickness of over two miles at its center, the Mothership's surface was composed of thousands of overlying panels that resembled scales. There were hundreds of view ports and massive access hatches in addition to the scores of gaping landing bays. This particular Mothership was unique in that it was the Flagship of the Visitor Armada. It hung four thousand feet in the sky dominating San Francisco like an ominous dark cloud and casting its huge shadow across the city and the people below. The two fighters were streaking down from it toward the Golden Gate to intercept Nathan.

Sarah chewed her lip nervously. "They're Class Fours."

Nathan had already noted that. They were the newest fighters, about five feet longer than the older twenty-five-foot Class Two that he and Sarah were in. The Fours still maintained the basic curved wing design that was a cross between a delta wing and the cowl of a king cobra snake. Even sitting on the ground or in a landing bay they had a very menacing appearance. In the air they were as deadly as they looked. Nathan and Sarah were both aware that the Fours were also faster and more maneuverable than their Class Two. Nathan knew he was facing a serious challenge.

The pilot in the lead interceptor was a female Patroller, a flight leader named Gina. Her false human face gave her the appearance of a striking Asian woman about thirty years of age. Her face was slightly more round than oval; her almond eyes were dark and quite sharp. She was a seasoned pilot, confident of her proven ability to bring down any combatant. She was a top gun killer.

She keyed her transmitter, and spoke with calm command, "Six one niner, you will form with us and follow to the Flagship."

In the rogue craft, Sarah was tapping the arm of her seat with growing anxiety. "We should've come in farther north."

"Nah, too far to walk"—Nathan looked out to check below them—"hang on, Sare."

Sarah felt her stomach go light as Nathan suddenly did a sharp wing-over to the left, diving the fighter toward the desert floor. Sarah's body went from near weightless to very heavy as he pulled out of the steep dive at the last second and flew level not more than ten feet over the parched dried mud. Sarah saw the Golden Gate Bridge flash past high overhead as they skimmed across the deep dry valley into what had once been San Francisco Bay. A few sun-baked hulks of rusting ships sunk long ago littered the cracked floor of the bay along with various pieces of flotsam, jetsam, and a lot of carelessly discarded junk. The only water remaining in the formerly broad estuary was a narrow, ankle-deep rivulet no more than ten yards wide that snaked down from the much-diminished Sacramento and San Joaquin Rivers far inland to the north.

In her Class Four, Gina reacted to his maneuver and transmitted, "Flagship, he's hostile. We're engaging. Break break." Then she spoke to her companion fighter, "Twenty-two, I'm going in. Drop back two klicks and try to stay with me."

"Roger that, Fourteen," came the response from the Patroller pilot in fighter 3122 just behind and off her left wing. Then Gina glanced at one of the ghostly controls that hung transparently in the air before her cockpit window. The instrument sensed her glance and reacted immediately. Gina felt the fighter's internal workings responding. Slim panels opened underneath each of the arched wings and the tubular pulse cannons lowered. A tone in Gina's cockpit indicated that they had locked into firing position. She pushed her hand control forward and to the right, diving her fighter in pursuit of Nathan.

In the Sierra Mountain cabin Bryke was dusting off her hands after disposing of the three men's bodies. "You say he *stole* the fighter?" She walked to where Kayta stood beside the old wooden table, looking down at its surface. Kayta's blue orb was projecting a high-altitude view of the fighters pursuing Nathan over San Francisco harbor.

Kayta nodded. "From the Mothership near Hawaii."

Bryke leaned closer over the table, assessing Nathan's ability as a pilot. "Very skillful. A real possibility."

"*If* he's legitimate," Kayta cautioned.

Nathan increased his speed as he banked his fighter around the rocky pinnacle in the center of San Francisco's dry harbor. The abandoned prison of Alcatraz still rested on top of the rock. Gina squeezed off the first blast from her pulse cannon. The baseball-sized charge of fiery electrical energy rocketed toward Nathan's fighter trailing a tight corkscrew of smoke like a thin filament. The projectile of pure energy missed Nathan but blew a hefty chunk of concrete from the north wall of Alcatraz.

Nathan heard the explosion behind him and banked his fighter steeper yet, forcing it into a tighter curve. His face quickly grew flushed and his arms heavy as lead. He strained against the extreme G-force as he rounded the pinnacle and looked for his quarry. As he'd hoped, the second fighter was holding a reasonable distance aft of Gina's. Nathan's extremely tight curve had brought him out directly behind it.

Nathan activated his pulse cannons and even before they were locked in to position beneath his wing, he opened fire. He saw the ball of energy flash from under his wing and score a hit on the underside of his adversary. The injured fighter immediately began to side-wind out of control downward toward what had been the shoreline of the city, but was now just a dusty hillside that sloped down into the dry harbor valley below. Nathan could see that the pilot was trying to pull up, but was unsuccessful. The fighter crashed into a long-unused pier, plowing inland 150 yards through the wooden structure before exploding.

In the cabin, Kayta and Bryke exchanged a look. They were both impressed with Nathan's skill. But they were not the only ones watching the combat.

In the back of a shadowy truck that had been rigged as a makeshift communications center, a battered TV was also showing the action. A Peruvian woman, who looked sensational for her seventy years, was at a small control console switching from one camera angle to another. The images came from various clandestine and stolen sources atop high buildings in San Francisco. The woman was Ysabel Encalada. Her thick black hair, a legacy from her Incan ancestors, had only begun getting sprinkles of gray a few years earlier. She kept it cut short in a no-nonsense style that perfectly complemented her feisty personality. She had spoken out strongly against the Visitors twenty years earlier. When three of her fellow workers at Microsoft had disappeared after voicing similar complaints, Ysabel realized the danger and slipped away into the Underground so she could continue her fight against Visitor tyranny. Her computer science and communications skills served the Resistance well.

Her compatriots were also cheered by her colorful blouses that echoed her South American heritage. A half-dozen thin bracelets were always clicking together on her wrist. She frequently peeled one off with a smile and gave it as a gift to lift the spirits of a disoriented child whose family had just come into hiding.

She was now peering at a monitor over the half-glasses attached to a beaded string around her neck, watching Nathan's dogfight very carefully. "Wow, Margarita, this guy is something."

A slender hand came to rest on Ysabel's shoulder, then the young woman to whom it belonged leaned down for a closer look at the monitor. Margarita Perry had the sort of face that always inspired both men and women to take a second look. She was in her twenty-seventh year but her eyes had a depth beyond that age. Her rich auburn hair was pulled back in a tight, utilitarian ponytail, but ringlet wisps of it always escaped to soften the edges around her face. Her eyebrows were the same rusty hue as her hair and a sprinkling of freckles saddled her nose. She was a curious blend: she had a tomboyish quality but her features also suggested royalty in her Scottish-Canadian heritage. When she was focused sharply, as she was now, her face took on a severity that could make people who didn't know her feel unsettled. She was aware of this effect and like any smart leader she utilized it to maximum effect whenever necessary. But as soon as a corner of her full lips turned upward or the twinkle reappeared in her hazel eyes those same people were calmed and reassured.

Ysabel glanced up at the younger woman. "He's very good . . . or very loco."

"Or both." Margarita was watching Nathan's skillful evasive maneuvers in the aerial dogfight with a practiced, analytical eye. "Put out the word to watch for him."

Ysabel nodded and rolled her stool over to a nearby radio console within the truck. Margarita continued to study the screen with a slight frown, unconsciously rubbing the back of her forefinger across the tip of her nose as she always seemed to do when considering something carefully.

In Nathan's fighter, Sarah was clutching the armrests tightly as the G-forces pressed her first one way and then another. Nathan was flying in above the city streets of San Francisco. As he banked sharply over Montgomery Street around the Transamerica pyramid he saw in his aft-facing vid screen that Gina had also dropped lower and was gaining on him. Gina fired again, the burst from her pulse cannon splashing off of an edge of the Transamerica skyscraper, shattering the windows of a corner office.

People on the street below heard the explosion overhead and ducked for cover as shards of glass came raining down. Nathan banked southwest and flew over broad Market Street, almost skimming the lampposts, swerving from side to side over the median to avoid Gina's continuing air-to-air cannon fire. He knew he was in trouble and was looking for an escape route or a place where he could set down and quickly flee with Sarah. But Gina curved in behind him, closing rapidly now. Pedestrians looked up fearfully as the two fighters flashed past overhead. A truck driver, momentarily distracted by them, smashed his ten-ton into the back of a trolley car.

Then Gina got a solid bead on Nathan and fired both of her pulse cannons. Nathan's fighter took the hit on its rear control surfaces. Inside his cockpit, alarms began sounding and Nathan felt a sudden sluggishness in his control stick. He grabbed it with both hands and struggled to get the nose of the fighter to respond upward, but there had been too much damage.

Nathan barely had time to shout, "Hang on, Sarah," before his right wingtip tagged a traffic light and he lost control completely. Fortunately for most of the people on the street below him, Gina's cannon fire had already attracted their attention. They were scattering frantically as Nathan's fighter dropped down. It snapped the electrical bus and trolley wires, sending them whipping and arcing like high-voltage snakes. Then the fighter skidded in on its belly along Market Street at nearly a hundred miles an hour. The landing gear was up so the bottom of the craft sent up a cascading flurry of sparks behind it. Inside the fighter the buffeting was so bone-jarring Nathan couldn't see the direction they were headed and couldn't have controlled it even if he had.

His fighter plowed through and across a dozen parked cars before it finally came to rest near the corner of Fifth Street as Gina's fighter whipped past overhead. The Asian-looking beauty glanced down at her handiwork with a tight smile.

Inside the ruined fighter, electrical panels were arcing and smoking with the acrid smell of ozone and burning insulation. But Nathan's only thought was of Sarah. He turned immediately back to her, disengaging her seat straps. "Sarah?" He saw that she had been shaken badly by the crash; he took her face in his hands and looked urgently into her eyes. "Sarah, we've gotta go. We've gotta go now. Come on." She nodded weakly. Disoriented from the trauma of the crash, she needed his help to extricate herself from the disarranged bucket seat.

Panicked people were still scattering on Market Street as Nathan kicked out the emergency panel on the fighter's roof and pulled Sarah from the smoking wreckage. A car lodged beneath the fighter was on fire. Above Nathan and Sarah, on the walls of a nearby building, a billboard-sized video presented cheery information from a doctor about the latest Visitor medical breakthrough that would finally put an end to all the deadly strains of the Ebola virus.

On another building opposite an equally large screen was showing the latest music vid of a sassy, sexy, cocoa-skinned singer named Emma. She was in her mid-twenties and at the top of her game as a popular music star. Emma was an eye-catching beauty who had been blessed with all the best genes from her fine-featured, athletic white mother and her lean, handsome black father. The lyrics of her song were extremely clever and the pounding rock beat was infectious. Her green eyes flashed and her long black hair tossed in rhythm with her tightly choreographed dance steps. To many of both sexes in her audience, Emma embodied perfection; she was totally appealing.

But Nathan's attention was fully on Sarah who slumped to the sidewalk, dizzy and very weak. She looked up at Nathan, her breathing labored. "Leave me. You have to leave me and go on."

He blew out a puff at that ridiculous suggestion. "Yeah, right." He scooped her up in his strong arms and quickly glanced around to find the best route. Several people nearby, who had taken shelter in doorways from the crashing fighter, saw his plight but avoided his eyes and hurried away. Nathan wasn't surprised. He knew the social climate very well. As a Teammate, he had helped to create it. Now he was reaping the whirlwind.

He was about to head south on Market when he saw an SFPD car speeding in to block escape in that direction. Nathan spun back around and saw a squad of Teammates in denim uniforms like his own rushing around the corner toward him from the north on Fifth Street, as they drew their pulse weapons.

Nathan ran south on Fifth toward Stevenson Street, passing beneath a large vid sign displaying two huge eyes looking back and forth with the flashing words: *See something suspicious? Report it!* Bullet-sized pulse bursts of electricity from the Teammates' hand weapons struck the building chipping off pieces of stone beside Nathan as he ran. Several sharp shards caught him on the cheek and neck. As he dashed toward a startled black businesswoman he saw one of the pulses meant for him burst against her right shoulder. She screamed in pain as the flaming impact of it spun her down to the sidewalk in agony. Nathan kept running but he had a flash of memory of innocent people whom he himself had wounded while pursuing Resistance fighters in years past.

As Bryke and Kayta watched an overhead view of his travails, Kayta was using a small needlelike instrument to follow Nathan's image on the tabletop while he ran along Stevenson Street. Bryke urged her impatiently, "Tag him. Hurry."

Kayta was calm and intent. "I'm endeavoring to."

Nathan was in excellent physical condition, but carrying Sarah as he ran was beginning to tell on him. He was breathing hard as he emerged from the other end of Stevenson onto Sixth Street. For a brief moment he thought himself in the clear, but then he saw Gina's fighter sweep around a corner two blocks away and arc sharply northward directly toward him. Gina's high-caliber cannons fired a half-dozen pulses. The balls of energy impacted in rapid succession along the street wounding several people who hadn't seen them coming. The final burst hit the back of a city bus only a few yards from Nathan and Sarah. It triggered the bus's hydrogen fuel cell into a furious explosion that engulfed the vehicle and its passengers in a broiling ball of flame. Its metal and glass became deadly shrapnel that flew in all directions cutting down many men, women, and children nearby.

Nathan was also blown down by the concussion. For a moment he could hear nothing as he lay dazed with his cheek on the cold rough sidewalk. When he raised his head the smoke-filled street with people dead or dying looked like a war zone. Many had their bones and bowels exposed. Some of the victims were in flames. Then Nathan realized Sarah was no longer in his arms. He saw her lying facedown against a brick wall. He crawled quickly to her and gently turned her over.

Some sharp piece of flying debris had slashed the side of Sarah's face and peeled back the false human skin on her cheek. It revealed her true reptilian face beneath and had cut deeply into that scaly tissue as well. Her green blood was flowing. Nathan was heartsick. He muttered, "Oh, God damn it," as he looked about frantically for something to stanch her bleeding.

Her weak hand caught his and grasped it tightly. She knew she was failing. She gazed up affectionately at him. He saw that the contact lens had been blown from her left eye revealing her yellow vertical reptilian iris. Her eyes were growing dim, but Nathan wasn't about to give up. "Sarah, now you listen—"

She squeezed his hand tighter to hush him, then she spoke with a hoarse whisper, "I love you, Nathan," and with her final breath she said, ". . . Make me proud . . ."

She died in his arms. Nathan stared at her, then clutched her limp body tightly to him, angry tears rising. A pulse burst flashed against a drainpipe beside him. He looked up and through the smoke he saw three Airborne Visitor Patrollers in their orange uniforms and dark-visored helmets flying down toward him from a rooftop. The Air-Pats used personal propulsion packs on their backs to take flight.

Nathan took a last look at Sarah, his jaw tightening as he engraved her final words in his mind. He kissed her forehead, then took off running past the flaming bus and across the smoky street. It was littered with debris, body parts, and bloody flesh, as well as many moaning, injured people. The incoming Air-Pats continued to shoot at him but being in flight their accuracy was poor. Several of their stray shots hit innocent people, including two already downed by the bus explosion. The Patrollers were within a block of him when he heard a loud whistle and saw a scruffy kid beckoning urgently to him from the nearby corner of Jessie Street. Then the youth ducked back around the corner. With his other options seemingly cut off Nathan ran around onto Jessie Street. He was stunned to see that it was a dead end and that the kid had vanished.

He realized that he was out of escape routes and stood there breathing hard, thoroughly infuriated with himself, when he felt something grasp his ankle. He looked down and saw the leathery hand of the kid, a scaly-faced, human-Visitor half-breed. The scrappy girl was about twelve years old. She had human blue eyes and Irish coloring with short, tousled, chestnut-colored hair, but the reptilian scales inherited from one of her parents radiated upward from her neck and onto her cheeks. Her right hand that grasped him was reptilian, but her left hand bore a predominance of human skin with only splotches of scales. She was dressed in piecemeal castoffs and a small crush cap with no brim. She was clearly a seasoned street kid with an Artful Dodger twinkle in her blue eyes. She had reached up to him out of a wide storm drain. She wiggled her eyebrows cheerily, inviting him down.

Nathan dropped quickly into the shadowy, steamy storm sewer. He turned to see the scaly-faced girl reaching out to shake his hand as her bright eyes grinned at him. "Hey, sailor. Welcome to San Francisco."

She jerked her thumb for him to follow, then turned and darted down the slimy, dark tunnel, nimbly dodging big rats as she ran. Nathan took a breath. He weighed his options, the kid's bravado, and decided to follow her.

In the mountain cabin, fair-skinned Kayta turned off the orb and its projected image faded. Bryke was eyeing her sternly. "Well? Did you manage it?" Kayta smiled and held up the needle instrument, which was blinking steadily.

Bryke nodded with stoic satisfaction. "Good. We should hasten."

3

IN PATRICK HENRY MIDDLE SCHOOL ON ORTEGA STREET AT FORTY-first, the second bell had already rung so the students were in their homerooms and the hallways were empty. But the hurried footsteps of two eighth-graders echoed softly off the shiny concrete floor and gray metal lockers. The taller of the two boys, Danny Stein, had aquiline features, thick brown curly hair, and a reputation among his peers for always pushing the envelope, which was exactly what he was doing this morning. That made his companion more nervous than usual.

Thomas Murakami was smaller, thinner, and more fastidious than casual Danny. Thomas's Japanese parents were decidedly old school with very definite and strict rules. They exerted constant pressure on Thomas to excel in all his academics, which he did. But that pressure had developed in Thomas a wariness from an early age. He wasn't merely paranoid. He positively *knew* that people were constantly looking over his shoulder and that created in him an innate nervousness about doing anything outside the rules. Forbidden fruit was always intriguing, however, so Thomas couldn't help but be drawn to Danny Stein's panache and the excitement of Danny's ability to dance along the edge of a precipice, generally managing to narrowly avoid taking a big fall.

Nonetheless, as they approached the closed door of their classroom, Thomas felt his pulse quicken. "I don't know, we're going to be so late."

Danny shrugged it off lightly. "So what? Monday morning's always the same. You know that. Check it out." Danny indicated the small rectangular window in the classroom door. Thomas edged closer and carefully peeked through into the classroom. He could see their heavyset, dowdy teacher, Mrs. Richmond, a study in drab, turning on the large, ceiling-mounted flat-screen TV.

Her voice was upbeat. "Okay, class. Time for our Monday movie. And I heard that this is a brand-new version. See how many new scenes you all can spot—then we'll talk about them afterward."

Rhythmic, energetic music started as a flashy title appeared on the TV screen, heralding a presentation titled *The Visitor Way*. A smaller version of the title appeared as an icon in the lower corner of the screen that was a subtle but constant reminder of the official vid that the students were watching.

In the hallway Thomas and Danny could hear the music coming not only from their own classroom, but from all the others up and down the corridor. Danny nodded to doubting Thomas. "I told you so. Come on." Danny started off without looking back. He knew Thomas would hesitate a moment, then quickly catch up.

"What's so important?" Thomas asked as they walked.

Danny spoke with conspiratorial seriousness, "I've got a *different* vid to show you."

Back inside their classroom and all the others not only at Patrick Henry but in every school in the Pacific Time Zone at that moment, *The Visitor Way* was beginning. It was an attention-grabbing vid that had been created with slick production value, trendy editing, and simultaneous, multiple images. At first it showed documentary scenes of real people in conflict: rebellious crowds that were tearing down symbols of authority or attacking police or fighting with an opposing mob of equally enraged people. Then came classic scenes of warfare with heavy artillery firing, buildings being hit and destroyed by their shells or by missiles launched from Predator-style drone aircraft. Then images of bloodied and crying people on streets where suicide bombers had blown themselves and others to bloody pieces. Then long lines of distressed and injured refugees. The totality of images seemed to contain examples of virtually every human ethnicity and recognizable culture.

An unseen narrator began speaking over all of the visuals. It was the voice of a concerned young woman. "Our old Earth was a real mess twenty years ago. International conflicts abounded. Just about every country in the world had some sort of internal strife. War and suffering were everywhere and it looked as though things would only get worse and worse. But then suddenly . . . *They* arrived."

Images appeared on the screen of the monumental alien Motherships approaching over Earth's major cities: New York, London, Moscow, Beijing, Rio de Janeiro, and of people everywhere reacting to the astonishing sight with understandable awe.

"And everything got better," the voice continued in a tone of friendliness and wonder. "The Visitors had arrived to bring us their gifts—and to bring peace in our time."

Emma, the green-eyed, African-American pop singer whose latest music vid had been playing on the billboard screen at Nathan's crash site, was smiling and speaking directly into the camera as she walked beside a huge Visitor tanker craft. "Hi, kids. I'm Emma." She was wearing faded blue jeans and a Hamlet-style blouse that was loose-fitting yet managed to show the curves of her picture-perfect figure. Her long, straight black hair flowed down over her shoulders. The pale yellow of her blouse ideally complemented the coffee-with-cream color of her smooth skin. Her outfit had been carefully selected to be particularly kid-friendly, just as she herself had been. Emma was a popular celebrity who set fashion trends for young women while also having the sex appeal to turn the heads of males of any age. She was a double treat because in addition to being beautiful, she also had the talent to back it up. As a songwriter as well as a performer she was respected and admired. Thus she was an ideal choice to speak on behalf of the Visitors.

In spite of the fact that the students in Danny's classroom had seen modified versions of this video every Monday morning for years, Emma was a relatively new addition and generally made the old information sound fresh. On the screen she had continued walking in the bright sunlight and came to join a natty, engaging Visitor, who looked to be in his mid-thirties. He had a friendly, open face topped with nicely coiffed dark hair.

"And this is a good buddy of mine," Emma said with a smile, "Paul is the Press Secretary for the Visitors." Emma turned to him. "You love your job, don't you, Paul?"

His smile was engaging, "I sure do, Emma." Like all Visitors, Paul wore sunglasses and his voice had the peculiar alien resonance. "I love it because I get to tell young people about us Visitors." He turned to look directly into the camera and address the kids in the viewing audience. "Being a reptilian race, we were afraid we'd look a little too *alien* to you"—he wiggled his fingers near his face with self-deprecating humor—"and since we needed protection from your ultraviolet radiation anyway, our doctors created this human-looking skin." He pulled gently at the skin of his cheek. "It was a good idea and helped us to fit in more easily among our new friends here on Earth. We also need the sunglasses to protect our eyes which are considerably more sensitive than yours." The vid image had changed to show numerous shots of human-looking Visitors all wearing sunglasses as they arrived en masse and began working cheerfully among welcoming humans.

Again on-camera, Paul nodded. "We were very happy to be here, but then . . ." His face grew sad and there was an abrupt cut to a Visitor fighter exploding. Then a factory was shown in flames. There were more explosions and scenes of many people injured. Human and Visitor victims were frightened and bloodied, clinging to each other. Paul's voice was heard over the images. "A conspiracy of jealous Earth scientists wanted to undermine our helping you. These *Scis*, as your people began to call them, committed vicious acts of sabotage and did horrific surgical experimentation on innocent Visitors."

Emma was seen, her head bowed in sadness and shame for the disgraceful behavior of her fellow humans, then the camera panned to Paul whose face also expressed distress. "The Scis finally confessed to causing much of Earth's turmoil for their own glory and financial gain."

In one of the school's custodial closets, which was dark and smelled of industrial-strength soap, Danny had sequestered himself and Thomas amid the buckets and cleaning supplies. As Danny pulled out his wallet-sized vid player Thomas was growing more nervous with anticipation. "It's not porn, is it?" Thomas was worried yet secretly hoped at the same time. "My parents said they'd kill me if I ever—"

"Relax. Just watch." Danny had turned the small unit on and the screen showed a grainy image of auburn-haired Margarita Perry speaking with passion directly into the camera. They could see she was standing in what looked like an abandoned building. Beside her stood a distinguished-looking man in his fifties. His black hair was flecked with gray and he had the look of a smart, friendly college professor but with the weathered tan of someone who had spent much time doing hands-on work in the field. His eyebrows were thick and black. They set off his dark, intensely intelligent eyes. Like Margarita he was dressed in simple, serviceable clothes.

Margarita introduced the man, "This is Nobel laureate anthropologist Robert Maxwell. Like most scientists and their families, Dr. Maxwell was made an object of scorn and hatred by Visitor lies."

Young Thomas's eyes flared open. "Omigod, Danny! Where'd you get this?"

"It's a bootleg vid from the Resistance," Danny was proud to say.

Robert Maxwell had begun to speak. "Visitors are afraid we scientists might find a way to stop them, so they want to contain us. Or worse. That's why all Scis are implanted with ID chips. And we're not the only ones singled out: anyone opposing the Visitors simply vanishes."

The vid graphically illustrated his point by showing grainy, clandestine, handheld, telephoto shots of disturbing scenes: Visitor Patrollers and human Teammates brutally squashing demonstrations at colleges, beating students to the ground; halting union meetings, clubbing those who resisted or shooting them with pulse pistols; breaking into people's homes and dragging them out and away into the foggy darkness.

Margarita was narrating: "These images were captured by ordinary people like you and me, at great personal risk to themselves, to show what the Visitors are *actually* doing across America and around the world. You won't see images like these on normal TV or in the press, of course, because for over twenty years the Visitors have *controlled and censored* all media and communication—including the Internet. They quickly destroy anything negative said against them. Or anyone saying it. Particularly if they have any connection to scientists."

In the classroom *The Visitor Way* was showing happy scientists in pristine laboratories, living in pleasant, colorful, parklike suburbs as Press Secretary Paul rapturously intoned, "Most scientists are rehabilitated now and gladly work alongside Visitors. Some of their fellow men haven't yet forgiven scientists' behavior as we Visitors have, so for their own protection Sci families live within their own lovely communities."

Then Paul continued on-camera, his face expressing sad regret. "But there are still a few misinformed social misfits who resist the help we're offering. So we must all be very vigilant and immediately report any suspicious behavior to authorities."

AT THAT SAME MOMENT, AMID THE GIGANTIC INTERWOVEN PIPES AND catwalks at a huge biochemical plant on the southwest side of the dry chasm that had been San Francisco Bay, a sweet-faced, middle-aged woman of Italian descent named Connie Leonetti was being arrested by a Visitor Patroller and two Teammates. She was frightened and completely confused. "What are you talking about? I am *not* an 'undocumented scientist'!"

"Just come along quietly, lady," said one of the Teammates, a young Pakistani woman, as she prodded Connie with a pulse pistol.

"But it's a lie!" Connie protested, with tears of panic welling in her dark eyes. "I'm not in the Resistance! Who told you that? Who would have—?" Then Connie's eyes fell upon another woman standing some distance away, who pretended not to be watching though she obviously was. Connie shouted at her, "It was *you*, wasn't it!"

The other woman, Stella Stein, was about forty with curly brown hair like her son Danny. Her full face reflected the fact that she was slightly overweight. Stella seemed to be watching the scene with curious concern. But Connie could read the smug satisfaction just beneath Stella's studied innocence.

"You just want my job!" Connie was raging tearfully now, then as the Teammates cuffed her and took hold of her arms, her voice cracked as she pleaded to the other woman, "Tell them it's not true, Stella! Please! Stella, *you tell them*!" But Connie was muscled away by the Patroller and the Teammates, passing a group of upscale humans and Visitors who were walking in the opposite direction. Connie seized the opportunity and called out desperately to the corpulent man who was leading the group, "Mr. Oliver! Please help me! There's been a mistake. Please!" But the Teammates jerked her roughly into a convenient doorway and out of sight.

Jowly J. D. Oliver had ignored her. He wore an expensive business suit. He was almost entirely bald, but refused to give in to it. He had combed his wisps of black hair back along the sides of his round head. He was the owner of the plant and spoke with an ingratiating tone to his guests regarding Connie's arrest. "As you see, we run a very tight ship."

He was addressing the local Visitor supervisor, Shawn, who had a long angular face and deep-set eyes that could be very penetrating when he chose to make them so, as he often did. Shawn was a shrewd political animal who had risen in the Visitor ranks but not yet to the heights to which he aspired. He was touring the factory along with several of his aides and the San Francisco mayor, Mark Ohanian, who had three or four people in his own human entourage. The mayor was in his thirty-eighth year and had the striking good looks of a dark-haired, 1950s movie star, which his grandfather had in fact been. Mark was popular among the people of San Francisco and his ongoing collaboration with the Visitors made the alien force feel very comfortable about keeping him in office.

Oliver was proudly pointing out an area of the plant. "That section over there was where we mass-produced the Visitor cure for Alzheimer's."

Mark Ohanian smiled. "Sure helped my granddad a lot."

"And millions of others, Mr. Mayor. Now down this way, Shawn, we've retooled to make your *new* chemical."

They moved on, nodding to Stella who was cheerfully heading

back inside one of the large industrial structures. Then Stella realized that a hefty black worker, whom everyone called Blue, was eyeing her. Stella glared at him. "What the hell are *you* looking at?"

Blue held up his hands to indicate he was staying out of it: no harm, no foul. Stella stared coldly at him a moment longer, as if in warning, then went on her way. Blue shook his head and sighed. He had liked Connie Leonetti and knew for certain that she wasn't involved with the Resistance. He hated to see her denounced and arrested, but also knew there was nothing he could do to save her.

Blue heard the nearby checkpoint gate beeping and looked up to see Dr. Charles Elgin entering. Charles was forty-six, only a few months older than Blue, but he looked years older. His shoulders were always slumped slightly forward, as though the weight of the world were upon him. He paused in the entry gate where a vid screen was flashing the word *Sci* and showing Charles's photo. A full-body scan pinpointed the ID implant in his left arm and presented all his vital statistics. The Patroller at the gate checked the data and admitted him. Charles took off his glasses to clean them and nodded a greeting to Blue, noticing the frown on the big man's face. "What?"

"Good ol' Stella screwed another one."

Charles also frowned. "Who?"

"Connie."

Charles sighed bitterly. The two men began to walk together. Though Charles was of average height and size he looked small beside Blue. Charles's mind was turning on distressing possibilities. "Could be any of us next."

"Yep. I hate that bitch."

"If she keeps it up, she's going to be a Player, too." Charles was looking across the complex to where the plant's owner Oliver was sucking up to the mayor and Visitor Shawn.

"They all deserve each other," Blue grumbled.

Charles looked away. "I didn't hear that."

"I didn't say it." Blue smirked. Then he drew a breath. "So what's this new crap we're making? Insecticide?"

"Very potent," Charles said, nodding, "weapons grade."

"What for?" Blue puzzled over the news. "Visitors got them some giant cockroaches somewhere?"

Charles shrugged, unconcerned and slightly preoccupied. He had spotted an electric drill that was lying behind some barrels, apparently misplaced or forgotten.

IN THE MIDDLE-SCHOOL CLASSROOM THE YOUNG STUDENTS WERE still watching *The Visitor Way*. It was now showing brisk shots of "industry on parade"—smiling people working alongside friendly Visitors. The vigilant Mrs. Richmond saw that one or two of the students were glancing out the window or doodling inattentively and she cruised by them like a dark cloud, tapping their shoulders to refocus them on the vid. On the TV screen Emma's voice was heard over the images of happy workers. "The Visitors soon got Earth running smoothly under the dynamic guidance of their Commandant, Diana."

The beautiful face of Visitor Diana appeared in a compelling close-up. She was a striking brunette with high cheekbones. Her large brown eyes bespoke great intelligence and innate wisdom, and were quite easy to get lost in. She was seen working as a benevolent organizer, meeting her own people and humans at their work places always with a smile and the Visitor greeting-salute, which was the right hand extended and slightly raised, palm up. Diana was shown talking to factory workers, nurturing children at a day-care center, visiting patients at a hospital, and addressing the United Nations General Assembly.

Visitor Press Secretary Paul's sonorous alien voice described the scenes, "Working in humanity's best interests, Diana settled petty disputes like the Middle East by suppressing unruly elements. With advanced Visitor surveillance technology, Diana also ferreted out rogue troublemakers and virtually snuffed out global terrorism. World leaders, like revered U.N. Secretary-General Alberto Mendez, quickly recognized that the Visitors were a powerful force for good. All the top human leaders happily stepped aside to let Visitor wisdom streamline government and bring peace."

Emma's voice chimed in cheerfully, "And so much more, Paul. 'Team Visitor' has shown us how to create cheap fuel cells that eliminated our dependence on oil. They ended famine and gave us miraculous cures for heart disease, AIDS, and most cancers."

In the school custodial closet, Danny Stein's clandestine Resistance vid was chronicling the darker side of the Visitors: stolen glimpses showed crowds of frightened people, their hands on their heads, under heavy Visitor guard, being shoved onto Visitor shuttle craft. People of both genders and sexes, including many disoriented and tearful children, were herded aboard the craft for deportation. Their faces and clothing indicated various ethnicities from different parts of the world. Dr. Robert Maxwell's voice was narrating, "Visitor cures for diseases *seem* like a good thing, but they also yield more healthy people for the Visitors to *take away*."

Margarita continued. "Under Diana's direction, elected leaders and others got herded into transports and flown to one of the many Motherships. All the prisoners have been cocooned in stasis capsules to be used later by the Visitors as soldiers, slaves . . . and even food."

In the dark closet, young Thomas chortled cynically. "No way. That's such bull."

Danny Stein met the Murakami boy's eyes grimly. "You really think so?"

In all school classrooms *The Visitor Way* was showing clean streets and cheery, denim-clad human Teammate units as Paul intoned, "Crime is nearly gone because Diana created *The Teammates*. All humans over the age of thirteen train and serve at least part-time in these grassroots groups that stress fitness, discipline,

and spirited camaraderie. All of Earth's armies have been transformed into Teammate units. Many assist local police forces
against antisocial troublemakers, and keep our neighborhoods
safe."

THAT SAME MORNING IN DOWNTOWN SAN FRANCISCO PEOPLE WERE
presenting their identification papers to smiling Teammates and
Patrollers at a Visitor checkpoint. From a large vid sign above
them, people were smiling out and applauding as the words
flashed: *Be a hero! Report suspicious activity!* Patrol craft, utility vehicles slightly larger than the Visitor fighters, quietly glided
overhead. On the surface, everyday life appeared to be proceeding fairly normally, but most people knew they were living in
a subtle, tightly disciplined, and ever-present police state. For
those old enough to remember World War II, it reminded them
of Paris in the early 1940s after the fall of France. On the surface
the Nazi occupation had not seemed as brutal on the general
populace as many had feared. The French could still go to the
theater, though the plays and films had been judiciously censored. One could still listen to music, though lyrics were carefully expunged of any inappropriate sentiments. A Parisian could
still enjoy an espresso while sitting at an outdoor café along the
Champs Élysées, though German soldiers in their crisp Wehrma-
cht uniforms were sitting at a nearby table or walking along the
wide boulevard and chatting, often in French.

   At that time it was still possible to have a reasonable life if one
were careful and wasn't Jewish or didn't espouse any important
connection to those unfortunates who had been disenfranchised
or denounced. In Fascist Italy during those years there was a
similar sense that if one didn't question authority and kept one's
head down, everyday life could go on and in many ways even improve. The Italian public was delighted that for the first time the
trains actually ran on time. Life in the streets of twenty-first-
century San Francisco, and virtually all the other cities and

towns of the world, had been proceeding for two decades in that same tonality.

The cocky half-breed girl who had saved Nathan peeked out from an alley, waving for him to stay back behind some trash cans as she scoped out the scene. She also didn't want him to see that she was whispering proudly into a tiny radio transceiver, "Hey, it's me. I've got him."

In the shadowy communications truck lovely Margarita smiled wisely. "Gee, why am I not surprised? Take him to Street-C."

The waif nodded to herself. "That's what I figured. I'm already on the way." She clicked off the radio and scurried back to Nathan, pointing a direction. "Down that way. Oh, and hey, I'm Ruby." She extended her leathery hand and he grasped it.

"Nathan. You Resistance?"

"You could say that, yeah," she said with a grin.

Nathan's face was stern. "I want to join up."

"More the merrier. Why'd you bail on the Teammates?"

Nathan saw a smiling Teammate troop moving away in the distance and glared in their direction. "I've got some issues."

They passed a dingy door in the alley and heard the sounds of a small but raucous crowd inside. A very sleazy, unwashed man leaned out to beckon them. "Hey, hey. Gladiator combat. Open betting."

Nathan kept walking. "We'll pass."

The man's grimy, unshaven face twisted into a come-hither grin revealing a broken tooth. "Fights are to the death."

Ruby kept hurrying on. "I'd say there's enough of that on the street."

"We got women, too, pal. Pretty sexy. You'd like!" Nathan and Ruby didn't look back, but the man kept eyeing Nathan, assessing him carefully.

THE MIDDLE-SCHOOL TV SCREEN SHOWED IMAGES OF AMAZON RAIN forests being felled, greasy industrial waste pouring into rivers, dense, ugly smog hanging over cities, seabirds trapped in oil, as Emma's voice said, "Most importantly: *The Visitors came to save our entire civilization.* They saw that Earth was going to die unless they helped immediately. Our industry had poisoned the oceans. The Visitors showed us how oceanic pollution was far deadlier than our very modest science understood. The poisoned oceans are the root cause of *all* our worldwide ecological problems, including the disappearing ozone layer which shields us from deadly cosmic radiation. Without that, we would die."

Then Emma appeared on-camera, her green eyes alight as she delivered the good news, "So the Visitors are taking our water to purge it of toxins, to purify it, *and then return it to us!*"

Paul smiled, using his hands to emphasize and shape the idea. "It's like dialysis on a planetary scale. We Visitors are masters at this sort of massive purification. Much of your polluted sea water has already been collected, compressed within our Motherships, and cleansed. But pouring it back into foul water would be wasteful and counterproductive. We have to wait until the bulk of your toxic water has been removed."

On Danny's Resistance vid, Margarita was looking directly into the camera. "Visitors taking our water is like how Mulholland dried out the Owens Valley to nourish Los Angeles. Only this time we'll all *die*. Look at the damage they've done so far." The supporting images appeared as she spoke. "They're increasingly strict about rationing our water because over half of it is now gone. A few brave Visitors sympathetic to us humans have told us the water *won't* be returned because it's so rare and valuable. Water not only sustains life but to the Visitors it's also like oil: it powers their ships and weapons. And our Earth will be left devastated."

"Earth will be saved and revitalized," smiling Paul said on *The Visitor Way*, "and advanced Visitor technologies will make it a much *healthier* world for the future."

Emma chimed in, "The impurities the Visitors remove are

actually *helpful* to them, so we all benefit. For their effort, the Visitors will keep about ten percent of our water to use as fuel for their spacecraft."

Paul nodded. "We'll also continue to use Earth as a base for further space exploration, which all the people of Earth will share the fruits of."

The vid's cheerful music began to swell as Emma smiled with pleasure and delight at being able to deliver the final, grand message, "Life has never been better or more promising. *We'll all have a terrific, harmonious future together! Thanks to . . . The Visitor Way!*"

The orchestral crescendo continued sweeping toward a grand, inspiring conclusion as Emma and Paul gave each other a warm, friendly hug and waved good-bye.

ON DANNY'S SMALL SCREEN THE RESISTANCE VID WAS SHOWING Margarita's focused, intense face. "Since most of us have seen only their human-looking faces for over twenty years it's easy to forget that underneath they are very different." Diana's beautiful face appeared in a shot that had clearly been captured by a hand-held, secret camera. She was seen admiring a live guinea pig in her hand, then she opened her mouth, which suddenly distended inhumanly wide, transforming into a frightening maw. She casually pushed the frightened animal into her gaping mouth, swallowing it whole and alive. It made her throat bulge out grotesquely as it traveled down into her gullet. "These images were recorded shortly after the Visitors' arrival by news cameraman Mike Donovan," Margarita narrated as another shot appeared, taken when Mike's camera had obviously fallen onto its side during a fight: it showed a Patroller in hand-to-hand combat with strong, rugged Donovan, who tore the false flesh of the Visitor's human face to reveal the startling and hideous creature beneath. It was green and covered with thick scales. A dozen tiny horns raised from its temples and across the top of its forehead. A reptilian forked tongue lashed out.

"This was our first revelation that the Visitors were not what they pretended to be, but rather a carnivorous, aggressive, and deadly reptilian race." Then Margarita reappeared, speaking directly into the camera. "The Visitors will annihilate humanity unless Earth's people *rise against them now*. This is our *last chance*: the Resistance was dealt a terrible blow in 1999 when Diana launched her Great Purge and killed or captured millions of us. You must join us to fight back now—before you, your loved ones, and our planet are destroyed. Please call this untraceable number and—"

Thomas reached out and stabbed the button to turn off Danny's vid player. He was shaking his nervous head vigorously. "No, no, this is all bullshit. My dad says—"

"Your dad's a damn *Player*, Thomas." Danny was vehement. "I've seen him play along and suck up to 'em."

"Yeah? Why don't you go suck a—"

Suddenly the closet door was opened by a seventeen-year-old, human-Visitor half-breed named Ted. He wore janitor's clothing. One of his eyes was human-looking and light brown, but the other was red and had the vertical yellow iris of a Visitor. The scales on his cheeks extended upward and into his brown hair. His ears lay flat against his head. What human skin he did have on his face was troubled by some acne. The leathery skin on his arms completely covered the back of his hands, though the palms were softer and human-looking. He was as surprised as the two boys he had found in his storage closet. "Hey, what're you doing in here?"

Danny was unrepentant and derisive, "Screw off, scale-face."

Even the milder Thomas was equally dismissive of the janitor. "None of your business, you stupid dreg."

Then an overly friendly male voice made their blood chill. "What's going on here?" Danny, and particularly Thomas,

blanched when they saw it was the vice principal of Patrick
Henry Middle School, Mr. Gabriel. He was approaching up the
hallway, a tall, robust man who always had a well-exercised,
healthy glow about him. His round cherubic face made him look
ten years younger than his actual age of thirty-nine. Though he
always spoke with a homey warmth and humor, Danny and many
others referred to Gabriel as the Angel of Death and dreaded
any encounter with him. They knew that his ever-present smile
disguised a very angry and therefore very dangerous man. Danny
knew that Gabriel had been passed over twice already for the
position as full principal and he had a nasty, underhanded way
of taking his frustrations out on the students. His cheery,
friendly smile was much more frightening than the glowering
face of Mrs. Miles, the uncompromising principal of Patrick
Henry. Mr. Gabriel was notorious for dealing out very harsh
sentences to after-school detention for even the most minor in-
fractions. Being sent to Gabriel's office or, worse, being captured by him personally in an inappropriate circumstance was
universally considered to be the ultimate bad news for any of
the middle schoolers.

Danny Stein had several times come under the glare of
Gabriel's overly bright eyes that glowed menacingly out from
beneath his arched, single eyebrow. The current instance could
prove uncomfortable indeed and Danny knew it. But the boy
was a very quick thinker. Before the vice principal glimpsed him
inside the closet, Danny shoved his vid player into a back pocket
and grabbed two sodden rags from the janitorial sink. He pushed
one of the rags into Thomas's hands and the smaller boy looked
at him with confusion just as Gabriel opened the door fully.
Danny immediately took the offensive, "Oh, Mr. Gabriel. Good.
You should know about this."

Gabriel inclined his head toward Danny with a comradely but
satanic wink. "What I know, Daniel Stein, is that you both
should be in class."

"You're absolutely right, sir," curly-haired Danny earnestly agreed. "And we were on the way but then we saw a big spill on the floor here."

Ted, the half-breed janitor, frowned as he glanced around the nearby spotless floor. "What spill?"

Gabriel addressed the boys as though the janitor were not even present, "What spill?" Ted glanced at Gabriel and started to protest again, but then looked away. Such dismissive treatment was an everyday occurrence for half-breeds such as Ted. They were called dregs for a reason.

Danny held out his rag. "I don't know what it was, sir. But it was coming out from under the door here and making a very slippery spot on the hallway floor."

Gabriel studied Danny and then flicked his dangerously friendly eyes over at Thomas, who jumped on Danny's bandwagon and nodded nervous agreement. "Yes, sir, it was some sort of soapy stuff."

"We were afraid some student might not see it," Danny continued earnestly, "might slip and hurt themselves, so we stopped to wipe it up. It was a real mess." As he spoke, Danny watched Gabriel carefully to see if the vice principal was buying the story. When he didn't immediately respond, Danny piled on some more, "Then we were going to report it to you, sir. We thought you should know that *somebody*"—Danny threw a not-so-subtle look toward the half-breed—"maybe wasn't doing his job as well as he needed to."

Ted's annoyance had increased, but he held his temper. He spoke quietly and respectfully toward the vice principal without looking directly at Gabriel's face. "Sir, I was by here ten minutes ago and I can assure you that there was absolutely no—"

Gabriel waved Ted to silence and spoke to the boys with a chilly grin. "Very well, Daniel, I'll look into it. Now you two little rascals get on immediately to your class."

"Right away, sir." Danny tossed his rag back into the sink.

Thomas did likewise, smiling wanly at the tall man. "Thank you, sir." Then the two boys headed down the hall.

Ted watched them go and felt a tightness building behind his eyes. He turned to inspect the telltale rags in the sink. Gabriel was continuing to study the boys, and particularly Danny, as they walked away. He had started to turn back to the half-breed when something registered in Gabriel's mind. The vice principal gazed back down the hall at the departing boys, looking particularly at something that was partially protruding from Danny's back pocket.

4

NATHAN HAD BEEN LETTING THE HALF-BREED TWELVE-YEAR-OLD girl lead him through back alleys northward across Chinatown from where he had crashed on Market Street. He was aware of the sights and sounds of the city around him, particularly the numerous Visitor shuttle craft that cruised by on patrol overhead, but he was focused inwardly.

In his mind's eye he could still see Sarah's dying face before him. He was furious that he'd had to leave her body in the uncaring possession of Patrollers and Teammates. He was infuriated at having had no time to properly absorb his loss of her, to honor what she had been to him, to grieve. He thought of Sarah's smiling face over the years, her infinite patience with him as a very angry young man. As his Teammate leader, she had been a mentor, but because of her gentleness and nurture, he had also come to think of her as family. She was like a knowing older sister, almost a mother, who had given him understanding and guidance.

From time to time during their years together, Nathan had noticed some very small hints from Sarah, an oddly shaded phrase or an averted eye. It was always something that seemed so trivial that only he who knew her the most intimately could discern. He had once seen an astronomer at work over a chart showing a thousand stars. The woman was so familiar with each individual star's placement that from the multitude of tiny spots she could tell immediately if one was out of place. So well did Nathan know Sarah. It was those tiny hints that gradually led him to the feeling that her allegiance to the Visitors might not be as unswerving and true as she professed. But he suppressed those suspicions because of their personal bond.

He performed his duties as a Teammate with great ardor. He knew that he owed it to his parents because of their sacrifice. Nathan was determined to make up for the untimely death that had claimed them at the hands of the Resistance. He was proud when he distinguished himself during the Great Purge eight years earlier by helping to track down and arrest, sometimes quite roughly, many members of the illegal and dangerous Resistance. And he had also brought to justice many Visitors who had aided and abetted the Resistance. He was much praised by his superiors for his achievements and had even been given a commendation by Diana herself, though he had not met her personally.

But throughout it all, Nathan had an ever-growing concern that Sarah, the person to whom he was closest, upon whose counsel, guidance, and even love he had always most counted, might herself be a traitor to the Visitors' cause.

His unease had come to a head only within the last twenty-four hours—when he at last found the courage to put to Sarah the questions that had kindled within him over the years and now were burning to be answered. He had held off asking her for so long because he feared her answers and feared the position in which he would then be put. His Teammate loyalty would demand that he denounce and inform on her.

All his fears were realized when Sarah admitted that his suspicions were justified. She was indeed part of a fifth column cadre, a supersecret network that existed between a tiny minority of the Visitors who did not believe in the grand cause espoused by the vast majority under the guidance of their Great Leader.

Though he had expected it, Sarah's admission was a stunning blow to Nathan and threw him immediately into a moral quandary. How could he possibly be loyal to the Visitors and Sarah both? She held him close as she had when he was first orphaned as a fifteen-year-old. She comforted him and quietly said that she understood his turmoil. She knew he couldn't possibly decide where to place his loyalties—unless he learned the entire truth. She herself had struggled for years with how and when she might reveal it to him. More than once she had been about to do it, only to have second thoughts, to protect his safety and his future. Like Nathan, Sarah also had anguished over the proper course to take.

But when he confronted her yesterday, she resolved that the time had come. Now they had both suffered the consequences. Sarah had been killed and Nathan was on the run.

"This way, come on," Ruby whispered urgently, bringing Nathan back into the moment. She was leading him through an alley off Clay Street in Chinatown. Nathan winced at the smells wafting out of the various establishments, fishy fumes of shrimp and other seafood sautéing in woks mixed in the air with the sour smells of rotting garbage from the trash cans and Dumpsters they were passing. Then Nathan sensed something. He stopped and glanced sharply back over his shoulder, studying the four- and five-story rooftops of the old brick buildings behind them. Looking through the filigree of fire escapes and pieces of laundry hanging from them he thought he caught a glimpse of a blond head ducking back into hiding.

"What?" Ruby had turned back, impatiently. "What is it?"

He was eyeing a particular roof's balustrade carefully. "I don't know." He was uncertain now, thinking that perhaps he was just being overly paranoid.

"Nobody's following us." Supremely confident, little Ruby was already scampering onward, calling back to him, "C'mon!"

Nathan still glanced back at the rooftops as he followed. His instincts were usually right on the money, yet there was nothing to be seen. It puzzled him as he and Ruby moved on, passing the back door of a small Chinese grocery. A moment later it opened. An occidental fourteen-year-old girl emerged.

Charlotte Elgin was pretty but thin and underdeveloped. She wore a simple thrift-shop dress, purchased two years earlier and washed so often that the colors in the delicate print had faded. She carried an old bushel basket to a Dumpster and was about to throw away some bruised, overripe apples when she paused to look at the fruit more carefully. Then she began to pick out a few.

A Chinese woman waddled out of the grocery's back door carrying a bag of trash. Charlotte smiled. Her employer's shape had always reminded the girl of a classic snowman: a small round head, a medium-sized round torso, with the bottom third of her roundest of all. The woman was not even five feet tall. She saw what the teenager was doing and shook her head. Her voice was heavily accented with her native language. "No, Charlotte. They all bad. No can sell. You throw way."

Charlotte tilted her head sweetly down toward the older woman who was a good foot shorter. "Oh, Mrs. Soon, if you don't mind, since they were just going to be thrown out, I was going to take some of them home."

Mrs. Soon looked carefully at the apples, scrutinizing each of them microscopically. Charlotte could almost hear the abacus clicking inside the woman's head as she calculated their worth.

"They not very good. Lotta bruise. Soft spots."

"Not good to sell, maybe. They'd be good enough for me," Charlotte said confidently. "I'll bet I can get lots of nice pieces off of them."

"Mmmm"—Mrs. Soon pursed her lips as she made a final

careful assessment, then finally nodded—"okay, Charlotte. You take."

"Thank you very much, Mrs. Soon." The teenager smiled and took a used plastic bag that the lady held out to her for the damaged fruit. Mrs. Soon liked Charlotte's smile and her ability to be friendly toward customers with whom Mrs. Soon often had little patience. Charlotte's mild temperament could charm the most aggravating of them. Mrs. Soon had also noted how her store's business had actually increased since Charlotte had begun working there several months ago, though she had never considered increasing the girl's pay.

Charlotte came after school every day plus she was there from opening until closing all day on Saturdays and Sundays. Mrs. Soon purposely never asked about Charlotte's family situation, but at their first meeting she had immediately deduced they must be struggling to survive. Probably Scis. Mrs. Soon carefully avoided any record of the girl's employment and paid Charlotte "under table" as she put it, which she had decided would be better—and safer—for them both.

Mrs. Soon had once been very poor herself, which accounted for her becoming the most infamous miser in the neighborhood. She knew all the earmarks of poverty. In all the many days Charlotte had come to the grocery, Mrs. Soon had never seen her wear more than three different dresses. They were all threadbare, but always neatly ironed and cared for. They were too thin for the San Francisco winter now that the climate had become more severe since the drying up of the bay and the Pacific Basin almost halfway to Hawaii. There had even been some snow during the last few years. On those colder days, Charlotte augmented her dresses with a thin, pale blue cardigan sweater. It was always the same sweater. Charlotte herself was as thin as her sweater. Once in a great while the tight-fisted Mrs. Soon would allow the girl to take something like the nearly spoiled apples.

Charlotte was always very grateful. Indeed, the girl had an unwavering graciousness about her that inspired most of those who came in contact with her. Her influence on people was subtle but definite. Many would begin to emulate her gentle charm. People left Mrs. Soon's store feeling better than they had upon arriving. One man had even told Mrs. Soon that seeing Charlotte always gave his immune system a boost. For her part, Charlotte was very happy just to have a job that allowed her to help support her family.

She was basically a pretty girl with nice features and gray-blue eyes, though to Mrs. Soon her face sometimes looked a bit drawn, as though Charlotte perhaps had some recurrent or chronic ailment. Charlotte had never mentioned that she had diabetes.

Charlotte did have wonderful hair, though. It was thick, long, and almost raven black. As Mrs. Soon watched Charlotte put the bruised apples in the bag, the older woman eyed Charlotte's shiny tresses appreciatively. "You hair beautiful, Charlotte."

Charlotte smiled. "You always say that, Mrs. Soon. Thank you."

"It look Chinese."

"So you tell me."

"My daughter, hair terrible." Mrs. Soon shook her round head in frustration. "You see her? Hair all ratty. Look like crap."

"But your May is a very nice young woman."

"But could be beautiful. If hair good. I tell her: you get wig. You hair terrible. Not like Charlotte."

Charlotte blushed slightly as she smiled and tied the top of the plastic bag. She then held it up in a thankful gesture and bowed to Mrs. Soon in proper Chinese fashion. The older lady received the acknowledgment with a tiny hesitation, wondering if she should keep the apples and try to sell them after all, but then she likewise bowed.

* * *

IN THE BEDROOM OF EMMA'S PLUSH, TRENDY CONDO AT THE PEAK OF Nob Hill on Clay Street, a flat-screen TV lay on its back on the thickly carpeted floor. Emma herself was lying facedown on a massage table, her tawny, well-toned dancer's body completely nude. She was looking through the table's padded circular head support at the screen on the floor. It was displaying the flashy images and staccato editing of Emma's most recent, unreleased music vid. The rhythms were kicky, infectious, and so toe-tapping they were irresistible. The striking young diva had thorough command of her latest song and the vocal strength to do it justice. The vid showed her backed up by human singer-dancers and even a couple of Visitors as she sang in various locations. At one point she was dancing atop a Visitor fighter craft. Anyone viewing it would instantly understand why Emma had become such a popular star. Quite simply, she was very talented and she used her talents extremely well.

But she wasn't happy with the particular performance she was watching. "I've got to change those lyrics, find a better way to say it. I need to reshoot it. Don't you think, Mary?"

Mary Elgin's mind had been wandering while she administered the massage. "Hmm? No, it sounds fine to me." Mary, a pale-complected woman of forty-six, looked considerably older than her years to Emma and always seemed emotionally frail. Like other scientists or their families whom Emma had encountered, Mary had a beleaguered quality. But she was a wonderful masseuse. She kneaded Emma's long, lovely neck and barely glanced at the music vid on the screen. "Relax your neck."

Emma closed her eyes and gave herself over to Mary's magical fingertips. "Mmmm," Emma murmured, "you are so good, Mary. All those years studying anatomy, huh?"

"I suppose," Mary sighed.

"Do you still do any sculpting?"

"No. Can't make a living at that." For a moment as she

worked her fingers carefully on the muscles in Emma's neck Mary remembered working clay with her fingers. She had loved the feel of it as she shaped and reshaped it. She remembered how she'd felt back in high school and later in the gracious neo-classical Fine Arts Building at Carnegie-Mellon. She'd felt that she wasn't merely shaping the clay, but actually shaping her own future, shaping the art that would speak for her, that would be her contribution to the world; that would be *her* and live on long after she was gone. That was the dream that first dawned within her as a child. She still had a visceral memory of the first piece of clay she held between her fingers when she was four or five: the clean, earthy smell of it. The infinite joy and possibilities it offered, until the Visitors arrived over twenty years ago. And suddenly all her hopes and dreams, like those of so many others, were quashed overnight. Her musing was interrupted as Emma raised up slightly to look at her.

"Oh, listen, Mary." Emma paused, seeming frustrated and sorry about what she had to say. "I tried my pharmacy, like I said I would."

Mary heard Emma's tone and grew disheartened, anticipating what Emma was about to say. "But they wouldn't do it?"

"No, I'm so sorry." There was genuine regret in her voice. "They wouldn't let me buy medicine for your family even under *my* name."

"I was pretty sure they wouldn't." Mary sighed. "Thanks for suggesting it—and for trying."

"It's so damned unfair"—Emma lay her face back down on the circular support with a frustrated puff—"I wish I could just *give* you the extra money again, Mary, but now they're watching every penny I might pay to Scis or their families. The curse of being sort of high profile, I guess."

Mary nodded with stoic resignation. "They monitor us very closely, too. Thanks, anyway."

"Is their diabetes very advanced?"

"My daughter Charlotte seems to be holding on, but my father-in-law is not doing so well."

The peculiarly resonant voice of a male Visitor interrupted, "Knock knock?"

The two women looked over to see Paul, the natty Visitor press secretary, peeking in around the thick, beautifully crafted wooden door that accessed Emma's peach-colored master bedroom suite.

Emma smiled at him, thoroughly unembarrassed by her lack of clothing. "Hey, you. Caught me with my pants down." Mary eased a sheet over Emma's exposed bronze curves.

"Sorry." Paul smiled, but Mary noted that he didn't back out of the room. "Your assistant was on the phone and pointed me this way."

"It's okay, we were just finishing up." Emma slid gracefully off the table while wrapping the sheet around herself. She did it a bit too gracefully for Paul's taste, because he was foiled from seeing as much of the singer's café au lait body as he would've liked. In the twenty years since his arrival on Earth he'd developed quite an eye and a sexual fascination for beautiful human women, not unlike many other male Visitors. Emma particularly inspired a savor of sensuality in him.

As Mary helped Emma with the sheet, the singer looked at her sincerely, speaking privately. "I'll try to think of some other way to help, Mary."

"Thanks, Emma, that means a lot." Then Mary stepped subserviently back as she nodded hello to Paul.

Emma, scarcely concealed in her sheet, went to him and gave him a friendly kiss on his cheek. "What brings you into my boudoir?"

"The Leader's Emissary arrives tomorrow," Paul said with some gravity, "I'd love to have you there."

Emma smiled cheerfully as she shook her long black hair from the clip that had been holding it. "Wherever you want me."

"Really?" He studied her. "Don't tease me, now."

But that was something Emma did very well and often without even realizing it. She winked at him. "I'll be out in a sec and you can tell me all about it." She padded barefoot across the thick carpet and into her cream-colored bathroom while Paul stood in the bedroom and imagined her naked.

THE FUNKY YOUNG MAN IN HIS SLOUCHY HIP-HOP CLOTHES KEPT A weathered eye on the street. He had learned from childhood to be very careful. He was constantly shifting his weight from one foot to the other on the top step of the old brownstone at Cordelia and Broadway in San Francisco's seamy Tenderloin District. Named Jerome Xavier Hernandez by his black mother and Mexican father, as a teenager he had created for himself what he thought was the way-cool nickname of Street-C. A few of his friends guffawed and said it was pretty stupid, which only aroused Jerome's pride of authorship, so he made sure that it had stuck. Jerome fostered his image as a funky, street-smart wise guy, but underneath he was extremely literate. There was always some dog-eared paperback stuffed into the back pocket of his slouchy jeans. It was generally a book banned by the Visitors, like his current choice, Will Durant's *The Story of Philosophy*.

Jerome had his father's Central American skin color, but his mother's dark eyes and tightly curled hair, which he'd done up in tiny cornrows. His passion for the Resistance was unsurpassed. As a boy he had lost his family members one at a time to the Visitors and by the age of ten Jerome had become an orphaned street urchin scraping by for survival. Then he'd made the wonderful mistake of trying to rob a Peruvian woman who proved to be much tougher than he was. She had boxed his ears severely and then proceeded to turn his life around. Ysabel Encalada had seen her own teenage son be corrupted by the Visitors and become an ardent Teammate some years earlier, so she too was without family. The spicy, no-bullshit Latina became Jerome's surrogate mother and raised him within San Francisco's prime Resistance cadre. Ysabel was the only one he allowed to call him Jerome.

He was chewing on a matchstick and casually searching the street over Nathan's shoulder for any slight indication that this new guy might not be what Ruby said he claimed to be: a deserter from the Teammates. "So why you want to join the Resistance?"

Nathan stood near the half-breed girl who was watching him carefully from just inside the alcove at the top of the stoop. She saw from his surly expression that he wasn't in the mood for a lot of questions. "I've got my reasons."

Street-C pressed darkly, "Gotta show me some proof, mofo."

"Proof?" Nathan had a short fuse and he was getting annoyed. "Why don't you haul your lazy ass over to Market and look at the fighter I stole and got shot down in?"

"Yeah, I heard about that," Street-C said with a nod. Nathan watched as the youth continued to survey the street. "But I'm afraid you gotta do better than that, my man."

"Better than—?!" Nathan flared, then stopped himself. His wounded cheek was throbbing and he wanted to blow off this street punk in the worst way, but knew he needed the contact. He pushed down his annoyance and spoke quietly but with thinly veiled sarcasm, "Just what did you have in mind, friend?"

Street-C twiddled the matchstick between his teeth, then looked into Nathan's eyes for the first time. "Gotta off a lizard. Kill a Patrol captain."

Nathan knew that Street-C was looking for any flicker of hesitation. There was none. "Fine. You got a specific one in mind?"

"Oh, yeah"—Street-C's eyes drifted back out toward the passing traffic—"he gets tips from a snitch over at Fremont and Mission."

Nathan nodded. "I'll need a weapon."

"You be there tomorrow. Noon. My old lady'll point him out and give you a piece."

A disturbance up the block distracted them. Nathan glanced off and saw a skinny, elderly man who looked like he might be homeless being roughed up by four Teammates. One of them was Debra Stein, a tough, short-haired, chunky seventeen-year-old. She was shouting derisively at the cowering old man, "Forgot your ID?" She shoved him abusively. "*Forgot it*! You some kind of antisocial! Huh? Or maybe a Sci?" She pushed him harder and he fell to the pavement between the four young fascists.

Nathan instinctively wanted to go to the man's defense, but he held himself in check and glanced back to see Ruby and Street-C's reactions. He was surprised to discover that he was alone on the stoop. They had disappeared inside the locked brownstone. Nathan waited until the rowdy Teammates were looking the other way, then he walked quickly across Cordelia into a narrow alley between two decrepit buildings.

On a rooftop above, a woman with short blond hair and a slight sheen to her skin had been observing Nathan intently. Kayta's violet eyes twinkled with pride as she spoke into a small pin on her suede vest. "I have him, Bryke. And I think our instincts are correct. I think he'll lead us to them. Where are you?"

Bryke's voice came back, "Investigating the Sci Section." The dark-skinned woman had just turned east off of Guerrero Street onto Twenty-second, heading toward the Mission District. She was cruising along slowly on a sleek, narrow, aerodynamic motorbike, scanning the scene with her strange pink eyes. "What of Ayden?"

"He's inbound." Kayta was moving along the rooftop keeping sharply focused on Nathan below. He had temporarily settled into a secluded nook in the alley behind a pile of trash. He sat beneath a rusty fire escape with his back against the weathered bricks and his knees drawn up close to his chest. Even from her distant vantage point, Kayta could see the dark, troubled frown on his face. Having witnessed much of the turmoil he had been through that day, she was desirous of learning more about the true nature and intent of this apparent Teammate deserter.

5

THE FINAL BELL HAD JUST RUNG AT PATRICK HENRY MIDDLE SCHOOL. Thomas Murakami was among the myriad young students pouring out the school's front door. He paused at the top of the broad concrete steps to open his backpack. He was checking to make certain he had the sheet music for his piano lesson. He wasn't fond of the lessons, but his strict, traditional parents insisted upon him taking them and practicing diligently. He located the music and was just closing his pack as he felt a strong hand grasp his shoulder. He looked back and his heart immediately dropped into his stomach.

It was the ever-friendly vice principal, Mr. Gabriel. He was staring down at Thomas with a knowing glint in his soft, cherubic eyes that unsettled the thirteen-year-old in the extreme. "Thomas, my boy," Gabriel said with a curious smile that made the boy's heart ice over and drop even farther, "I need to talk to you for a moment. In my office."

THAT EVENING A BILLBOARD-SIZED VID SCREEN ON THE WALL OF A building at Potrero and Eighteenth was displaying the latest news to passing pedestrians. Anyone listening carefully would also have heard the identical broadcast echoing from all of the other televisions and radios in the downscale urban residential neighborhood. The huge screen showed a Hispanic man, well into his seventies, with shaggy white eyebrows and a full head of thick white hair combed carefully back. He was seen approaching microphones that had been set up outside a hospital. A Visitor shuttle craft was visible in the parking lot behind him, as were several Visitor Patrollers. A newsman's voice was saying, "And continuing his visit to his home here in San Francisco, U.N. Secretary-General Alberto Mendez, the much-revered Nobel Peace Prize winner, had more praise today for the Visitors."

The Secretary-General spoke in a matter-of-fact tone. "The new work in genetics being done by the Visitors is truly remarkable. I'm given to understand that, with their help, there will soon be no more human children born with birth defects."

Several people passing on the nighttime street noted and nodded to each other approvingly. It was yet another achievement in the plus column for life under the Visitors. And since it was being reported by the Secretary-General, whom everyone held in high regard, it was clearly the reliable truth.

But one person walking along the sidewalk had an angry frown caught on his scaly forehead. It was Ted, the half-breed school custodian. His mismatched human-alien eyes stared down at the pavement. He kicked at a crumpled soda can. He was brooding darkly about the reprimand that Vice Principal Gabriel had given him that morning for something that certainly wasn't his fault because he damn well knew it had never happened. Such a dressing-down wasn't unusual for him to receive. Ted often grumbled accusingly that trouble always came to rest upon the nearest half-breed.

Ted was approaching a group of sanitation workers who were laboring at a steamy, foul-smelling manhole beside the roadway of the James Lick Freeway that curved nearby. Their yellow jumpsuits were stained and grimy with filth. They were half-breeds, of course. Janitors, sewer workers, garbage collectors, most all of those who worked at the lowest end of the social spectrum now came mostly from the ranks of the half-breeds. All were under the age of twenty, since inter-species breeding had begun about four years after the Visitors' arrival.

One of the half-breeds, a female about Ted's age with a broad swash of green scales across the human skin of her face, noticed he was looking in their direction and she smiled. Ted turned his eyes away, he wanted no part of her or the others. He dodged a bus and crossed the street to avoid passing too close to them. He saw several Visitor Patrollers ahead and the envy he felt toward them kicked in. He smiled toward one. "Hey. How's it going?"

The Patroller scowled at Ted's effrontery, shoving him across the sidewalk into a pair of human teens, who reacted with equal distaste. "Watch out, you fucking dreg!" They shoved him off the curb and into the gutter. As they continued on, the teens wiped off their hands on their jeans as though they had touched fecal matter. Ted stood in the street staring after them. Half-breeds were the lowest caste, it was no wonder that everyone above them, human and Visitor alike, had long ago begun to call them dregs. They were the disinherited, the bottom of everyone's barrel. Every day Ted encountered the bitter truth that he and his kind existed only on the dim fringes of life. They were literally beings without a world or even a race to call their own. It was with that sour mind-set, which was normal for him, that Ted climbed the creaking wooden stairs toward the cheap third-floor walk-up on Twenty-first Street where he lived.

Ted's human mother was already inside the apartment, having arrived a moment earlier. She shed the jacket over her waitress's uniform, which bore her name tag: Harmy. It was short for Harmony. She kissed her fingertips and touched them to the feet of the Christ that hung on a small cross on the wall. It had been a confirmation gift when she was thirteen and was always nearby since. She flipped on the TV and began humming along with Emma's latest cheery hit as she entered the kitchenette. Emma's tune fit well with Harmy's naturally optimistic approach to life. Though pushing fifty, her frazzled, strawberry blond hair added an extra glow of youth and no one seeing her at that moment would've known she'd just been working hard on her feet for eight hours.

She brightened further when she saw her son enter. "Hi, Teddy. Just got home myself." She gave him a kiss on his scaly cheek, then noted Ted's dour face. "You okay, honey?"

"I'm the same, Mom," was his monotone reply.

Harmy was determined to stay upbeat. She was accustomed to Ted's depressive moods, which increasingly had been the order of the day, but she refused to be drawn into his negative energy. She was certain that she could be more beneficial to him by accentuating the positive, so she worked to leaven his discontented spirit. "Hey, I graded your math paper on my lunch break"—she was pulling out the sheet Ted had wrinkled uncaringly while writing it—"you did really good!"

At that moment, one floor below them in the stairwell of the dingy tenement, a woman with curlers in her hair and a cigarette drooping from her lips was shaking the dust from a small rug when her expression went vinegary. The male Visitor was coming up the stairs like he did every few days to visit the frizzy-haired woman in 3D. But he always arrived without his human-looking face. Only rarely did anyone ever see a Visitor's actual face. They weren't supposed to be shown. Diana had made it a regulation. The woman with curlers thought they were ugly as sin with their green scales and those small horns that lay flat against the sides and tops of their heads. She hated the way their noses looked all smashed down, and their lipless mouths truly put her off. The Visitor nodded to her politely as he passed and went on up. The woman stubbed out her cigarette on the ratty banister and dropped the butt down the stairwell. She shook her head, wondering how that woman up in 3D could be involved with one of them? Have sex with him? Give birth to one of those ungodly half-breed bastards? It was positively stomach-turning.

In the apartment above, Harmy was working to lighten Ted's mood. "Oh, and I found another mom who's setting up a real school for kids like you and I thought maybe—"

"You should've just aborted me." Her son stared coldly out the window at the dark city.

His words went into Harmy like a knife. She paused a moment. "It makes me so sad to hear you say that, Teddy."

Neither of them had noticed that Harmy's Visitor husband William had quietly opened the front door. He had paused outside to affix his human face over his real one. He had short, tightly curled hair that was light brown like his eyes. His chin was rather weak, but there were tiny wrinkles at the corners of his eyes from smiling. Though rather nondescript, his face reflected a gentle nature. He had overheard Ted's cutting remark and instantly surmised the boy's mood. He walked to them, putting his arm around Harmy's waist with an easy smile. "We loved each other, Teddy. You know that. We loved the thought of having you."

Harmy nodded, leaning toward her son and trying to catch his sullen eyes. "You know how we hope that kids like you will be—"

"'A bridge between your two peoples,' yeah, yeah," the teenager said in a sarcastic, singsongy voice. He'd heard it all before ad nauseum. "Well, in case you haven't noticed, the bridge is out."

Willy had watched Ted's eyebrows along with the scaly skin of his forehead rising and falling as he talked. Willy knew how that contraction and expansion went on involuntarily whenever his son was deeply distraught. Willy sat against the edge of their small dinette table trying to take a new tack. He spoke sympathetically, "Look, Teddy, we all have hard days sometimes and—"

"Sometimes!" Ted chortled darkly, then he looked directly at his father, anger and frustration burning in both his human eye and the one that was reptilian. "Dad, you've got *no idea* what it's like to be me! No fucking idea!"

"Teddy." Harmy reached a calming hand toward his arm, but he pulled it away.

"Shit rolls downhill, don't you know that? And do you know who it lands on? Huh!" Ted cast his eyes toward the ceiling searching for something impossible to find, then he looked back forcefully at Willy. "I wish I was full-blooded like you."

Willy gazed levelly at his son and spoke quietly, "Beware what you wish for."

"Right, right"—Ted's head bobbed sarcastically—"easy for you to say."

His mother touched his shoulder. "These have been rough years, I know."

"But we're trying to make the best of things, Teddy," his father counseled, "day by day."

"And I truly believe things are gonna get better, honey." Then Harmy remembered, "Oh, and I got you a new book at that bargain place." She smiled as she pulled a ragged paperback from her ten-year-old purse and handed it to him. It was Charles Dickens's *Great Expectations*.

"Perfect, Mom"—Ted smirked, his eyebrows knit and then smoothed again—"really. That's just perfect." He shuffled off into his small room and closed the door.

Willy and Harmy both stared at the closed door for a long moment, then looked deeply into each other's eyes, sharing parental angst. Harmy leaned against the gentle Visitor's chest and breathed a long, sad sigh.

Willy put his arms around her and held her, wishing he had some answers for Ted's dismay and reluctant to have to tell her his news. "I've got to go back to the ship tonight."

Harmy sagged with disappointment as she looked up at him. "Oh, Willy, why?"

"They want everybody, even my maintenance crew. Some large-hair is arriving tomorrow."

"'Large-hair'?" Harmy screwed up her face, trying to fathom what he meant. Willy stared at her, realizing that he had misspoken, but not knowing how. Harmy continued to puzzle over it, " 'Large-hair'?"

"I . . . thought that's what they said," he was trying to remember exactly.

Then Harmy's face brightened. "Do you mean *bigwig*?"

"Ah. Right"—Willy nodded, pleased—"bigwig. Yes."

She gave him a kiss on the cheek. She loved Willy and also the fact that he was often slightly out-of-sync with the language and thus unconsciously humorous. That was partly what had endeared him to her and drawn them together at the beginning. Despite the fact that they were literally from two different worlds they had slowly discovered that they were soul mates. The kindness of their hearts was much stronger than their physical differences. Harmy knew that Willy had a reptilian physiognomy beneath his human-looking exterior. She of course had seen his true face, though he had been very reluctant to show it to her that first time. But by then they were already in love and she knew his heart.

The spark between them had been struck on his very first day on the planet, when he was wandering around the chemical plant lost and unable to communicate. He had been trained to speak Arabic, but through a foul-up typical of all bureaucracies, human or alien, he had found himself deposited in America. Harmy had helped him acclimate and later she actually saved his life. She'd discovered a bomb that had been planted in the chemical factory by the Resistance. She was anguishing over whether or not to report it when she saw Willy pause right beneath it. Her shout of alarm had saved him.

Harmy and Willy were not unique in their relationship. Thousands of other interspecies couples around the world had had similar experiences and had, purposely or not, given birth to half-breed offspring. Others had experienced momentarily lustful moments that led to such births and of course many human females had simply been raped and for personal or religious reasons were unable to terminate the pregnancy.

The mutual affection that Harmy and Willy felt was genuine, however, as were their concerns for each other's safety. That was why Willy always entered the apartment without his human face, so that neighbors like the nosy woman in curlers wouldn't recognize him. Most humans couldn't distinguish the subtle differences in the reptilian faces, so to humans, Willy liked to joke, "We all look alike."

Willy drew out a small gray envelope from within his shirt and gave it to Harmy. "Be careful. Our snoopy neighbor was in the stairwell."

Harmy turned the envelope over in her hands, knowing her mission with it. "I wish we didn't have to worry about what people thought of us. Or worry about us helping the Resistance."

"Well, we have to do what's right"—Willy hugged her close to him—"and someone I love a lot truly believes things are going to get better."

Harmy pressed her cheek against his shoulder and closed her eyes, praying that her hope might come true.

CHARLOTTE ELGIN WAS IN THE TINY, CHEAPLY PANELED BATHROOM that also served as a storage room for the Chinese grocery. She hadn't been feeling well and was splashing cold water on her face over the stained, cracked sink. She heard Mrs. Soon turning out the lights in the store and calling to her impatiently, "Charlotte? You ready go?"

"Just a sec, Mrs. Soon." The teenager took some breaths and looked at her reflection in the fragment of mirror. More and more lately Charlotte had felt like a mere fragment herself. She opened a prescription pill bottle and poured the pills carefully into her soft palm to count them, though she already knew there were only two. She replaced one of them, contemplated the remaining pill for a long moment and decided not to take it. She returned it to the bottle. Then she picked up the plastic bag that contained the four bruised apples she had rescued from the garbage. The little treasure made her smile because it meant there would be an apple for each one in her family.

A LARGE BLACK RAT SKITTERED UP THE DAMP ALLEY BEHIND THE Chinese grocery as Nathan cautiously returned toward the Dumpster he'd passed earlier. He was cold and hungry. He lifted the metal lid and was digging through the day's discarded remnants, mostly paper and cardboard, when he heard a gentle voice, "I'm afraid there's really nothing edible in there."

He turned around to see the young teenager with raven black hair whom he'd passed earlier. Charlotte was just coming out the grocery's back door, leaving for the night. Nathan looked at her and sighed. He closed the Dumpster as Charlotte studied him and considered his plight. She noticed his Teammate uniform was badly smudged and from the sight of his bruised jaw and the fresh wound on his left cheek she easily surmised that he was in some kind of trouble. He also looked very hungry. "Here." She reached into her small plastic bag, "Take one of these. It's not perfect, but . . ." As she fished out one of her discolored apples, Nathan noticed that her shoes were badly worn and her thin pale sweater was very frayed at the cuffs.

He held up his hands resisting. "No, no, that's very kind, but I couldn't take your food."

"Oh, it's okay. I've got more than enough." She smiled sweetly. Nathan paused, he didn't really believe her, but she extended the apple toward him. "Really. Please."

He took it and nodded appreciatively. "Thanks."

From the entrance to the alley, Ruby had been secretly watching their exchange. Now she whispered into her radio, "So far he looks legit, Margarita. Seems like a nice guy . . . and he's really cute. Got a great butt."

In the communications truck Margarita smiled as she sipped

some chamomile tea. "Ah. The important criteria. Okay, Rube, I'll send you relief by nine. Keep a close eye on him."

Ruby's eyes twinkled. "That will be my pleasure." Then she clicked off cheerfully. She took off her crush cap, ran her scaly hand through her chestnut hair, then pulled the cap back onto her head as she settled in happily to wait and watch. She was unaware that from a rooftop above her she and Nathan were *both* being carefully observed by Kayta.

AN HOUR AFTER WILLY HAD LEFT, HARMY EMERGED FROM THEIR apartment building into the chill February night. She casually sauntered up Potrero Street, then turned left onto Seventeenth as a Patrol shuttle glided by overhead. Harmy checked her watch, pacing her walk so that she would time it properly and not arrive too late or, worse, too soon, which might make her look suspiciously like she was loitering.

Nodding to a passing Teammate unit, Harmy arrived at Franklin Square Park and saw the cyclist approaching on his bike. He was a clean-cut, handsome man in his thirties, his skin was smooth and close shaven and his smoke-colored hair carefully blow-dried, as always. For security reasons they didn't know each other's names and they never really looked at each other as Harmy deftly handed off the gray envelope to him and he went pedaling on. Harmy then continued walking, planning to circle the park as she always did, even when she didn't have to make a drop-off. She barely noticed the lean black woman who was sitting on an unusual motorcycle parked on Hampshire.

Bryke had been there for some time, absorbing the ambience and the details of the street life. She fidgeted in her clothes, which continued to annoy her. She much preferred being naked. She had spotted the exchange of the gray envelope and now started her motorcycle, which purred quietly beneath her. She waited for a break in the traffic to wheel around into the other direction and follow the cyclist who had turned a corner onto Bryant. But when Bryke turned the same corner she was puzzled not to see him up the street ahead of her. Curious as to where he could have gone, she continued along Bryant toward the Sci Section in the Mission District that she had earlier reconnoitered. She had seen that the city neighborhood within the Sci area was effectively cordoned off by a fence made of parallel laser beams. Bryke slowed as she approached a checkpoint door frame in the fence that was manned by several Teammates and Visitor Patrollers.

Just going through the entrance at that particular moment was the chemical-plant scientist, Dr. Charles Elgin. With his head down and his shoulders slightly stooped as always, he passed through the security frame, which beeped recognition. One of the Teammate guards checked the screen showing Charles's statistics and waved him on inside. Bryke had noted this procedure earlier. She looked through the gateway trying to see if the cyclist was on the Sci street within, but he wasn't and she continued down Bryant.

The street in the Sci Section looked nothing like the parklike communities for scientists as shown in *The Visitor Way*. It was more crowded and grimy than Harmy's street. There was more obvious surveillance. Two Patrol shuttles were gliding overhead. To Charles they emphasized the claustrophobic feel of the ghetto. He walked past two fellow scientists. They were meteorologists checking makeshift instruments they had jerry-built together. Charles heard one saying, ". . . Yeah, of course the climate's changing from the water loss. It has to. Look how it's sped up global warming, dropped the humidity."

The other scientist shook her head in frustration. "It's terrible. Did you hear about that latest dust storm down in the Amazon Basin?"

Charles trod on up the street toward the tenement where his

family lived. He felt deeply fatigued. Not merely from his long days at the plant or the three hours it took him every day to make the round trip by bus and trolley, but from the weight of surety he felt that things were never going to change. Except probably for the worse.

NEAR THE MOUTH OF THE CHINATOWN ALLEY, RUBY WAS GETTING stiff from being so scrunched up in hiding. She shifted her position slightly as she glanced down at Nathan. He hadn't moved for the last hour. He was huddled against the grocery Dumpster, trying to stay out of the cold night breeze. Then Ruby heard a pair of raucous voices drawing near.

On the rooftop above, Kayta also heard them. She saw two men stumble into the alley below, walking awkwardly as they leaned heavily against each other. They were apparently very drunk and singing boozily. They walked right past Nathan who sized them up, then he drew his arms closer around himself for warmth and shut his eyes. In that split second a heavy cloth bag dropped over his head and the two men, whose awkward drunkenness had vanished, began to bludgeon him.

Ruby shouted from her distant vantage point, "Hey! *Hey!* Leave him the hell alone!" She scrambled to her feet, looking around for something to use as a weapon. Then she saw an old step van swerve into the far end of the alley.

On the rooftop, Kayta also watched as she spoke calmly but quickly into her pin, "Bryke. We have a situation."

In the alley below, the two men shoved Nathan into the side door of the van, which then screeched right toward Ruby. The girl had to dive out of the way to avoid being hit. She leaped back up furiously. "God *damn it*!" She watched with great frustration as the van sped away from her into the night.

6

DANNY STEIN'S FAMILY LIVED ON MORAGA STREET NEAR THIRTY-first, five blocks south of Golden Gate Park. The modest old house was slightly too small for them. It was decorated in Sears/Wal-Mart Traditional. All the furniture was sturdy and service-able if lacking in much style. The small menorah that sat on a side shelf was pretty much ignored except on Hanukkah.

Their plasma TV was showing news coverage of the bus that the pulse cannon bursts from Gina's fighter had exploded that afternoon. There were also visuals of the smoking devastation on the street and the many people who'd been wounded, maimed, or killed by Gina and the Patrollers who'd shot at Nathan.

A newsman's voice was describing the scene and relating the Visitor version of what had happened: "Six people were killed, thirty-seven others severely injured today by renegade Nathan Avery, a mentally unbalanced Teammate deserter. He was responsible for the bombing of the city bus seen here and then he went on a rampage, firing a pulse weapon at many innocent bystanders."

Nathan's photo appeared, covering half the screen as the newsman continued portentously: "He is armed, extremely dangerous, and is likely a part of the criminal faction calling themselves the Resistance. All Teammate and SFPD officers have been authorized to shoot to kill. Anyone with any information about him should call—" The newscast was muted by Debra, the chunky, short-haired, teenage Teammate who, among her other activities that day, had accosted an old homeless man at Cordelia and Broadway. She was still in her uniform, minus her baseball cap, curled on their small couch working a crossword puzzle. She called out to her younger brother, "Danny? Three-letter word for untrustworthy?" Before he could answer she figured it out herself, "Oh. Duh: *S-c-i.*"

Danny was doing his homework at the knotty pine dinner table when his father Sidney entered from the bathroom, nervously pulling the belt of his blue Teammate uniform around his middle-aged spread. He was a pasty-faced man with a growing bald spot on the back of his graying head. Danny heard the toilet empty but not refill, which meant the water had been shut off again. He also knew his father must have had another bout of irritable bowel syndrome that even Visitor medicines had yet to cure. "Where's my cap?" Sidney was asking anyone who could hear him. "I'm gonna be late."

Debra didn't look up from her puzzle. "Your roll call's not till seven, Dad."

"But I'm riding the bike over to save gas."

His stocky, matronly wife, Stella, was just coming in the front door from her job at the chemical plant. There was a coy light in her eyes. "We'll do okay"—she was pulling her coat off—"Connie Leonetti got arrested today. So I got promoted."

Debra reached up and high-fived her mother. "Aw-right, Mom!" Stella smiled haughtily at her daughter. Just then the doorbell rang and Stella turned back to answer it.

Sidney had paused and was looking at his wife curiously. "Someone denounced the Leonetti woman?"

"Mmm"—Stella felt some private pride—"*someone* did." Then she opened the front door and was startled to see two SFPD uniformed officers. They were backing up a Visitor Patroller who spoke immediately, "We're here for Daniel Stein."

The entire family reacted as the helmeted Patroller stepped boldly in, focusing on young Danny whose blood suddenly turned to ice.

Stella was nonplussed. "Well, Danny's our son, but—"

The Patroller waved the police officers over to Danny who was getting up shakily. "Daniel Stein, you're under arrest for possessing an illegal vid."

His confused father stammered, "Wait a minute, what?"

"Search his room," the Patroller directed one of the cops, who headed off as the other cuffed Danny.

"Wait, wait," the frightened boy said, "I don't know what you're talking about."

Debra had already convicted him and was glowering. "Danny! How could you?"

Danny protested, "I didn't!"

Stella tried to maintain a calm tone as she spoke to the stony Patroller, "It can't be true. Really, I'm sure that—"

The Patroller took Danny's arm firmly. "You were denounced by two eyewitnesses."

Sidney was completely flustered. "But wait, wait . . . I've been a loyal Teammate for over nineteen years—"

The Patroller cut him off, "Then you know the law." He pulled the fearful boy out the front door as the other cop went deeper into the house to join the search.

Danny was calling back tearfully now, "Dad? *Dad!*"

"It's got to be a mistake!" his father called out to the Patroller.

Debra was spitting nails, but mindful of the police. "The stupid little shit!"

Stella glared fearfully at her husband. "We've got to do *something*! Sid!"

"I know, I know"—his eyes were searching around—"I'm going down there. Where's my damn cap?"

Debra was continuing on her own rant, "They'll be watching us *all* now. Tapping our phone and—God!" She stabbed her hands up into the air. *"I hate him!"*

Stella found the uniform cap and thrust it into Sidney's hands. He rushed out to pursue the Patroller as the police emerged from Danny's room holding the illegal vid.

"Listen," Debra said hurriedly to the officers, "I had absolutely nothing to do with that, you understand? If I had known it was here I would have denounced him myself." They barely glanced at her as they walked out into the night. Debra watched them go for a moment, then turned away irately to stare at the TV news that was now showing U.N. Secretary-General Mendez and his aides disembarking a shuttle with an entourage of Patrollers.

STALE, MOIST, HEAVY AIR MADE ITS WAY INTO THE DIRTY CLOTH BAG that was over Nathan's head. He could smell cigarette smoke and alcohol fumes that had been exhaled by the noisy crowd through which he was being muscled. Then he was suddenly lifted off of his feet and thrown forward onto a wet and gritty stone floor.

Realizing his hands had been freed, Nathan jerked the bag off of his head. His sandy hair was soaked with sweat. He saw that he was on the floor of a very smoky cellar. He was in a grimy circular arena of sorts some twelve feet in diameter, surrounded by the rowdy crowd he'd heard. He stood and tried to push his way out, but was shoved roughly back by the juiced-up mob that encircled him. He saw that among them were men and women, some wearing Teammate uniforms, and also a few Visitors. Through their jostling shoulders Nathan also saw behind them the sleazy, unwashed man whom he and Ruby had passed earlier in the alley. The unsavory man was being paid in cash, obviously for delivering Nathan.

Then the crowd reacted with a shout of greeting. A brutish, muscle-bound female wrestler who outweighed Nathan by at least a hundred pounds was pushed into the arena from the other side. She had an ugly, jagged gouge where her left eye used to be. She wore tight ratty shorts, and an ancient sweatshirt over her voluminous breasts. The shirt was stained with blood, sweat, and likely the tears of her previous victims. She snarled at Nathan, waving her fat hands that had fingers like swollen sausages. An unsavory Master of Ceremonies shouted with delight to the assemblage, "The contest begins! To the Death!"

Nathan's one-eyed opponent roared furiously, showing sharp teeth, some missing and broken. She began to slowly circle toward him as the crowd of enthusiastic gamblers shouted encouragement. Among the loudest was the portly chemical factory owner, J. D. Oliver. He was sweating heavily in his business suit, but unmindful of it as he cheered heartily. One-Eye circled closer to Nathan, who was countering in the opposite direction.

"Hey, hey." Nathan's hands were out, fingers spread, trying to calm the snarling behemoth. His foot slipped on the wet stone floor and glancing down he realized that there were pools of blood smeared across it. He looked back at the grisly woman. "I'm not here to fight you. Okay?"

But One-Eye leaped at him and the battle was on. The crowd roared excitedly. Hands waved money. Bets were taken. The odds were three-to-one on the big woman.

With the crowd's attention focused on the combat, Bryke and Kayta easily edged in through the battered steel door that opened onto the alley. Their strange beauty turned a few heads of those nearby, but most eyes were on the fight. The mysterious women could see that Nathan was already bloodied and had been wrestled down by the vicious One-Eye. Kayta held back strategically as Bryke maneuvered closer to the arena, where One-Eye was now a juggernaut, pummeling Nathan mercilessly. Nathan managed to duck beneath one of her massive, reeking, flabby arms. He swung a furious roundhouse, slugging One-Eye very hard and spinning her bulky body against the crowd, which shouted their mass approval.

The Master of Ceremonies was right in front of One-Eye at ringside and slipped her a butane lighter. The bestial woman smiled with dangerous pleasure. She wheeled and ignited a ten-inch flame. Some in the crowd booed, shouting angrily about the altered odds. But the majority loved the new wrinkle and cheered louder. One-Eye brandished the fire dangerously, like a dagger, toward Nathan. He was bleeding, angry, and steeling himself for what he now understood would be mortal combat.

Then Bryke suddenly vaulted gracefully into the arena, her fisherman's vest catching some air. Nathan was as startled as were the crowd and One-Eye. Bryke dealt One-Eye a single, powerful kick in the stomach, folding the big woman over. The amazed crowd cheered.

Standing at the oily bar in the back, Kayta was watching carefully. A very short, round, and greasy man with a scruffy beard sidled up eyeing her shapely figure. "Hey, baby"—he grinned lasciviously—"what would you say to a little fuck?" He reached his hand around the back of her neck, then jerked it back with a yelp. He saw that his hand was bleeding.

Kayta eyed him sadly. "Good-bye, Little Fuck."

The man suddenly choked. One hand grabbed spasmodically for the bar but he missed and dropped to the floor gasping and twisting, unnoticed by the cheering people who were entirely focused on the arena.

Bryke had laid hold of One-Eye's ears with both hands and pulled the porcine, repulsive woman into a *kiss*! Everyone was stunned and amazed. One-Eye was pounding against Bryke, but the blows had no consequence. There was no breaking Bryke's powerful hold, no unsealing of her lips on the woman's.

The crowd was aroused, shouting with one voice, "GO, GO, GO!" One-Eye suddenly convulsed violently several times. Then when Bryke released her from the kiss, the big woman went limp and dropped like a rag doll, facedown on the grimy arena floor.

Bryke swung around, addressing the cheering crowd, "Fire is cowardly! Kill with *hands*!" Then before Nathan could speak, she leaped onto him, driving him down onto the floor, but by holding tightly to his collar, she prevented the back of his head from cracking on the bloody stone. Her face was inches from his own; he noticed her breath smelled like carnations and saw that her eyes were a startling bright pink. She whispered to him with calm but firm direction, "Prepare to run. —Now, strike me."

Nathan was totally befuddled. "What—!"

"*Strike me*!" she hissed emphatically. "*Do it*!"

Nathan hauled off and slugged her. But her reaction made his blow seem much more powerful than he knew it had been. It was as though Bryke were using his blow as a mere excuse to spin back against the cheering crowd.

Nathan was gaining his feet and felt his eyes must be deceiving him. He thought he saw Bryke's arm seem to *hinge backward* as her hand grabbed a bottle of liquor from someone behind her. She took a big mouthful as the juiced-up crowd shouted encouragement.

Then, with the easy grace of a ballet dancer, she swept her hand across the floor picking up the butane lighter that was still aflame. She held it in front of her mouth and spewed her mouthful of liquor, which the lighter ignited. She had created a fountain of flame that set fire to a dozen nearby spectators—including the Master of Ceremonies.

The mob's shouts of encouragement instantly became shrieks of pain. People around those afire climbed over each other to get away. And at that moment the wall behind Kayta suddenly exploded outward. Everyone was startled, except Kayta who slipped a small pistol-like device back under her suede vest. Water sprayed from broken pipes as dirt and debris rained from the low rafters. Panic was spreading, many were screaming in pain, and all were desperately trying to shove their way out of the growing chaos.

Nathan was momentarily as stupefied as everyone else. He lost sight of Bryke in the pandemonium, but realized the opportunity she'd given him to escape and he took it. He clambered over several fallen people, including Oliver, and bolted out into the alley where a misty rain was hanging in the dark air.

He ran breathlessly down the alley and around a corner, the sounds of the fleeing crowd gradually diminishing behind him. He looked about, but there was no sign of the strange woman who had saved his life. Whoever she was, he felt grateful. He flexed his hand; it was sore from hitting her. He started to wipe what he thought was her blood off of his fist, but quickly realized that the liquid on his hand was not red. It was a pale yellow.

He studied it for a moment, greatly confused, his head still throbbing from the fight. Then angry shouts from the alley encouraged him to hurry on through Chinatown and into the foggy night.

CHARLES ELGIN LEANED OVER THE SECONDHAND KITCHEN TABLE IN his family's exceedingly small, run-down tenement in the Sci ghetto. His head bumped against the cracked, faux Tiffany plastic lamp that hung over the scratched Formica surface of the table.

"We'll get a few bucks for this." He was unwrapping the electric drill he had found at the plant. It was small but heavy and as it rolled from the newspaper wrapping it made a dent in the tabletop.

His wife Mary flinched slightly. "Careful."

Charles emitted a dark chuckle. "Oh, yeah, like it really matters with this priceless piece of furniture." He reached down into his sock. "Blue helped me sneak out some bits for it, too." He retrieved the drill bits and was lining them up on the table when he noticed Mary's sad eyes. He often saw that expression on her face and he was never sure if it was better to just let it pass or whether talking about what was troubling her might help. This time he decided to engage, speaking gently, "What is it, honey?"

She was staring down at the stained and faded green Formica, but her eyes were looking beyond it into the past. "I always wonder where they took *our* table"—she crossed her arms in front of her, closing her fingers around her thumbs protectively—"where they took all our beautiful furniture, all those years ago." Charles touched her cheek gently; he knew how emotionally fragile she was. He knew that she was near tears as she murmured, "I loved that table."

Charlotte had just come in and immediately discerned her mother's melancholia. She eased closer and slipped her arm around Mary's waist. "Well, I like *this* table, Momma. Because we can all still sit around it *together*. And look," she said. A pleased smile danced across her pretty face and caught in her cheerful eyes as she opened the plastic bag from the Chinese grocery. She took out the three bruised apples. Mary frowned with worry, but Charlotte calmed her concern. "Mrs. Soon let me have them. These are for you two and Poppy."

Her mother looked from the three apples to Charlotte. "But what about you?"

Charlotte shrugged it off. "Oh, I ate mine on the way home." Then she leaned closer, squeezing her mother's arm. "We're really very lucky, Momma." Charlotte kissed her on the cheek. "I'll check on Poppy."

She moved across the thin Persian rug with threadbare patches that covered part of the uneven wooden floor of their cramped flat. She drew back a makeshift curtain along the rope from which it hung. Her grandfather, Charles Senior, was reclining on a lumpy, brown corduroy sofa. He was seventy-three but looked easily ten years older. His mottled face was wrinkled and careworn, but it brightened considerably when he saw Charlotte's optimistic face.

Across the room Charles and Mary were still standing beside the kitchen table. Mary spoke quietly, "I'm sorry, Charles. Some days it just . . ." Her voice trailed off.

But he completed the thought, "It just all closes in. I know."

"It's like the world's gone mad"—Mary's eyes searched the middle distance—"I feel so helpless. If it weren't for you, we'd—"

"All fly off to Acapulco? Have a nice vacation?" He was grinning. "Little surf and turf maybe?"

She looked at him, then smiled sadly, appreciating his attempted humor. She hugged him close with her forehead against his shoulder and her eyes closed. She didn't see his look of deep concern about his family's future.

Charlotte was fluffing and rearranging the meager pillows for her weak, ailing grandfather as she spoke good-naturedly, "You look better today, Poppy."

"You're the worst liar in San Francisco." He smiled back, then narrowed his gaze as he studied her with eyes that had been dimmed by macular degeneration propelled by his diabetes. "And *you* looked kind of peaked this morning, sugar."

"What?" Her face crinkled up incredulously. "Don't be silly, I'm fine. I'll get your meds."

She turned to a small wooden cabinet nearby, searching among the books, pencils, and glasses that were crowded atop it. She found his pill bottle and with her back to the old man she noted that only one pill remained within. As she turned to him, she dropped the bottle, endeavoring to make it look accidental. "Oopsie. Good one, Char." She knelt down and pretended to be searching for it beneath his couch. She felt her grandfather's creped hands lovingly stroke her long, beautiful black hair. She knew how deeply he cared for her. He'd often said that her presence alone always improved his outlook and that he was very fond of the faint fragrance of jasmine that accompanied her.

Unseen by him, Charlotte had pulled her *own* pill bottle from her pocket. Except for her name on it, the bottles and medications were identical. Charlotte poured her last two pills into the old man's bottle.

THE PARNASSAS POLICE STATION WAS ACROSS FROM THE U.C. MEDICAL Center at the southeast corner of Golden Gate Park. A boxy, bland, mid-twentieth-century building, it was equally uninspiring on the inside. The air bore a faint green glow from the fluorescent lights in the ceiling and there was always a lingering smell of industrial soap common to bureaucratic environs. Due to the uncertain hygiene of the people constantly coming and going there were also occasional whiffs of potent body odor. The squad room was a large space with numerous desks pushed back to back creating a maze. Various SFPD officers, Teammates, and Patrollers were busy at their various tasks, talking on phones, checking computers, or questioning the cross section of humanity who sat by their desks. Through this buzz of activity Danny Stein's nervous father Sidney was following a Visitor Patrol captain who had the strong face of a thirty-something African-American. The captain was tall, square-shouldered, and imposing. His alien voice resonance was lower-pitched than most, lending it gravitas. "Your son agreed to identify the dealer who's dispensing the vids. As soon as he does we'll release him."

"Oh, thank God"—Sidney sagged with relief—"I really appreciate you taking time to check it out for me. It was so unlike Danny to ever do—"

"No problem, Sidney"—the captain was making notes on a large PDA—"now, you're late for training. Get on in there."

"Yes, sir"—Sidney gave the palm-up salute—"and thank you again, sir. Thanks."

Sid hurried quickly toward the assembly room passing a frightened, bearded, wide-eyed vagrant who smelled of cheap wine. He stood at the booking desk rambling a mile a minute to a preoccupied Hispanic cop and a stout middle-aged female Teammate. "I ain't never seen nothing like it, I tell ya!" The vagrant was shaping the air in front of him with gnarled hands. "I seen that big one-eyed bitch break people in half that were twice her size. But tonight"—he was searching for the best way to describe the indescribable—"tonight was different. One minute she was this 250-pound wrestler, but then this wiry black chick jumps into the ring and kisses her—*kisses her*, you understand? When they turned the wrestler over she was all *caved-in*."

The cop looked up, thinking the story ludicrous. He said, deadpan, "Caved-in?"

"I mean to tell ya." The vagrant nodded, grateful he'd finally gotten their attention. "Her face was all dried-out. Like a goddamn *husk. Transparentlike.* You could see her veins and bones inside and she was all flaky, like something had sucked all the bodily fluids right outta her."

"Like you sucked all the fluids out of a case of Ripple?" The overworked cop motioned to the Teammate. "Get him the hell out of here."

Adjoining the squad room was a bland, square assembly room where a Teammate unit was forming ranks. Sid scrambled in and found his place among the others. The unit consisted of thirty-two men and women of various ethnicities from age thirteen up through their mid-fifties. They all snapped to attention as the black Patrol captain entered and moved to the podium facing them, his deep voice resonating, "At ease, Teammates."

There was a long folding table beside him with an array of pulse weapons carefully laid out. A Visitor Patroller was dismantling one of the sleek, high-tech rifles. The captain gestured toward the guns. "Tonight we'll begin training you with the new upgrade of our pulse weapons."

There were grins and other positive reactions among the Teammates. Several glanced at each other with enthusiasm.

"I knew you'd like that." The captain smiled. "But first, Teammate Sidney Stein?"

Sidney snapped back to stiff attention. "Sir!"

The captain strolled slowly along the line of Teammates in front of Sidney while glancing at the PDA in his hands. "We've been reviewing your record, Teammate Stein." Sidney felt his stomach lighten as though it were being filled uncomfortably with helium. There was a pause. "It's very clean."

Sidney was greatly relieved. "Yes, sir. Thank you, sir."

"But it's also very undistinguished."

Sidney frowned, confused now. "Sir?"

"It is the record of someone only fulfilling the minimum requirements, someone just going through the motions." The captain was eyeing him with disappointment.

Sidney was a bookish accountant and had never been good at thinking on his feet. He was thoroughly ill at ease. "But, sir, no, I've—"

"You've just never had that level of total commitment and enthusiasm that your fellow Teammates demand."

Sidney realized that the other members of his unit were all looking at him now and that two strong young Teammates had appeared on either side of him.

"Sir, please." Sidney felt a drop of perspiration slide from his armpit and trail down his skin beneath his blue uniform shirt. "This is a mistake. I—"

"The mistakes have been yours, Sidney," the captain said sadly. He grasped his own hands behind his back and rocked slightly on his heels. "And your lack of parental inspiration has allowed your son Daniel to wander down illegal paths. You've disappointed your fellow Teammates who know that strict discipline is always necessary." The captain's deep voice lowered portentously. "You're going to be sent to our Motivational Unit." The two younger Teammates took Sidney's arms into their firm grips and began to lead him out.

"Sir. Please"—Sidney was getting panicky now—"just let me speak to you a moment. Sir?"

The captain turned away as Sidney was led past several of the ardently dedicated Teammates who sneered at him and also past some of those who were just like Sidney—who were "going along to get along." In that moment all of the go-alongs knew that the fearful message was meant for them. A trip to the Motivational Unit was always one-way. Unless they wanted to suffer Sidney's unknown fate they'd better shape up quickly, toe the line, and work in support of the Visitors.

In his holding cell within the police station, young Danny Stein was standing nervously to one side among the seven other people being held there. One was a sour-smelling, drugged-out street person who had threatened Danny at first, but now seemed to be in a pharmacological haze. The other six were apparently ordinary citizens like Danny. They were all silent and wore looks of distress. Danny heard a low hum begin and turned to look out the barred window of the cell that faced the parking lot behind the station.

A Visitor shuttle craft about the size of a city bus was waiting in the police station lot. It had started its magnetic engine. Then Danny saw his father Sidney, with his hands on his head, being prodded toward the vehicle amid other prisoners about to be transported. The window was smudged badly but Danny could still make out the tears on his distraught father's cheek.

Danny felt his own throat tightening with emotion as he watched his father disappear into the craft and the upper hatch come down overtop the lower one. The shuttle hatches had always reminded Danny of a large metal mouth closing. The hum of the shuttle's engines increased and it lifted off. Danny was grieved and felt a great burden of guilt lowering upon him as he watched the shuttle carry his father upward and away toward the mammoth Flagship overhead, only partly visible in the night and fog.

7

AS DAWN CAME THE NEXT DAY THE AIR WAS VERY CLEAR. VISITOR fighter pilots heading out on patrol from the Flagship over San Francisco could look westward and see all the way to the horizon across the Pacific Desert. There was heightened activity all around the huge Mothership that hung in the sky four thousand feet above the city. Numerous shuttle craft as well as many two-hundred-foot-long tanker craft were outbound or inbound as usual, but twice the normal number of fighters were flying on patrol.

Inside Hangar Bay Eighteen, Willy was emerging with several

other Visitors from one of the transport tubes that laced through the gigantic ship like the capillary blood vessels inside a whale. Hangar Bay Eighteen was like the other landing bays, about two hundred yards square with proportionally large hangar doors that opened to allow the various Visitor craft to enter and exit. The shiny gray floor of the main deck had sequential landing lights built into it. On either side of the broad central landing area were smaller bays designed to accommodate individual shuttles, tankers, or fighters, depending upon the particular mission requirement of each of the 250 landing bays.

Above the main flight deck there were twenty-five additional levels of individual platformed bays that from below looked like so many balconies overhanging the central atrium. As with all Visitor facilities, the hangar bays were kept very clean by custodians who were primarily of the half-breed caste. The walls were a medium gray and the numerous metal catwalks were slightly darker. To accommodate the Visitors' sensitive eyes, the built-in lighting was as subdued as possible, though with the fifty-ton hangar bay doors fully open, the sunlight from outside illuminated the lower regions quite thoroughly during the daytime. Many large pieces of test and maintenance equipment were scattered around the various craft on the main deck level as well as on each of the landing platforms above. A legion of Visitor technicians busied themselves loading, off-loading, and servicing the ships. Higher-ranked Visitor supervisors moved among the techs pointing out the smallest examples of inattention. On that special morning the supervisors were anxious that everything be particularly shipshape.

Hangar Bay Eighteen was a general purpose bay, primarily for use by shuttles rather than tankers. But it was also the landing area aboard the Flagship generally reserved for special ceremonial receptions such as the one about to take place.

Willy moved along the pipes and electrical conduits that lined a side bulkhead to join the assembling ranks of Visitors, Teammates, and other humans known as Players. These were key civilians who enjoyed privileged access to the Visitors. A less-kindly but more apt description of them, particularly among the Resistance, was *Collaborators*. They reminded those with the longest memories of the Vichy French who, for their own gain, had cooperated with their Nazi occupiers during World War II.

Willy hurried past a shuttle craft that was disembarking prisoners nearby. Among them, though Willy didn't know her, was a very frightened Connie Leonetti, the innocent woman whom Stella Stein had denounced at the chemical factory. Willy saw the natty Visitor Press Secretary Paul bustle onto the scene. Paul was angry and agitated as he addressed a Patroller: "What is this? I gave strict orders for all prisoner shuttles to be sent to other bays. Get those prisoners out of here! Diana's on her way!"

The Patroller nodded and along with his cohorts prodded the worried prisoners quickly toward a tube entrance.

Willy came to stand among the gathering ranks next to a Visitor named Martin whose human face made him look mid-forties. He had blond hair, soft blue eyes, and a thoughtful, quiet demeanor. There was also a touch of sadness about him. He nodded to Willy with a private camaraderie because, like Willy, Martin had long been risking death by being an ally of the Resistance. They looked across to where a Visitor red carpet escort was guiding Emma toward the large contingent of local Players. The beautiful young star was wearing a rose-hued, one-piece jersey dress that was quite tasteful, yet managed to accentuate her fine curves and show a reasonable amount of those famous fawn-colored legs. Among the Players was the chemical plant owner Oliver. "Emma, my dear! Greetings!" He leaned his jowly face very close to hers. "Why haven't you come to visit, you naughty girl?"

"Sorry," she said with a polite smile, "new song. We'll catch up." Turning to avoid his cigarette breath she found herself face-to-face with Mayor Ohanian. Suddenly there was no one else in the huge bay for either of them. Each had flashes of memory of the other: their first meeting backstage at one of her concerts; the snowy weekend at her cabin in Tahoe; the warmth of their bodies together. Time paused for a moment as they gazed fondly at each other. Each could see in the other's eyes that there was definitely still a spark.

Continuing to hold his eyes, Emma inclined her pretty head gracefully toward him. ". . . Mr. Mayor."

A faint smile crossed his face as well. ". . . My friends call me Mark."

She leaned up and kissed his cheek, whispering, "Am I still a friend?"

He squeezed her arm gently. "Always." Their gazes held a moment longer as embers glowed.

Even though Willy was a good twenty yards distant, he noted the connection. So did the jealous Press Secretary Paul who had appeared right beside the pair. "Excuse me, Mr. Mayor, Emma, could I . . . ?" He gently ushered her a few feet away, leaning covetously closer and chiding her, "Little nuzzly there. I know that history."

Emma smiled charmingly. "Then you know it *is* history." She kissed Paul's cheek while Willy noted *their* personal dynamic as well.

Then narrow-eyed Visitor Shawn appeared on the catwalk above. "Attention on deck. The Commandant."

The amassed ranks of a thousand Visitors, Patrollers, and Teammates on the main deck and all of the platforms above immediately snapped smartly to attention as Diana appeared from within. She stepped out onto the catwalk with a regal bearing. Her presence instantly filled the entire landing bay. Hers was a persona that demanded respect and instantly received it. Everyone beneath her extended their arms up toward her at the proscribed thirty-degree angle in the palm-up Visitor salute.

Diana was the most powerful creature on the planet. She enjoyed that dark supremacy. But she was also an astute diplomat who presented a friendly face to those assembled below and on the platforms above her as well as to the billions whom she knew were watching her around the world at that moment. She knew precisely where the cameras were placed within the landing bay; knew her image was being flashed out globally, filling vid screens from Boston to Kuala Lumpur.

Diana wore the standard dark trousers and ivory blouse with her Commandant insignia on the collar. She filled out the blouse nicely, some would even have said invitingly. She had carefully calculated and designed her face and figure to be appealing to humans both male and female. Her nearly black hair was perfectly, yet casually coiffed. Her large brown eyes carefully surveyed all those beneath her.

To Martin she always called to mind a sensuous, smiling cobra. He knew well exactly how treacherous she could be. Diana relished her dangerous reputation, but generally chose to play it lightly. As her keen eyes scanned the invited Players, her gaze riveted on Emma, who was offering a friendly and respectful smile. Diana had met Emma before, but the young singer looked particularly delectable that morning. Diana continued to gaze at Emma and weigh her possibilities until a resonating Visitor voice came echoing over the hangar's speakers, "Attention: the Emissary's ship is on final approach."

A well-rehearsed Teammate band began to play martial music. The people within the hangar looked out of the hundred-foot-wide door and murmured with surprise when they caught their first glimpse of a distant fleck of silver against the blue sky. Vid cameras in the hangar bay captured the image and transmitted it around the world. From Stockholm to Capetown, Anchorage to Tierra del Fuego, Kamchatka to Auckland, people of every age, gender, and ethnicity watched on their home screens, their vid phones, or on one of the thousands of billboard-sized screens that the Visitors had installed on the walls of buildings seemingly everywhere.

From a San Francisco alleyway Kayta and Bryke watched one of the wall-sized screens, then Kayta sensed something and looked skyward. Bryke saw it, too. And then people nearby in the street began to notice it and talk excitedly. A shuttle unlike any that had ever been seen, its shining surface giving the appearance of liquid silver, was approaching the great Flagship at a high altitude from the north.

A faint tone attracted Kayta's notice. She looked at the pin on her vest, which was blinking a complicated sequence.

"He's arriving."

Bryke was already on the move, nodding. "I'll see to him."

Nathan was on Fremont Street en route to his assassination assignment. He also looked up into the bright sky and saw the incoming Visitor vehicle.

Vid screens across the world showed images of the silver ship gliding grandly over the San Francisco skyline and into Hangar Bay Eighteen of the Flagship. On the flight deck, a Visitor crew chief guided the pilot to a gentle landing.

Visitor Shawn, always acutely attuned to the slightest clue about Diana's thinking, saw her arch one of her perfect dark eyebrows in a faintly critical gesture as she eyed the striking, unusual craft. She began to move down the catwalk stairs to the hangar deck. Shawn followed, only a half step behind. Diana's personal Patroller guardsmen had arranged a wide path for her down the red carpet between the massed, regimented troops and the Players. Diana heard some among the group whispering among themselves about the amazing reflective appearance of the silver shuttle.

Diana walked slowly, watching the shuttle's hatch unseal and the ramp extend downward like a long silver tongue. Shawn, walking just behind, knew that she was carefully timing her arrival. She did not want to arrive at the base of the ramp a moment too soon and have to be seen waiting.

As the ramp touched the deck Diana slowed slightly, knowing

that the individual inside the shuttle would be calculating his appearance with the same care as she. Finally the Emissary appeared in the hatch. From the vantage point of the Players, Emma, craning her head for a better look, could see that he appeared to be in his late thirties. He was very lean and handsome with dark hair and coloring that was somewhat like Diana's.

Mark Ohanian, who hadn't risen to mayor without being able to read people exceedingly well, was also watching carefully and was sure he caught a calculating glint in the Emissary's eyes.

For her part, Diana had immediately noticed something about the newcomer that piqued her ire, but she managed to show no reaction. Then she raised her hand casually in the palm-up greeting, which signalled all the other Visitors and Teammates attending to follow suit. A thousand arms shot up and out in greeting. The Emissary acknowledged the assemblage with a modest salute of his own, then nodded politely to Diana.

He slowly descended the ramp, and Diana nodded with a queenly attitude, saying merely, ". . . Jeremy."

He was equally self-assured and smiled. ". . . Diana."

What she had noted, and been slightly annoyed by seeing, was his rank insignia. "Full Commandant? I hadn't heard."

Jeremy stood at the base of the ramp facing her with a self-effacing shrug. "Our Great Leader's whim."

"Congratulations," Diana said dryly. "And the face: nice choice."

Jeremy chuckled and looked past her to where Shawn was waiting patiently. Shawn saluted respectfully and added his personal emphasis to Diana's comment, "Indeed it is, sir!"

"Thank you, Shawn." Jeremy seemed to be measuring something about Shawn, his allegiance perhaps? "It's good to see you again."

"And you, Commandant"—Shawn clicked his heels smartly—"welcome to the Flagship, sir."

Among the Visitor contingent Willy and Martin were watching carefully. Willy frowned as he whispered to his compatriot, "Wait, they're both the *same rank* now?"

"Mmmm"—Martin nodded—"but I've heard that Jeremy has more than just the Leader's *ear*."

Willy's eyebrows went up in surprise. "You mean . . . ?" He let the sexual innuendo hang unspoken.

Martin understood and nodded slightly. "Mmmm-hmmm."

Willy was amazed. "But wasn't that *Diana's* act?"

"It *was*."

Willy mulled the new situation. "Well, this could get very interesting."

He and Martin could feel the chill between the two Commandants who continued to take watchful measure of each other as Diana guided Jeremy slowly past the welcoming group. She introduced him to several individually, including the mayor who was cordial, J. D. Oliver who was practically drooling, and to Emma, of whom Diana spoke fondly as she studied the lovely young woman up close. "She is one of Earth's most popular musical artists."

Jeremy was polite to Emma and each of the others, but Mark's seasoned political eye recognized a dignitary just going through the motions. Jeremy did not even seem particularly interested when Diana introduced him to grandfatherly Secretary-General Mendez, who also seemed to be merely going through the motions of politeness himself.

Overall, however, the impression transmitted to those billions watching around the world was one of cordiality and friendship. In the Resistance communications truck, Margarita and Ysabel were also studying the ceremony as it unfolded on TV. Margarita's hazel eyes narrowed. "I wonder why the Secretary-General is always so closely guarded? And always looks so . . . ?"

"Troubled? Yeah." Ysabel had often noticed it, too.

In the hangar bay Jeremy and Diana moved away from the

Players and were now proceeding past the ranks of Visitor fighter pilots. One of the flight leaders stood in the forefront. She was Gina, the striking Asian-looking Visitor who had gunned down Nathan's fighter. Her sharp almond eyes were focused like lasers on Jeremy. When his gaze crossed hers, they locked on to one another for a fleeting, but potent moment.

Willy whispered again to Martin, "Did you catch *that* look?"

Martin remained motionless. "Mmmm-hmmm."

IN DANNY'S CLASSROOM AT THE MIDDLE SCHOOL, THE TEACHER HAD lowered the volume on the overhead plasma screen as the ceremony aboard the Flagship drew to a conclusion. The eighth-graders were working quietly. Thomas Murakami glanced over toward the unoccupied desk where his friend Danny normally sat. A low wave of guilt folded uncomfortably over Thomas's heart. He hadn't wanted to tell about Danny's vid, but Vice Principal Gabriel had made it clear that Thomas would share Danny's punishment if he didn't denounce his friend. A metallic squeak attracted Thomas's notice. Glancing out the open classroom door he saw the half-breed janitor Ted passing by in the hall.

Ted had his mop in a large metal bucket that he was pushing up the hall. One of its small wheels needed oil. Since the incident with Danny, Ted had been ordered to mop all the floors twice a day. Ted's own attention was focused up the hall where he saw the sunny-faced vice principal receiving a small gift from a local Patroller who smiled. "In appreciation of your help."

Gabriel was surprised and pleased, but reluctant. "Really, I told your captain that it was unnecessary. I was just doing my part."

"And for that you are rewarded." The Patroller smiled.

Gabriel opened the small box. As Ted passed by he saw that it contained a signet ring inset with a diamond. Gabriel inhaled with amazement. "Oh, no, this is really too extravagant."

"Nonsense," the uniformed Patroller sloughed it off. "And the captain said he'd been looking into that question you had about the new position opening up over at Benjamin Franklin. I think you'll find yourself occupying the principal's office very soon."

Gabriel's round face glowed with delight; Ted turned away, his eyebrows bunching sourly.

NATHAN WAS TRYING TO APPEAR INCONSPICUOUS AS HE GLANCED over the magazines at a small newsstand near the corner of Fremont and Mission. He kept looking casually up and down the street waiting for the female contact that Street-C had told him to expect. In the meantime he had been thumbing through the magazines and realizing how bland they were. Many of the articles were identical from one magazine to another. Of course he had always known that the Visitors exercised careful censorship over all of the media. As a former Teammate he had helped enforce that censorship by seizing and destroying material the Visitors deemed inappropriate or aberrant and arresting those responsible for it. But he had always believed that his work was in the best interests of a public that was vulnerable to Resistance lies and Sci propaganda. Only in the last twenty-four hours had his perspective altered drastically.

Looking down Fremont, Nathan was startled to see a large vid sign suddenly display his face with the flashing words: *Seen this traitor? Report it!* He shrank back into a doorway and pulled the brim of his Teammate baseball cap lower. Then he spotted a young Hispanic woman crossing the street. She seemed to be angling toward him. His anticipation grew, but then she flagged down a cab. Tight-lipped, he blew out a small, antsy puff through his nose. Where was his contact?

Kayta was patiently watching Nathan from an apartment building rooftop. Then her keen senses detected a new presence behind her. She glanced across the roof and saw Bryke approaching with Ayden, the amber-eyed man with whom she had communicated via the holographic transmission in the mountain cabin. Ayden walked with an unusual, heel-to-toe, measured gait that added a curious majesty and strangeness to his imposing, steely affect. Ayden's skin had a more pronounced sheen than Kayta's. He was no longer naked, but clothed in the black leather pants, gray turtleneck, and bomber jacket that had been taken from the dead outdoorsman Burton.

"Welcome, Ayden." Kayta nodded with great respect as she interlaced her fingers before her in greeting. She noticed the irritation he felt from his clothing and that his breathing was slightly labored.

"Is the air always this bad?" he asked.

"I'm afraid so, sir. And I know the garments are uncomfortable. But on the brighter side . . ." She nodded toward Nathan below.

Ayden carefully assessed the sandy-haired man down on the sidewalk. "Bryke told me he made initial contact with them?"

"Yes, last night."

"Why haven't they taken him in yet?"

"Perhaps they're as cautious as we are."

On the sidewalk below, Nathan was reaching for another magazine when he suddenly felt a pulse pistol being pressed into his hand. He turned to see his contact and was surprised to be facing a stoop-shouldered eighty-year-old woman. Her thin, stringy gray hair hung out of the cheap knit cap pulled over her ears. Her deeply wrinkled face also had a gray pallor to it and her eyes looked as though they had cataracts. Nathan blinked incredulously. "*You're* Street-C's 'Old Lady'?"

The crone nodded as she pulled her thin shawl closer around her and pointed across the street at a black Visitor patrol captain who wore a Parnassas Precinct patch on his uniform. The captain was getting information from a young Native American woman who had a small bead stand on the sidewalk. The old woman beside Nathan nudged him and spoke in a rasping voice, "Do him. In the back. Now."

Nathan saw that the captain had left the Indian and was walking away up the Fremont Street sidewalk. Nathan quickly crossed the street and fell into step behind the Visitor. His quarry's path forced Nathan to walk directly beneath the six-foot-wide vid screen displaying his face and branding him a traitor. He kept his chin down and his shoulders up, trying to hide as much as possible. Had Nathan looked back he would've seen that the old lady was hobbling along, following as closely as her aged legs would allow.

Nathan gained on the captain and when he got within six feet he raised the pistol. But he found he couldn't pull the trigger. He couldn't shoot anyone in the back, even a damned Visitor. He grabbed the startled captain and spun him around, confronting him, "Say good-bye."

Nathan pulled the trigger. But nothing happened. He tried again, then realized that the gun was empty. During Nathan's confusion the captain was unholstering his own pulse weapon. Nathan felt a strong hand jerk him aside and watched with amazement as the old lady performed a flying spin-kick that caught the captain right in the throat and dropped him. Then the old woman grabbed Nathan, hissing angrily, "Come on, you idiot!"

Three young Teammates were among those on the street who had witnessed the encounter and were running to the captain's assistance. The old lady executed some well-practiced martial arts moves, catching one Teammate assailant in the stomach with her pile-driver foot while slinging a second through the plate-glass window of a bakery. Nathan managed to take down the third Teammate.

On the rooftop across the street Kayta and Ayden exchanged a glance. They were as surprised and impressed by the old woman as Nathan was. Then Kayta pointed down toward an old Chevy sedan that was careering up the street toward Nathan and the old lady. With its back door flapping open, it slowed beside them just long enough for the crone to shove Nathan in and climb in behind him. Then the car peeled away.

While Kayta's and Ayden's focus was on the street below a Visitor Patroller had appeared from a doorway on the rooftop behind them, making his rounds. He saw Kayta and Ayden watching the action below and crossed toward them, gesturing at them with his rifle. "Hey," he said officiously, "you're not allowed up here. Let's see some ID right now."

Ayden barely glanced at him. Then, so lightning-fast that the Patroller never saw it coming, Ayden slashed out with a gleaming white fourteen-inch sword. The Patroller's severed head rolled away, with a startled expression frozen on the face.

Kayta, her focus still on the street below, emitted a crackling chirp. On the street level, Bryke came out of an alley. She saw Street-C driving the Chevy containing the old woman and Nathan. Bryke raised an odd-looking small pistol and shot a tiny jellied blob of goo onto the passing car.

Inside the getaway car the old lady was breathing hard as she pulled off her gray wig and peeled the latex from her face. Nathan was surprised to see a sultry auburn-haired beauty emerging from beneath the disguise. And he was thoroughly pissed off. "What the hell is going on! Why'd you give me an empty gun?"

"Just to see if you'd pull the trigger," Margarita said angrily. "If you'd done it from behind there'd have been no trouble. You're not much on following orders are you?"

The scruffy kid riding shotgun in the front seat turned to look back at Nathan. It was bright-eyed little Ruby. She lifted a stun gun and wiggled her eyebrows.

Nathan raised his hand. "Hey, now wait just a minute—"

But by then Ruby had already shot him and Nathan's world swirled down into darkness.

8

LEVEL 125 OF THE FLAGSHIP WAS THE SECTION AT THE THINNEST
outer edge of the dish-shaped, sixteen-mile-wide interstellar
spacecraft. It was an area reserved for the highest strata of the
Visitor command and their invited guests. Pundits, when there
had been pundits before they had all disappeared, used to refer
to Level 125 as a combination Visitor White House, Pentagon,
Kremlin, and Mount Olympus. The corridors within it were similar to those elsewhere in the general-access areas of the vast
ship. They were seven and a half feet in height, ten feet in width,
a medium gray color, and octagonally shaped. The lighting was
indirect and subdued except where it pooled at various intersec-
tions. Small control panels presented themselves near the numerous hatch doors that slid open into the bulkheads with a
touch to reveal chambers whose sizes differed depending upon
their intended use. Most Flagship corridors bore pipes or electrical conduit in their upper corners, but the bulkheads and ceil-
ings on Level 125 were smooth, uncluttered, and elegant.

The hatch to a transport tube at the end of the corridor
opened. Diana stepped out of the small car leading Jeremy and
several aides including Shawn and Press Secretary Paul. Martin,
who was one of Diana's secondary aides, brought up the rear
while listening carefully.

Jeremy was saying to Diana, "I was sorry to hear of the original Commandant's 'accident'"—he glanced sideways at her—
"but you've obviously taken firm control."

Diana felt his intimation and said with a calm and firm voice,
"Indeed I have."

Jeremy was picking tiny pieces of lint from his uniform as he
walked. "Unfortunately our Leader feels your efforts here have
been insufficient."

"Indeed?" Diana smiled smugly as she paused beside the Patrollers who stood at attention outside her personal conference room. "Well, Jeremy," she continued with some heat, "our Leader certainly hasn't conveyed those sentiments to me."

Jeremy met her superior gaze with an equally self-satisfied look. "Consider them conveyed." Then he walked past her and into her conference chamber as though he now owned it.

Diana contained her ire for the moment and followed him in, trailed by her three aides. The chamber was slightly darker gray than the corridor outside. A floor-to-ceiling window made of thick, darkly tinted Visitor glass formed the long outside wall. It was facing south so the southern portion of the San Francisco peninsula stretched into the hazy distance beneath them, with the Pacific Desert off to the right. Visitor fighters or shuttle craft occasionally glided by outside the window. At the far end of the room was what in an earthbound conference room would be called a small wet bar. Jeremy had noticed a nice selection of small live animals nosing around in tiny cubicles next to the bar and walked toward it. A short male janitor stood up from behind the bar where he'd been using a small vacuum cleaning tool. When Jeremy saw the janitor's face his eyes grew cold with displeasure.

The janitor, an eighteen-year-old half-breed named Jon, was short for his age and slight of build. His blue human eyes stood out in stark contrast to the flat, reptilian nose and the leathery scales that covered two-thirds of his face. Jeremy saw that his mouth seemed particularly misshapen, as though it had never quite decided whether to be human or reptilian. The scaly forehead curved up into unruly, brownish human hair that formed a widow's peak in the front. The boy's hands were small, delicate, and human-looking with only patches of scales here and there. His overall demeanor was gentle and very polite.

Reading Jeremy's distasteful expression, the young janitor

bowed subserviently and walked toward the exit. He passed behind Shawn who, Martin noticed, seemed to make a particular point of averting his eyes as Jon went past.

Diana registered Jeremy's obvious aversion for the half-breed and goaded, "You don't find them attractive?"

"How can you have such lowlifes around you?"

"They're useful for the unpleasant work."

"So that prompted you to relax our strict rules against fraternization with an occupied species?"

"I know that your personal experience at overseeing an occupying force is very limited, Jeremy," she explained with a patient, patronizing tone. "A good field commander must always grasp the *realities* of a situation and adjust her, or *his*, standards as best suits the situation. No matter how strict the rules, on an operation of this duration it was inevitable that some of our troops would transgress." She glanced subtly toward Shawn who looked away with slight embarrassment. Then she refocused on Jeremy. "We certainly don't encourage it, but no harm has been done by the presence of the half-breeds. And overall the opportunity for sexual release has aided troop morale."

Jeremy was doing his best to avoid her lecture and had been eyeing the food that was displayed in covered containers behind the bar. There were chunks and shreds of flesh in some of them, twining entrails in others, small organs and glandular meats in still others. All were raw and coated with a thin film of red blood.

"This is fresh, I trust," he sniffed aristocratically.

"Killed within the hour, of course," she confirmed.

He eyed the selection carefully. "Anything human here?"

"Not yet," Diana said, smiling. "We're saving them for dessert. After we've selected out those suitable for other uses." She watched as Jeremy also inspected each of the small animals pawing around inside translucent containers. "Anything look interesting to you?"

"I'd heard these were quite nice." Jeremy opened one of the built-in cubicles and took out a yellow parakeet.

"Yes, indeed they are, sir," said Paul. The unctuous press secretary had been looking for a neutral opportunity to insert himself into their conversation. "Careful of its little claws, though, sir."

Jeremy turned the parakeet around in his hand, admiring the feathers. Then he opened his mouth and his jaw popped loose as it distended inhumanly wide. He pushed the fluttering bird in and swallowed it whole.

Diana watched his throat bulge unevenly as the still-living bird slid down his gullet. She wondered if Jeremy thought he could dispense with her as easily.

For his part, Jeremy seemed focused entirely on his dining experience. He was, Diana knew, a connoisseur who much preferred live food such as the parakeet. He liked experiencing the deep satisfaction that resulted from the sensation of the creature's passage downward, alive and squirming, within his throat. He greatly enjoyed that feeling as he would also enjoy the animal's panicked, drowning flutters deep within his stomach for the next few minutes.

Diana moved to her chair at the end of the table and sat. "So. You're here to improve our efficiency?"

"Yes. There are pressing reasons." He was picking a small piece of yellow fluff from the corner of his mouth.

"Oh, I know there are, of course." Diana nodded, smiling as she traced a finger over the smooth tabletop and said casually, "The approaching *war*."

Martin stopped breathing. Had he heard correctly? From his position near the door, Martin saw that Paul was also stunned at the mention of a coming war, but the ever-cagey Shawn was unruffled, apparently in on the secret. Jeremy's eyes had quickly flicked over to Diana. She had not looked up, but she knew that he was surprised and it pleased her. "So you see I'm not completely uninformed." She raised her smoldering eyes slowly to meet Jeremy's. "Martin, will you please see to tonight's gathering?"

As Martin emerged from the conference chamber and walked down the shadowy passageway, Willy, who had been pretending to do some maintenance work nearby, fell into step beside him. Willy could feel Martin's unease bubbling near the surface. He whispered to his friend, "What is it?"

"Oh, just the casual mention of a coming *war.*"

Willy was shocked. "War! Against the Resistance?"

"No, it was something else, something new." Martin exhaled with frustration. "I *wish* I could be among her innermost group."

When they were well past a Patroller, Willy said in a whisper, "Listen, I had an idea about that. Someone who might help. I sent off a message to Margarita . . . about Emma."

AS IN ALL OF THE OTHER 250 MOTHERSHIPS, THE FLAGSHIP'S LOWER, inner passageways were narrower and much less inviting than those frequented by Diana and her command staff. The walls were an oily black. They were covered from top to bottom with electrical conduit or pipes of various sizes. Many of the pipes were transparent so the various colored liquids within them could be seen flowing; some were thick and moved sluggishly while others flowed at great speed. The inner corridors were also much darker and since they were steamy most were perpetually damp. The temperature was as high as the humidity, which made the air feel even more close and claustrophobic as it pressed against Sidney Stein's sweaty skin.

His clothes were soaked from his own perspiration that traced down his face and neck. Danny Stein's father was among thirteen very worried human prisoners being led by three Patrollers along a dark passageway deeper and deeper into the bowels of the great behemoth of a ship, where even the most trusted Teammates were never allowed. The prisoners continually glanced at one another, seeking some comfort or at least connection with

a fellow human. Sidney had seen the panic in the tearful eyes of
the woman just in front of him. He didn't know her name and
had never seen her before they were thrown together as prisoners. "I shouldn't be here," she was murmuring to the uncaring
Patroller walking in front of her. "The woman who denounced
me was lying. I'm not in the Resistance."

As they passed a hatch, a female Visitor technician suddenly
popped her head out at nervous Sidney, and shouted, "Boo!"

Sidney was startled and unnerved by the Visitor's appearance.
The technician had a human face with a Hispanic cast to it, but
one of her eyes was violet. Sidney also noticed there was an odd
sheen on one of her cheeks. A Patroller prodded Sidney to move
along as the technician laughed, then went back inside the hatch
and into one of the Flagship's many chemical laboratories.

There were perhaps twenty-five Visitor technicians and doctors working at various tables and consoles. The lab was similar
to those of Earth. It contained numerous racks of flasks, tubes,
and other containers, but also some devices and instrumentation
that a human chemist would have thought unsettlingly alien. The
technician, Teresa, who had scared Sidney, looked in a mirror assessing the sheen on her face. "So, what do you think?"

The human blue eyes of the gentle half-breed custodian, Jon,
glanced up eagerly from where he was electronically scrubbing
the floor. He was delighted to be called upon. "Very interesting,
ma'am. What exactly are you—?"

"I'm not talking to you, you stupid dreg." The tech gruffly
shoved Jon aside and approached a Visitor research doctor.
"Well, Eric?" The doctor turned to look at her. He had a good,
square, honest face and thick, slightly graying hair that gave him
the look of a respectable fifty-year-old Caucasian. He was in the
midst of using a syringe to extract puslike fluid from a bulbous
insect.

Teresa displayed her violet eye and the sheen on her cheek. "Is
Jeremy going to be happy?"

"Only if we finish quickly." Eric scrutinized the details of Teresa's face while she picked up one of his fat insects and popped it into her mouth, chewing it with enjoyment. Then Eric concluded in his characteristically soft-spoken manner, "Yes, it looks better. And please stop eating my research."

"But those brown ones are killer." Teresa was reaching for another when Eric's serious expression stopped her. She smirked and turned back to her own work as Eric gathered some scrap material and smiled down toward the young janitor.

"Jon, do you think you could dispose of this?"

"Certainly, sir." Jon nodded graciously at the kindly doctor. Eric was one of the very few who ever showed tolerance to halfbreeds such as Jon. "Oh, and, sir," Jon spoke quietly to avoid the notice of the other doctors and technicians, "you had also discarded this molecular analyzer." The teenager opened a door on the side of his floating custodial module to show Eric the small device.

"Yes, I did, the power cell was faulty"—then Eric smiled knowingly—"something new for your collection?"

"If you wouldn't mind, sir," Jon said hopefully.

"By all means." Eric gave the misshapen boy a fatherly pat on the shoulder and returned to his work.

Jon put the waste materials into the top of his floating module and eased it out the hatch ahead of him. Once in the corridor he used his access key to enter a transport tube designated as *Restricted Entry*.

As the tube carried the teenager downward and at the diagonal angle necessary, his facile mind was turning over the possibilities of recalibrating a micro-fuel cell already in his possession to reactivate the molecular analyzer. He was confident he could construct the proper algorithms and create the necessary quantum interface. Numerous possible equations spun through his busy brain and began forming into exciting coherence.

The elevator eased to a stop and the control panel demanded

a *High Security* code key, which Jon supplied. Then the door hissed open to reveal a corridor much larger than those he had just left. It was dark. The walls were the same slick black and circumscribed with conduits and piping through which the bodily fluids of the great ship surged, pulsed, or slowly flowed. The air here was even heavier with heat and humidity, though Jon seemed not to notice. He walked along the floor, a metal grid that allowed him to see down through to other such walkways below his feet, the sublevels disappearing downward into the hazy distance.

Jon guided his custodial unit toward a larger open hatch. The gurgling sound of thick liquid intensified around him. There were also thousands of intermittent hissing and percolating noises that blended together into a low, pervasive white noise like a wide swath of a shallow river flowing over small stones. But this was no sylvan landscape. Crossing the threshold into the Storage Chamber was like suddenly stepping from an ordinary room into a dark, towering cathedral, but much larger, like a domed sports stadium. Yet this Storage Chamber was far larger even than that. It seemed immeasurably vast, stretching a mile above and below Jon's vantage point and more than a mile across. And it was not empty.

It was filled with opaque, membranous capsules, each about the size of a coffin. They stood upright, side by side. There were row upon row of them, stretching upward, downward, and away from Jon with access catwalks and open lifts interwoven among them. Jon looked at the capsules nearest him, which were representative of all the tens of thousands of others. Bloated, flexible, intestinelike tubes coiled and pulsed around each of the capsules creating the undulating sounds that filled the chamber. Inside each capsule was a human being, sightlessly staring out, comatose.

Several of those near Jon wore U.S. military uniforms, while others wore clothing that suggested their profession. There were mechanics, people in lab coats, business suits, firemen. A little girl wore the white blouse and pleated, plaid jumper of a Catholic-school girl. But the majority of them were dressed in everyday clothes such as might be seen on any city street. Each of the people entombed was fitted with a neurological unit that covered head and ears like a helmet. The cables snaking upward from the head unit always reminded Jon of the mythological Medusa.

Jon was fascinated by human mythology. Unlike many half-breeds, Jon had embraced the human side of his heritage and was an avid reader of whatever books from Earth he could get his hands on. Many books that were no longer available to people on Earth were stored in the restricted vaults on the Flagship, to which Jon had custodial access. He had secretly read such forbidden works as *Brave New World*, *1984*, *Huckleberry Finn*, *All the President's Men* as well as hundreds of other books both fictional and fact. His thirst for knowledge was intense and he took great advantage of his privileged access. He particularly enjoyed scientific works. He counted himself very lucky, because the education of most half-breeds was ignored among the Visitors much as it was among the humans.

Jon had moved farther along the catwalk amid the storage capsules. Though he had seen these complex, cocoonlike mechanisms all his life, they fascinated him. He was intrigued by how they had been designed to keep the people within in a state of suspension, just barely alive, for years. He slowed his pace as he approached a particular capsule. He stopped and with his hand gently wiped the collected moisture from its surface so he could better see the woman within. She was about thirty years of age and her hair and eyes were similar in color to Jon's.

He gazed at her glazed, unseeing blue eyes for a long moment, then he sighed and walked on. Rounding a corner he came in sight of a Capsule Operations Control. There were many such operational platforms scattered throughout the gargantuan storage chamber, but this was the principal one and the largest. It was semicircular, its flat side about forty feet long. Monitoring consoles were built into that back wall with hundreds of thick conduits channeling into the top of them. There were two long desk-style consoles along the front of the curve with a wide space in the center to allow access from the platform to the catwalks that fanned out among the myriad capsules.

Jon saw that Diana's chief lieutenant Shawn was showing the operation to the newly arrived Commandant. Not wanting to incur Jeremy's further displeasure, Jon held back discreetly but watched the proceedings. He saw the thirteen most recent human prisoners being led to an equal number of open capsules. The frightened people were being directed to step into them, as a storage technician moved closer. Like many of the Visitors who worked in the innermost regions of the ship, storage technicians rarely wore human faces. This one leaned his scaly reptilian head with its several tiny horns along the temples close to the woman who had been walking in front of Sidney Stein and who was now standing in the capsule next to his. Though Sidney did not know it, she was Connie Leonetti, the woman whom Sidney's wife Stella had falsely denounced at the chemical plant.

Connie drew back instinctively from the reptile's sour breath and sharp teeth. His forked tongue flicked out and toyed with her ear a moment. Jon knew that the technician enjoyed his position of superiority and often harassed the new prisoners. Then the technician's yellow eyes with their vertical irises flashed as his green lipless mouth grinned at them. "Welcome to our little hotel. We've got some nice bedtime stories for you."

Other storage technicians, also with reptilian faces, were using their scaly, clawed hands to affix the neuro clamps onto the heads of the prisoners, including Sidney who was near panic now. "This is a mistake! I'm a loyal Teammate! Please, Commandant!"

Sidney's plea opened the floodgates and suddenly the other

prisoners also began crying out, begging for their lives, as the plasticine shells began to slowly close them in. Connie was screaming through her tears, "Please! I'm not with the Resistance! Don't do this! My little girl has only me! Please don't—!"

The capsules sealed around Connie and the others whose voices could no longer be heard though Jon could still see them pleading within. Jon glanced at Commandant Jeremy, who was watching with bored impatience as the interiors of the capsules swirled with a greenish gas. Jon saw the people within reacting with terror as they tried to breathe, but couldn't. Jon held his own breath while mentally urging the desperate people not to fight it. He knew that struggling against the gas was useless. Yet several of them did, particularly Connie whose mouth was gaping wide again and again seeking the oxygen that was no longer available. Jon hated to see the bizarre, unnerving process. But he forced himself to watch, thinking that perhaps his presence, his bearing witness, might somehow ease their suffering.

After an interminable moment, the clenched muscles in Connie's face and neck began to relax and she ceased to move. Like Sidney and the others, she had become impassive, staring sightlessly, without motion.

Jon glanced at Jeremy. The Commandant was picking another tiny piece of lint from his pristine sleeve, apparently anxious to get on to more important matters.

9

THE AFTERNOON SHADOWS WERE LENGTHENING ON HEMLOCK STREET just west of Van Ness where there were a number of small shops. One was a modest, mom-and-pop vid store, selling mostly used merchandise. An old table set out in front displayed the cheapest inventory. The vid dealer, a turbaned Arab named Ahmed, was arranging his wares as a middle-aged businesswoman paused by the table and flipped through the vids. Then she casually checked to be sure no one was listening and whispered to him, "I'm looking for *The Truth*."

Ahmed reacted cautiously, then chuckled. "Hard to come by. No CNN, no Voice of America. Just like in my old country."

They both became aware that a Patrol shuttle was gliding by overhead. They waited for it to pass. Then the woman poked at the cheap merchandise again and spoke without looking at the dealer, "I think I'm supposed to say 'Street-C sent me.'"

Ahmed had already been sizing her up. These were very dangerous times, but he also knew they were critical times. He and his wife Viella had been working with the Resistance for sixteen years, ever since they had barely escaped a Visitor dragnet in Riyadh. He glanced again at the businesswoman. The look in her eyes was earnest. Ahmed reached under the table and gave her a vid disk like the one Danny Stein had been viewing at his school. The customer smiled and opened her purse, but Ahmed stayed her hand. "No charge. Just please pass it on."

The woman met his eyes with a conspiratorial twinkle. "You can be sure I will." Then she moved on up the sidewalk.

Across the street the black Visitor Patrol captain who had condemned Sidney Stein was holding Danny's arm as the boy reluctantly looked across at Ahmed in front of his shop. Danny's voice was low; he was very reluctant. "Yeah. That's where I got the vid." Danny looked up at the Visitor's dark face. "Now will you let my father go?"

THAT EVENING THE GRAND BALLROOM AT SAN FRANCISCO'S FAMED Mark Hopkins Hotel was rocking with the latest popular hit being sung by America's sexy sweetheart, Emma. The music carried out into the large elegant foyer that was deserted except for Commandant Jeremy, who had just emerged from the ballroom onto the thick burgundy carpet. He'd had quite enough music. He looked impatiently around the lovely high-ceilinged room with its gold rococo chandelier, its beautifully carved mahogany woodwork, its tasteful and expensive artwork, and he saw none of it. The thick, king-sized door he'd just come through opened again as Diana paused there to study him. Behind her could be seen a narrow sliver of the chic gathering within, people in black tie or in Visitor and Teammate dress uniforms seated at tables flowing within linen cloths and set with crystal. Emma could be glimpsed singing on the small stage, but Jeremy was uninterested. Diana walked slowly toward her fellow Commandant with a look of feigned concern on her face. "Something wrong?"

His tone was curt. "We should just get to business."

Diana smiled wisely. "This *is* business, Jeremy."

"This is fluff. All of that in there"—he gestured deprecatingly toward the ballroom—"it's mere nonsense."

"Exactly. And humans thrive on it," Diana spoke easily, a twenty-year student of human sociology. "Gatherings like this, and entertainment in general—with embedded propaganda," she added pointedly, "is the best way to achieve our goals."

He didn't believe her. He'd made his own assessment. "You've gone soft."

She smiled patiently. "Let me tell you something. All those Teammates and Players in there will *kill* for us. Some already have." The satisfied coldness in her eyes made it clear she was speaking the truth. She moved toward the ornate circular oak table that graced the center of the foyer. "I let them have their little entertainments to encourage camaraderie. I encourage sports to maintain fitness; business to serve our needs and sustain infrastructure; procreation to give us more . . . raw material." She was amused by her little pun. "I'm forging an entire conquered people into loyal Teammates."

Jeremy thought he knew better. "What about the Resistance?"

Diana took a single lily from a huge bouquet on the oaken table. "I broke their back in my Great Purge of '99."

"I've heard there's been a new resurgence," he prodded.

She was examining the lily with unconcern. "They'll be crushed by the time we begin our new enterprise."

"Really?" Jeremy affected surprise and watched her carefully as he said, "By the end of this week?"

He was rewarded when Diana glanced sharply at him. He had trumped her again. From inside the ballroom came loud applause.

Emma had concluded her song and was taking a bow before the grateful audience. She was slightly flushed from the exertion of the song and it looked good on her. She was wearing a short dress that seemed to be made up merely of a number of strategically placed veils. The dapper black Patrol captain who had been with Danny two hours earlier helped Emma step down to the closest table. He held onto her hand longer than necessary. "You are extraordinary."

"Oh, thank you, Captain. Thank you so much." She moved to her table where Press Secretary Paul was raising a glass to her. She smiled graciously, then let her eyes find and linger on Mayor Ohanian who was sitting near one of his mayoral aides. Mark's glance increased the flush on Emma's cheeks. She had noted the rush she felt upon seeing him aboard the Flagship and felt it rise within her again now. She began to consider that perhaps she had ended their relationship prematurely. Ever-present Player J. D. Oliver held her chair and leaned his double chin down close to the bronze curve of her shoulder. "You really *must* come visit. I have a trinket for you—and a case of '96 Evian."

NINE-YEAR-OLD ALI HAD HIS HAND ON THE OLD IRON LAMPPOST IN front of his parents' vid store. He was half swinging in a slow circle around it as he waited patiently for his parents Ahmed and Viella to lock up for the night. Ali often had bouts of asthma, but tonight he was feeling pretty good, particularly because he knew that his mother was going to make *bastia* for dinner. The

Moroccan chicken pastry with powdered sugar was his favorite. Viella had already lowered the metal screen over the vid store window and Ahmed was just emerging when Ali saw an SFPD squad car, four Visitor Patrollers, and a Teammate unit suddenly converging on the store.

"On the ground!" a big Patroller shouted, brandishing her pulse rifle. "All of you! Now!"

Ahmed and Viella were startled, they looked about fearfully. Another Patroller fired a warning shot that shattered the neon sign above Ahmed. "Get on the fucking ground," the Patroller shouted more forcefully. Ahmed held out his hands in compliance and urged Viella down to the sidewalk. Then Ahmed's eyes met Ali's and the little boy suddenly turned and ran.

"Ali! No!" Ahmed shouted urgently. "Don't run!"

Teammate Debra Stein stepped out and raised her pulse weapon. She drew a bead on the fleeing boy and casually fired her pistol. The fiery ball of energy flashed through the darkness and burst brightly against the boy's back, driving him to the pavement.

"Ali!" Ahmed screamed through frantic tears. Viella also wailed her son's name and tried to move toward him, but the troops shoved her brutally back down, skinning her face badly. Ahmed felt the gritty sole of a Patroller's jackboot against the back of his neck but managed to turn his head against the concrete just enough to see his fallen son. Ali was lying motionless thirty yards away, his limbs at odd angles. Ahmed heard the Teammates smash open the vid store and begin gutting it.

At the corner a block away, the SFPD had cordoned off the area. Some people tried to walk on by without looking, since it was always better not to get involved. But a few had paused to witness the police activity. One of them was a young hip-hop man with his hair in cornrows and a matchstick clenched tightly between his teeth. Street-C's stomach had hardened into a knot, his brow was lowered, his face grim and angry. He watched

Ahmed and Viella being pulled to their feet as the Teammates roughly dragged away little Ali's lifeless body.

MALE AND FEMALE VOICES WERE ECHOING IN THE DARKNESS AND slowly growing more intelligible. Then a painful brightness stabbed in as Nathan's eye was pried open. His vision was still very blurry, as though he were looking up from underwater, but he recognized Margarita's auburn hair as she leaned in to check his pupils. Her voice thrummed distantly. "You can get the scan now."

Nathan blinked heavily and thought he saw Ruby sitting nearby thumbing through a textbook and glancing at him while she did schoolwork in a looseleaf binder, but his head was still swimming. Then a man he recognized from the Resistance vid as Robert Maxwell, the Nobel Prize–winning anthropologist, leaned in with an optical instrument and Nathan realized his retina was being scanned. He heard Margarita directing Robert briskly, "Have Ysabel run his stats and get me the results asap, Robert." Then she added, "Please."

Nathan saw Robert's dark eyes smile at Margarita's energy and head off. Then Nathan determined to shake off the effects of what he knew must have been a tranquilizer. He forced himself to rise up onto one elbow and take some deep breaths. He tried to sit up straighter, but the cot he was lying on suddenly felt like a raft atop a wavy ocean.

"Not too fast, hotshot. You'll fall on your face."

He didn't want to admit it, but he knew she was right. He turned more slowly to look in the direction of Margarita's voice. She was sitting on a crate nearby, expertly cleaning an AK-47 assault rifle while she kept an eye on him. He took some more breaths as he groggily surveyed his surroundings. They were in what appeared to be a funky abandoned warehouse, complete with a few pigeons fluttering about in the vaulted wooden rafters. Nathan saw a large letter "V" spray-painted in red on various walls. He also saw nine or ten trucks of various sizes parked inside the building. Their sides or backs had been opened out to afford easy access to equipment and supplies within. He understood: the Resistance needed to be ready to relocate at a moment's notice. He could see that two trucks held foodstuffs, one was rigged as a mobile emergency room, one flickered with vid images and was clearly a communications center. He saw numerous weapons both conventional and Visitor-style, energy pulse types in a steel-clad garbage truck that was obviously an armory. Several of the vehicles contained advanced electronic and biomedical equipment as might be found in an extensive science laboratory.

Along one side of the warehouse's interior were some ratty cubicles that had once been small offices but had now been pressed into service as living quarters for those in the Resistance who had to remain permanently in hiding. The doors of many cubicles were open and Nathan could see they had been personalized with pictures and other items, to keep those in the Underground in touch with their former lives.

There were several low concrete islands built into the broad floor with thick metal mounting brackets as though they had once supported heavy machinery. Across the large central space Nathan saw Street-C and about two dozen other Resistance members sitting on mismatched chairs or boxes. The people were a cross-section of race, gender, ethnic backgrounds, age, and class. Among them was Gary Lavine, the clean-cut, nicely coiffed cyclist to whom Harmy had handed off Willy's envelope. Beefy Blue, the chemical plant worker, was also in attendance.

Street-C had been talking to the group. Now he was shaking his head, sad and angry. "It was bad. Little Ali didn't have a chance." A pall fell over them all and there was respectful silence for a moment. Then a far door opened and Nathan noticed that everyone in the room drew a breath of respect as a diminutive blond woman entered.

Nathan immediately recognized Juliet Parish. Though she was only five-foot-two, he could feel that she was a major presence. She was carrying a cardboard box under her left arm. Her right hand managed a polished wooden cane. Nathan knew that she was about forty-six, and was surprised that she still had the figure and fresh face of a college girl with clear skin and sky blue eyes the color of the old sweatshirt she was wearing. Her hair was pulled back into a simple bun. Nathan saw that her cheeks had deep dimples, particularly when she smiled. "Hey, Ruby, grab this, would you?"

The little half-breed was already skipping over to help and to get a hug from Julie. "Whatcha got, Mom?" Ruby said with hopeful enthusiasm. "Explosives?"

"Better yet, Rube: fresh eggs, oranges." She gestured over her shoulder. "There's more in the car, guys."

Several of the others went out to gather it while from across the room bleary Nathan studied Julie with some surprise, muttering to Margarita, "Wait a minute, that's her? *She's* Juliet Parish?"

The redhead was mildly amused. "You were expecting a 'Hallelujah Chorus'?"

"After all the legends about her: 'the heart and soul of the Resistance,' all that stuff, yeah, I guess I was." Nathan measured the small woman against her enormous reputation and all of the wanted posters and Visitor vids bearing Juliet's photo that he had seen over the years. Like all good Teammates, Nathan knew her history by heart.

Juliet Parish had been an intern at the UCLA Medical School when the Visitors first arrived. She had displayed a strong talent for biochemistry and was being urged by her mentors toward a career in that field. Her background gave no hint of any future civil disobedience. Born in Michigan and raised on a farm, she came from straight-arrow, conservative, middle-American stock. Like her family she had been a Republican, but not active in politics. An only child, Juliet did well in school and was near the top of her class as an intern. When the "scientific conspiracy" was unearthed and Scis became persona non grata Juliet had seen many colleagues disappear and finally felt the need to go into hiding herself. She left her fiancé, a stockbroker who was relieved by her departure and later spoke vehemently against her and the Resistance. Over the years he became a trusted Player with the Visitors. Though Nathan had seen many psychological profiles that the Visitors had worked up on Juliet he knew the only common agreement among them was the mystery of why she of all people had become a key leader of the worldwide Resistance.

Some early documentation suggested it was because of her connection to another Resistance leader, TV news cameraman Michael Donovan. It was later shown that they had not met until after Juliet was already recognized as chief of the first and prime Resistance cell. Her personal relationship with Donovan was also sketchy. Clearly they had been close compatriots, and each had saved the other's life more than once. Several reports concluded a definite romantic link between them, even calling them lovers, but there had been no conclusive evidence to support that theory.

As for her becoming the key figure of the international Resistance movement, it was as though she had risen to the top by pure happenstance.

As Nathan watched her interact with the others, she seemed completely average, down-to-earth, unassuming, and accessible. He was a bit surprised by her use of the cane. "She limps?"

"Wounded in her very first fight with your Patroller pals," Margarita said, checking the Kalashnikov's magazine. "She went back to rescue a doctor who had been left behind when they were stealing biomedical equipment. She barely got him away and he died in her arms." Nathan saw Margarita's gaze turn inward, as though she were remembering a loss of her own.

Nathan looked back at Julie. "So how come she's the top dog? She just stand up one day and say 'I'm the leader'?"

"No." Margarita chuckled as she snapped the rifle back together. "Everyone else had to tell her. We still have to."

"But why her?"

Margarita shrugged as though it were obvious. "She's the Natural."

Street-C had walked somberly to Julie and was about to speak when she said, "I heard about Ali." She stared off sadly toward the medical truck. "I just treated his asthma last Thursday."

"Well, the Teammates just *cured* him. Permanently." Street-C had a bitter taste in his mouth, thinking about the little guy.

Julie was also pained, but asked, "What about Ahmed's contacts?"

"We're spreading the word, but they're in danger," Margarita said, walking toward her.

Gary ran his hand through his smooth, smoky-colored hair, frustrated. "God, can't we get a break?"

Ysabel, the feisty Peruvian grandmother who had raised Jerome a.k.a. Street-C, brought Margarita and Julie the latest messages. "Feels like '99 all over again. Tighter than a gnat's ass in Europe and Asia." Ysabel pointed to one of the dispatches. "Melbourne is starting to get out the new vids, though. They want to talk to you two."

Margarita had shuffled through the dispatches. "Still no word from Tokyo?"

Ysabel sighed as she took off her half-glasses, letting them dangle on the beaded chain around her neck. "Not since they recontacted us last week. They may have gone under again. Teammate training's ramping up everywhere. And disappearances."

"More denouncements, too," Blue said as he rubbed the stubble on his thick, dark chin. "Took a woman from my plant yesterday. And the water's shut off more than half the time now."

"It's only going to get worse as the water diminishes further," Julie pondered as she leaned against a wooden crate.

Street-C nodded dourly. "Gonna be dog-eat-dog, man."

"Or Visitor-eat-man, dog," Ruby quipped darkly.

Street-C popped the girl's fist. "Got that right, Rube."

Julie was mulling it over. "Only the very strongest people will be left."

"Yeah"—Ysabel was discomfited at the thought, fiddling with the thin bracelets on her wrist—"to be the best slaves, or soldiers . . ."

"Or *dinner*," Ruby said emphatically.

They all glanced at the half-breed girl, knowing she was so very right. "Shoot"—big Blue was shaking his head—"feels like we're at the damn Alamo. And what's up with this big new Emissary guy coming?" His question was aimed at Margarita.

"History would say: big new trouble, Blue," Margarita said, then saw Nathan approaching. "Oh, and speaking of . . ."

Nathan was still unsteady on his feet, but his attitude was brash and focused on Julie. "I'd like to know why the hell you needed to have me shoot at—"

Margarita interrupted, addressing Julie, "I already told him the assignment was a loyalty test—"

"Which was pretty weird," he cut in sarcastically, "since, let's see, I already stole a fighter and shot down one of theirs. *Hello?*"

Ruby piped up in his defense, "It's true, Mom, I saw them seriously shooting at him." Nathan had impressed Ruby from the beginning in more ways than one.

But Julie smiled patiently. "I know, Ruby." Then she addressed the former Teammate, "All of which could've been set up for our benefit."

Nathan blinked, incredulous. "You've got to be kidding."

"We're a little suspicious when a longtime, loyal Teammate suddenly wants to join us," Julie continued.

Nathan smirked. "I just wasn't motivated before, okay?"

Robert brought the results of Nathan's retinal scan. "Visitor database lists him as 'a decorated Teammate major. Now a deserter. Mentally unbalanced. A dangerous fugitive.'"

Street-C's eyes narrowed. "Don't mean he's on our side."

"*Doesn't*, Jerome"—Ysabel poked her adopted son—"stop with that street talk."

Nathan chuckled darkly at all of them. "So how the hell do I convince you?"

Margarita met his eyes. "Just tell us the truth, hotshot."

Nathan was flippant. "You got a lie detector, Red?"

"Yeah"—she held his intense gaze—"you're looking at 'em." Nathan stared at her for a moment, then surveyed the intent group surrounding him.

He decided to back off a notch, then spoke, "When I was fifteen the Visitors told me the Resistance killed my parents. Showed me what was left of their mutilated corpses. And the 'confession' of the Resistance people who killed them." He sighed, studying the scarred concrete floor a moment. "What can I say? I was a kid and an orphan overnight. And very pissed off. I joined the Teammates to fight against the Resistance. Shot up through the ranks because I did the job."

The others knew what that meant. That he had captured or killed compatriots of theirs. They watched him carefully. Julie particularly noted that what he said next was very difficult for him. "Over the years I had a very close Visitor friend named Sarah who'd always watched out for me. She knew that this week I was going to be promoted to a much higher command in the Pacific. She said she didn't want me fighting for the wrong side anymore and she told me the truth about herself: that she was one of the fifth column. One of the few Visitors who didn't believe in their almighty Leader's agenda. I had wondered occasionally about her loyalty to them, but I never said anything. So she was taking a big chance. She knew I was a gung-ho Team-mate. She knew I might turn her in immediately. But she snuck me into the prisoner storage chamber on the Hawaiian Mother-ship. She showed me my mom and dad." Nathan's jaw set with emotion as the image reappeared in his mind's eye. "They hadn't been killed. They were inside two of those goddamn alien cap-sules. I realized what an idiot I'd been. So I deserted with Sarah to fight back." He paused as he remembered her last words in his arms on the smoky street. "And I got her killed."

"I'm very sorry," Julie said softly.

But Margarita was hanging tough. "Why didn't you work from the inside?"

"Because I was too pissed off."

"How 'bout too impulsive. Too impetuous."

Nathan bristled at her, "How 'bout when *your* parents get pickled you come talk to me!"

"Her parents were," Julie said. "And her brother was killed by Teammates."

Nathan glanced at Julie, then looked into Margarita's strong eyes. He nodded an apology.

"We've all lost people, Nathan," Julie went on sympathetically, "family, friends. Loved ones. We can't afford to lose any more. And we can't allow any spies among us. Or any loose cannons."

Ysabel cocked her sprightly head toward him. "We need *teamwork* action, amigo."

Nathan emitted a caustic little laugh. "Yeah, well your 'ac-tions' haven't been all that effective lately."

"When you're right, you're right." Julie sighed as she stood to relieve the pain from the old pulse wound in her hip. "When Di-ana created the Teammates the odds really swung against us."

Street-C nodded. "Got that right. Then her 'Great Purge' back in '99 all but kicked our ass for good." His eyes narrowed at Nathan. "Guess you were one of the ass-kickers, huh?"

"Yeah, I'm sorry to say I was." Nathan was sincere and genuinely curious. "But how'd Diana ever get so much inside intelligence?"

"We never found out who betrayed us"—Margarita took a cup of tea that Blue was offering her—"but we had to start all over again. And it's gotten steadily harder."

"You know what it's like out there, Nathan." Julie paced slowly among the group, leaning on her cane. "Over time millions of people have been seduced just like you were into believing *The Big Lie*—that the Visitors are actually a good thing."

"Or people go along because the Visitors are such an intimidating hyper-power," Gary added. "Most Visitors on *our* side, like your friend Sarah, have been ferreted out and killed. Only a few of our bravest spies are still alive."

"They're in constant danger." Clearly Julie was concerned for them. "And we have no one inside the Visitor High Command."

"Actually," Gary said, opening the gray envelope he'd gotten from Harmy, "Willy had an idea for a new recruit who might have some access."

Margarita's auburn eyebrows went up when she read the name. "Emma. Well, she's certainly connected."

"Let's figure out the best approach to her," Julie counseled, then looked at their newest volunteer. "Meantime you're welcome here, Nathan. If you think you can work our way."

Nathan gazed at her a moment, uncertain about that himself, but he finally nodded tersely.

Margarita was watching him closely as she rubbed the back of her forefinger against the tip of her nose. She was not thoroughly convinced about him.

Outside the warehouse, violet-eyed Kayta was moving stealthily through the abandoned and rusting industrial area as her remarkably sensitive nostrils sniffed the air. She had already spotted and avoided the female lookout nestled in a pile of tires and junk at the far end of the ratty complex. Kayta began to hear a buzzing sound and her nose led her toward a dark, greasy garage where she saw the car that Margarita had used for her get-away with Nathan. A thick swarm of insects was buzzing around the gelatinous blob of pheromone Bryke had shot onto the side of the car. Kayta assessed the location and the old warehouse carefully.

Then she spoke quietly into her pin, "I think Phase Two has been achieved, Ayden. I believe he has led us to their principal base." A ragged crow was watching Kayta from a broken fence, but when the bird caught sight of the gleam in her strange violet eyes it grew uncomfortable and took flight. A faintly ironic smile slowly formed on Kayta's lips and she settled in to wait.

10

THE IMPOSING, SQUARE-SHOULDERED VISITOR PATROL CAPTAIN WHO headed Debra Stein's Teammate unit was just stepping out the front door of the Stein house. He held his uniform cap in his hands. His strong African-American features bore a sad expression. His deep bass voice was solemn. "I am so very sorry." He gently touched Stella Stein's shoulder. The stout woman had suffered an emotional shock and was crying. The captain said goodbye and walked slowly out toward his shuttle craft, which was idling in the street.

Stella watched him go, still stunned by his news. Her daughter Debra stood nearby in her Teammate uniform trying to tough it out and hold her own emotions in check, but young Danny could barely wait for the door to close before he exploded in fury, "It's a damn lie!"

Stella was feeling weak in the knees. "Danny, please . . ."

"He lied to you, Mom!"

Debra glared at him. "Watch your mouth, Dan."

"Oh, sit on it, Debra," he fumed. "Dad wasn't 'killed by the

Resistance' like that captain said. The Visitors took him away! I saw it!"

"Oh, yeah," his sister said with a smirk. "Like I'm so sure the captain would *lie* to us."

"*I saw it, Debra!* You've just got your fat head so far up their asses that—"

"Stop it! Both of you!" Stella blurted through her tears. "Do you think I want to believe that your father's dead?"

"If he is it was *the Visitors* that killed him."

Debra turned on her heel. "I won't listen to your bullshit"— but then she spun back and looked daggers at him—"and let me tell you something, Dan: you keep it up and *I'll* report you."

Danny watched her storm down the short hallway into her room. Then he turned to his mother and tried his best to present a calm, rational demeanor. "I *saw* them take him, Mom. Up there." He pointed upward toward their ceiling and the Flagship above it.

Stella stared at her boy, her insides churning from the conflict between Danny's firm conviction, Debra's fiery Teammate dedication, her own distress over her missing husband, and the mystery of Sidney's actual fate.

JEREMY WAS ENJOYING HIS POSITION AT THE CENTCOM'S TOPMOST level. A large portion on the north side of the Flagship's Executive Level 125 housed all of the command and control facilities for the great Mothership. It also contained the Command Center for the entire Visitor Armada. It was from this Centcom that fleet operations were coordinated and directed for all of the 250 Motherships. It was nearly the size of a football field and four stories tall, with each higher level set back slightly from the one below it. All the levels faced the transparent outer wall of the great ship through which could be seen the sky above and San Francisco below. The window wall was heavily tinted during the day to protect the sensitive eyes of the Visitors. Inbound and outbound Visitor craft were constantly seen cruising past.

On all levels of the Centcom there were charting sections for strategizing military movements and following ongoing maneuvers. Virtually all of the thousands of Visitor craft in the air anywhere in the world were represented on one or more of the many visualizers. All of the optical information was realized in high-definition, three-dimensional, holographic-style displays that could be rotated for examination from any angle. The same could be done from the hundreds of smaller, individual stations that crowded the huge space. Holographic projections hovered in the air above each station's console. They were interactive so that Visitor technicians could literally reach into the image before them and make adjustments. On other visualizers, data and statistics were constantly changing and updating. Scores of technicians glided from one level to a higher or lower one on small pallets, which floated by means of Visitor antigravity technology.

There was a low buzz of dialogue from the technicians reflecting their constant communication with similar control centers on various Motherships or specific vehicles in transit, in departure, or on approach.

Jeremy sat in the commandant's chair that was always reserved solely for Diana, but since Jeremy was at that moment addressing by teleconference all of the captains aboard their individual Motherships, Diana had courteously relinquished it to him, temporarily.

Watching from a seat nearby, Diana's graciousness was merely on the surface. She was still seething over Jeremy's elevation to equal rank with her. What was gnawing at Diana even more than his promotion was the uncertainty of Jeremy's new closeness and personal relationship with their Leader. Diana had always enjoyed the privilege of being the one most intimate with the

Leader, both professionally and personally. While Diana was wise enough to know that the Leader enjoyed occasional dalliances, Diana had also been given to understand that the Leader held her in the highest regard both as a Commandant and as a sexual partner.

The Leader's few communications with Diana since Jeremy's arrival, however, had seemed to Diana to be ever so slightly off-key from their normal personal intimacy. Diana was also wise to the ways of palace intrigue, having been the author of many such maneuverings herself. She knew that Jeremy was an extremely astute and dangerous challenger. She had resolved to scrutinize his every move and turn of phrase from which she might gain advantage.

Martin, standing to the rear, was taking it all in. As Jeremy spoke to the Mothership captains, Martin saw that Diana was determined not to show how much she was chafed by Jeremy crowding her authority. Her closest aide, Shawn, exercising that subtle cleverness that Martin knew was inherent in his nature, had strategically positioned himself behind and between the two Commandants. Martin could tell that Shawn was already beginning to play both ends against the middle, so that whichever Commandant came out on top, shrewd Shawn would be in the winning camp. Martin watched the subtle expressions playing across Diana's face and felt he had correctly deduced much of what she had been thinking. He also saw that she was idly toying with the controls of a vid screen while Jeremy was talking.

"And I'm speaking with the full personal authority of our Great Leader," Jeremy was saying firmly, causing Diana to shift slightly in her chair. "Our main Earth-based research facility here in San Francisco has developed a new chemical compound that will be our principal weapon in a grand new conquest against an old and dangerous enemy. I want the senior Patrol captains from each of your ships to report here immediately for training with this new weaponry."

Martin noticed that during Jeremy's discourse Diana had brought up on her holographic display a view of a detention cell somewhere in the dark bowels of the Flagship. A guard could be seen tossing scraps through the laser grid at the mouth of the dark cell. Martin could barely see the ragged prisoner within. With wild hair and beard that had gone uncut for years, the human crawled on all-fours and looked to be a crippled, skittish beast.

Jeremy concluded his transmission to the Motherships and signed off. As he rose, he glanced at the prisoner on Diana's screen and chuckled. "Bigfoot?"

Diana clicked off the image, and smiled privately. "No. A personal souvenir. A special prisoner."

Jeremy ignored her comment and headed out, motioning to the press secretary. "Paul, we'll be getting a VIP very soon. We need to talk." Shawn waited diplomatically for Diana to stand, then followed her out. Martin held back, he was curious about the unique, bestial prisoner Diana had been viewing. He traded a private look with a brown-haired Centcom technician who had the face of a thirty-year-old human. Her large eyes were as soft as they were dark. Martin knew her name was Lee and that she was one of the few remaining Visitors stationed in the Centcom who was sympathetic to the Resistance. Lee understood Martin's silent glance. She began to casually search out the location of the cell holding the peculiar prisoner.

AT ABOUT THE SAME TIME, JULIET PARISH WAS IN HER BATTERED, LOW-rent communications truck speaking fluent French with one of the key European Resistance chiefs. "That's excellent, Michel. Try to reach Anthony in Brussels. It's critical for him to get those new vids out and also up into the Netherlands. Let's talk again at 1400 Zulu. Good-bye."

Ysabel broke off the contact, impressed as always by Julie. "You go, girl."

Julie sighed. "But we've got to do better, Ysie. See if you can get a signal through to New Delhi. Give me a yell."

As she climbed out of the truck she saw that scruffy Ruby had been listening nearby while eating a banana. Ruby spoke to her in halting French, "I think I actually understood most of that."

Julie kissed the girl's scaly cheek and continued in French, "I've got a very smart daughter."

"I've got a very cool momma." Then Ruby said softly in English with shyness that was uncharacteristic and therefore charming, "Don't you think he's sorta cute?" Ruby threw a quick, bashful glance toward Nathan across the warehouse. Ruby had noticed that she often felt a fluttering lightness like butterflies in her stomach when she looked at Nathan. And when she found herself physically near him she would often be surprised by a flood of feeling. She still wasn't quite sure what it all meant, but she had noticed how she always contrived to be near to where he was. She'd also realized that when she was close to him an unusual warmth seemed to pervade her young body.

Julie correctly diagnosed that the girl had developed a crush on the young man. Julie scrunched up her nose sourly and gently teased Ruby, "*Him? Eeeyew.*"

Ruby punched Julie's arm playfully and giggled with embarrassment. "*Mom!* Not funny."

Julie laughed, making her dimples deepen. Then she tousled Ruby's bright chestnut hair as she whispered, "Yes, I think he's cute, too. But you might be a little too mature for him."

Ruby felt encouraged. "You know his dad was a native Hawaiian but his mom came from Europe, so he's sort of a half-breed, too."

"Like I always told you, Rube . . ." Julie smiled as Ruby nodded and finished the catechism.

"'One way or another we're *all* half-breeds.'" Then Ruby concluded in French, "What a smart mom." They walked on together,

Ruby holding Julie's arm and leaning against it as Julie inquired after the progress of her other schoolwork. In spite of their circumstances, Julie insisted on Ruby putting in an appropriate number of study hours every day. As with many children forced to live in hiding, Ruby's education continued in as organized a fashion as possible. The other adults also lent a hand. They all enjoyed helping Ruby because she was more than just an eager student. She found such sheer enjoyment in merely being alive that when she came into a room people often felt inclined to laugh with delight.

Across the large warehouse, Nathan had been watching curiously from where he and Margarita were unpacking blank vid disks from a van. He felt a bit confused. "Julie's her mother?"

Margarita shook her head. "No, Ruby's mother died in childbirth. Julie delivered her, raised her. Me, too, since I was seven."

"After your parents got . . . ?"

"Yeah. They caught my dad twenty years ago. It was just after he helped Julie send a distress call into space. They were trying to contact an enemy of the Visitors."

"What, hoping that 'the enemy of my enemy might be my friend'?"

"Yeah. Never got a response, though. Listen, there's another box of disks in the back of that truck." She pointed to it as she snagged Ysabel. "Hey, Ysie, you get that background info on Emma?"

"Still working on it, Margarita."

Nathan pulled open the truck's back door. Dozens of snapshots of men, women, and children formed a mosaic covering the inside of the door. He paused to look at them as Margarita stepped closer. "A little memorial. A few of the people we've lost."

Nathan's eyes zeroed in on a familiar face, "Isn't that one . . . ?"

"Yeah. Mike Donovan. First one to expose the Visitor agenda."

Nathan studied the photo. Donovan's expression was intense,

his eyes keen. He was in his mid-thirties, lean but broad-shouldered. His face was angular and rugged-looking. Even in the loose-fitting shirt Nathan could sense Donovan's muscularity and athletic physique. His longish hair was a light brown, just slightly darker than Nathan's own. Nathan considered the photo for a long moment, then read the handwriting on the bottom, " 'Killed, 1991.' The London Uprising?"

"Yeah. He was leading it. He was an enormous loss to the movement. And to Julie."

"Were they . . . ?"

"Close," she said emphatically, making clear that the extent of their intimacy was none of Nathan's business. "They were close. A very dangerous thing to be—then or now." She lifted out the box of vid disks and turned away from Nathan, having a private flash of bad memory:

A rainy night in Portland. An alleyway. Margarita, then seventeen, leaned out of a grungy doorway, shouting, "Jimmy! This way!" The boy, a year younger with the same auburn hair and freckles as hers, was running fearfully toward her when a fiery burst from a pulse weapon somewhere overhead knifed through the rain and blasted him full on the back of the head. He crashed into some metal trash cans and landed hard on the wet cobblestones. Margarita was over him immediately, frantic, lifting his limp, bleeding head into her lap. Raindrops coursed down her face, mixing with her tears. "Jimmy! Jesus! Jimmy!"

A deep male voice brought Margarita back into the present, "Hey, young lady . . ."

Margarita looked up to see the plant worker, Blue, smiling with sad understanding and holding out a turkey sandwich to her. "You're getting way too skinny to go skipping breakfast again."

Nathan watched her carefully as she said, "Thanks, Blue," taking the sandwich and drawing a breath. "Got busy, you know.

But I took the vitamins you gave me. Oh, hey, you got any more on that new chemical?"

"Not yet. This Sci guy I work with thinks it's weapons grade stuff. He don't know for sure, but thinks it don't affect humans."

"So who're they going to use it against?"

Blue shrugged. "Beats the shit outta me." All three of them puzzled over it. But Nathan's mind was churning the hardest.

A SLIGHT BREEZE RUFFLED THE THIN, FLIMSY CURTAIN IN THE WINdow of the Elgin family's tenement in the Sci ghetto. As the current of air drifted across the wrinkled, age-spotted face of Charlotte's ailing grandfather, his eyes flickered open from the short nap. He had a faint smile on his face because he'd been dreaming about Charlotte as a little girl, about how she loved for him to comb her long raven hair because he'd always sneak a hand down to her third rib and find her tickle spot. Now in his old age she occasionally combed what was left of his hair and searched for *his* tickle spot.

His vision was failing because of the diabetes, but he knew that Charlotte was nearby because of the fragrance of jasmine. He turned slightly and saw her hazy form at his arm, pouring some water for him. "Oh, I'm sorry, Poppy," she said sweetly, "I didn't mean to wake you. Go back to sleep."

"No, no, I'm all right," but a frown had settled into the old man's brow and he was reaching for his glasses. He put them on and looked at her with concern.

Charlotte's beautiful long hair was gone. She had a buzz-cut. She smiled warmly. "Well, it's time for your medicine, anyway."

"Charlotte? What'd you do to your hair?"

She shrugged lightly. "I decided this was much less trouble. Here you go." She shook pills from his prescription bottle that was now half full.

Her grandfather looked at the bottle, confused. "Where'd we get this much?"

"I bought it," Charlotte said proudly. "You've got plenty now."

"But how'd you ever get enough money to . . . ?" His voice trailed off as he looked at her shaved head and his breathing grew shallow. "Oh, Charlotte . . . no . . . ."

The teenager laughed, totally dismissing his concern. "Oh, I was tired of it being so long. Mrs. Soon paid me way more than it was worth. Now you take your meds, young man." She pressed the pills into his fragile hand.

The old man, stirred by deep emotion, looked deeply into his granddaughter's bright, encouraging eyes.

THE GENTLE, HALF-BREED TEENAGER JON PAUSED IN HIS JANITORIAL duties and looked around the high-tech chamber he had been cleaning. It was one of the Flagship's numerous Data Storage Sections. It had row upon row of racks so tall that for the most part they were accessible only by riding up on a floating pallet. Jon looked around stealthily, then secretly opened one of the racks and took out some data plugs. But he jumped when he heard the coarse voice of a Visitor clerk call out, "Hey, you! Dreg. What exactly do you think you're doing?"

The Visitor, who had the face of an ancient reptile and was wrinkled as a prune, walked toward him. Jon's stomach dropped. He knew this female didn't like his kind at all. He had seen her look with disgust at his human eyes and hands. He stammered, "Oh. Well, ma'am. I was . . . uh . . . just . . ."

"Just picking up some data I need," a voice behind them said. Jon was surprised to see a friendly faced Willy nearby. Willy took the data plugs from Jon, looked them over, and smiled. "Good, Jon. This is exactly right."

The shrewish Visitor clerk eyed them suspiciously, not entirely convinced. "All right. But see that you check them out properly." She turned and shuffled away.

Jon whispered gratefully to Willy, "Thank *you*, sir. I'm most appreciative."

Willy spoke warmly, explaining, "I have a son like you."

"Ah. He has a passion for learning, sir?"

"No, he's . . . sort of confused right now." Willy thought of Ted's angst, then drew a fresh breath and smiled at Jon. "As long as you're here, are there any other plugs you want?"

Jon looked up at Willy as though he were a gift from the gods. He nodded eagerly. "Oh, yes, sir!"

IN THE INDUSTRIAL AREA NEAR THE ROTTING PIERS THAT ONCE SER-viced ships before the East Bay became a dust bowl, Ayden and Bryke were joining Kayta. From a discreet vantage point they observed the Resistance warehouse. Ayden was still unaccustomed to his clothing and annoyed by it, but pleased that Kayta had successfully tracked Nathan.

"Well done, Kayta. Let's reconnoiter." They moved off carefully in separate directions.

Inside the warehouse Nathan was making dupe disks of the Resistance vid and he wasn't happy about it. He called out to Margarita as she passed with some reports, "Hey, Red. I didn't sign on to do grunt work. How 'bout some war action?"

"That's what this is: a war for *minds*." She walked over to check his progress.

Nathan thought he knew exactly what she was going to say, "Yeah, yeah I know: propaganda is important and all. But—"

"*The Truth* is what's important." She picked up a few of the disks like they were beloved old friends. "These vids are just like the illegal leaflets that kick-started the American Revolution. And Julie's tactics are pretty much the same: we're trying to wake people up by getting out *The Truth*."

"So she's George Washington?"

"More like Thomas Paine actually. Remember *Common Sense*?"

Nathan chuckled. "The very words I live by."

"Yeah, right," she said with a smirk. "But Julie's also like

Themistocles"—Margarita saw his look of curiosity—"the Athenian general who seized opportunities, improvised strategies?" She saw that Nathan still looked vague. "Led his outnumbered troops to beat the Persian army at Marathon? 490 B.C.?"

"Oh, *that* Themistocles. History buff, are we, Red?"

" 'Those who can't remember the past . . . ' "

" 'Are condemned to repeat it.' " He was pleased to see the flicker of surprise on her freckled face. He puffed up a little. "Santayana. I know some stuff."

Their eyes held for a moment in mutual appreciation, then Julie called from across the warehouse, "Margarita? We got the info on Emma."

"Great. Let's go recruit us a spy."

She handed the vids to Nathan who immediately set them aside. "I'm for that."

He started to follow her, but her hand went up. "Sorry, hotshot, this is girl talk. You just keep those vids coming," then she softened slightly, "please."

Nathan watched the two women depart. Then he looked back at the boxes of vids and at the ten other people nearby who were also busy duping them. This was not what he wanted to be doing. He felt like the young, antsy mustang he'd once seen on the Big Island in a corral that was too small for it.

A half block away outside, Ayden, Bryke, and Kayta had regrouped to share what they'd discovered. "No other outbuildings on my side either," Bryke was saying.

"Good." Ayden nodded, his amber eyes turning again toward the Resistance warehouse. "Then their entire prime operation would seem to be centered in there."

Kayta had been distracted by something she sensed to one side of the warehouse. She indicated that the other two should watch and they saw the small getaway sedan round the corner. Street-C was driving off through the deserted industrial complex with Julie and Margarita aboard.

Ayden glanced significantly at Bryke. The dark-skinned woman understood and left to follow them.

Inside the headquarters Nathan had all of his vid machines duping away. More than ever he was chafing for some action. He looked around at the other Resistance members busy at their own tasks. Then he walked casually toward a door, took a final glance back to be certain he was unobserved, and snuck out.

Ayden and Kayta were taking some strange instruments out of the back of their sleek motorcycle when Kayta turned her head sharply toward the warehouse. Ayden knew her keen senses had detected something else and he followed her eye line. They both watched as Nathan appeared and went into a small attached garage. He emerged a moment later driving a dusty, sputtering Honda Civic in a direction opposite the one Julie and Margarita had taken.

Kayta turned her violet eyes to Ayden. "I told you he was impetuous."

"Or perhaps duplicitous," Ayden pointed out. "Try to discover which."

Kayta started the motorcycle, which made almost no sound, and expertly drove away, leaving Ayden to calibrate one of the handheld instruments and train it carefully on the Resistance headquarters.

11

BY MIDDAY, NATHAN AVERY WAS AT THE CHEMICAL FACTORY WHERE he knew Blue worked. He had hidden the Honda several blocks away and had been skirting the factory's fenced perimeter looking for an access point. He reached the front parking lot opposite the entrance, which was gated by a heavy Cyclone fence that opened electrically on rollers. A security guard station was just outside the gate. Nathan stayed low among the parked cars as he squinted from the sunlight and tried to figure a way in.

He saw a large tractor trailer tank truck approach and stop by the guard shack. The security guard checked some paperwork, then opened the gate and waved the driver in. As the eighteen-wheeler lumbered past the guard, he nodded to the smiling Teammate who was riding on the back. It was Nathan.

Chemical engineer Dr. Charles Elgin stood frowning and stoop-shouldered as he took readings from one of the factory's numerous control panels in the midst of a forest of pipes. He jotted notations on a clipboard-sized PDA as Stella Stein approached with concern on her face. She whispered urgently to him, "My husband disappeared."

Charles looked at her curiously, pushing up his glasses. His frown intensified. "Excuse me? What?"

"A Patrol captain said he'd been killed by the Resistance"— she leaned closer, more confidentially—"but my son swears the Visitors took him away." She waited for Charles to speak but he just stared at her. "Can you find out anything about him?"

"What are you talking about? Why would I have any idea—?"

"I figured, you being a Sci, you might be able to help me."

Charles was completely confused and put off by her. "How could I do that?"

Stella glanced over her shoulder nervously whispering, "I thought you probably know people in the Resistance."

"What? No!" Charles hissed angrily, "For God's sake, Stella. I'm just doing my job here, doing the best I can to keep my family alive. I don't know anything about the Resistance. And I never heard you even ask me about it, okay?" He turned sharply and walked away, passing Blue who had been adjusting a valve nearby and whose eyes were trained on Stella.

Another area within the pipes of the factory was characterized by a circular tank large enough to hold an elephant. Red signs on the side of it warned of *Danger* and *Corrosive Acid*. Beside it was a wall of vertical parallel pipes that looked like those of a huge church organ. Nathan paused there to snag a PDA notebook and a hard hat, which he felt would make him look more authoritative. Then he officiously asked a passing employee, "Where's that new Visitor chemical in the works?" The man pointed a direction and Nathan headed that way.

At the factory's front gate the tractor of the eighteen-wheeler had dropped off its tanker trailer and was now driving out, but the gate guard waved it to a stop, calling to the driver, "Hey, where's your buddy who was riding on the back?"

The driver frowned, puzzled. "What the hell are you talking about? I didn't have anybody with me."

Nathan had reached a section with massive pipes, each the size of a mature oak tree trunk. His sharp eyes were taking in every detail, but not finding the information he was looking for. He approached a worried-looking man who was taking readings from a control panel. "Hey, there." Charles Elgin jumped slightly as he turned to see Nathan strolling up. "Hi"—Nathan was treating Charles like an old acquaintance—"listen, the front office needs up-to-date stats on the new chemical, but I got turned around and I don't remember where exactly the work is going on."

Then a shout attracted their attention, "You!" The gate guard was coming toward them along with two plant security guards and several Teammates. "Hold it right there!"

Nathan grinned tightly at Charles. "We'll talk later." Then Nathan took off running.

The Teammate leader already had his pulse weapon out and when he saw Nathan bolt, he raised it to fire. The security guard shouted for him not to shoot, but the warning came too late. The Teammate fired two shots. Charles had ducked down and the energy bursts flashed overhead. One blasted against a pipe behind him and ruptured it, triggering a fiery explosion that blew

Charles flat. He was pinned down mere inches beneath boiling gas flames that were spraying out horizontally right over his head. Uncaring about Charles, the guards and Teammates rushed around the flames pursuing Nathan.

Big Blue had witnessed the attack and saw the fiery blast that was threatening to incinerate Charles alive. Blue grabbed a coil of electrical cable and hurled one end in to Charles. "Grab it, Charles! Quick!"

Charles stretched for it but the cable had fallen short. He cried out, "I can't reach it!"

Blue pulled the cable back. Then, risking his own life, he edged closer to the roiling flames. He saw Charles's clothes beginning to ignite. Blue threw the cable a second time for all he was worth. Charles grabbed it with hands that were already reddening from the raging inferno just inches above him.

"Hang on, man!" Blue began dragging him out. "*Hang on*!" Though his own face was scorching, Blue persevered and pulled Charles clear of the flames. Soaked with sweat and with their clothes smoldering, they collapsed against each other, breathing hard.

Near the front gate Nathan came running out from amid the pipes of the five-story industrial complex as pulse bursts from his pursuers exploded closer and closer to him. He saw a small truck headed for the gate and he jumped onto the running board. Pulling the door open he yanked the startled driver right out and sent him somersaulting onto the pavement. Then Nathan dropped into the driver's seat himself and burned rubber toward the gate just as a Teammate Humvee from within the plant screeched around a corner in hot pursuit.

The heavy gate was closed but Nathan floored his accelerator and crashed right through it, setting off a loud alarm. He looked in his rearview and saw that the Teammate Humvee was gaining on him, but then Nathan's ears popped as a powerful sonic concussion blew the Humvee right over onto its top.

Nathan looked back, as startled as everyone else who had witnessed the amazing phenomenon. He was completely confused about what in the world could have caused the one-and-a-half-ton Humvee to go flying.

Neither Nathan nor anyone else saw Kayta duck down among the parked cars near the front gate. Her violet eyes had the calm, focused look of a dangerous professional soldier. She was holding a weapon the size of a thick sawed-off shotgun. Though small, it was obviously formidable. On its business end there was a palm-sized, wire mesh dish antenna that snapped closed and back, disappearing inside the weapon like a startled sea anemone while Kayta watched Nathan drive away.

WILLY WAS LEADING MARTIN QUICKLY THROUGH THE DARK, HUMID, labyrinthine passageways that laced like arteries through the bowels of the Flagship.

"Jon was one of the first half-breeds," Willy was saying. "His no-good father got the human mother cocooned and tossed his infant son down into the janitor unit."

Martin was appalled by such behavior. "Do you know who his father was?"

"Shawn."

Martin glanced at Willy, then shook his head in disgust. "Why am I not surprised?"

"Jon's a nice boy though. He's educated himself."

"And you said he's very intelligent?"

Willy nodded emphatically. "Off the carts."

"You mean *charts*?"

"Ah. *Charts*. Yes. Down this way."

They reached the small chamber where Jon's custodial equipment was housed. The floating module was docked and recharging. As Martin went slightly deeper into the low-ceilinged area he was surprised to discover that Jon had fashioned this hovel into a combination nest, laboratory, and library. Martin smiled at the half-breed's inventiveness. Jon had used discarded parts and supplies, cleverly crafting and adapting them to his use. The boy's back was partly to them and Martin saw that Jon was intently studying some kind of complicated technical text on a vid. Then Jon realized they were there and beamed. "William!"

"I brought a friend to meet you. This is Martin."

They exchanged greetings and Martin complimented the eighteen-year-old. "Quite an impressive lodging you've created."

Jon's human-looking eyes glowed with modest humor. "Oh, just a bit of Swiss Family Robinson Crusoe, sir. Necessity being the mother of all invention."

Willy proffered a small packet. "Take a look."

Jon's blue eyes widened. "New data plugs!" He examined them and got even more excited. "*Tentonese biogeometrics*! I'd been searching for this one. You are indeed a prince, sir!"

"I'm glad you like them." Then Willy's tone grew more serious. "Jon, I'm hoping you might be able to help us."

The boy looked up quizzically, and Willy explained.

A few minutes later the transport tube door opened on a still-lower level and Jon guided his floating module out into the dim, steamy passageway followed by Willy and Martin, the latter of whom was saying, "I didn't realize that the custodial crew had such extensive access to these levels."

Jon's scaly, misshapen reptilian mouth twisted into what Martin assumed was a knowing smile. "Ever read *The Invisible Man,* sir? That's rather like being a dreg janitor." He glanced playfully at Martin. "No one really sees you." Then Jon bowed acknowledgment toward Willy. "Present company excepted. But as you surmised, sir, it does give one access to almost the entire ship. Including this next section."

They had reached an oily black hatch with *Restricted Entry* warnings on it. Jon entered his key code and the heavy hatch slid open revealing another dark passage where moisture was condensing on the low, variegated ceiling and dripping from it. He indicated for them to be quiet and stay back. Then he cautiously walked ahead of them toward an intersection.

As Jon rounded the corner he could see the laser-barred cell that Martin had described. He caught a brief glimpse of the bearded, bestial prisoner huddled deep in one dark corner. A muscular Visitor guard was on station and very grouchy about his assignment there. His reptilian face had a long scar across one of his brown, scaly cheeks, which lent him an additional aura of menace. The fingers on one of his leathery hands were dripping with blood that he sucked off, then he reached again into a nearby food container. He extracted a short length of some medium-sized mammal's intestines and thrust it into his mouth, making a small gulping motion upward with his chin to encourage passage of the entrails down his thick throat.

He was looking at his personal viz unit that was projecting a motion hologram showing three of his fellow reptiles naked and engaged in a sexual ménage à trois. He glanced up with annoyance as Jon took a container of cleaning fluid from his module. "Be quick about it, dreg. I hate the smell of that shit."

Jon was feigning some difficulty in opening the cleaning container. "Yes, sir. I will, sir." Then the lid suddenly popped loose, "accidentally" spilling some of the fluid onto the guard.

The big Visitor leaped up and slapped Jon very hard. "Ahk! You stupid dreg!"

"I'm so sorry, sir. You must wash it off. Quickly! This way!" Jon hurried the guard farther down the dingy passage and out of sight. Martin quickly walked into the cell area and held one of Jon's cleaning tools up over the security camera lens while Willy turned off the laser bars that crisscrossed the cell's entrance. Then Willy moved cautiously toward the fetid cell. He saw small, empty drug packets on the malodorous, smeary floor as he gently approached the crippled, bestial prisoner who was staring at him with wild and fearful eyes.

"Easy"—Willy held out a calming hand—"we're here to help

you. Can you speak?" Willy only heard a grunt of warning. "Why does Diana keep you in this special cell? Were you with the Resistance?"

The prisoner growled and clawed at the air threateningly toward Willy, who continued to speak soothingly. "Easy now, we want to get you out of here." Though the prisoner couldn't walk, he suddenly lunged violently, but Willy was prepared and shot him with a stunner. The brutish prisoner screeched and then, glaring at Willy, slumped to the greasy metal floor.

THE BRIGHT SUNLIGHT FILTERED THROUGH THE LEAVES OF THE TREES in Lafayette Park and mottled the sidewalk along posh Washington Street where Emma had just been shopping. Despite her vast popularity as a celebrity, it was not unusual for her to be out alone. She certainly was aware of and appreciated the nods of recognition from passersby and the special treatment she received in the boutiques. But she preferred to be—and to be thought of as—an open, friendly person. She only relied on handlers or an entourage for security among the enthusiastic crowds at her concerts. Nor was it unusual for her to pause as she had on this day to graciously sign an autograph for a star-struck young fan. On the upscale building behind them one of the ubiquitous large vid screens was silently flashing: *Suspect anti-Visitor activity? Tell a Teammate!* After a last smile to her fan, Emma got into the driver's seat of her silver Lexus. She was startled when the passenger door suddenly opened and a small blond woman got in beside her. Emma's voice, however, was firm. "I'm sorry, but—"

Margarita rose up behind her in the backseat. "Drive straight ahead, past Franklin."

Emma was shocked. But the blonde's voice was calm, nonthreatening. "We just want to talk."

Emma looked more closely at the woman in her passenger seat and her blood chilled as recognition dawned. "Oh, my God, you're—you're—!"

"That's right, she is," Margarita interrupted. "Now, please drive."

Emma nervously pulled from the curb. She was too rattled to notice that following a short distance behind was a striking black woman on a sleek motorbike. Bryke adjusted a tiny hearing device, listening to the conversation in the car ahead of her.

Julie had come right to the point. "Emma, the Resistance needs your access to the Visitor High Command."

"What?" Emma was incredulous. "You want me to *spy* for you?" She laughed nervously. "Are you crazy? Why would I do that?"

"To help us get solid proof we can show the world that the Visitors are taking our water and our people *permanently*."

"Oh, come on, I don't believe those ridiculous Sci rumors. I've never seen the remotest shred of evidence that—"

"Of course you haven't," Margarita was less patient than Julie, "because *who* controls all the media?"

Emma's mind was racing. She saw a Patrol shuttle passing overhead, but she had no way of alerting it. Her eyes flitted around the busy intersection ahead, but she couldn't see any Visitor Patrollers. She did spot a Teammate unit one block to her right on Franklin, which unfortunately ran one-way against her. Margarita knew what Emma was thinking and cautioned her, "The northbound traffic is too heavy against you. And your horn's been disconnected. Go on across, turn right into the next alley, then stop by the end of it. You won't be harmed, I promise." Emma's fear was turning to anger, but she drove on.

Julie said quietly, "We know that we're asking a lot, Emma." The singer practically chortled at the understatement, but Julie continued earnestly, "We do know that. Just please look at this vid." Julie put it in the console pocket between them.

"No, I won't look at it," Emma had found her voice. She was a strong young woman and determined not to be intimidated even under these dangerous circumstances. "So you might as well just get the hell out of my car and—"

"What happened to your cousin Tim?" Margarita's question stopped Emma cold. The singer glanced in the rearview mirror at the redhead's intense hazel eyes.

Before Emma could respond, Julie spoke up, "A Visitor Patroller told you Tim was killed in a car wreck."

"Yes," Emma said, vividly recalling that awful moment. Then, as if defending the statement, "Yes, and that's exactly what happened."

"Did you or anyone ever see his body?" Margarita's voice was lower now, with an assurance that was troubling.

Emma shook her head. "His car was burned up. Tim was—"

"Not in that wreck," Julie said, pausing a moment to let the notion sink in. "He was taken. Tim worked with us. He was in the San Jose Resistance."

"Tim? There is no way." Emma stopped the car at the end of the alley, trying to cover her uncertainty with anger. "Now get out of my car!"

Julie was not one to give up. "Emma, please—"

"Listen"—Emma gripped the steering wheel tightly—"I struggled very hard to get where I am, okay? And I'm not going to risk losing everything, including my *life* just to . . . to . . ."

"Help save humanity?" Margarita wouldn't let her off the hook.

There was a moment of silence, then Julie said quietly, "Please . . . just look at the vid, Emma. It won't kill you. But you could save a lot of good people from *being* killed if you'd consider helping us. Like Tim did."

Having trailed them into the alley, Bryke saw Emma's Lexus idling at the end of it. Then she saw Margarita and Julie get out, trade a frustrated glance as they got into Street-C's waiting car and speed away. Behind Bryke a burly Hispanic Teammate with a thick, black handlebar mustache had entered the alley and was eyeing Bryke suspiciously. He walked up beside her, his hand resting pointedly on his holstered pulse pistol. "Hey, bitch," he said arrogantly, "let's see some ID."

Bryke slowly turned to gaze at him. He was surprised to see that her eyes were bright pink.

Had anyone been passing the mouth of the alley at that moment they would have been confused by the image within its shadows. The dark-skinned woman had pulled the hefty Teammate into what looked like a passionate *kiss*. Their faces were locked together. But it was a curious embrace because the man was beating and clawing against her viselike hold on him as his body gyrated in a macabre dance of death. At length there came from him a horrific, gurgling scream and then Bryke released him. He collapsed backward into a pile of trash and lay motionless. From a distance his body looked somehow less robust than it had moments earlier.

Bryke guided her purring motorcycle toward the mouth of the alley wiping some of his fresh red blood from around her nose, then she glided on out to intermingle with the San Francisco traffic.

12

IT WAS LATE AFTERNOON BY THE TIME WILLY AND JON REACHED Hangar Bay Thirty-seven and were guiding their trunk-sized floating cargo container into the back of a shuttle craft. The dispatch Patroller stopped them, requesting the appropriate authorization, and Willy presented an electronic clipboard. Willy also called the Patroller's attention to the large biohazard symbol on the side of the container. "They told me not to open it or we'd be dead in twelve seconds and the hangar bay would be contaminated and sealed off with us in it."

The Patroller gingerly stepped back from the container, and

waved them up the ramp and onto the shuttle. Eric, the research doctor from the Visitor lab, was also boarding and lent them a hand, smiling at his young half-breed friend. "Let me help you there, Jon."

"That's very good of you, sir." Jon nodded to the doctor who always had a kind word for the boy. Then Jon touched the container and cautioned Willy, "Handle this very carefully, sir."

"Oh, yes. Indeed."

They shared a final conspiratorial look and Jon jumped off just as the hatch began to close. Eric glanced curiously at the container in Willy's charge. "What exactly is in there?"

Willy also studied the container and spoke the truth. "Actually, I'm not quite sure."

The mouthlike hatch of the shuttle sealed closed and the craft began to rise for departure.

THE BLACK-MARKET ARMS DEALER, A GOTH YOUNG WOMAN WITH many piercings, always enjoyed doing business with Gary Lavine. He was a charming, gregarious guy who always had the right cash. Gary had left early from the midtown office of the computer company where he worked as a graphic designer. After concealing the two stolen Visitor pulse rifles in his large portfolio case, he walked quickly to his apartment at Fifth and Howard.

He carefully locked the door of his sunny, cheery loft and walked through the tastefully Victorian-style living room. He opened a secret panel on a window seat and proceeded to hide the new rifles amid the conventional weapons already in the compartment. He glanced out the window just above it. It looked eastward across the top of the old Moscone Convention Center, which was now used primarily for Teammate training sessions. He looked beyond that, to a commanding view of the Bay Bridge, which stretched from San Francisco across the desolate valley of the dry bay to Oakland. Seeing the rusting hulks of several sunken ships, which had been revealed when the waters receded, he was reminded of his resolution that they would not be metaphoric harbingers of the future of human civilization. Their physical presence fueled his personal determination to prevent that fate. Seeing them out there every day always kept his commitment to the Resistance burning brightly. That commitment had been made to his father years earlier, just before his father had become a victim of Diana's Great Purge.

Gary was startled to hear the front door open behind him. He hurriedly closed up the cache and replaced the flowered cushion back atop the window seat as he called out happily, "Hey there. You're home early." He stood up from the hiding place and smoothed his already smooth, smoke-colored hair, "Nice day at the office, dear?"

The Visitor doctor Eric had entered tiredly. He tossed his uniform cap aside. "About like usual."

Gary gave him a loving hug and a welcoming kiss. "Like usual? Just another little miracle cure? Like mine?"

Eric's arms were comfortably around Gary's waist. "I'm glad I could help cure you. Otherwise we might never have met."

"Otherwise my adorable ass would be *dead*, honey." Gary nuzzled his lover, then sensed that Eric was troubled. "But what is it? What's wrong?" Gary saw immediately the veiled expression develop on the doctor's face and quickly recanted, "Sorry, sorry. Bite my tongue. I know we agreed: no questions." He changed the subject lightly, "Hey, I got you a new E-string."

He slipped gracefully from Eric's arms, gathered up an acoustic guitar off of their fuchsia paisley couch, and presented it to his partner. Eric smiled appreciatively and took it. He checked the tuning and strummed a blues lick. Gary watched him fondly, remembering how part of their initial attraction to each other had derived from their mutual love of ethnic music. Gary recalled the first time he had taken Eric to hear Mississippi Delta blues being played by one of the genre's oldest living practitioners. Sitting with Gary in that Tenderloin dive, Eric had become completely enthralled with the funky music, which to Eric was "earthy" in more ways than one. He in turn had introduced Gary to some of the music from his own planet and had gifted Gary with a flutelike alien instrument.

"Nice," Eric said as he felt the quality of the new string on his fingertips. "How are you doing with mine?"

"Still learning the nuances." Gary lifted the Visitor instrument and after a squeaky false start played a simple blues melody. Eric touched Gary's cheek fondly, then began to accompany his partner in a rhythmic bluesy duet.

THE BIG BLACK LABORER WAS IN A FURY. "YOU 'BOUT GOT MY HEAD blowed off!" Blue was angrily confronting Nathan at the Resistance warehouse.

"Take it easy, man," Nathan said coolly, "I was just trying to get info on that new chemical."

Margarita was mediating, but clearly on the side of her hefty compatriot. "Blue was already working on that."

Nathan was cavalier. "Just trying to cut to the chase."

With his powerful, thick hands, Blue snatched Nathan up by the shirt collar. "How 'bout I cut *your* chase, motherfucker!"

Margarita touched his broad shoulder. "Blue."

But the plant worker stayed focused on Nathan. "You know what happened after you breezed outta there? They had a roundup. The Patrollers came and picked four people at random. Innocent people who hadn't done nothin' wrong. And they *transported 'em*! You know what that means, hotshot! Ain't nobody gonna ever *see* 'em again!" He tightened his grip. "You stupid—"

Margarita was calm but emphatic now. "Blue."

The big man glared heatedly in Nathan's face, then gruffly slung him aside and walked away. Margarita looked sharply at Nathan, who noticed that her freckles were flushed redder than usual as she said, "Listen, you've obviously got skills we can use, but this is a coordinated team. You go off wildcatting again and"—she spoke the words one at a time—"we will cut you loose." She held his eyes for a moment to impress upon him that she was very serious. When she headed off she made brief eye contact with Julie who had watched the whole exchange. Then Julie's cell phone rang.

Outside the warehouse in the growing twilight, Ayden, Bryke, and Kayta were scanning the building with several alien instruments. Ayden was using a viewer that revealed the shapes of the people within. They had overheard the heated exchange between Nathan and Blue. Bryke looked at Ayden and said, "What do you think?"

Ayden continued to scan the building. "Soon. Very soon. Keep collecting data and tracking all their comm channels."

"Here's a new one." Kayta had fine-tuned a scanner.

They could hear Julie's voice answering her cell, "Hello, this is Lexington Base. Go ahead, Harmy, this line's secure."

From his bedroom in the run-down Twenty-first Street apartment, half-breed Ted could hear his mother talking on her cell phone in the kitchen. "Mr. W. is smuggling down some weird prisoner he thinks may have been Resistance," Harmy said. "Can you guys come check him out?"

Ted had spent yet another day of slaving subservience at the middle school and he was as angry as ever about his lot in life. As he listened to his mother's conversation conclude, the boy's scaly brow furrowed.

Ten minutes later the sun had just set but the western sky was still glowing as Julie and Nathan emerged from the warehouse and headed for the car. Julie tossed him the keys. He was pleased. "Thanks for letting me come along."

"I'll tell you something, Nathan," Julie said as they climbed into the car, "you remind me a lot of an old friend. He was pretty impetuous, too."

"Mike Donovan?"

"Yeah." Nathan saw her gaze turn inward for a sad moment as she said, "A lot of times his passion got ahead of his reasoning. But he was a great asset to our cause once he realized that hitting the Visitors piecemeal wasn't as important as working together to win back the *minds* of our people."

Nathan nodded. Though he didn't yet completely agree with Julie's way of doing things, her understated style was much more appealing than Margarita's in-your-face attitude. He was beginning to understand why the others considered Julie to be the natural leader. Being near her was like discovering a welcoming campfire in a dark, cold forest. Julie radiated light and warmth. Nathan thought that if he held his hands out toward her he might almost feel a campfire's comfort.

The three strangers with the slight sheen to their skin had witnessed the exchange from their hidden vantage point. Ayden, beckoning Kayta to accompany him, moved toward a motorbike to follow Julie and Nathan. Bryke stayed busy refocusing their unusual surveillance and recording instruments toward the Resistance warehouse.

COMMANDANT JEREMY'S QUARTERS ABOARD THE FLAGSHIP HAD BEEN arranged to his liking. Like Jeremy himself, everything was Spartan and well organized. Though the food containers built into his wall contained various body parts, flesh and organs of freshly killed animals, his patrician tastes drew him to the living examples available. He had been surprised and pleased by the quality of the rodents on Earth. He examined a fat, healthy gray rat that stared back at him. Its beady black eyes were shining, its whiskers twitching, as Jeremy turned it in his hand. Then he distended his jaw for greater ease of ingestion and thrust the living creature into his gaping mouth. Jeremy felt the rat biting and scratching within his leathery throat as it passed down his esophagus. Then began the animal's terrified wiggling, quivering death throes deep within Jeremy's abdomen, which would be so very agreeable to him for the next few minutes.

The hatch to his quarters sounded its subtle tone advising him that he had a visitor. Shawn, Diana's aide de camp, looked up from the viz pad on which he had been taking notes from Jeremy. "Shall I answer, sir?"

Jeremy waved him off as he wiped his lips and activated the hatch himself. It opened to reveal Gina, the fighter pilot. She snapped to attention, looking straight ahead. "You sent for me, sir?"

"Yes, Flight Leader, I did." Jeremy eyed her lazily, then glanced at Shawn. "That'll be all, Shawn. And secure the hatch."

"Very good, sir." Shawn nodded obsequiously and departed, brushing past the lovely pilot as he exited. Once in the passageway Shawn closed the hatch, but didn't immediately depart. Instead, he stood outside the Commandant's hatch supposedly checking through his notes in case anyone should pass by. But what he actually did was affix a tiny listening device to the wall beside Jeremy's quarters. Shawn drew a sharp intake of breath when he heard Gina say brazenly to the Commandant, "It's about time."

Inside his quarters, Jeremy agreed, "Yes, it is." He pulled Gina into a passionate kiss, their long forked tongues probing deeply down into one another's throats. Then she bit his lip, causing him to look at her sharply. "What was that for?"

"What do you think? I heard about you and the Leader. Where exactly does that leave *us*?"

"In an excellent place, my dear." His attitude was low-key but exultant. "My intimacy with the Leader merely advances my own interests"—his hand was caressing Gina's hard body, sliding lower toward her loins—"*our* own interests." He nibbled at Gina's long neck. "I've already superseded Diana. Her star is falling. Once I'm in total control she will be snuffed out entirely."

Gina frowned, not certain she understood. "'Total control'?"

"Mmmm. Someday our Leader will require a successor"—an expression of feigned innocence crossed his face—"perhaps sooner rather than later, one never knows what fate has in store." Gina was astounded at the audacity of what he was hinting. "Believe me," Jeremy continued with supreme confidence, "very big things are in the offing."

Gina's almond eyes flashed provocatively as she now slid her hand down the front of his pants. "I'm very glad to hear that." Then she submerged him into another succulent kiss.

In the passage outside, Shawn disconnected his listening device and walked slowly away, considering his options.

DARKNESS HAD FALLEN AND THE STREETLIGHTS WERE ON AS THE black limousine glided to a stop in front of Emma's condominium on Nob Hill's upscale Clay Street. Emma and Visitor Press Secretary Paul had been ensconced in the backseat. As she gathered up her things she said, "Well, I'm really glad to hear that Diana liked the new vid."

"She didn't just like it, she loved it." With the tip of his forefinger, he touched Emma's nose playfully. "I'm telling you, she watched your parts several times."

"That's great, Paul. And thanks for the lift." She slid out, sensing that Paul was watching her parts at that moment.

He caught her wrist lightly. "Hey, are you busy right now?"

The pretty singer looked back in at him. He had been getting increasingly chummy of late and it was obviously more than just professional enthusiasm. She wanted neither to encourage him nor alienate him, so she spoke as though she had completely missed his real subtext. "Yeah, my accountant's coming. Some other time?"

He looked at her a moment. "Sure," he said smoothly, "I'd really enjoy sharing some of the perks of the High Command. Little shuttle ride out to the moon?"

She was genuinely surprised. "Really!"

"Mmmm," he sounded as though he was striving to keep his voice as casual as possible, "but it'll get pretty busy for me after our Leader arrives."

Emma was stunned. In the two decades of occupation the Visitor Leader had never come to the Earth. It was portentous news that Emma didn't know quite how to process. She stared at Paul, speaking slowly, "Your Leader is coming here!"

"Yes. To rally our troops and your people."

She frowned, confused. "Rally them for what?"

Paul smiled as coquettishly as Emma herself might have. "Well, if we ever get some alone time, I'll fill you in." He gave her a meaningful wink, then signaled his driver.

Emma watched the limo driving away, trying to fathom the importance of what she had just learned.

AS PAUL'S LIMO GLIDED DOWN CLAY STREET FROM NOB HILL TOWARD Chinatown, he contemplated his forthcoming conquest of Emma. The human species hadn't been particularly inviting to him at first, but after several sexual encounters with human women over the years he had discovered that they could be nearly as gratifying as his own kind, particularly if he kept his eyes closed. And even more than the sexual release, he enjoyed his triumphal domination of them.

The proximity to the very alluring pop star that he had enjoyed for over a year had awakened a definite curiosity about how it would be with her. He was determined to find out and felt sure that he would soon have dominion over her.

He breathed a long, contented sigh of anticipated enjoyment as he gazed out the window at the passing scene, at the colorful neon signs flickering their Chinese messages. He did not notice the frail figure walking slowly toward a bus stop.

Charlotte Elgin had been feeling very light-headed. She suddenly became even more unsteady and paused to lean against a mailbox. She felt extremely weak. The February night had turned colder and the wind was gusting down from the north. Until she had shaved off her thick black hair Charlotte hadn't realized how much it had contributed to keeping her head warm. She pulled the thin scarf tighter around her buzz-cut scalp and slowly continued toward the bus stop.

THAT SAME EVENING, RUBY WAS BOUNCING CHEERFULLY DOWN Washington Street. Having read many works of Charles Dickens at her mother's suggestion, Ruby had adopted the Artful Dodger as her role model and studied his panache. On this night she felt more than ever like him. She had just scored a load of peppermint chewing gum from the back of a truck at Lafayette Square, and while she knew that in the grand scheme of things chewing gum wasn't very important, she had noted how everyone at the Resistance warehouse brightened up when she brought some once before. Ruby figured that every little bit helped. As she passed the alley east of Franklin she caught a glimpse of something weird in her peripheral vision. She stopped and backed up to look more carefully into the alley, then her blue eyes widened. "Holy shit!"

Sticking out of a trash pile against one wall of the alley were the arm and hand of a Teammate, frozen in death. But Ruby could see that something was very strange about it. She moved closer cautiously, frightened but keeping her cool. She saw that the flesh didn't look human any longer, but rather had a dried, orangey, semitransparent quality to it. She could see the withered veins and the bones within. She picked up a stick and poked it. It seemed almost like thin fiberglass. It was unlike anything she had ever seen. Very gingerly Ruby used the stick to ease back some pieces of trash for a better look, but then she heard the voices and radios of an approaching Teammate unit. Thinking quickly, Ruby grabbed a piece of newspaper and broke off a piece of the crusty hand. Then she dashed away just before Teammate Debra Stein appeared at the mouth of the alley.

"This one was part of his patrol," Debra called off to those behind her. "I'll go see if—Oh, my God!" Debra had seen the strange arm and what remained of the hand sticking out of the Teammate sleeve. She came to it and pulled the trash away to reveal a chrysalis-like husk of the burly Hispanic Teammate with the thick mustache who'd had a close encounter with Bryke.

Debra drew back in horror as her Teammate companions gathered beside her. They all stared down at the fearful face of the husk. It was skeletal. The eyeballs were shriveled like raisins. Its gaping mouth had many broken teeth and it was contorted in gruesome final agony.

AYDEN AND KAYTA HAD FOLLOWED JULIE AND NATHAN TO THE downscale urban neighborhood at Twenty-first Street and Potrero, then watched as the two freedom fighters climbed up the back fire escape to the third floor, Julie struggling somewhat because of her game hip. Ayden and Kayta had immediately sought a higher vantage point on a building opposite. The streetlights from below made the sheen on their skin seem to glow. Once on the rooftop, Kayta patched her audio scanner to Ayden's optical device. He scanned with it until he found the apartment that Willy shared with Harmy, who was just letting in the Resistance pair. Julie hugged the waitress and tousled her frizzy, strawberry blond hair. "Boy, I've missed seeing you guys."

Harmy hugged Julie tightly in return. "Us, too, you."

As Julie embraced Willy, Nathan nodded toward Harmy. "Hi, I'm Nathan."

"Ah." Harmy pressed his hand. "As seen on TV: 'the mentally unbalanced deserter.' Welcome to the asylum, Nathan."

"He's over here," Willy said as he led them to the filthy, hairy, motionless figure that lay askew across their couch. The liberated prisoner's head was turned away. "No one else was kept like this. He was crazed. Must've been in that cell for years. He's crippled. There were morphalyne packets everywhere."

"They must have addicted him to it." Julie was feeling the man's grimy wrist, checking his pulse.

"Morphalyne"—Nathan shook his head—"no wonder he was acting crazy."

Harmy looked at the crippled man sympathetically. "Why would they do such a horrible thing?" Then she rolled her eyes with immediate realization. "And why do I even ask."

Julie looked at Nathan. "Turn him toward me. I'll do the ret scan." The prisoner groaned deliriously as Nathan turned him over. The man's thick, brownish gray hair had been filthy and uncut for years. Like his beard it was thickly matted with grime and clotted blood. What skin they could see between his beard and hair was pocked and mottled with grit ground deeply into the pores.

Willy leaned closer, and said, "Jon, the young janitor who helped us get him out, said the Flagship lab was developing a voice modifier to make us Visitors sound like humans."

Nathan understood the implications immediately. "To try to infiltrate us."

"So it would seem," Willy said with a nod. "They may even be able to mimic specific people's voices. They're also injecting experimental insect pheromones into some Patrollers. And creating faces and skin that have a peculiar sheen." Nathan and Julie looked at each other, puzzled over that one, but on the rooftop across the street Kayta and Ayden traded a sharp glance and their concern grew as Willy continued. "Oh, and they're also creating contact lenses that make their eyes violent."

"*Violent*?" Julie frowned. "You mean *violet*?"

"Ah," Willy affirmed, "violet, yes. Other odd colors, too, Jon thinks."

"But why are they doing it all? Did your friend tell you?"

"He didn't know yet."

Julie turned her attention to scanning the prisoner's bloodshot eye. Then she checked the readout. What she saw made her literally stop breathing. Her face turned ashen as she looked sharply back down at the prisoner's filthy face.

The others were disconcerted by her reaction. Nathan spoke for all three of them, "What's wrong? Julie? . . . Who is he?"

Julie glanced up at them with a very strange, fearful look in her eyes. Her mouth worked, but she was too stunned to speak. She stared again breathlessly at the bestial figure as Willy took the scanner from her limp hand and read what it had reported.

"He's . . . *Mike Donovan*?!"

13

ON THE ROOF ACROSS THE STREET, AYDEN AND KAYTA ALSO REACTED with surprise upon hearing Donovan's name. Ayden refocused his viewer on the group inside Harmy's flat. Though the image flickered occasionally, they could be seen in a fair amount of detail, enhanced by an infrared filter. Kayta and Ayden could hear their voices through intermittent static.

Harmy was staring in amazement at Willy. "How could it possibly be Mike?"

Nathan checked the readout and saw the information was solid. "I thought he was killed back in '91, in London."

"We all did," Willy said, frowning. "Why'd Diana keep him alive?"

Julie was working to regain her composure. "We have to get him out of here, Willy. It's very dangerous for you and Harmy."

Outside, Kayta touched the leather sleeve of Ayden's bomber jacket, indicating down toward Potrero Street where an SFPD squad car was quietly driving in from the north to block a nearby intersection. A squad of helmeted Visitor Patrollers, their pulse weapons at the ready, moved stealthily past the police vehicle in the direction of Harmy's tenement. Ayden quickly checked the other direction and saw a Teammate unit also converging on it from the east.

Kayta's violet eyes looked urgently at Ayden, ready for his orders, but the steely man indicated patience. He pointed down to where Nathan, Willy, and Julie were already carrying the unconscious Mike Donovan toward Julie's car. "And look there." Ayden was indicating the Visitor Patrol, whose leader had brought her troops to a halt. Kayta also saw that the Teammate unit had likewise paused in their advance, though neither group could yet see the Resistance people on the near side of the building.

"What's going on?" Kayta wondered. "They seem confused."

Ayden was puzzling over it as well. "Perhaps they got conflicting orders."

They watched silently as Julie and Nathan drove Mike safely away, but Ayden and Kayta remained perplexed by the Visitor troops' peculiar behavior.

THE LIGHTS WERE LOW AND EMMA HAD CAREFULLY DRAWN THE rich curtains tightly closed in her elegant living room. She was watching a vid, but had purposely chosen not to use her wall-sized plasma. Instead she was sitting nervously in a large, over-stuffed chair with her legs curled securely beneath her. It was as though she were trying to make the smallest profile possible as she watched the tiny vid screen on her lap. The volume was very low, barely whispering in her ear, but Emma hadn't missed a word.

She had been watching the Resistance vid given to her by Julie and Margarita. It was the same vid that young Danny had shown his friend Thomas. When it ended Emma sat motionless. Her heart was greatly troubled by all the compelling images she had seen and the startling information she had heard. But her mind was struggling with how it could all be true. It was as though she'd always believed the Earth was flat but in the last few minutes a disquieting possibility of roundness had developed.

She was having great difficulty getting her mind around the concepts the vid had presented and with the consequences those concepts might have for her. She stared past the small blank vid screen, past the beautifully appointed stylishness of her home, into the darkness of an uncertain future.

The door chime went through her like an electric jolt. "Jesus!" she exclaimed and with jittery hands she quickly pulled the damning disk from the vid unit and thrust it deep into the cushions of the chair. Then she took a breath to try to calm herself and touched the intercom. "Yes?"

She heard a woman's frantic voice call out, "Miss Emma? Thank God you're there! It's Mary Elgin! I need your help!"

Emma emerged from her condo a moment later pulling her heavy sable coat over the pale green silk dressing gown she'd been wearing. Her feet were in unlaced running sneakers. Mary beckoned her quickly toward the backseat of a waiting taxi. "Here! She's in here with Charles."

Emma saw a man she took to be Mary's husband inside the cab holding Charlotte in his arms. The girl was ghostly pale, her eyes dark and sunken.

Mary had opened the door. "We think it's insulin shock. We found out she'd been giving *her* medicine to my father-in-law."

"Oh, Mary, I'm so sorry," Emma said with concern, "but I don't understand. What can I do to help?"

Charles spoke up urgently, "Come to a hospital with us. Please. They might let her in if we're with *you*."

Emma was still totally confused. "What do you mean, if—"

"Please!" Mary was desperate. "She could die!"

"Okay, Mary, okay"—Emma pulled open the taxi's front door—"let's go."

* * *

IN THE RESISTANCE WAREHOUSE ANTHROPOLOGIST ROBERT MAXWELL
and Margarita both wore latex gloves as they examined the
strange husklike hand Ruby had found.

"It's been drained dry." Margarita turned it slowly under the
bright surgical light they had stolen a year earlier. "As if all the
fluids had been drawn right out of it."

"Mmm," Robert acknowledged, thoroughly intrigued. His
thick black brows furrowed as his dark eyes examined the tiniest
details while he probed the crusty skin with a thin scalpel. "But
this chrysalis effect is so strange. I've only ever seen anything
like it in insects."

They heard Julie call softly to them from the darkened corner of
the warehouse that served as their infirmary, "I think he's waking."

Julie looked back down toward Mike Donovan, who lay on the
cot beside which she was sitting. He was stirring very slightly.
Julie and Nathan had cut away the foul prison rags, then washed
and considerably trimmed the filthy matted hair and beard. Julie
had started an IV drip to replenish his fluids and begin medication. She had worked carefully with cotton swabs, soap, and mild
astringents to gently coax the grime from Donovan's face while
Nathan tried to cleanse the rest of his body. Julie saw that Mike
was at least forty pounds thinner than when she'd last seen him a
decade and a half earlier. His cheeks were hollow, and his collar-
bone and ribs had an unnatural prominence. But what troubled
her most were his legs, which were very emaciated. Her physician's eye immediately deduced that the muscles were atrophied
from lack of use and she examined an ugly series of scars that
were raised above and behind his knees. His hands, so supple and
strong the last time she'd seen them, were skeletal now and their
skin, like the rest of his body, bore a sickly yellow pallor.

At the foot of the cot, Nathan was stuffing the last of the foul
prison rags into a plastic garbage bag when Donovan suddenly
snapped awake with a shout that startled everyone.

"Easy, easy, it's okay," Julie said soothingly as she touched his shoulder. He jerked back and looked hastily around like a cornered wild animal. Then he seemed to realize that his wrists were restrained to the cot. "It's okay," Julie spoke calmly, but Nathan noticed that she was exhibiting an emotional awkwardness as she withdrew her hand from his shoulder. The beleaguered patient looked at her and tried to focus his vision. Julie searched for words and finally said, "Mr. Donovan. Welcome back. We've . . . we've missed you." He pulled again at the binders that held his wrists. "Easy," she counseled, "we just restrained you so you wouldn't hurt yourself or pull out the IV. I'm going to loosen them now, okay?" She began to do so as she went on softly, "Just breathe easy . . . Do you remember us?"

Donovan looked at her numbly, but with recognition. Robert leaned in, his dark eyes alight and smiling. "Hey, Mike. It's Robert. *I* sure remember how you saved my daughters."

Mike looked vaguely at Robert while Julie adjusted the small bandage that had come unstuck on his upper arm when he started awake. She checked the inch-long incision that she had made earlier and then reapplied the bandage. Donovan was fighting the glaze over his eyes as he looked at Julie and squinted. His voice was hoarse and listless. ". . . Doc . . . ?"

"Yeah. Can't get rid of me," Julie tried to say lightly, but there was a much heavier emotion in her eyes. "So, how're you feeling?"

". . . Some water?"

"Here." Margarita, who had quietly arrived behind Julie, filled a paper cup. Donovan's bony, quivering hand took the cup, brought it to his thin, parched lips, and he slowly drank. Some of the water escaped at the corner of his mouth and dribbled down his chin. They all watched, trying to comprehend how this feeble graying man could once have been the most robust freedom fighter of them all. It was a sobering lesson in mortality. If this was what had become of the legendary Mike Donovan what might become of them?

Donovan finished the water and looked hazily back at Julie. She saw a question in his eyes and asked, "What?"

His voice came low and hopeful, his speech was slurred. "You got some dope?"

"We're going to get you off the morph. You're on an antipsychotic drip with some methadone to ease you down."

Margarita retrieved the paper cup. "They tried to make you talk by addicting you?"

Donovan's rheumy eyes searched for and found the striking redhead who had given him the water. "Yeah"—his voice was lethargic as he chuckled darkly—"among other things."

Nathan spoke quietly, "*Did* you talk?"

Donovan looked at Nathan and instantly sensed the young man was an upstart. "Not for the first few years. After that"—his eyes wandered blearily across the dim warehouse and his mind seemed to wander for a moment as well—"after that . . . I didn't even know I was alive. I'm still not sure." Then he looked back at Nathan and tried to focus, though he seemed only mildly curious. "Who the hell are you?"

Nathan shrugged slightly. "The Second Generation."

Donovan chuckled bitterly again, looking away with disinterest. "More like The Last Generation, kid."

Julie did her best to sound encouraging. "Well, it was pretty hard trying to get along without you, Mr. Donovan. We've been beaten down badly, almost got destroyed in 'ninety-nine, but—"

" 'Ninety-nine?" Donovan glanced sharply back at her, working hard to hold her in focus. She and the others saw that the date somehow troubled him.

"Diana launched a Great Purge," Julie explained. "The Resistance was nearly crushed. But we haven't given up." She touched the bandage on his upper arm. "I took out your ID implant."

"They won't find you," Margarita said confidently.

He leveled his eyes at her with a profound wisdom though his voice had a drunken quality. "Honey, lemme tell you something: they'll find everybody."

Robert tried to ease the moment genially. "Hey, you'll feel different once you're up and around."

That occasioned the most derisive laugh of all from Donovan. "Up and around?" His eyes rolled as he tried unsuccessfully to clear his vision. "On which legs, exactly? Diana had the nerves severed. One at a time as I recall."

Julie swallowed, trying to find the right words. "I know we can't imagine what you've been through. But we all want to help you to—"

"Get a grip, Doc." Through what seemed like an angry and supreme effort his voice was suddenly matter-of-fact. "We lost. Okay? We fuckin' *lost*. Now, I just want to avoid as much pain as possible. So just give me my morph, okay?"

Nathan saw Margarita's freckles getting redder. He sensed she was getting annoyed whether Donovan was sick or not, legend or no, and her tone confirmed it. "What about the pain of the ones who already died fighting?"

Donovan waved a hand, exhausted and dismissive. "They'll never know you gave up."

"But *we'll* know," Julie said.

"Not for long. Trust me, it's over. You should've just left me in that cage." He started to turn away, but Julie said softly, "What about your son?" Donovan's movement was arrested halfway. She continued gently, "Wasn't Sean only eleven when they took him? He still would be if he's been in a stasis capsule. Isn't he still their prisoner somewhere?"

Silence hung heavily in the air over Donovan's cot. He continued to face away from them. Finally the others heard his hoarse voice whisper, "It's a lost cause. You should've just left me in that cage." He turned his head further away.

Julie was trying to figure another approach when Ysabel arrived out of breath. "Hey. We just intercepted a police call. The vid dealer Ahmed must have cracked, poor bastard. He gave up the names of his connections on the South Side. They're heading down to bust some of our Hunter's Point group. Gary's trying to make contact and warn them."

Julie headed for the comm truck. "I have a couple other numbers."

Margarita was also already in motion toward their makeshift armory. "We'll get down there." She grabbed a pair of pulse rifles and tossed one to Nathan. Little Ruby watched Nathan follow Margarita out, then glanced back to see if Julie was watching *her*.

When Julie reached the comm truck Gary was saying, "I'm trying to double-down on the circuits to Hunter's Point, but—Oh, my God," he suddenly interrupted himself. "Oh. My. God. Look at *that*!" He had noticed a staticky picture appear on a tiny monitor to one side. He punched it up onto the larger flat screen that hung loosely from the ceiling of the truck. He adjusted the very intermittent video signal. "It's coming in on the secret sideband from what's-her-name, our spy up in the Flagship Centcom."

"Lee, her name is Lee." Julie was hovering over his shoulder now, handing Ysabel the additional Hunter's Point numbers while she tried to make out the image. Then it suddenly came clearer, astonishing them all.

On the screen a massive, segmented spacecraft was seen cruising slowly past the moon. It gave the appearance of an enormous spinal column, with section after section attached in a long line like vertebrae. On the screen there appeared textual calibrations and tracking data being attached to the image. Gary translated for the others, "*It's over thirty miles long! And headed right for Earth!*"

At their hidden monitoring station outside the Resistance warehouse, Ayden and Bryke were approached by Kayta who displayed for them the same image of the gigantic new spacecraft hovering holographically over her blue communications orb. The three of them exchanged a glance of surprise.

AT EMMA'S DIRECTION, THE TAXI DRIVER HAD TAKEN HER AND THE Elgins to the nearby hospital on Hyde Street. Emma had gone to the Emergency Room there when she'd broken her wrist. The personnel had all been very kind, solicitous, and a bit starstruck. On this night, however, it was proving to be a much different story. Emma was thoroughly baffled by the attitude of the nurse on duty behind the thick glass at the security entrance. Charles was listening anxiously from the back of the nearby taxi. His arm was around his badly ailing daughter. Mary stood close to Emma who had Charlotte's ID papers in her hand. The Elgins listened to the exchange between the sturdy Philippine nurse and Emma who simply didn't understand. "*Why* won't you let her in?"

"It's against the rules, miss, sorry."

"What?" Emma was used to having the sea part for her and she was getting irate. "What 'rules' are you talking about?"

The nurse glanced toward Charlotte in the taxi. "We're not allowed to take in *her* kind."

"Oh, come on, that's ridiculous." But seeing that the nurse was not about to change her mind, Emma tried a different approach. She took note of the woman's name tag and played the chummy celebrity card. "Look, Amanda, do you know who I am?"

"Certainly, I like your new song."

"Thanks. And I'd be happy to get you some backstage passes to the next concert if you could help out my friends here. Their daughter—"

"Can't come in, I'm sorry."

Emma boiled over. "Listen, honey, I want to talk to your supervisor right now." She started toward the entrance, but two bouncer-quality Teammate guards blocked her way. She glared at them emphatically. "Excuse me."

But they were unintimidated and unmoving.

"All right"—the lovely singer switched gears again, dropping into a sarcastically sweet mode—"would one of you two nice gentlemen please ask her supervisor to step out here?"

The two Teammates merely stared at her. Emma was severely taken aback. She wasn't accustomed to such disregard, particularly from those like herself who worked closely with the Visitors. But it had become clear to her that entry to this hospital was impossible for the Elgin girl.

"Miss?" the nurse called softly. When Emma stepped back to the security window the nurse whispered, "I'm sorry. Really. You might try this place." She had written down an address and slipped it through the narrow slot at the bottom of the thick glass. Emma read the address and reacted with astonishment.

AFTER JULIE AND NATHAN HAD CARRIED MIKE DONOVAN AWAY, WILLY had gone on to a store to buy some groceries that Harmy needed. He returned a half hour later. He'd removed his human face as always and was climbing up the stairs to the third-floor landing when he paused. He saw the front door of their apartment standing open. He sensed something was amiss. Approaching the apartment cautiously, he peered in, but saw no one. He entered and set the groceries aside as he called out quietly, "Harmy? . . . Ted?"

There was no answer. Then a squeaky door across the hall opened a crack and an old man in a stained T-shirt peeked out sourly. Willy turned to look at the man who had the ruddy face and strawberry nose of a chronic alcoholic. "Your dreg boy just ran out a minute ago," the man said with a judgmental air. "He got real upset when he came up and I told him how the Teammates had arrested his slut mother."

* * *

TED WAS DISCONCERTED AND SHAKY, HIS BROW ALTERNATING BE-
tween being smooth and tightly knit. He was struggling to contain
his anger as he followed the African-American–looking Patrol
captain through the busy squad room at the Parnassas Police Station. "Sir, you promised that my family wouldn't be taken. Only
that prisoner guy I told you about."

"It's just routine, Ted"—the captain was busily looking at a
report—"your mother will be released shortly."

"They won't hurt her or anything, will they?"

The captain glanced at Ted as though the question were inane.
"Of course not. You absolutely did the right thing by coming to
me." He focused intently on the half-breed. He was always put off
by the boy's looks, with his face half scaly, his left eye pleasingly
reptilian yellow, but the right one human and blue. The captain
covered his distaste. "And I'll honor our agreement." He opened
the door to a closet and pulled a Teammate uniform from among
a dozen hanging within. "I think this one ought to fit you." He
held it in front of the young custodian's piecemeal clothing measuring by eye and was satisfied. "So, you're one of us now. Welcome aboard, *Teammate Ted.*"

Ted carefully took the uniform into his leathery hands. It was
a treasure he had coveted for so long it was hard to believe he'd
finally attained it. He handled the simple blue chambray shirt,
navy cord trousers, and baseball cap with utmost respect. He felt
a rush of prideful joy swelling within his chest, but it was in coun-
terpoint to the conflicting emotions surrounding his mother's
arrest.

COMMANDANT DIANA SWEPT QUICKLY INTO THE UPPER COMMAND
level of the Flagship Centcom. Her large dark eyes focused
sharply on the multiple views of the massive incoming ship. All
of the Visitor Centcom staff at their various monitoring and control stations looked to her as she began snapping orders.

"Alert the entire Armada to sound General Quarters. Scramble all the fighter squadrons. Bring up primary and secondary defense shields. Give me the coordinates for expected first contact."

Jeremy had strolled in casually behind her and was watching with an odd grin. "Oh, Diana, Diana"—his tone was one of mild amusement—"at ease, my dear. It's not attacking us . . . It's *mine*."

Diana's fiery eyes flashed angrily at Jeremy who merely smiled smugly.

14

HUNTER'S POINT WAS JUST ABOVE THE BORDER BETWEEN LOWER SAN Francisco County and San Mateo County. It had been home to the Naval Shipyard when there was still water for the ships to float upon. Like all coastal facilities over the last two decades it had fallen into increasing disuse. The giant cranes that once serviced the U.S. Pacific Fleet now stood as silent sentinels, rusting away, as was much of the nearby industrial complex.

Near one of the dilapidated cargo depots a group of twenty-three Resistance people was being herded out of a low building by Patrollers and Teammates. The prisoners had their hands on their heads and were being prodded toward a waiting shuttle craft. As Nathan and Margarita inched closer among some barrels to survey the scene, Margarita saw that many of the prisoners were frightened, but equally as many had faces expressing pure anger. Nathan touched her sleeve and pointed toward a tank truck some thirty yards from the shuttle. He silently mouthed to Margarita, "Boom," and she nodded. She watched as he stole away, skirting along the barrels, then moving behind some tumbled-down rotting crates to get closer for a cleaner shot. Margarita began edging in the opposite direction, which took her on a line toward the scene of the arrest.

Close to the truck that Nathan had targeted sat the hulk of a gutted car, which provided him with good cover. He snuck up behind it and unslung the pulse rifle he carried. He was priming it when he caught a glimpse in the car's cracked side mirror of a half-breed's face in the dark behind him. He whipped the rifle around and was about to fire when he saw it was Ruby. "Jesus!" He whispered angrily, "You almost got shot. What the hell are *you* doing here?"

Her eyes twinkled in the shadows. "Watching your butt."

"Well get over here and stay down!" She scrambled over to him. He saw that she too was carrying a pulse rifle. "You know how to use that?"

"Hey, I was born with it in my hands," she said with a grin as she expertly primed it.

"Well, you just keep your head down," he said as he pushed her lower. Ruby enjoyed the contact. She looked up and studied his handsome face as he looked through the data sight on the pulse rifle. He settled himself and fired at the tanker.

He scored a direct hit, which ruptured the undercarriage. The truck exploded in a ball of flame that blossomed out to a twenty-yard diameter startling everyone nearby.

Margarita instantly opened precision pulse fire from her new position ninety degrees to the left of Nathan. The Resistance fighters understood at once what was happening. With a defiant shout they attacked their keepers. Though some of the Patrollers and Teammates had handguns, they were outnumbered by their charges. Nonetheless, the Teammates fought back ferociously, firing point-blank and killing some of the nearest freedom fighters. The fighting quickly went hand-to-hand.

At that point it became such a melee that Margarita and Nathan couldn't shoot for fear of hitting their compatriots. They both headed into the fray as the smoke from the burning truck billowed around them and secondary explosions detonated.

Nathan shouted back at Ruby, "Don't. You. Move!"

Margarita used her rifle like a quarterstaff, clubbing a Patroller, then taking out two Teammates.

Nathan had leaped onto the back of a large female Patroller who was struggling with a smaller man. Nathan grabbed the female Patroller's face from behind and in the process his fingers dug in and ripped off a large chunk of her false human face, dislodging a contact lens. The reptile's yellow eye glared at Nathan and she fought back fiercely.

Several pulse weapon bursts hit amid the combatants, injuring Resistance members and Visitors alike. Margarita looked up and saw an Air-Pat flying in using his personal propulsion pack. She raised her pulse rifle to shoot at him, but she was blindsided by a Teammate who knocked her to the ground.

Behind the ruined car Ruby had also seen the inbound Air-Pat and was raising her own pulse rifle. "'Keep down,' my ass," she muttered as she aimed quickly, held her breath as Julie had taught her, and squeezed the trigger. The pulse of energy flashed upward trailing its thin smoky filament. It burst against the Air-Pat's shoulder spinning him off and into a bruising collision with the supporting girders of a huge service crane.

As the ground combat intensified, Ruby saw two more Air-Pats winging in from the distance. She fired at them repeatedly but their distance made them difficult targets.

Another Teammate unit was also rushing onto the scene. Nathan was fighting valiantly among the others flailing around him, but he sensed that the battle was turning against the Resistance. He saw two freedom fighters being brutally assailed by fearsome Patrollers, but he was so embroiled with his own combat at hand that he couldn't help them.

Then suddenly Nathan was startled to see a new face jump to the assistance of the freedom fighters. It was the sleek black woman with pink eyes, close-cropped hair, and an odd sheen to her skin who had helped him escape the gladiatorial cellar. Though much preoccupied with his own struggle, Nathan caught a glimpse of her exhibiting prodigious strength. Bryke grabbed a Teammate with one hand and slung him off the fallen compatriot. Her moves were fluid, graceful beyond athletic, and somewhat unearthly.

Then he caught sight of a striking blond woman in a suede vest entering the skirmish. Her lovely face also had a peculiar shine. When she was attacked from behind by a Teammate, Nathan saw short, spiky quills fan up from the back of her neck, penetrating deeply into her assailant who gasped with surprise and began to convulse. Nathan downed his own attacker and shouted to the blonde, "Who are *you*?" Before Kayta could respond, she and Nathan were both set upon by the newly arrived Teammates.

The Air-Pats were getting closer and beginning to fire randomly into the crowd when one of them saw the pulse fire directed toward them from a half-breed behind the hulk of a car.

Margarita had been bravely fighting multiple adversaries, but they were about to overwhelm her when a sturdy man in a bomber jacket came to her aid. Margarita thought she saw a flat white bone flash out of the man's wrist. It extended about eighteen inches, like a white sword. In an amazing blur he had suddenly filleted two Patrollers. Green blood gushed from their slashed throats and they fell where they'd been standing.

Margarita was clubbed from behind and driven to the ground by a Teammate, but Ayden pulled the man off of Margarita with one hand and tossed him thirty feet over the heads of the fighters. Margarita's jaw dropped. "Who *are* you?"

Then she heard Nathan shouting, "Into the shuttle! I'll fly us out!" Nathan was knocking down a Teammate and urging his Resistance allies toward the shuttle, "Go! Go!" Then he shouted back toward the hulk of car, "Ruby?! This way!"

Many Resistance fighters scrambled aboard the shuttle. Nathan and Margarita headed for it. He was looking back for Ruby and for the mysterious strangers as he shouted to Margarita, "Did you see a black woman with pink eyes?!"

"I can't believe what I *did* see!"

As they turned back toward the shuttle into which their allies were climbing they saw three Visitor fighters diving in from the night sky with their pulse cannons blazing. The bursts strafed in a staccato line up to the shuttle and blasted the large craft, which exploded to pieces. The powerful concussion knocked Nathan and Margarita to the ground.

Inside the quiet cockpit of the lead fighter Flight Leader Gina grinned at the results of her prowess. She pulled her control pad back and to the right, feeling the increasing G-force press her into the seat as she banked her fighter hard up and to the right for another pass.

On the smoking debris field that surrounded the exploded shuttle, the few Resistance fighters who had survived were helping each other to their feet. Margarita and Nathan, soaked with sweat and spattered with blood, were struggling to rise. Margarita surveyed the devastation, the destroyed and burning shuttle, the body parts and entrails that lay everywhere. She looked at the wounded with an aching heart, then she saw another squad of heavily armed Patrollers coming and she shouted to her remaining people, "North! Go north! Go underground!"

Nathan saw one of the airborne Air-Pats dodging fire from Ruby and returning pulse bursts toward the burned-out car. He shouted, "Ruby! Dammit," and dashed off toward her.

Hearing the girl's name, Margarita looked back and fleetingly saw Nathan running through the blowing smoke. Then one of the bloodied freedom fighters caught her sleeve shouting, "Come on, Margarita! You're right, the only way out is north."

Margarita looked back again but Nathan had disappeared into the dense smoke.

* * *

THE TAXI HAD CARRIED EMMA AND THE ELGINS HALFWAY ACROSS THE Bay Bridge. It was only after Emma agreed to pay the driver extra that he turned off onto Yerba Buena Island, which gave access to the man-made Treasure Island Naval Reservation.

With no water left in the bay, the four-hundred-acre island was now a mesa that rose in isolation above the dry bay valley. Over the last twenty years it had gone to seed and become a haven for squatters and indigents who were routinely rounded up by the Visitors and "relocated" to the storage capsules.

Amid the falling-down wood-frame structures one old steel edifice loomed over all the rest. It was a truly gigantic hangar designed to house blimps. Long out of use, it had several low maintenance buildings attached to it that were in frightful disrepair.

Inside one of those structures Emma, Mary, and Charles hurried along pushing a secondhand gurney with a rattling wheel that bore the weakening Charlotte. Emma cringed in disgust at the smell of urine that permeated the ratty hallway. Dimly lit by dusty, broken, or flickering fixtures, the walls, with their paint blistered or peeling, looked leprous. As they hurried down the dismal corridor they passed shuffling patients in street clothes or mismatched hospital gowns. Some were merely slouched against the wall. The patients outnumbered the beleaguered medical staff to a far greater extent than at a normal hospital.

The hospice doctor attending Charlotte was a thin woman in her fifties with gray streaks in her light brown hair and a careworn look in her tired eyes. "We do what we can," she was telling the Elgins and Emma. "We don't have much equipment or meds, but we're really the only place that scientists can go."

She guided them across the uneven floor into a makeshift E.R. with battered cabinets and sparse supplies stacked haphazardly. A half-breed male nurse who looked exhausted rose to help.

Emma stayed near the door, but Mary was at her daughter's side, holding Charlotte's slender hand. "Charlotte honey, hang on. It's going to be okay now."

The tired doctor saw that the nurse was already about his business. "Good, Charlie, you get her hooked up. Start a drip. I'll try to find some *diatome*."

As the nurse searched for a vein on Charlotte's frail arm Charles also leaned close to his daughter as Mary repeated, "It's going to be okay."

Charlotte was exceedingly weak, but still managed a faint smile, though her breath was short and her voice halting. "I know it will be, Momma . . ." The teenager was genuinely more concerned about her parents than herself as the light in her eyes grew dimmer. "Just don't lose hope or . . ." Her shaved head lolled limply to one side.

Charles reached in and cupped her head with both hands. "Charlotte . . . Charlotte!"

Mary was frantic. "Oh, please God! Charlotte!"

The doctor stepped quickly in and injected the girl as the nurse dropped the IV gear and started urgent CPR heart massage.

Charles saw an old defibrillator unit in the corner and grabbed the paddles from it. "Here! Use these! Quickly!"

The doctor had clapped an oxygen mask over the girl's nose and mouth as she said to Charles, "It's broken." She was seeking a pulse on Charlotte's willowy neck.

"Please, please," Mary was crying.

But after a moment the physician sighed and touched the nurse for him to cease his CPR efforts.

Mary grew frantic. "No, no—*NO*! Charlotte!" Mary was not about to give up. She pumped her hands desperately on her daughter's shallow chest. "Charlotte! Please! Come on!"

After several moments Charles reached slowly from behind Mary and gently tried to enfold his distraught wife in his arms, but she pulled away, disconsolate. Mary collapsed across her daughter's chest, sobbing inconsolably. Charles stood by feeling helpless, numb, empty.

The doctor and nurse quietly left the room to see to their living patients. They passed by Emma, who hadn't moved from beside the scuffed and dented doorway. When Charlotte died Emma had felt a sudden, subtle, but very physical change in the shabby room. It was an abrupt vacancy, as though the very air had somehow become thinner. The only sounds now were the choked sobs of the grieving mother.

Emma slowly eased out the doorway to give them privacy. Turning into the rancid corridor she found herself looking toward a matching doorway on the opposite wall. She could see that the room inside it wasn't small. And she heard a strange low sound coming from it, a soft dissonant chorus of human moans. Curiosity compelled her forward. She pulled her sable coat closer around her throat and as she stepped through the doorway the room opened out breathtakingly around and above her.

It was the inside of the blimp hangar. Shadowy and vast, it was at least three hundred feet tall, equally wide, and twice that length. It was the largest interior space Emma had ever stood within. There were pools of light from an eclectic collection of floor lamps scattered into the dim distance.

Between the mismatched lamps in dozens upon dozens of uneven rows were beds, metal bunks, cots, and wooden pallets of sick or dying people who very much needed a real hospital. It called to Emma's mind pictures she had seen of disaster victims who had become refugees and been crowded onto the floor of some domed sports stadium. But this forbidding place was much darker and more crowded. Emma walked slowly among the patients. She saw that hospital gowns were scarce, most of the patients wore their own clothes and far more than half of the beds had no sheets, but only a single meager blanket if anything at all. Some beds were mere frames with no mattresses. The sour, pungent smells of bodily fluids, vomit, and excrement combined with medicinal scents and the stale, humid breath of the unwell.

Emma looked at those individuals nearest her. She looked at

the withered, drawn, perspiring face of one young man who seemed to be fighting severe abdominal pain; at a beautiful thirty-year-old Latina with dark, sunken eyes and a festering pustule on her cheek who vomited a small amount of dark blood into a used paper cup.

Emma looked up from the woman. The suffering people multiplied and expanded to the extent of her vision on all sides. She realized there was only a very small handful of nurses and doctors attending to the multitude. The labored breathing and groans of the ill and injured intermingled to create the low inharmonious hum that lay like an invisible, undulating carpet over them all. The effect was smothering.

It added to the increasing emotional weight that Emma had felt pressing down upon her since entering the cavernous space. She realized what she was feeling was shame. She felt like a latter-day Scarlett O'Hara, who had always been egocentric and utterly self-absorbed in her own privileged world, until she suddenly discovered the thousands of wounded Civil War soldiers spread across the enormous train yard in Atlanta. The war, with all of its unspeakable horrors, suddenly became grievously tangible and undeniable because she was looking into the very face of it.

Emma, the blithe young singer, the popular star, the Player, the engaging spokeswoman for her alien friends, was now confronting a very different side of *The Visitor Way*.

She felt a wispy touch on her leg. She looked down at a very small blond boy who lay on a bare, stained mattress. His fingertips were brushing the soft luxurious black fur of her sable coat. His angelic face was fevered, damp with perspiration. The child's exhausted eyes stared up into Emma's.

SHE FOUND HERSELF WALKING BLINDLY ALONG THE DARK AND DIRTY street outside the blimp hangar. She passed a few scruffy people who were gathered around a fire in a rusted oil drum, but she barely noticed them or the trash blowing in the street or the empty morphalyne packages and used syringes in the gutter. She'd been stunned into a trancelike numbness by the multitude of sick and dying people she had seen in the huge hangar. When the taxi had not been waiting she had just begun to walk. As she came upon an intersection, red and blue flashing lights began to play rhythmically across her face.

Emma slowed, becoming aware of the emergency lights and the raspy squawk from police radios. She was passing an ugly auto accident. There was twisted metal and bodies covered with rubber sheets. Businesslike SFPD officers and paramedics were exchanging information. Then she noticed a Visitor Patroller near one crashed car as he bent to pick up something flesh-colored. He glanced around cautiously, didn't notice Emma, and seemed content that he was unobserved. He slipped into an alley.

Emma inched forward and carefully peered into the alley. The Patroller was unaware that she was watching him as he examined what Emma realized was a severed human finger. The Patroller smiled. Emma watched him open his mouth and swallow it whole.

IN THE RESISTANCE WAREHOUSE ALL THE LOOSE EQUIPMENT HAD been gathered and secured within the trucks ready for speedy departure at a moment's notice. It was a precaution they always took when there was the slightest possibility that their current location might have been compromised. Gary, Street-C, Blue, and others had been called in to help. Everyone's nerves were tightly wound as they awaited word. Ysabel looked over her half-glasses at Julie, whom she saw was particularly restive. With Blue's help, Julie was at one of the medical trucks taking out some of their first aid supplies, to be handy in case there were injuries incoming from Hunter's Point. Ysabel knew that the lack of contact from Margarita down there was eating into Julie. Ysabel poured them both a cup of tea and took one to Julie, who started slightly. "Oh. Thanks, Ysie."

The older woman was looking around for a way to distract her beloved leader when her eyes fell upon Mike Donovan who was frowning with an introspective expression as he lay on his cot across the room.

Ysabel sipped her own tea. "Was it just me or did he seem to react funny when he heard that the Great Purge was in '99?"

Julie blew across the vapory surface of the hot tea as she nodded slowly. "Yeah. I saw it, too."

"We always wondered who could've given Diana so much detailed information about the Resistance."

Blue had paused in his work to listen and said to them, "He must've been captured in the London Uprising back in '91."

"Yeah"—Julie gazed at Mike trying to imagine—"if he was the one that gave them information . . ." She couldn't finish the thought, but Ysabel did.

"Then he must've gone through eight years of Diana's torture before he caved."

At the mention of torture, Blue instantly felt a surge of electrical discomfort originate deep in his groin. It spread upward through his bowels with a searing, high-voltage intensity. It was his invariable reaction to seeing someone injured or particularly to thoughts of torture. That was the one part of being a Christian that unnerved him; the thought of the torments Jesus had undergone on Golgotha. He knew that day had actually happened; that so many other days of hideous agonies had been visited upon so many innocents, like the young girls forced to undergo the pain of female circumcision. Such horrors always made him queasy and tightened his stomach. He would break out in a cold sweat as though all of the air conditioners in the world had suddenly been turned on. Though Blue was a big sturdy man and physically quite strong, the prospect of torture and the horrifying pain he imagined from it turned his innards watery.

Julie's eyes grew distant as she tried to fathom the unspeakable experience Mike must have undergone. "What he must have suffered through."

"And if they got him on morphalyne"—Ysabel shook her head; she had been studying Mike—"once they got him hooked he might not even *know* he told them."

"But if he suspects he did," Julie was trying to envision Mike's feelings, "can you imagine the burden of guilt he's carrying?"

The three of them looked at the fallen hero, lying immobilized in the shadowy warehouse. Then Julie's cell rang and she grabbed it quickly. "Yes! Lexington Base."

Emma was leaning against one of the dingy brick buildings on Treasure Island. The police emergency lights still flashed on her from the accident scene down the street. Her cheeks were streaked with tears, her breathing was shallow. Her nerves were raw, her voice shaky, but resolute. "Juliet . . . It's Emma."

In the headquarters, Gary gravitated to where Ysabel was watching Julie listen carefully to her phone. Then Julie drew a large breath in reaction to something she heard. She nodded, saying into the phone, "Yes. I understand. We'll be in touch. And, Emma . . . please be careful." She clicked off the phone as she looked at Ysabel and Gary. "Emma is with us."

"Good," Ysabel said. But she could see Julie's extremely serious expression, her reaction to something else Emma had just told her.

Gary also recognized there was more. He inclined his head toward Julie. "And what's the bad news . . . ?"

Julie drew a breath. "She says the Visitor Leader is coming."

"Holy Mother of God." Ysabel's voice was low, dumbfounded. "What does *that* mean?"

"Maybe a special treat?" Gary offered. "Like . . . Armageddon?"

Street-C was coming from a back room and had overheard Gary. "Looks like it's already started." Then they saw what he referred to: Margarita and several combatants were straggling in, badly battered from their losing battle.

Julie, Ysabel, and the others hurried to bring them first aid. From his cot in the makeshift infirmary corner, Mike watched with a grim, world-weary expression as the injured were brought in around him.

Margarita took Julie aside. The grimy, scraped, and bloodied redhead was out of breath and quaking with nervous distress, "Oh, Julie, I handled it terribly. Lots of casualties. Nathan and Ruby are missing."

Julie blanched. "*Ruby* was there!"

"Nathan went after her, but I lost them. A whole shuttle full of our people got blown up. It was"—she was fighting tears of anger and guilt for losing the battle—"oh, God, Julie. This is all a nightmare. I think the bastards really *are* unbeatable."

A man's voice called to them, "Maybe not."

They looked toward the doorway and saw Nathan standing in it. He was as filthy and bloodied as Margarita, but suffused with a peculiarly optimistic spirit. He looked at Julie. "First off: nobody could've done better than Red. Second: I think Ruby escaped. Thirdly: I didn't. The lizards had my sorry ass big time. But I got rescued by a very interesting trio."

He stepped in and motioned to those still outside the doorway. The three with the shiny skin and the strangely colored eyes entered. They examined the Resistance gathering and glanced around to take stock of the room. Julie and all the others sensed that an unsettling new presence had arrived among them.

Julie immediately noticed that the newcomers were slightly wounded, but Street-C's eyes went wide as he pointed at Bryke. "Whoa, hang on. If that's her blood how come it's *yellow*?"

Gary had seen that Ayden's blood seemed to be thick and white.

Ysabel was stunned by something else unearthly and instinctively crossed herself. "*Madre Mia!* Look at their eyes."

Nathan smiled. "Yeah, we'll get to all that. But first may I present for your approval, Ayden, Kayta, and Bryke." The Resistance gang all studied the three with wary uncertainty. Then Nathan looked again at Julie. "Remember that distress call you sent out twenty years ago?" He grinned broadly. "Well, guess what: *they got it.*"

15

MARGARITA AND ALL THE OTHERS WERE THUNDERSTRUCK. THEY stared at the three mysterious and clearly powerful aliens. Julie saw that Ayden was looking at her specifically and she asked, "You've come to help us?"

He nodded. "To try."

"Awright!" Street-C pumped his fist. "Now that's some *good* news!"

Margarita was still eyeing them warily. "Let's hope so."

Julie beckoned them toward the infirmary. "But you're injured . . . Please . . ." She guided Ayden to a chair where he removed his bomber jacket and pushed back the sleeve of his gray turtleneck, revealing the cut on his arm.

Kayta opened a small med kit she carried as Robert edged nearer, his dark eyes studying the thick, milky liquid on Ayden's arm. Blue also looked at it and said the obvious, "That . . . don't look like blood." He glanced questioningly toward Robert, aware of his expertise in anthropology.

Robert explained, "They've obviously evolved differently from us."

"Yeah"—Nathan grinned knowledgeably—"from insects."

"Insects?" Street-C stepped back. "No fuckin' way!"

Even Robert's eyes had widened. "Are you serious?!"

Nathan nodded. "Their race is called the *Zedti.*"

Margarita came closer. "I'm Margarita and this is—"

"Ysabel, yes, we know," Kayta said, adding with a hint of apology, "We have listened." Her soft violet eyes met Margarita's, then she sensed something else and her gaze drifted toward Mike Donovan who was watching from his cot on the periphery.

To all of the Resistance team, Kayta seemed less aloof than either steely-eyed Ayden or silent Bryke. Ayden addressed Julie as Kayta tended his wound. "We know that you are the eye of this hurricane, Dr. Parish, the one who sent the distress call. We three are each different species. Our communicator Kayta is a physician and a *sensitive*. Particularly to pheromones."

"They shot a blob of pheromone goop onto our car," Nathan explained, "Kayta sniffed it out. Tracked us here. Ayden's sort of like a Samurai knight with a built-in sword and—"

"Very strong, among other things," Margarita interjected.

"Extraordinary strength is natural to insects," Robert said. He'd been studying the three. "Like your hardened skin . . . an *exoskeleton*?"

"Of sorts, yes," said Kayta. "We each have that in varying degrees. Which makes us each look different."

Gary was staring at something. "Uh . . . I'd say there're some *other* differences, too." They followed his amazed glance to Bryke who was scratching her back. Her shoulder and elbow joints were hinged entirely backward.

They all stared for a silent moment. Then Ysabel said, "Just a wild guess: you folks were responsible for that weird *husk*?"

Julie noticed Ayden glance at Bryke with mild annoyance, as he acknowledged, "Yes."

IN DIMLY LIT HANGAR BAY TWELVE ABOARD THE FLAGSHIP AT THAT same moment, two dried husks were being laid on the flight deck. One was the burly, mustachioed Teammate and the other a Visitor Patroller whom Bryke had downed at Hunter's Point. Shawn and Martin stood by as Diana surveyed them with some recognition. She poked at one with her booted foot as she addressed the Visitor doctor, "Nothing from Earth can cause this?"

Eric shook his head. "Nothing we know of, Commandant."

Two Patrollers brought the grungy reptilian guard who had been stationed at Donovan's cell. Diana turned her sloe eyes to him. "*You* let my prisoner escape?"

The frightened guard protested, "It was a dreg did it, Commandant! I swear."

"Which dreg?"

"Forgive me, Commandant, but they all look alike. I'm not sure which it was." Then he noticed two half-breed janitors who were cleaning a smelly mess beneath a nearby shuttle, "Could've been one of them! Yes! I think it was one of them!"

"No, it wasn't," Martin spoke up, "those two only work the hangar bays."

Shawn looked disdainfully at the guard, then at Diana, "He obviously has no idea which dreg it was, Commandant."

Diana didn't even glance at the Patrollers holding the guard. "Kill the fool. Slowly."

"No! Please, Commandant," the guard pleaded desperately and continued to protest his innocence as the Patrollers dragged him away. Diana was already looking back down at the bizarre husks. Martin thought that her expression indicated she had knowledge of what had caused them.

THOUGH RUBY'S WRIST HAD THE TOUGH LEATHERY SKIN INHERITED from her reptilian father, the handcuff was chafing her. The other end of the handcuff was secured to the arm of the wooden bench she was sitting on in the police station. Nathan had been mistaken. Ruby had not escaped at Hunter's Point. She had been captured and brought north to the Parnassas Station at the southeast corner of Golden Gate Park, a clearinghouse for those suspected of Resistance involvement. The twelve-year-old was worried, but with her innate bravado she was carefully observing the bustling police squad room trying to formulate an escape plan. So far she was batting zero.

Then her stomach dropped when she heard the stern black Patrol captain's deep voice. "Bring her in for interrogation." She looked around sharply and realized he was talking about someone else. She saw that it was terrified Harmy who was being led through the fluorescent haze into a forbidding anteroom.

BY MORNING JULIE WAS GETTING VERY WORRIED FOR HER DAUGHTER and having trouble keeping her mind on X-rays of the Zedti that she and Robert Maxwell were examining. She grew expectant when she saw Ysabel coming, but the older woman shook her head and waved negatively, clicking the thin bracelets on her wrist. "No Ruby yet. But everybody's looking."

Robert couldn't think of any comforting words that Julie would believe, so he tried to refocus her on examining the X-rays. "They are definitely *not* Visitors."

Gary was nearby, sipping coffee, but his eyes were unsettled. "So why do I feel just a tad uncomfortable?"

"Because they're very unemotional," Margarita said as she and Street-C brought some breakfast burritos to Julie and Robert. Everyone had been up all night.

"Yeah. Talk about *chillin'*," said Street-C.

"That'd be consistent with their physiology," Julie said. "There's no sentiment in the lives of insects."

Kayta spoke up from a short distance away where she had been examining their human medicines. "Yes. We Zedti experience less emotion than we have observed in humans." They turned to her and Kayta glanced downward, shyly. "Forgive me. Often I overhear without meaning to."

"Hey," Nathan quipped, glancing at Margarita, "a lot of us have minimal emotion."

Margarita ignored his barb. "Please tell us more, Kayta."

In a gesture designed to emphasize the interconnectivity of

her people, the blond Zedti raised her hands before her and interlaced her fingers. "Our strongest individual desire is to work for the good of our society."

Blue, who had been keeping a weathered eye on the three newcomers, drifted closer. "Sounds kinda communist, huh?"

"It's the *Hive Mentality*," Robert clarified. "Let me tell you: if ants were bigger, humans would've been gone long ago."

Nathan had been thinking. "You said you came from the star we call Altair? That's about sixteen light-years away, right?" Kayta nodded affirmation. "So Julie's distress call took sixteen years to reach you."

"It did," Ayden's voice was authoritative, "we then came immediately."

Dark-skinned Bryke had joined them. "No one should have to live under such tyranny." The others looked at her with some surprise. Her voice was much softer than her warrior's demeanor suggested.

"Bryke piloted us here in four years," Ayden said.

Nathan's face scrunched curiously. "Faster than light speed?"

"Utilizing what you would call *wormhole technology*," Bryke explained.

Julie asked the obviously key question, "And you're an enemy of the Visitors? You've defeated them before?" She noted that Bryke's pink eyes looked away, perhaps from a bad memory.

Ayden confirmed for Julie, "Yes. But at enormous cost to our people."

"Their Leader is ruthless," Kayta said. "With an enormous ego and a deep hatred of the Zedti because we defeated them. Barely."

Ysabel was beginning to suspect something. "Are you afraid Earth's just a stopover on their way back to smack you good?"

"We do have intelligence that they may be planning just such an attack, yes," Ayden acknowledged.

Street-C's eyes narrowed as he got Ysabel's drift. "So y'all ain't just come to help us."

Kayta clarified, "If we can stop them here, both you and we would benefit."

"But to do that we need *your* help," Ayden said. "We must discover their exact plans, strategy, and weaponry."

Margarita had been studying the three Zedti. "We know they're creating eye coloring like yours, human-sounding voices, and a sheen like your skin has."

"Obviously to infiltrate our outposts," Ayden reasoned. "To undermine our security en route to attacking our home planet."

Julie had picked up on Margarita's line of thinking. "And they'd need those pheromone injections—"

"Or the Zedti could sniff out spies," Robert agreed.

"Yes," said Kayta, "from our previous encounter we've learned to never underestimate their treachery. We narrowly defeated them before."

Bryke was resolved. "But we're determined to stop them permanently this time."

Nathan looked at her. "So how many of you are here?"

Ayden answered, "Just we three."

"Three?" Blue blinked, frowning.

Street-C groaned, "Shit, man, that ain't gonna do no good."

Then Ayden continued. "But our *fleet* is standing by."

Street-C immediately reversed attitude, "*Fleet!* Yeah! Now *that's* what I'm talkin' about. Where are they?"

"Marshaled behind the planet Saturn to avoid detection," Ayden explained. "We have 177 warships. Kayta will call them in once we learn everything you know." He looked directly at Julie. "Will you share all your information with us?"

The freedom fighters grew silent, weighing the situation. Julie remembered the Visitors' arrival twenty years earlier when they also had professed to need "our help." Blue and the others were equally wary. Nathan saw that Margarita was rubbing the back of her forefinger against the tip of her nose as her keen eyes flicked from one Zedti to another. Nathan knew she was pondering the same critical question that was worrying all of the Resistance members: could *these* aliens be trusted?

And, as she had for twenty years, Julie felt unequal to the grave responsibility thrust upon her as all of her compatriots' eyes eventually looked to her to make the call.

IN EMMA'S CONDO EARLY THAT SAME MORNING, SAN FRANCISCO'S mayor was surprised when Emma greeted him with a deeply romantic kiss. She ran her fingers through his thick dark hair. Then, as her moist lips grazed along his cheek, Mark whispered, "I thought you'd invited me to have breakfast."

"We'll get to that," she purred, easing off his suit jacket. She was wearing a thin, lavender silk robe and when he put his arms around her he could feel the warmth and smoothness of her tawny skin beneath it. Under the silk she was wearing nothing. She kissed him again.

"Mmm," he hummed, "I guess you *have* missed me."

"When I saw you again . . . all those important Visitors courting you"—she was loosening his tie—"I suddenly remembered what a prize you are."

"Ah . . . the lure of power . . ." Mark said lightly and with humor. "Let me tell you, it's not all it's cracked up to be."

"You let me be the judge of that," she said and kissed him deeply again. He responded as her robe slipped away, and his hands glided down over her bronze curves. Emma glimpsed herself in a mirror over his shoulder. She was truly fond of Mark and felt a stab of guilt about her new career as a Mata Hari.

THE BROAD VIZ SCREEN ON THE WALL OF THE DARKENED FLAGSHIP conference room was displaying multiple views of Earth's greatly diminished oceans. At the top of North America, Hudson Bay had vanished along with all the bays and basins that had held less than a thousand feet of water. To the north and east to Greenland all of that water was gone. The east coast of Canada had swelled outward to include all of Newfoundland. The formerly prime fishing grounds of the Grand Banks were high and dry. The great harbors of Boston, New York, and Norfolk were empty, as was the entire Chesapeake Bay. The rivers that flowed into them—the Charles, the Hudson, the Potomac, the Delaware, and others—had all diminished and now snaked out shallowly across the arid land. Along the entire former Eastern Seaboard of the United States there was dry land for at least two hundred miles eastward to the precipitous slope of the continental shelf. From there steep cliffs slanted down over a thousand feet before reaching the new level of the sea.

The Gulf of Mexico had shrunk to half of its size, enlarging the Mississippi Delta. The great muddy river now did not reach the Gulf until it had traveled an additional 120 miles south of New Orleans. The Florida peninsula had widened on either side and from space it looked swollen. The Florida Keys and the Bahamas were no longer isolated islands but part of the mainland.

On the Pacific side of North America, from the Bering Straits to the Aleutian Islands a broad land bridge had formed between Russia and Alaska as it had existed during the last Ice Age when sea levels were lower, though never this low. All along the western United States dry land now extended outward for several hundred miles. Puget Sound was empty and the great ports of Vancouver, Seattle, Los Angeles, and San Diego were as waterless and arid as San Francisco's former bay. At Portland, the Columbia River fanned out westward into a wide, shallow delta and was mostly absorbed into the parched ground before it could reach the new edge of the Pacific Ocean.

The continent of South America had likewise grown, particularly on its southeastern side where the continental shelf was now dry land all the way east to and beyond the Falkland Islands.

The water in the deepest abyssal plains of all the oceans, normally from five to seven thousand feet deep, had diminished by more than half. Africa, which possessed the narrowest continental shelf, now had steep cliff sides that plunged two thousand feet and more down to the waters that remained in the Angola Basin to the west and the Somali Abyssal Plain on the east.

The northern two-thirds of the Adriatic Sea that had previously separated Italy from the Balkan Peninsula was dry. The Red Sea had become a new section of the Arabian and Egyptian deserts. The Mediterranean and Black Seas had shrunk to half their normal size. The North Sea, English Channel, the Celtic and Baltic Seas had simply disappeared. Scandinavia and the former British Isles were now entirely linked by land to Western Europe and Holland's dikes now held back only the wind.

The Indian subcontinent had grown by nearly a third and connected itself to Sri Lanka. The Indochinese Peninsula now continued far to the south encompassing Sumatra and Borneo. The East China Sea and the Yellow Sea were also dry beds connecting the Chinese mainland to Korea, Taiwan, and Japan. Proportionately, Australia had grown most of all, increasing its size by fully half. The living coral of its Great Barrier Reef, left exposed to the intense sunlight, had dried out and died.

Transportation by sea had thus been severely hampered because the worldwide ports were now either well inland or much farther above sea level than they had ever been in human history. In spite of new facilities, which the Visitors had helped construct to connect the ports with the ever-diminishing oceans, commerce by sea had become difficult at best. Transport was made even more arduous because of the closing of the landlocked Panama and Suez Canals.

Diana proudly pointed out to Jeremy all the statistics and the vast quantity of water that had already been taken up and, using Visitor technology, had been compressed for storage aboard the

Motherships. Many of the gigantic vessels had already quietly departed for their home planet.

Jeremy was thoroughly unimpressed. "It's simply not happening fast enough to suit our Leader. Hence, my new creation." He nodded for Shawn to switch the viz screen to show the recently arrived, thirty-mile-long, segmented spacecraft, which was now in a low orbit around the Earth. "I suppose that here they would refer to it as 'Visitor 2.0.'" He smiled with mild self-amusement.

Diana's stony expression did not change, however, as she watched the individual vertebraelike segments of the massive craft beginning to separate and divide off from the elongated ship. "Each segment is a plug-in for a Mothership which will greatly accelerate water collection and compression," he explained with self-satisfaction. "Our work here will thus be finished not in years, as under your plan, but *weeks*. Which, of course, will allow us to commence our attack against the Zedti." He sat down comfortably into one of the conference room chairs and stretched his arms expansively. "I must say, our Leader was extremely pleased."

Diana was not. But she contained her ire as she stared at him and considered her best countermoves.

EMMA AND MARK LAY BESIDE EACH OTHER, NAKED IN HER BED. IF people still smoked, they would've been. They were snuggled closely and the mayor was talking softly: "Oh, they've done remarkable things for us, of course. But I still have . . ." His voice trailed off. Like everyone, Mark was wise enough to take care when speaking about the Visitors in any way that might be considered critical. In his position as San Francisco's mayor he had to exercise particular caution.

But Emma was anxious to keep him talking and gently coaxed him, "Still have what?"

He glanced at her. It was so good to be lying close to her again. He loved her perfume with its subtle rosy fragrance. They had become lovers several years after the death of his wife, drawn together at first merely as people with celebrity often are. They had quickly found that they shared many common sensibilities and the same understated humor. Mark had been very disappointed when Emma drifted away and he was glad that she had now decided to renew their closeness. Their lovemaking was both very comfortable and very inventive. He greatly enjoyed their renewed intimacy and was convinced that she also did.

Emma, in fact, truly did enjoy it. But she also had a mission now and prompted him again, "You still have what?"

"Some ambivalence, maybe. The whole anti-Sci thing troubled me from the beginning and . . ." Again he hesitated, weighing a decision. Then he finally said, "Can you keep a secret?"

Emma's pulse rate increased slightly, but she maintained her casual manner. "Of course."

"I've been able to sneak a little humanitarian aid to scientists and their families. I set up a hospice in an old blimp hangar over on Treasure Island to provide them with some medical assistance."

Emma blinked. "*You* did that?"

Mark was surprised and a bit concerned that she knew of it. "You heard about it? How?"

"I . . . have a masseuse who's married to a Sci. She told me."

"Well, it's not much, but it's something. If you're interested, maybe you could go by there sometime. I'm sure it'd bolster the spirits of the patients." Then he had second thoughts and quickly backpedaled. "But of course, I wouldn't want you to do anything that might seem inappropriate to you or compromise your position with the Visitors."

Before she could answer, his cell-phone rang. As Mark sat up to answer, Emma studied him. This unforeseen information had furthered her new awakening of caring for him. Simultaneously Emma felt all the more guilty for spying on him.

Mark held his vid phone in front of him as he clicked on the tiny viewer. The Visitor Patrol captain's face appeared. He was seen in the rear of a moving vehicle. "Mr. Mayor . . . I was on the way to our meeting, but I'm afraid I'll have to postpone it."

"Not a problem. Nothing too serious, I hope?"

In the car, the mayor's face was on the vid phone of the captain who had also glimpsed half-naked Emma on the bed behind Mark. The captain struggled to speak while he was so distracted. "Uh, no, sir . . . Actually very good: I was just informed that we've caught Juliet Parish's little dreg bitch. I'm going back to interrogate her."

In the bedroom Emma overheard and turned away to hide her alarm.

AT THE PARNASSAS POLICE STATION BOOKING DESK, WILLY WAS TRYing to stay cool as he watched a crew-cut SFPD sergeant checking the paperwork Willy had presented. A Visitor-Asian half-breed edged past to empty the sergeant's trash. Finally the sergeant stamped the papers. "Looks in order. I'll go get her." He went off, passing a Teammate unit that was heading out on patrol. Willy was stunned to see that among the unit was his half-breed son Ted who was now wearing a Teammate uniform.

Willy turned away quickly so he wouldn't be noticed by Ted. The scaly-faced teen was introducing himself to Teammate Debra Stein, who looked particularly aggravated. "Debra? I'm Ted. They told me I was partnered up with you." He held out his scaly hand to her, but she ignored it.

"Just not too close, okay, pal," she couldn't have been sourer, "I can't believe they stuck me with a goddamn dreg."

Out of the corner of his eye, Willy watched Ted departing among the enemy. Willy sadly realized that it must have been his son who had informed on Harmy and gotten her arrested.

"Here's your prisoner," the sergeant called out and Willy turned to see his wife. Harmy looked terrible. Her cheek and arms were bruised. When she finally raised her downcast eyes and realized her escort was Willy he gave her a sharp warning look to quell her reaction as he grabbed her roughly.

"Come on, you." Then he nodded thanks to the sergeant, adding, "She's in good hands."

As Willy guided her out of the busy station Harmy whispered worriedly to him, "Oh, my God, you forged the transfer papers!"

"I would've done anything." They left by a side door and were so intent upon each other that they didn't notice the pre-teen half-breed handcuffed to a bench nearby.

Ruby did not see them either. A few minutes earlier she had been moved to the bench just outside of the interrogation room. She was putting on a brave front, but the twelve-year-old was truly frightened by the ordeal that she knew lay ahead of her.

16

WHETHER OR NOT TO TAKE THE THREE MYSTERIOUS NEWCOMERS into the confidence of the Resistance was a major decision for Julie. She had, as always, listened to the thoughts of her compatriots. Some were in favor of it, some opposed. Even more than their words and ideas, Julie tried to feel the temperature of their various emotions. In the midst of doing that she recalled, as she had so many times during leadership crises over the years, the moment two decades earlier when she'd had a breakdown over the huge responsibility that had somehow been thrust upon her.

The fledgling Resistance group had just established its first piecemeal headquarters in the partially collapsed basement of an old bank building. Julie had stepped forward a couple of times to volunteer her energies and take on a task when no one else was willing. Because of that, everyone somehow had assumed that Julie was the prime coordinator of the Resistance. They proceeded to barrage her with a thousand questions and problems. She had never sought the weight of leadership and often tried to dodge it because it was becoming an increasingly overwhelming burden for her. But like nature itself, Julie abhorred a vacuum. Whenever one occurred, whenever a pressing need appeared and no one else came forward to deal with it, Julie stepped up and took it on.

At the end of a particularly long and trying day back then, a day filled with dozens of other tribulations, which Julie had already struggled to resolve, she had been attending to one of those myriad troubles. She was trying to fix a leaky pipe in a dark basement corner. It was spewing icy water in her face as she struggled alone with an outsized wrench to shut it off. When the heavy wrench slipped and bashed her knuckles, painfully bloodying them, she finally lost control, beating the iron tool furiously against the pipe in an angry tantrum, then slamming it to the concrete floor while her diminutive body shook with infuriated sobs.

The oldest member of her company was passing and saw Julie's distress. Ruby Brown, gray-haired and seventy-five years old, came immediately to Julie's aid. The young intern literally collapsed into Ruby's grandmotherly arms, saying that she simply wasn't up to the challenges of this kind of leadership. She was just an intern, not some kind of rebel leader. Julie couldn't handle it. She wanted out. Old Ruby held her tightly, quietly saying that these were the times that tried men's souls. And women's. Then she gazed into Julie's eyes and went on, "I'll tell you why we all look to you: because you're a Natural Leader."

"Oh, but Ruby," Julie said through exhausted tears, "I don't feel that."

"It doesn't matter," the older lady said confidently, "*we* feel it." Then she focused on Julie's liquid blue eyes to drive home the point, "Trust yourself, Juliet. Trust your instincts."

Julie tried to absorb the advice, yet she was unconvinced she truly had the mettle that Ruby ascribed to her. "But what if I don't know all the answers?"

The older woman looked away momentarily, considering,

then she finally met Julie's eyes again and shrugged. "Fake it. What the hell. We won't know the difference."

Julie had laughed through her tears in that moment. And two decades later it still made her smile to think about it. Julie certainly hadn't always been right, but her batting average was well above five hundred.

A few years later, Ruby Brown was killed, shot in the back by a teenage Teammate. But Julie felt that the wise older woman was nonetheless always with her. And when Julie delivered a little half-breed girl whose mother died without giving the child a name, Julie memorialized her dear old friend by passing along her name to the infant who became Julie's own adopted daughter.

And now, when faced with perhaps the biggest decision she'd ever faced as a leader, a decision that might either mean the end of the Resistance or its salvation, Julie remembered old Ruby's wisdom and sage advice. Julie studied the Zedti carefully, weighed all the options, looked deep within her heart, and went with her instincts. She inhaled a deep breath and decided to take the three aliens into the confidence of the Resistance.

In the communications truck at the Resistance headquarters Margarita was standing beside a rack of small screens. Their sizes were mismatched and many had been jury-rigged to fit into the old metal rack. The screens showed glimpses of various cities in other countries as she explained to the Zedti, "We coordinate 207 Resistance cells worldwide. What you see here in this warehouse is typical of our operations in cities around this country and the world. We're linked by radio channels that Ysabel encrypted. The encoding also makes our cell phones and two-ways untraceable." She rested her hand on the proud Latina's shoulder. "There used to be many more of us, until Diana created her Teammates."

Julie leaned on her cane nearby and picked up the story, "And we were *severely* crippled by Diana's Great Purge in 1999.

We've been regrouping as fast as we can, because we know this will be our last stand."

"We do still have a few spies among them. One in their Flagship's Centcom," Margarita added.

Ayden was encouraged. "So some still oppose their Leader?"

"A *very* few," said Margarita, "but they're devoted to us."

Ayden's strong eyes held theirs. "And what is your strategy?"

"We've been working on a number of fronts simultaneously," Julie said. "Dr. Robert Maxwell leads a team trying to create a biological weapon we could use against them. Some sort of magic bullet that would spread like a virus and either kill or incapacitate the Visitors."

"For a lot of us, including Julie," Margarita elaborated, "that poses a thorny moral question, particularly as regards those Visitors who are on our side becoming infected and dying."

"Our scientists have also sought such a biological weapon," Ayden said, "without success. Have you achieved one?"

"No, not yet." Julie sighed. "The work continues, but we don't have a lot of hope. So we're focused primarily on trying to move from isolated guerrilla warfare to inciting *mass insurrection*." Her hand had emphasized the words. "We feel that's our only real hope."

Margarita, the student of history, carried on, "Revolutions are only won when the masses of people mobilize to act. So far, most people are too scared by the Visitors' hyper-power and strength."

Julie held up a vid disk. "We're getting out more and more of these that show the truth, but Visitor media control is so pervasive it's like trying to climb up Niagara Falls."

"When there *was* a Niagara Falls," Ysabel interjected. "What the people of Earth need is a major catalyst to jump-start 'em."

Julie agreed, "Hopefully your arrival will be that, Ayden."

The Zedti was thoughtful. "Hopefully."

As Ayden and the others stepped out of the truck, Street-C who had been watching from nearby whispered warily to Blue and Gary, "You think these suckers are legit?"

The blue-collar worker shrugged. "They were fighting on our side, man."

Gary was more wary, quoting a classic Oscar Hammerstein lyric, "'If allies are strong with power to protect me, might they not protect me *out* of all I own?'"

Across the warehouse, Kayta moved closer to where Donovan was propped up on his cot wearing someone's faded Berkeley sweatshirt and a pair of gray boxer shorts. From the moment she'd first seen him her keen senses had detected something out of the ordinary and it was puzzling her. Mike noticed her expression. "What is it?"

Kayta frowned, unable to determine precisely what she was detecting. "I was . . . sensing something . . . odd."

He chortled darkly. "Probably just my bad vibes."

She looked at him a moment longer, but couldn't quite discern what was troubling her. Then she asked quietly, "May I touch your legs?"

He shrugged. "I wouldn't know if you did."

She sat down on a box nearby. Her fingertips lightly touched the skin just above and below his knees. She examined him carefully, with her eyes closed. Then she sat up and seemed to be considering several options. Finally she looked directly at Mike. "Can you stand some pain?"

He frowned derisively. "What are you talking about?"

"Do you want to walk again?"

Mike stared at her, studying her violet eyes, as Ysabel leaned out of the comm truck, calling to Julie, "Emma found out that Ruby *was* captured!"

"Oh, my God!" Julie was on her feet instantly. "Where is she?"

Ysabel was reluctant to say, "Parnassas."

"Jesus"—Blue felt his blood congeal—"she's just a kid! If they torture her—"

"Yeah"—Street-C swallowed hard—"and she knows everything." He was grabbing a weapon. "It could be worse than '99!"

"We've got to get her out of there!" Julie was headed toward the door, but Margarita snagged her.

"No. You pack up this place; we'll get her out."

Julie was more fiery than Margarita had ever seen her. *"She's my daughter!"*

Nathan was right beside her. "And they know that. They'd like nothing better than to lure you in. Let us get her out, Julie, we'll do it"—then he looked pointedly at the Zedti, throwing down the gauntlet—"won't we?"

Ayden's firm amber eyes met Nathan's and accepted the challenge.

EMMA WAS IN THE CONTROL ROOM OF THE SMALL RECORDING STUdio that she had built into the lower level of her condo. With her favorite audio technician, Westie, the graying grandson of hippies and a long-haired throwback, she had been remixing a new vocal track into her latest song. But her mind had been on the amorous morning she'd spent with Mark and even more focused on the fate of Julie's young daughter who was facing interrogation.

When the phone rang on the console she saw the caller ID and said to Westie, "Give me a second, will you?" He got the message and left her alone. She picked up the receiver and turned on her considerable charm. "I thought you'd forgotten me."

Paul was in his office aboard the Flagship, stroking a squirmy young ferret as he spoke into his speakerphone. "I could never. But I wanted to apologize."

"For what?"

"I've been pressing you too hard, I think."

She listened more attentively. "Pressing me? To do what?"

"To take our relationship to the next level," he said, pausing to be certain she understood. "So I'll ease back, hope that absence makes your heart grow fonder."

They were not talking on vid phones so Emma couldn't see Paul open his mouth to the size of a grapefruit and swallow the ferret whole and alive. But she clearly understood his innuendo. Thinking of intimate sex with a reptilian creature made her chest tighten. Yet she knew that Paul would be an invaluable source of intelligence. Emma steeled herself, took a breath, and answered in a low, suggestive voice, "My heart is fonder than you know, Paul."

ON ONE OF THE BILLBOARD VIZ SCREENS IN THE POTRERO SECTION, U.N. Secretary-General Mendez was seen with his ever-present Visitor handlers among grateful, happy young patients in a beautifully appointed children's hospital. Then he was shown saying directly into the camera, "Visitor medicine is now even curing youngsters with mental disabilities." He went on to describe the wonders of their medicine, but Willy, who was walking beneath the screen with his weak human wife, wasn't paying attention. They were warily skirting past a squad of Patrollers.

Harmy was cradling her injured arm, and feeling shaky. "I'm gonna need to sit down pretty soon."

"They may be watching the apartment," Willy cautioned as he looked about for a sanctuary and spotted one. "Over there."

It was an old movie theater, the sort that played retrospectives of Visitor-approved cinema classics. Willy paid, got the tickets, and helped Harmy in through the door. "You look so pale. What did they do?"

Tears welled in her eyes. "I told you I don't want to talk about it."

* * *

A TOUGH-AS-NAILS PATROLLER CLUTCHED RUBY'S ARM WITH AN IRON grip as he led her into the Parnassas interrogation room where she had seen Harmy taken. Though the door was very thick, Ruby had heard Harmy cry out several times. The scrappy, courageous girl rubbed off a tear that had escaped down her scaly cheek. She was determined to tough it out. The Patroller secured her to a steel chair in the center of the room. Ruby saw a drain in the floor beneath the chair and dark red stains around it. The Patroller unlocked and opened a nearby cabinet revealing a collection of gleaming, sharp surgical instruments. Some of them had long, needlelike prongs and were peculiarly twisted. Ruby feared to imagine for what purpose they had been designed. She also saw electrodes that could be attached to various parts of someone's anatomy. As she took it all in, Ruby's young heart began to flutter.

GARY PULLED THE OLD VAN TO A STOP IN A LOADING ZONE ON PRE-sidio Avenue. Caddy-corner across from it was the Euclid Fire Station that housed Engine Company 34. Ayden remained in the front seat while Nathan hopped out and went to open the back door of the van. Margarita was inside in a remarkably short miniskirt. She was buttoning a sexy, scoop-necked T-shirt that, since she was without a bra, really showed off her freckled chest and shapely breasts. Nathan was impressed. "Bringing out the big guns, are we?"

Margarita was all business. "Any distraction helps."

Nathan was trying not to gawk. "Red, you could teach a master class in distraction."

She hopped out to the street, reaching back in to gather up a large wicker basket filled with something covered by a calico cloth. Nathan couldn't help but take the moment to enjoy the beauty of her long legs and fine figure. Then she turned to him. "Just be ready."

"I'm getting readier by the second," he dead-panned.

She smirked at him and headed for the fire station.

In its office, four young firemen of various ethnic backgrounds looked up from their work as Margarita jiggled in. Their collective thought was decidedly carnal.

"Hi guys," she said, smiling like Little Mary Sunshine, "I live over on Lake. Just wanted to drop off a little thank-you for you guys always being here for us." She opened the basket revealing baked goods. "Made some oatmeal-raisin, chocolate chippers, and some muffins."

As the young firemen happily stepped closer to check out her muffins, Margarita pulled from her purse a pair of stun guns.

IN THE PARNASSAS INTERROGATION ROOM RUBY WAS FIGHTING BACK tears, trying to keep her breathing regular and remain cocky as the Patroller charged up the capacitor on one of the electrode devices. He briefly touched two of them together as a test and was rewarded by the sharp zap of an electric spark. Ruby swallowed nervously. Then the square-shouldered Visitor Patrol captain entered, closing the door quietly behind him.

Ruby went cheerily on the offensive. "You know, sir, all us dregs look alike. I think that *you* think I'm someone else, so—"

"Ruby," his deep bass voice cut her off as he smiled darkly, "we know exactly who you are."

A fire truck from Engine Company 34 was speeding south on Stanyan, passing alongside Golden Gate Park, its siren wailing. Nathan was in the driver's seat, grinning broadly like a little kid. "Man, I have *always* wanted to do this!"

Margarita and Ayden were in the front beside him. All of them wore San Francisco Fire Department fire-fighting gear. Nathan eyed Margarita's new outfit. "Definitely not as flattering."

"Listen," Ayden said, his eyes focused straight ahead, "I want to keep the presence of my team as low-key as possible." Margarita nodded agreement as she keyed her radio.

In an alley across from the Parnassas Station, Blue, Street-C, and Bryke were waiting near her sleek motorbike as Blue's radio crackled with Margarita's voice saying, "We're just passing Hayes. Go for it!"

Blue and Street-C fired two rocket-propelled grenades that broke through the basement windows of the police station. They heard a pair of small concussive thumps, then they saw puffs of billowy white smoke start to pour out the windows as an alarm began clanging loudly inside the basement.

Fire alarms had also begun ringing in the squad room above the basement as the white smoke started billowing up into the room. There was sudden confusion, then shouted orders from the duty officer and others to evacuate quickly.

Police officers, Teammates, Patrollers, perps, and various civilians were spilling out of the front as the fire truck arrived. Nathan, Ayden, and Margarita pulled on smoke masks as they headed inside, pushing through the evacuees and shouting authoritatively, "Out of the building! Everybody out, quickly!"

The Patrol captain had peered out from the interrogation anteroom into the emptying squad room. He had a sixth sense that something more than just fire might be going on. As he grabbed Ruby's wrist his dark eyes drilled into her and his bass voice rumbled threateningly, "Stay with me or I'll kill you."

Across the squad room, Margarita and Nathan hurried in while Ayden covered their backs. They shouted evacuation orders and shoved people toward the front door while scanning the large smoky room. Nathan spotted Ruby being brought out of interrogation and ran to intercept her. "Let's go! Let's go! This way, Captain! Quick!"

Ruby's young heart raced as she recognized Nathan's voice and realized that her white knight had come to rescue her. But the wily Visitor captain sensed the ruse and pulled down Nathan's mask. Seeing the deserter's face, his powerful voice boomed, "It's the Resistance! Stop them!"

The dozen remaining cops, Teammates, and Patrollers looked back. And then they attacked. Ayden's white blade flashed out of his wrist and he dismembered the closest pair.

Nathan struggled with the captain as Margarita grabbed a police pistol and returned hostile gunfire. Bullets ripped the desks, computer screens, and corkboards around her.

In the alley opposite, Street-C, Blue, and Bryke heard the trouble. Bryke lifted her sonic weapon. Its palm-sized, wire-mesh dish antenna snapped open on the muzzle. She aimed at a police car parked near the station and fired. The squad car was blown over causing shock and distraction to the troops outside who had been about to reenter the building. Then Bryke peered at the station through her wall-penetrating gunscope.

More hostile troops were coming through the front door but Ayden used his extraordinary strength to shove a heavy desk and send it screeching across the floor. It bowled over six of the incoming enemy. Nathan had just managed to subdue the captain temporarily. He grabbed Ruby, who was thrilled. But across the room Margarita was still pinned down. Bullets zinged past her and electrical pulse bursts smacked and sizzled against the file cabinets. The smell of gunpowder and burning paper filled the air as the room grew smokier still. Margarita knew by their gunfire that the troops were edging closer and flanking her.

Outside, Bryke was totally calm as she sighted through her scope. She zeroed in for a narrow surgical strike and squeezed the firing button on her sonic weapon.

Inside the squad room a wall exploded onto the cops and Patrollers, bowling them over with chunks of concrete, brick, and plaster. Most were stunned, but a few recovered to continue pressing the attack. Ayden was dueling with two, and Nathan protected Ruby from another, but two more had reached Margarita and she was definitely outgunned. Then Bryke was suddenly beside her, choking one assailant with her right hand as her left arm hinged backward to grab the second man. Margarita gasped as she saw Bryke's head twist around 180 degrees. Ruby saw it, too, and then they both witnessed an even more remarkable occurrence: two thin tubes flashed from the black Zedti's nose, jabbing down into the man's throat. In a flash Bryke drained his fluids, transforming his face into a mere husk.

Margarita was breathless. "So much for low-profile."

Ayden and Nathan were shouting to them, "This way! Quickly!"

Ayden hurried them out through the hole Bryke had blown in the wall. Big Blue was waiting just outside. He scooped up little Ruby in his strong arms, ignoring her repeated shouts of "Wait! I want to go with *Nathan!*"

Blue carried her quickly toward the alley where Street-C was peering out of an open manhole. "Come on, you guys! Hustle it up!"

Blue passed Ruby down to Street-C, helped Margarita drop in, and then clambered down after them. Ayden reached it but paused to look back for Nathan and Bryke. The black Zedti had just run to her motorcycle. She waved for Ayden to go on with the others, which he did.

Bryke started her bike as Nathan jumped on behind. "I got your six!"

Bryke nodded and peeled out of the alley as Nathan shot a Patroller behind them. But then Nathan looked forward over Bryke's shoulder and saw two SFPD cars screeching in to block off the street ahead of them. Bryke didn't even blink. She drove right toward them, gaining speed and adjusting a control on her bike. Nathan was trying his best to stay calm. "Uh . . . maybe not the best plan?"

The cops and Patrollers took cover, readying their weapons to fire as Bryke rocketed directly for them. Her head suddenly spun around 180 degrees to look Nathan right in the face. Nathan was stupefied. The effect was surreal as Bryke calmly directed him, "Hold tight to me."

Then her head twisted forward again and just as the enemy began to open fire Nathan felt the bike lurch forward faster as though something had suddenly pushed it from behind. He looked back and saw that a thick blast of ion particles had exploded out from the rear of the bike and was pushing in a powerful steady stream like a jet-assisted takeoff. Indeed, Nathan felt an odd pressure on the seat of his pants and realized that the bike was rising beneath him. He looked down to the side and saw that they had left the ground. The bike was airborne.

As surprised as Nathan was, the enemy was even more stunned. They fired wildly but Bryke was weaving through the air over their heads, providing a very difficult moving target. She continued to gain altitude, reaching fifty, then seventy-five, then a hundred feet as she banked left and swept over Golden Gate Park. Nathan was bedazzled and laughing like a schoolboy as he looked down at the flat rooftop and skylights of the California Academy of Sciences they were skimming over. Bryke skillfully guided their amazing little vehicle through the sky toward Presidio Heights. Like a kid in the world's biggest candy store, Nathan was beaming all the way.

THE TEAMMATE UNIT TO WHICH HALF-BREED TED HAD BEEN AT-tached was patrolling along Baker Street at the eastern edge of the Presidio. All six of the individuals in Ted's group were under twenty years of age and enjoyed flaunting their authority, chunky Debra Stein the most of all. As they moved along the sidewalk parallel to the circular, classically domed Palace of Fine Arts a half-breed girl was approaching from the opposite direction. She was about fourteen and wore the stained hand-me-down white uniform dress of a domestic. Both of her eyes had vertical pupils, but rather than yellow they were a sickly shade of green. She had a human nose and forehead that gave way to a dark head of hair, but her cheeks were scaly and she had no ears.

When she saw the Teammate unit approaching the girl dutifully stepped down into the gutter to let them pass. As she did she heard one of the Teammates, a chubby male with pock-marked skin, chortle to the others, "Shit, that one really got whomped with the ugly stick." His fellow Teammates chuckled and Ted forced a laugh along with them.

The half-breed girl paused with surprise when she saw Ted among them. Never had half-breeds been allowed to wear a Teammate uniform. She was amazed. Ted gave her a condescending, superior glance and continued on with his troop. After a few paces he even felt emboldened enough to comment, "Yeah, some of 'em are really ugly."

His partner, Debra Stein, didn't even glance at him as she muttered sourly, "Look who's talking."

HUMPHREY BOGART GAZED INTO THE LIQUID EYES OF INGRID Bergman and offered melancholy encouragement, "We'll always have Paris."

In the last row of the nearly-empty small theater, which often played such classic movies, Willy was attending to his distraught wife. He had gotten a cup of ice from the concession stand and held it against her bruised arm. Harmy was in great turmoil. She whispered with painful distraction, "I think it's all been a mistake, Willy."

"I don't believe that," Willy said sincerely. "Ted's just lost right now. Confused. That happens to a lot of kids, particularly to kids like him."

Harmy was staring downward into nothingness. Her face still had a film of perspiration from her ordeal, the bruise on her cheek throbbed. "It was unfair of us to ever have him."

"I know it's been hard but—"

"We should just separate, Willy." A tear spilled out.

The gentle Visitor put his arms around her. "No, I could never. I love you, Harmy."

She leaned into him, weeping. She loved him, too. He cradled her and his fingers stroked her frizzy, strawberry blond hair. Despite his determination to rally her spirits, Willy too was very worried about Ted and about their future as a family now that the boy had denounced his mother and given his loyalty over to the Teammates.

MIKE DONOVAN GASPED. THE PAIN WAS SEARING.

"Hold on," Kayta's soft voice encouraged, "I'm almost done." She was using a Zedti electrical syringe to inject and stimulate his leg at the same time. Mike was sitting up in an old wheelchair clutching the armrests so tightly that his bony knuckles were white. He had barely made it through the treatment to his other leg. The pain had been truly exquisite. Now the air in the room was getting sickeningly milky and grainy around him just as Kayta stopped the process. "There."

Mike slumped, breathing hard, blowing great puffs trying to stay conscious through the residual pain that still came in surges. In an effort to distract him, Kayta touched a nearby wall where a big red "V" had been spray-painted. "Tell me: this means . . . ?"

"For Victory," Mike said disagreeably, panting, "an old concept." He was still trying to get on top of the severe pain as she picked a small bug off of his nearby cot.

"Ah. You've got a friend."

"Your cousin?" He grunted.

Kayta smiled. "Only distantly. You and I are more alike, really. Except that humans have a desire for individual luxury. So they created technology which could leave your Earth uninhabitable." She examined the bug. "Except for insects."

"Or your kind?" He put it to her harshly, "Do the Zedti want the Earth for themselves?"

"No," she said, "we do not."

But Mike noted that she seemed uneasy about the question.

Kayta sensed that and changed the subject, fidgeting in her clothes. "What I *want* is to take these clothes off."

Mike's eyebrows went up. "Really? Well don't hold back on my account."

"On our world we wear nothing," she explained.

Mike visualized the concept. "Interesting place to visit."

She got to her feet. "Lean on me and try to stand."

"What? Already?"

"Yes, to help the nerve endings relocate." She assisted Mike, who rose about halfway out of the wheelchair. But the pain was excruciating. He shouted loudly and fell onto the nearby cot, angrily waving her away.

"Forget it, dammit! Forget about it!" He sagged onto the cot, feeling defeated.

"It will improve, you'll see." Kayta wanted to be more encouraging, but saw the timing was wrong. She stepped away. Mike secretly opened a packet of morphalyne he had boosted. He rubbed a dab of it into his ear. His eyes slowly glazed as the world turned soft and warm and his pain eased somewhat. Across the room, Julie watched him sadly, but then her face lit up brightly as Ruby ran in.

"Momma!" The scruffy little half-breed ran to embrace Julie, who hugged her tightly. The Resistance gang entered behind her. Margarita had shed her firefighting gear but Nathan still wore his. Ayden and Bryke came inside last.

Ruby was spouting privately and proudly to Julie, "You should've seen Nathan, Mom, he was so cool." Then the girl looked up at Julie with apprehension. "And I know: I'm seriously grounded." Julie laughed, wiping her own tears.

Margarita caught Julie's eye and nodded toward the Zedti. "They were rather incredible."

"And wait till you get a load of their goddamn airbikes." Nathan grinned, still on a high from his airy ride.

Julie went to each of them, extending a hand in gratitude. "Thank you," she said. Then she looked particularly at Ayden and Bryke, and added, "*All* of you."

Nathan saw Margarita move to one side nursing an injured hand. Ruby watched a bit jealously as Nathan went to her. "Get hurt?"

"Just stubbed my thumb." Margarita was rubbing her right one. He reached out to help. She hesitated, then let him take her hand. It was the first time they had really touched. A small current of feeling swept from one to the other. He felt her thumb carefully, then gently popped it back into place.

"Yow!" She saw stars for a brief second, then recovered as he continued to massage her hand soothingly. "Thanks. And nice work back there, hotshot."

"You, too, Red." He was still holding her hand and enjoying the softer, feminine side of her again, particularly since she was back in the very flattering T-shirt and skirt. After a moment she withdrew her hand and turned away. Nathan sensed that she wanted to look back at him, but that she wouldn't let herself.

Ruby watched the interaction between the two of them and then noticed Bryke looking at her. The half-breed girl went to the Zedti, extending her hand, which Bryke took into her own.

"Thank you," Ruby said, "for saving me. And for getting Nathan out okay, too." The dark-skinned Zedti didn't smile, but the expression of her pink, focused eyes reflected pleasure in receiving Ruby's thanks. "My mom really appreciated it, too."

Bryke glanced over at Julie, whose smile back underlined Ruby's statement. Then Bryke asked the girl, "What does 'mom' mean?"

Ruby was confused by the question. "What? Um, well, it's sort of a nickname." She saw from Bryke's stare that she was further bewildered. "Nickname. That means like short for something.

Like people might call me Rube instead of Ruby. Instead of saying mother sometimes we say mom."

"Ah." Bryke nodded.

"What do you call your mother?"

Bryke shrugged. "I never knew her."

Ruby frowned sympathetically. "Oh, I'm sorry. Actually Julie isn't my biological mother. Mine died when I was born and Julie adopted me. What happened to yours?"

"I don't know. Very likely she had other children."

"Okay, wait a minute"—Ruby frowned—"now *I'm* confused."

Bryke explained; "My mother deposited me as a larva in a birthing colony."

Ruby blinked, then realized, "Oh. Of course. The insect thing. That's so weird."

"Not to us."

"Well, duh, Ruby, no. I guess not. Sorry, that was very rude." Bryke actually formed a very slight grin. "So I guess you don't miss not having parents or a family?"

"But I do have a family," Bryke said in her soft voice, interlacing her fingers. "All Zedti are my family. They are all my parents, my siblings, my offspring."

"The hive thing, like Robert said, huh?"

"Exactly"—Bryke enjoyed the youngster—"the hive 'thing.' "

Ruby looked at her again, weighing something. "Okay, as long as we're into it here, can I ask you another question?" Bryke nodded. "Those things that came out of your nose . . ."

"The proboscis tubes," Bryke offered. "That's most likely what you'd call them."

"Oh, right," Ruby said blankly. "Proboscis tubes. Exactly what I was thinking. For sure."

"You have insects here on Earth with similar attributes, do you not?"

"Well"—Ruby thought a moment—"yeah, I guess we do, like mosquitoes, huh?"

"Among many others, yes," Bryke acknowledged.

Ruby suddenly felt a touch of embarrassment. "Hey, look. I'm sorry about all my stupid questions."

"I don't think any questions are stupid, Ruby. In fact, I have one for you." Ruby looked quizzical and indicated for Bryke to ask it. "I heard someone say you were twelve years old. Is that true, Ruby?"

"Yeah, why?"

"I thought you might be interested to know that I also am twelve years old."

Ruby's blue eyes grew wide. "No way! There is no way!"

But Bryke's expression showed confirmation of her statement. "Our growth patterns are somewhat different from yours."

"No. Really? Would you say that?" Ruby was still stupefied. She looked deeply into Bryke's friendly pink eyes, then finally said, "I just love getting to know new people."

THAT NIGHT EMMA STOOD IN THE DOORWAY OF HER ELEGANT boudoir. She was silhouetted by the light behind her and the outline of her naked body could clearly be seen through the thin, diaphanous teddy. She was trying, unsuccessfully, not to be nervous. Her breathing was shallow. The Visitor, wearing only boxers, moved closer and stroked his fingers like an artist's brush slowly up her arm. Paul whispered, "You're trembling?"

Emma's voice was very small, "A little."

She felt the palm of his other hand press against her side. His body temperature seemed cooler than hers. She felt his hand slide very slowly down to her hip as he murmured, "Am I your first of my kind?"

"Yes."

"You won't be disappointed," he murmured, his lips tracing along her mahogany shoulder, then her neck. Emma reacted with fear, but tried to make it appear as arousal. She steeled herself for what was to come.

17

SHAWN HAD PASSED THROUGH THE OUTER CHAMBERS WHERE DIANA'S lower-echelon aides were attentive to their evening business. After sounding the notification tone, he had been admitted into her inner sanctum. It was more comfortably appointed than Jeremy's Spartan quarters. Her suite had a sitting area with a soft couch and matching chairs near the large viewing port, which commanded a magnificent view. The nighttime lights of San Francisco twinkled directly below, with those of San Mateo in the distance.

Shawn saw that Diana and Jeremy were in the more formal area reserved for business. They were looking at a large screen that was presenting a three-dimensional holographic view of a Mothership. They watched as one of the huge segments from Jeremy's massive new craft attached itself to the underbelly of the Mothership over an ocean.

"The progress is excellent," Jeremy said matter-of-factly, though Diana was aware of his thinly veiled pride. "Within seventy-two hours *all* the Motherships will have my new plug-ins."

Shawn had been waiting for the Commandants' attention. When they looked toward him, he clicked his heels respectfully and said, "Commandants. Another husk has been reported. And an airbike was sighted."

Jeremy took the news in stride. "Ah, Zedti scouts rear their ugly heads. Excellent timing. Capture me one, Shawn."

Diana smiled sweetly. "I already ordered that. As soon as I saw those first husks. I also ordered a deep-space scan for Zedti warships."

Jeremy refused to be ruffled by her. "Good. Our Leader would be pleased. Thank you, Shawn."

Shawn bowed out, craftily eyeing his two sparring commanders. Once the hatch had closed Diana moved casually toward the sitting area. She had finally decided to broach a subject that had been preoccupying her, but she kept her tone airy and light. "I've heard rumors that you'd become rather intimate with our Leader."

"Intimate," Jeremy considered the word carefully, as a connoisseur might mull over a vintage wine. He was also enjoying keeping her in suspense. "Yes. One could say that."

"A liaison you doubtless encouraged?"

"Well, Diana, I didn't *dis*courage it." He was moving toward the hatch, which opened as he approached. He paused in the hatchway and looked back. "Any more than you did in your day."

He saw from her calculating, dangerous eyes that she felt it was *still* her day. Jeremy, however, was unintimidated. He smiled at her with a faint, private superiority and departed.

EMMA WAS STRUGGLING TO ENDURE PAUL'S ACT OF SEX THAT HAD continued in numerous variations far longer than she would've thought possible or ever wanted. He was now finally atop her, passionately pumping rhythmically into her harder and harder with his eyes squinted tightly closed. Emma was flinching and gasping in pain, which he interpreted as extreme gratification. Her fingernails dug into his back so sharply that she pierced through his faux human outer skin. Her fingertips felt his true leathery reptilian skin beneath. It so shocked Emma that she inadvertently cried out in horror. The Visitor took it to be her supreme libidinous encouragement and it inspired his action to an intensely fevered peak as he climaxed inside her. His entire body convulsed with a strange and frighteningly nonhuman quivering that started at the tip of his toes and swept in forceful, successive waves up through his body to the top of his head. Emma gasped again in fear, but her outcry was overpowered by his climactic bellow, which sounded all the more bestial because of the resonant alien quality of his voice.

After a long moment that felt endless to Emma he rolled off and laid beside her, glowing. They both were breathing heavily. The curiously inhuman quivering coursed through him again and Emma wanted nothing so much as to leap from the bed. It was only by the greatest exertion of will that she was able to pretend calmness.

At length he spoke without looking at her, "Are you all right?"

"Mmm . . . wonderful," she lied gracefully as she slid from the bed. "I'll be right back."

Alone in her designer bathroom, Emma leaned over the sink, gagging with dry heaves that wrenched her whole frame. She continued trembling with silent tears as she cupped water in her hands to wash away his spittle from her mouth and cheeks. Then she sat on the cold white tiles at the edge of her spa tub and wiped the blood from the inside of her upper thighs where he had bitten her. There was also a fine trickle of blood from within her. She sat there stunned, her stomach churning, detesting what she had just endured. She was startled when her phone rang. She instinctively grabbed for it, then saw the caller ID and wished she hadn't answered. She whispered meekly, "Hi . . ."

Mark Ohanian was in the shirtsleeves of his business attire, working late in his mayoral office at City Hall. "Oh, I'm sorry, honey, did I wake you?"

"No," she felt dazed, "I mean. It's okay."

"Just having some warm thoughts about you"—he smiled as he toyed with the chopsticks in his Chinese take-out dinner box and leaned closer into the phone—"some very warm thoughts."

"Me, too, you." Emma was choking back tears. "Um, can I call you back?"

Paul was enjoying the feel of the silk sheets on Emma's bed as she slid her satiny, cocoa butter body back in beside him. She was determined to play her role perfectly, to be perceived as comfortable and composed. "Do you think your Leader will like me?"

"Mmmm"—he nodded as he reached over and cupped her nearest breast—"who wouldn't? And particularly after what you'll do at the war rally."

"Well, I'll certainly do whatever I can." She kissed his cheek and snuggled closer, seemingly relaxed and nonchalant. "How imminent is this war anyway? And against *whom*?"

BY THE FOLLOWING NIGHT, JULIE WAS ABLE TO GATHER HER GROUP and the Zedti into a circle in the Resistance warehouse. "Emma has done some extraordinary intelligence work. She found out for certain that the prime reason the Visitors came to Earth is to establish an advance base for launching attacks."

"Using our water to power their Armada," Robert said.

"Yes," Julie said, "and our people as troops. That's what they've been building up to over the years. Emma said Teammates are already training with the Visitors' new chemical weaponry. As soon as all Teammates are trained and the chemical is replicated in volume aboard the Motherships the Visitors will attack the Zedti outposts and then the Zedti home planet."

Bryke and Kayta glanced at Ayden. All three realized that their worst suspicions had been confirmed. Nathan looked sharply at the Zedti. "So why the hell doesn't your fleet just come *now* and blow them away?"

"It is not that easy," Ayden said, "the Visitors are a true hyperpower. We must do methodical reconnaissance first."

Margarita drew a breath. "Ayden, no offense, but we need to talk to your people's *leader* so that—"

"You *are* talking to him," said Kayta.

The humans all blinked. Then they regarded Ayden with even more respect, though it didn't change his own attitude in the slightest as he went on, "We need a sample of that chemical weapon to analyze and—"

Bryke suddenly hissed and jumped reflexively to her feet, ready for combat. She was looking toward the door behind the others who turned and saw that Willy and Harmy had entered.

"She'll be safer here," Willy said. "She was arrested and they . . ." He had become aware of the three with the sheen to their skin. And their pink, blue, and amber eyes, which were all staring daggers at him. His heart fluttered with fear.

Julie understood what was happening and calmed the Zedti. "This is Willy, one of our most trusted allies. He's saved many lives and is married to Harmy." Then she turned toward Willy as she introduced the Zedti. "This is Ayden, Kayta, and Bryke. They saved Ruby's life and Nathan's. They're working with us, Willy." She turned back toward Ayden with a gesture that encouraged him to continue.

Ayden eyed Willy a moment longer, then he seemed to accept Julie's explanation, and resumed. "We need a sample of their chemical to analyze and determine its exact nature and its danger to our kind." Ayden turned his steely gaze back at Willy, who was very edgy.

Margarita had gone to Willy. "Are you all right?"

He tried to speak quietly and without showing any emotion, though his voice was urgent and nervous. "The Zedti are notorious for being devious and self-swerving." He corrected himself, "Self-*serving.*"

"You've experienced that yourself?"

"Not personally, no," he had to admit, "but still . . ."

"Listen"—Margarita touched his arm comfortingly—"Winston Churchill said the only thing worse than having allies is *not* having allies."

Willy weighed her words. He looked at the Zedti, then back at Margarita. His expression was concerned and fearful.

* * *

AT ABOUT THAT SAME TIME, WITHIN DIANA'S INNER SANCTUM, SHAWN was reporting to his Commandant, who was sitting at her conference table. She had her finger on the tail of a mouse that was sniffing the tabletop in a small circle. She was frowning thoughtfully as Shawn spoke. "The meeting to plan for our Leader's grand arrival rally has been arranged as you ordered. We'll meet at Candlestick Park Stadium at noon tomorrow."

"That planning session and the rally itself must be *flawless*. The Leader must see how we are in firm control."

"Of course, Commandant"—Shawn clicked his heels—"will that be all?"

"Yes." Then as he started toward the door, the dark-eyed Commandant had another thought. "No. There is something else."

He turned back and inclined his head respectfully toward her. "I serve at your pleasure."

Diana looked up slowly from the mouse, the tip of whose tail she kept firmly beneath her finger. "Do you, indeed?"

"Of course, Commandant." He took a step closer. "And if I may say, these years as your lieutenant have been most . . . educational."

"Then I'm sure you realize that you must take care, Shawn, never to let your ambition outweigh your loyalty."

He feigned slight confusion. "Your advice is always welcome, Commandant."

"My advice," she wanted to phrase this carefully, to be certain that it never came back to haunt her, "my advice is for you to observe Commandant Jeremy with utmost care. There is much to learn from him also. And about him. Of course any information that might impact on our person would naturally be the most valuable. And the most appreciated."

With a faint, wise smile that implied an *entre nous* understanding, Shawn nodded. "Of course, Commandant."

She had been studying him and thought she detected something hidden. "Have you such information already, Shawn?"

He met her gaze directly. "Certainly not, Commandant, or I would have already brought it to your attention. But I will absolutely be vigilant. And, of course, discreet."

"I'm sure you will. That will be all."

He bowed respectfully and exited. Diana stared after him.

In the corridor outside her chamber, Shawn breathed a sigh of relief. Then as he walked slowly away he continued to carefully weigh the options of where to place his loyalty.

MIKE HAD BEEN ENCOURAGED BY KAYTA TO TRY WALKING AGAIN. SHE and Ruby were on either side of him lending support. But he faltered, then collapsed in agony, laughing bitterly.

Kayta was undeterred. "Good. You are improving."

"Yeah, right. Look, it doesn't matter anyway."

"It does *too* matter, Mike!" Ruby was vehement. "It matters to the whole Resistance."

"No, it doesn't." Mike sloughed her off, "You don't know what you're talking about, kid."

"Yes, I do!" Ruby was fired up. "Don't you realize that back at the beginning you were the *whole, entire* Resistance! All by yourself. You were the one who discovered the stuff that started it all."

Mike was acerbic. "Fat lot of good it did."

"You're damn right"—Ruby was in his face—"it *did* do a fat lot of good. Saved a lot of people's lives, gave a lot of people hope that maybe we could somehow figure out a way to beat these bastards."

"Yeah?" He feigned innocent interest. "And how exactly are you doing on that, Rube?"

She flared angrily, "Not great, I know that! But do you think I'm gonna quit?" She swept an arm around angrily, indicating the other freedom fighters in the warehouse, some of whom had paused in their tasks to watch her confrontation with Mike. "Do you think any of *them* are gonna quit? Or any of the others who are working out of dumps like this all over the friggin' world?" She stepped closer to him again, standing tall to her full four feet eleven inches. "Let me tell you something, Mr. Donovan, your own personal rehab is important, but not nearly as important as what Mom told me you've always *represented*: The Fighting Spirit. For all the people in the Resistance to hear you were back on your feet and back in action—I'm telling you, that would be like a shot in the arm to everybody and—"

"Kid, kid, hang on"—he waved for her to calm down—"I love your enthusiasm, I really do. And I hate to burst your bubble, but even these Zedti guys are running scared." He spoke the rest one word at a time for emphasis: "We are stuck with the damn Visitors, Ruby."

Julie was passing with Ysabel and said casually, "We're stuck with mortality, too, Mr. Donovan, but that doesn't mean we should just lie around waiting to die." Then Julie continued her business as usual, looking at her compatriot. "Ysie, try to get the new Hong Kong cell in the loop next time we talk to Asia."

Julie moved on, busy and committed. Mike stared irately, watching her go. Then he realized Kayta's violet eyes were watching *him*.

"Please," the lovely blonde said with gentle encouragement, "take another step or two."

"Or ten, how about ten?" Ruby insisted with a very sharp edge of determination. Mike looked down into the half-breed's blue eyes. They were bright and supportive, but definitely, positively demanding.

A PAIR OF VISITOR SHUTTLE CRAFT WERE CRISSCROSSING IN THE BLUE sky over the Bay Bridge. Emma had a fleeting thought about how rarely there were big fluffy clouds in the sky anymore. She had heard it was a result of the water diminishing around the world. She was standing on the Embarcadero a few blocks south of the old Ferry Building. She gazed out across the dried, cracked mud of the empty harbor toward Treasure Island. She could clearly see the huge blimp hangar and she pictured the suffering patients within it. She thought of the sickly little boy who had touched her coat the night she had been there.

Street-C was nearby chewing on a matchstick and appearing to loiter while he checked out his cornrows in a small mirror, but his sharp eyes were actually on the lookout for any sign of trouble in front or behind them.

Margarita leaned against the wooden railing. Anyone observing might not have even known she was talking to Emma. "There's an important meeting tomorrow at noon."

"Yes," Emma said, "at Candlestick. They want me there to help plan for the Leader's big arrival rally."

"Good, I thought they might." Margarita nodded. "Martin said that Diana, Jeremy, Shawn, and other key aides will also be there."

Emma concurred, "I've heard that."

"If we could take them out it would very likely delay the Leader's arrival. That would give us and the Zedti more time to plan for—"

"Wait," Emma interrupted, "what do you mean 'take them out'?" She frowned as she studied the redhead's face carefully.

Margarita weighed her words and spoke slowly, "Emma, there's a terrible irony about fighting against brutal tyranny. Because those like us who're opposed to it often have to use brutal methods to defeat it." She saw that Emma was still staring at her, not certain she understood or even wanted to. So Margarita got specific. "When you go to that meeting we want you to carry in a device."

Emma felt the blood draining from her face. "What?"

Margarita clarified, "It will be a small surgical strike."

" 'Device'? You mean some kind of explosive!"

"You only have to get it there," Margarita said. "Then Martin will plant it beside Diana and Jeremy. It'll be triggered remotely once you've gotten to safety."

Emma wanted to laugh or scream or run. "Margarita. No. I mean"—she was fumbling to find words—"look. Gathering information is one thing"—she thought of her appalling sexual encounter with Paul—"and it's way bad enough, believe me, but—"

"Hey, Emma, listen up." Street-C had jumped in angrily, throwing down his toothpick. "It's them or us, don't you get it? They killed my family. My momma, my dad, my little sister. Wiped out my whole fuckin' 'hood and about a zillion others. We've got to do *whatever* to stop 'em."

Emma's mouth had suddenly gone dry. She looked fearfully at the impassioned young man, then at Margarita.

THAT NIGHT JEREMY'S SILVER SHUTTLE HAD FLOWN OUT ACROSS THE Pacific Desert past the edge of the continental shelf where the ocean now began. It had continued on some fifteen hundred miles west of San Francisco. The pilot, Gina, called back to her passengers, "Commandants? . . . It's just ahead."

She dimmed the cockpit lights so that they could all have a better view. Jeremy stepped forward and Shawn noticed that he placed a congenial hand on Gina's shoulder as he looked over it and out the cockpit window. Diana, somewhat tight-lipped, also stepped forward to look out.

The light from a full moon was glittering off of the corrugated surface of the sea a thousand feet beneath them. About twenty miles ahead of them and at a slightly higher altitude was a hovering Mothership.

"Our Honolulu ship," Jeremy surmised.

"Yes," Diana said, "although there's not much water left around Hawaii any longer."

"Very soon there'll be none left anywhere," he said as he smiled and squeezed Gina's shoulder gently. Shawn noticed.

As their shuttle drew closer to the Mothership they could clearly see one of Jeremy's huge new plug-ins attached beneath the great ship. It was drawing up a funnel of water that looked to be at least a half mile wide, rising like a gigantic, upside-down tornado sucking Earth's lifeblood up into the massive belly of the Mothership.

IN THE RESISTANCE COMMUNICATIONS TRUCK, YSABEL HAD PUNCHED up the same image, which their spy Lee was secretly forwarding from the Flagship Centcom. The freedom fighters were gathered closely, greatly disturbed.

"God. It looks like it's about a thousand times more efficient," Julie said gravely.

Nathan nodded. "Good-bye Earth. Watch out Zedti."

Kayta had stepped away from them, softly answering her pin radio. "Yes, sir?"

Ayden was also out over what remained of the Pacific Ocean on his airbike. He was several miles north of Gina's shuttle and above it. Like the Visitors he was also surveying the new Mothership device and its astonishing effectiveness at taking in the water as he spoke into his communicator, "Their progress has gained speed exponentially. Alert the fleet to prepare for attack on the Visitor Armada here."

In the warehouse Kayta stepped farther away from the others as she whispered urgently, "But, sir, you know what that attack will *do* to the Earth and its people?"

Ayden's voice held no trace of emotion. "Of course I know, Kayta. *Make the call.*"

WAITING IN DEEP SPACE, HIDDEN BEHIND MAGNIFICENTLY RINGED Saturn, lurking in the darkness of that gigantic planet's shadow, was an immense spacecraft nearly twice the size of a Visitor Mothership. It did not have the clean, simple lines of the Visitors' huge saucer-shaped star cruisers, however. The Zedti Flagship looked ungainly, irregular. It didn't give the appearance of having been mechanically constructed, but rather looked as though it had been *organically grown*. A human eye might have likened its design to the quality of termite mounds or a large wasp nest. But the wasps necessary to create this colossal ship would have been of truly Brobdingnagian proportions such as Gulliver might have encountered during his visit to the land of the giants.

Tiny craft with a similar look buzzed around it, traveling in and out of deep cavities that pitted the surface of the central vessel. Any person from Earth who looked upon the scene would have found it unsettlingly alien.

The Zedti Flagship's Executive Officer stood in the shadowy, organic, cavernlike control chamber from which Ayden had first communicated with Bryke and Kayta in the Sierra cabin. The officer was a striking, mature woman with Ayden's coloring and amber eyes. She was nude as were all of the other Zedti at various stations behind her. Data flashed on illuminated crystalline sections of the walls. Some of the Zedti technicians seemed to defy gravity as they sat with their feet on the walls and their backs parallel to the floor.

The Executive Officer was handed Kayta's communication by one of her male lieutenants. She stared at it for a long moment, then she looked sharply back at the lieutenant for confirmation. He nodded solemnly.

Still the Executive Officer hesitated. Though she was accustomed to the responsibilities of high command and knew her duty well, this was an extremely difficult moment. But she drew a breath and touched a glistening panel at her side. She spoke in the Zedti language. It had a hissing, clicking quality as though it were made up mostly of consonants. Her voice was firm and resolute. "Fleet Command to all stations. Make all preparations for imminent battle. This is no drill."

Strange internal alarms began to sound as the Executive Officer's voice echoed throughout the Flagship and across the fleet.

"Repeat, this is no drill. Make all preparations for imminent battle."

She looked back at her lieutenant who had brought Kayta's message. They were both veterans of the previous campaign against the Visitor Armada, which had very nearly been disastrous for the Zedti. They knew the situation must be dire indeed for Ayden to alert them in this fashion. They feared for their three compatriots on Earth and for the future of their entire race. But they also knew their duty, and would follow Ayden's order unquestioningly and, if necessary, to the death.

The officer turned to look through the irregularly shaped view port that bulged out like a huge fishbowl behind her. Against the darkness of space within Saturn's shadow she saw the running lights of other nearby Zedti starships flash from standby yellow to preparatory orange. She knew the lights were changing on all 177 ships in the fleet. They stretched away into the distance farther than her very keen eyes could see.

She knew that within each ship, the powerful Zedti army under her command was buzzing with activity, readying for battle action.

18

FOR THE THIRD TIME IN AS MANY MINUTES EMMA LOOKED AT HER watch: 11:33 A.M. She was waiting for someone who was late. She had dressed for the Candlestick Park planning session in a red sweater and an ankle-length peasant skirt. Now she kicked in irritation at the hem of it and paced tensely beside her Lexus parked on a deserted Berry Street. The traffic on the I-280 moved along the overpass behind her as she looked out eastward over the dry China Basin at the desolate valley of dried mud that used to be San Francisco Bay. Then a brown, rattletrap Toyota finally pulled up nearby. She hurried toward it as Street-C and

Gary climbed out. They looked hot and tired, as though they'd been working very hard with little sleep.

"Jesus! Where were you?" Emma snapped. "I'm going to be late."

Gary was apologetic. "Sorry, we had a problem with it."

"Here ya go." Street-C was opening the creaky back door of the old car. He gingerly extracted the device that Emma was to carry to Candlestick Park: a large, portable CD player.

She hadn't been sure what the device would look like, but she certainly didn't expect what she saw. "A *boom box*?"

Gary shrugged. "Little gallows humor."

Street-C explained, "We figured you could say some of your music was on it and all."

Emma was eyeing the audio unit nervously. "How much is in there?"

The men glanced at each other, then Street-C estimated, "Let's just say you want to be a good fifty yards off when it 'plays.'" He slipped it onto the backseat of her Lexus.

Emma watched, very uneasy. "And the 'problem' you had with it was . . . ?"

Gary hated to admit, "We can't get the remote trigger to work."

"What!" She nearly shouted, "Now wait a minute!"

"Easy, easy"—Gary's smooth hands patted the air in front of her—"it'll be okay. Martin's aware. All you have to do is get it to him. He'll place it."

"But how will it be triggered?"

"Automatically," Street-C said. "It's on an internal timer that's set to pop exactly at 12:05."

Emma looked at her watch again. "Are you crazy? It's already 11:35! What if Diana and Jeremy don't get there on time or—"

Street-C knew better. "Hey. That bitch is never late."

Emma looked at the deadly CD player resting on her backseat. She was barely breathing. Gary put a calming hand on her arm.

"Emma, if we show them we can strike at the very heart of their High Command, shake their confidence, throw them into disarray, then their Leader may postpone coming. That'd give us and the Zedti the time and leverage we need. Maybe we'd all finally win."

Street-C nodded encouragingly. "And we'll be on your six all the way, girl."

Emma's insides were knotting up as she stared at them, then she fluttered her hands angrily in front of herself. "All right, all right." She hurriedly got in her car and the two men headed to theirs.

IN A RURAL AREA THIRTY MILES EAST OF THE CITY, SEVERAL HUN-dred Teammates were training and being watched clandestinely through a high-powered telephoto viewer. From a vantage point within the forest that bordered the training area, Ayden and Margarita were spying on the Visitor Patrollers who were teaching the members of a Teammate unit the correct ways to use the various new chemical weapons. Margarita snapped digital photos. "I see three types of hardware."

"Four, I believe." The Zedti pointed. "See over there?"

He was indicating a pair of Teammates in the distance among the hundreds of others. One was a stocky, short-haired teenage female who was working with her partner, a half-breed male. Margarita looked through the telephoto lens of her camera and frowned curiously. "That's odd. I've never seen a half-breed Teammate before." Then she remembered that Harmy had told her about being arrested because of Ted. "He must be Willy's son"—Margarita sighed sadly—"that's heartbreaking." Even from their considerable distance and without hearing the two, Ayden and Margarita could see that the female was dealing harshly with the half-breed.

"Not like that, you stupid dreg," Debra Stein was saying to Ted. "Jesus, why the hell'd they make you a Teammate?"

He looked at her with cold confidence, determined to impress. "Because I informed on my parents."

She glanced at him a moment, taking that in. But then shrugged it off dismissively. "Well, it takes more than just that, scale-face." She grabbed the weapon, which looked like a cross between a rocket launcher and a flamethrower. "You're supposed to shoot it like this."

The weapon was heavy but Debra was determined to show him up. She took careful aim through the video rangefinder sight atop the thick barrel and fired it. The swirling charge shot across the open space a hundred yards to where heavy plastic targets had been set up. Just short of the target the charge burst into a vaporous orange cloud.

Ayden looked hard at it as he trained a spectrometer on the gas trying to analyze its composition.

THE SECURITY SECTION OF THE CHEMICAL PLANT LOOKED LIKE MOST of the other low, metal-walled buildings that were nestled within the industrial pipes of the facility. The exception was that its access doors were clearly marked with a red sign denoting that the area within was *Restricted*. A short distance away from one entrance, Charles Elgin stood in front of a control panel with various gauges and readouts near the large tank that contained corrosive acid. He was taking notes and adjusting the control panel, but his mind wandered again back to the recent night when Charlotte had died in that godforsaken hospital.

He had often heard that topping the list of psychological traumas a person could experience was the death of a spouse. And he knew that second on the list was the death of a child. Charles had become living proof of that thesis. He felt that his soul had been drained. His grief was deeper and more profound than he would have thought possible. And it was made all the more difficult for him because of the responsibility he felt to support his wife in her equally unbearable anguish. Charles had returned to the plant the very next morning after Charlotte died, because he couldn't risk giving his overseers any excuse to dismiss him. The survival of Mary and his ailing father depended upon him. So he was on the job, but he was merely going through the motions like a somnambulist.

Blue quietly walked up beside him. Blue knew about the enormous tragedy that had befallen Charles and had tried to be a one-man support group to ease his friend's heartache. Charles appreciated it as much as he was able. He knew that a great tragedy had also touched Blue's life. The big man's sister had been a history teacher. The Visitors felt that she was a bit too outspoken for her students' good, regarding the parallels between the Visitors and several of the totalitarian regimes of the twentieth century. On her way home from a school meeting one night she had been harassed by a brash Teammate unit. Several people watching saw her standing tall and resolute, refusing to be intimidated by the young thugs. But one of the Teammates bludgeoned her from behind. Then they dragged her into an empty lot between two apartment buildings and decided to enjoy themselves while they taught her a lesson. Before they strangled her they had each raped her.

Many people heard her cries but did nothing, fearful of the consequences of getting involved. Quite a few actually saw the entire incident from their apartment windows and could've intervened at the time or at least identified the Teammates later. But despite Blue's impassioned appeals afterward, no one would come forward. The witnesses all feared reprisals. They knew that others who'd spoken out about similar incidents had disappeared. That sort of crime, committed by Teammates or Visitors who went unpunished, was not unusual in cities around the world.

Charles knew only that much of Blue's story. Blue had never told Charles how he had managed to discover two of his sister's assailants; how he had tracked them down and killed them with his bare hands. Nor had he told Charles that when the others fled the city and eluded him Blue decided to fight back on a larger scale and had sought out Julie's group.

Charles was thus completely unprepared when Blue quietly said, "I need you to do something for me, man."

"Of course. What is it?"

"I need you to get me a sample of their new insecticide stuff."

Charles looked at him in astonishment. "What!" They had been friendly over the last few years and beyond that Charles felt deeply indebted to Blue for pulling him out from under the explosive flames that almost killed them both last week. But this was asking too much. "I can't do that."

"Sure you can," Blue urged.

"No, I can't, Blue. What do you need it for, anyway?" Charles saw the look in the big man's eyes and suddenly he understood. His voice dropped to a whisper. "Oh, my God. You're with the Resistance!"

"Come on, man. That new chemical is a weapon. All I need is a tiny sample."

Charles's voice took on a pleading tone. "Blue . . ."

"You got access, Charlie. I don't." Blue was glancing around to be certain they weren't being observed. There was only a half-breed maintenance worker picking up trash among the pipes and the scaly girl was well out of earshot. "You can do it."

"Yes, I do have access," Charles said tensely, "but if they catch me taking anything out I'll not only lose that access, I'll lose my job. Then probably get transported and my whole family would be history." Charles's stomach had begun to tighten. He took off his glasses and rubbed his eyes. "I've already lost my daughter, for God's sake."

"And I've lost my sister. Charlie, please"—Blue grasped his arm insistently—"we're all gonna lose everything unless we fight back."

The scientist shook his head adamantly. "I know I owe you, Blue, but I can't do this. I can't. I won't."

Charles jammed his glasses back on and walked nervously away. Blue watched him go, then he looked back at the door marked *Restricted*.

EMMA WAS DRIVING HER LEXUS SOUTHBOUND ALONG THIRD STREET, which paralleled the arid bay on her left. The traffic was sluggish but moving consistently. She was stiff with apprehension. She was just passing the abandoned Bethlehem Shipyards as she glanced at the LCD clock on her dashboard that showed the time to be 11:43.

Then a sudden burst of noise made Emma jump out of her skin. It was her cell phone. She grabbed for it angrily. "Yes? Hello?"

She heard Mark's cheerful voice say, "Good morning, how're you doing?"

"Oh, just fine," she said lightly as she glanced at the explosive device on her backseat.

"Are you already on the road?"

"Yes, I'm over on Third, why?" For some reason, Emma felt a tiny dark cloud appearing.

"Oh, too bad," he said with obvious disappointment. Emma had noted that Mark's voice sounded as though he was also on a mobile phone, which indeed he was. He was speaking to her from the expansive black leather backseat of his mayoral limousine. Two of his aides sat facing him, going over some notes and schedules as he spoke, "I thought I might try to pick you up so we could go down there together."

"Down where?" Her dark cloud was increasing in size.

"To Candlestick."

Icicles crystallized in Emma's veins. *"You're* going to that planning session?"

"The mayor's work is never done." He chuckled as he took a sheaf of papers that one of his aides extended to him.

Emma envisioned the conference room at Candlestick. She thought of Mark sitting there near Diana and the others. And what would happen at 12:05. "Where are you now?"

"Just leaving City Hall"—he glanced out at the motorcycle cops preceding his car—"but I've got an escort so I'll probably beat you there."

"Mark, listen"—Emma's mind was racing—"I need you to . . ."

When she paused he frowned curiously. "To what?"

"I've got to talk to you beforehand." She was scanning the GPS map on her car's instrument panel to show the area around Candlestick. "Look, meet me at Gilman Park. It's on Griffith just north of the stadium. I can't get there till about ten after twelve. But it's vital that you meet me there."

He was confused. "But, Emma, the meeting is at noon. We'll both be late for it."

"Better late than never. Please. You've got to do this for me. Ten after twelve." She waited but heard nothing. "Mark?"

"Yeah, I'm here." He was weighing her intensity against his own responsibilities. He finally said, "All right."

Emma clicked off the cell phone and chewed her lip nervously as she glanced again at her clock: 11:45.

AT THE RURAL TRAINING AREA, A NUMBER OF VIPS WERE SURVEYING the Visitor Patrollers as they instructed the dozens of Teammate units in the proper use of the new chemical weapons. The observers watched from atop a raised, tented platform that had been set up especially for them. It was about ten feet higher than the wide field, which was surrounded by forest and a stretch of marshland that had long since dried up. A pair of Air-Pats were gliding overhead, patrolling the perimeter.

Some twenty yards directly in front of the observers, the firing line was closely monitored by many Patrollers while others of their kind educated the myriad Teammates in the hands-on operation of the new weapons systems. The targets were a hundred yards beyond and downwind.

J. D. Oliver and several of his aides were intently watching this field test of their chemical. A smaller, thin man with white hair stood nearby quietly dictating notes to an assistant. Alexander Smithson owned the armament firm that had worked with Visitor technicians using their designs to create the actual weapons and the support hardware. His factories had benefited greatly from being retooled to supply the thousands of guns that had come off of his assembly lines.

Commandant Jeremy was also watching the training very closely, as was Shawn who was there as Diana's representative. Oliver puffed up proudly to them, "I must say, they all seem to be learning very quickly, sir."

"Not quickly enough," Jeremy said with effete displeasure. "Double their hours, Shawn."

"Very good, sir"—Shawn looked at two other Visitor functionaries nearby—"Lynette, you and Albert see to that." The two whom he addressed nodded and seeing that Jeremy was preparing to leave they gave him the palm-up salute.

"Let's get to this Candlestick place," Jeremy said to Shawn, "Diana is never late and I don't wish to be."

Shawn clicked his heels and bowed. "Very well, Commandant." Then Shawn followed Jeremy as he walked down the metal steps and to the nearby silver shuttle. At the bottom of the ramp Gina snapped to attention as Jeremy brushed past her and went aboard. Shawn, trailing slightly behind his superior, slowed as his eyes meet Gina's.

She gazed back at him curiously. "Yes?"

"Just thinking what a privilege it is to be flown personally by our newest Wing Commander," he said with a knowing grin.

Gina colored slightly, but said only, "It's my pleasure, sir."

"On the contrary," he said, with his lips pursing slightly, "I'm sure that it's all of our pleasures, isn't it?"

He held her eyes a moment longer, then climbed aboard. She studied him a moment, sensing that he was not someone to turn her back on.

From Margarita and Ayden's secret vantage point beneath a stand of elm trees nearby they heard the whine of the shuttle's magnetic engine starting up. Then they watched as it lifted off, passing almost directly overhead. Margarita had often noted how the pattern on the underside of their craft bore a resemblance to the scales of a large reptile.

"They should be headed for your Candlestick Park," Ayden said as he watched them pass over the trees and out of sight.

Margarita checked her watch. "I hope Emma's on schedule."

GARY WAS ALSO LOOKING AT HIS WATCH, WHICH SHOWED 11:50. THE rattletrap Toyota, which Street-C was driving with Gary at his side, was about half a block behind Emma's car on congested Third Street.

Gary inhaled nervously, then frowned with distaste. "I hate the way this car smells."

"Sorta like an old taxicab, huh," Street-C agreed. "Like about three hundred people been sick in it."

"Yeah," Gary said, swallowing hard, "I may make it three hundred and one." He looked out toward the back of Emma's car ahead of theirs. "But so far so good, I guess."

"Shit, man!" Street-C pounded the steering wheel.

"What, what, what?!" Gary looked around and behind them.

"You shouldn't have said nothing. Look!" He was pointing in front of them and upward. Gary saw that one of the Airborne Visitor Patrol craft was dropping down directly behind Emma's car. Its red lights were flashing.

Emma's heart skipped a beat when she saw the craft's flashers in her rearview and she practically fibrillated when she heard an amplified Visitor voice commanding her, "In the Lexus. Pull over and stop."

Emma couldn't believe it. She slowed to a stop on the side of the four-lane road and glanced at her clock. It was 11:51. Fourteen minutes to go. Emma's heart continued to pound as she looked into her side-view mirror and saw the uniform of a Visitor Patroller approaching. Then to her surprise she saw it was the African-American Visitor captain who smiled into her window. He peered at her through his sunglasses and touched his cap in greeting, his basso profundo voice resonated, "Thought that was you, pretty lady."

"Oh . . . Captain"—she smiled charmingly—"hi, there. So nice to see you."

"And you, miss," he said. Emma realized he was looking down at her partially exposed legs. "You headed for Candlestick?"

"Yes, and I'm running pretty late." Her antsy expression clearly indicated that she needed to get moving.

"I'm headed there, too," the captain said, then more confidentially, "but I'd sure rather ride with you than those guys. Would you mind some company?"

Street-C had eased his old car to a stop some distance back. He and Gary watched incredulously as the captain waved for the shuttle to lift off without him, which it did. Then he walked around and climbed into Emma's passenger seat.

Gary was confounded. "What the hell? Is he arresting her?"

Street-C smirked. "Looks to me like it has more to do with gettin' a little. You understand the term *booty*?"

"Fucking males," Gary said with exasperation as he glanced at his watch. It was 11:53. He looked up as Emma steered her Lexus back into the traffic. Gary's palms were sweaty.

So were Emma's as she looked back to check the traffic and also see if Street-C was still with her. She took some small comfort in seeing his car falling in behind her again, but she also knew that wouldn't help her much if she was too near the device at 12:05. She looked at the boom box on her backseat, which she knew was ticking down.

19

THE TEAMMATE TRAINEES HAD BEEN PRACTICE-FIRING THEIR WEAPONS repeatedly and a low cloud of the gaseous orange chemical now hung vaporously over the target area.

Margarita was dictating into a small digital recorder. "The weapons had been firing at targets only about a hundred meters distant, but now they're increasing their range to about twice that. We need to get our hands on some of the hardware so we can determine the precise extent of—" She stopped abruptly as she looked over at Ayden. She realized that his breathing had become very labored. "Ayden? Are you okay?"

Unable to get a good breath, he shook his head. Margarita glanced back toward the firing range and realized that the wind had shifted. Some of the airborne chemical weapon had begun wafting their way. "Oh, my God, that chemical's affecting you!" She jammed the recorder into the pocket of her faded jeans and grabbed his arm. "We've got to get you away from here!"

He managed to get to his feet, but Margarita was amazed by how potent the chemical weapon must be to have so affected the normally powerful Ayden. She needed to support his weight as they headed through the trees to where they had left his airbike. He grew increasingly unsteady.

Margarita urged him on, "Come on, we can make it."

As they reached the sleek motorcycle he finally managed to inhale enough breath to say, "You . . ."

"Me?" Margarita frowned. "Me, what?"

"You . . . better fly it." He leaned heavily against the bike, his breathing labored.

Margarita was staring at him. "*Me*!" Then she realized that he was right. He was in no condition to be anything but a passenger. "Yeah. Sure. Okay. Get on," she stammered as she helped him get his leg over the bike and settle onto the backseat. Then she climbed nervously onto the front. "Show me."

The weakened Zedti reached around her with one hand to point out the controls, which were designated in a language she had no hope of reading. "Start. Throttle. And that one is Lift. The trim is over there," then he slumped against her back.

"Ayden? Ayden, dammit, stay awake!" She manipulated the starter and felt the bike thrum to life beneath her. She was trying to get a feel for the vehicle before she started moving, but looking up she saw something that she would have much preferred not to have seen. The two Visitor Air-Pats who had been patrolling the perimeter with their propulsion packs had spotted her through the trees and were flying in toward her as they radioed for backup.

"Perfect," Margarita muttered sardonically. "Timing is everything. Okay, now," she was speaking to the bike, "be gentle with me." She slipped it into gear and the sleek machine started to roll forward through the forest. She wheeled it around in the opposite direction to avoid the oncoming Air-Pats. A pulse burst hit a tree just to her left and startled her. She twisted the throttle slightly and the bike bucked forward doing a wheelie on the back tire. Margarita yelped and fought for control, slowing the bike as another pulse burst flashed on the ground very near her right foot.

Then Ayden's hand reached around and covered her own on the throttle. "Wait! Wait!" she shouted. "I haven't got the feel of it yet!"

But Ayden twisted the throttle sharply and the bike took off like a thoroughbred out of a starting gate. Margarita fought to

steer as straight a course as possible while dodging trees. The vehicle careered across the forest's uneven floor, jostling her and
Ayden. The Patrollers soared in pursuit, lowering altitude to
drop in behind the bike. Margarita was still struggling to get control of it as two more balls of energy from the Air-Pats' pulse rifles burst much too close by.

"Ayden, help me out here!"

His voice was weak. "Lift . . . use the lift . . ."

She turned the control he indicated and suddenly a hot blast
erupted from the back of the bike. Margarita felt the downward
G-force pressing her into the seat as the bike shot upward into
the air and she exclaimed, "Holy shit!" She was simultaneously
gleeful and terrified.

The nose of the bike tilted upward more and more steeply until they passed through vertical and continued into a loop. The
strong centrifugal force of the tight loop kept them in the saddle
while they were upside down. Then Margarita saw she was now
in a dive straight down toward the forest below. She adjusted the
lift control and brought the bike's nose up only a fraction of a
second before they would have hit the Earth. Her back wheel actually tagged the ground, but she was beginning to get the hang
of flying the airbike. Even better than that was the fact that her
very swift, tight loop had carried her right over her pursuers. She
had now dropped down and in behind them.

The Air-Pats were disoriented by her maneuver and were trying to turn so that they could get a bead on her, but Margarita
swept in at them doing about sixty miles an hour. She plowed
hard into the two airborne soldiers as if they were bowling pins,
dashing one to the ground and spinning the other face first into
the trunk of a large oak.

Then Margarita dodged on between the trees, testing her feel
for the bike and quickly gaining confidence. Ahead she saw two
more Air-Pats who were obviously inbound as backup, but they
hadn't spotted her yet.

Ayden was wheezing painfully behind her, ". . . Stealth. Mode. . . . There." He was pointing toward a small control that he couldn't reach. Margarita touched it and felt a curious static electricity suddenly permeate and blur the air around them with a curious wavering.

"They . . . can't see us," Ayden managed to explain.

Indeed, the airbike with them on it had become nearly invisible, mirroring its surroundings.

Inside the stealth shroud Margarita grinned broadly as she and Ayden whipped right past the unsuspecting Air-Pats. Once they were well behind her, Margarita laughed. "Where can I buy one of these? I love this bike!"

She flew it on through the forest and was relieved to feel Ayden regaining his breath as they found cleaner air.

AT THE INTERSECTION OF CARGO WAY AND THIRD STREET, JUST PAST the small bridge over the dry shipping channel that had been Islais Creek, a water main had ruptured and was spewing a fountain of water. The flood in the intersection was a foot deep. The traffic was badly snarled in all four directions. Department of Water and Power workers had brought in some heavy equipment to attend to the problem while drenched SFPD officers were endeavoring to clear stalled cars and relieve the traffic jam. Emma's car was half a block back in the midst of the congestion and barely moving.

Emma drummed on her steering wheel with growing and very palpable fear. The captain on the contrary was completely relaxed and enjoying his private time with her. His eyes carefully examined her shapely body as his deep voice rambled, "It's just another example of how the city infrastructure is falling apart. Some people just don't seem to care about doing a thorough job anymore."

Emma wasn't really listening to him. She was muttering at the traffic, "Come on . . . come on . . ."

The captain leaned back against the soft gray leather seat and drew an expansive breath. "Don't fret. Pretty soon we'll blow through this."

Emma glanced at him, knowing that he might be literally correct. She looked at her clock as it clicked from 11:57 to 11:58, leaving her only seven minutes until the bomb sitting behind her would detonate.

DIANA GLANCED DOWN AT THE HUGE EMPTY STADIUM AS HER SHUTtle glided inbound five hundred feet over it. She was well pleased with her choice of the open air arena as the venue for the Leader's arrival and rally. She knew how the Leader enjoyed playing to vast gatherings in such a setting and how mass audiences always responded to the Leader's charisma and oratory. It was much better than greeting them merely by vid. The rally would of course be telecast worldwide on all channels, but the living presence of one hundred thousand passionate devotees would further inspire those watching the broadcast.

Diana was also hopeful that orchestrating such a powerful welcome would underscore her own many achievements here on Earth. She was anxious to rekindle the Leader's respect for her professionally and, just as importantly, on a personal level.

As her shuttle slowed its descent over the expanse of the parking lot Diana saw that only a handful of cars were present. Jeremy's silver shuttle had yet to arrive. That small fact pleased her immensely. Whenever she could one-up the snobbish Jeremy in any way it helped to strengthen her self-confidence.

Martin stood at the foot of her shuttle's ramp as she disembarked from the craft with several of her other aides trailing her. Martin extended the palm-up Visitor salute that she acknowledged with only a slight lifting of one index finger.

"Good afternoon, Commandant," he said, smiling.

She was all business as she followed his guidance toward the imposing twelve-story stadium. "Is everything attended to, Martin?"

"Very nearly," he said with a nod. Then they both caught sight of Jeremy's silver shuttle heading in from the east over the bay valley. Martin saw that Diana was annoyed that Jeremy was so close to being on time. "If I may, I'll just stay here to receive the others." Martin was indicating Jeremy's incoming shuttle.

"Of course," Diana grunted, adding acerbically, "I wouldn't want them to get lost."

Martin pointed across the parking lot. "The conference room is straight in and to your left. That guide at the door is awaiting you."

"Very well"—she cast a final vinegary glance toward the silver shuttle as it settled down onto the broad lot—"get them inside. Tell them I intend to start precisely on time."

"As do I, Diana." Martin knew how very critical it was for the session to commence on schedule. He hurried to the silver shuttle just as its ramp touched the macadam. Shawn was the first in the hatch and Martin coaxed him gently, "Good to see you, Shawn. Commandant Diana intends to start on time."

The narrow-eyed aide exuded confidence. "I'm sure we'll make it"—he glanced at his watch—"it's still one minute to twelve."

Jeremy appeared behind Shawn and followed him down the ramp, examining the impressive steel and concrete exterior of Candlestick Park's stadium as Martin saluted him. "Commandant Jeremy."

Jeremy condescended to give Martin only the faintest of greetings. Martin indicated the path for them to follow toward another aide who was in the entrance doorway. "If you'll just walk that way, sir. He'll show you in." Jeremy and Shawn proceeded as directed. Gina also disembarked and followed the other two along with three Visitor aides.

Then Martin quickly scanned around the streets that fed into the parking lot. There were three SFPD cars on station as well as two Visitor fighter craft and a Teammate unit.

But Martin saw no sign of Emma. He looked again anxiously at his watch. Shawn had been right. It was 11:59. Martin knew that the bomb would explode in six minutes. Wherever it was.

A TEN-FOOT CHAIN-LINK FENCE RAN ALONG THE SOUTH PERIMETER of the chemical plant. From there a low dusty hillside sloped downward toward a junkyard that had been abandoned and gone to seed. Nathan peered out from between a pile of rusting auto frames and a stack of discarded truck tires, watching the fence carefully. Then he spoke to someone whom he thought was right behind him, "Blue said he'd make the drop along here. Should be pretty soon now." He looked around and realized that the person he thought was just over his shoulder was actually several yards away in a flat area of the dirt lot.

Bryke was deeply engrossed in a pastoral tai chi-type exercise. Her arms and legs moved slowly, blending the military precision of a Samurai warrior with the grace of a ballerina. Nathan had of course seen such focused exercises before, but this was the first time he'd ever witnessed the practitioner's arms hinging completely backward at the shoulders, elbows, and wrists. He watched in fascination for a long moment as Bryke performed the ritualistic moves like a Zen dancer-soldier in extreme slow motion. He was captivated by the unique physical display and the quiet intensity of Bryke's concentration.

Nathan also reflected on Bryke's tremendous proficiency as a warrior. It wasn't merely her prodigious strength, or her mind-bending physiognomy, or her frightening ability to literally suck the bodily fluids from an assailant that made her so remarkable. What amazed him most was the calm focus of a true Zen master that Bryke demonstrated in this gentle exercise.

A new thought struck Nathan. He saw Bryke not merely as a singular, peculiarly alien individual, but rather as a representative of her entire subspecies of Zedti. He imagined the thousands, the millions that were like her. He fashioned a mental picture of them all engaged in an exercise similar to that upon which Bryke was now intent. What a formidable army they would be. What formidable allies for Earth's Resistance.

Nathan smiled faintly at the thought. But concurrent with that came the shadow of concern that was still gnawing inside him and Julie and the other freedom fighters. Bryke along with the legions like her and Ayden and Kayta might also be an even more formidable enemy. Could they truly be trusted?

He watched her flowing movements a moment longer. One arm moved in front of her while the other moved like a reflection behind her. It was both beautiful and unsettling. Then he quietly asked, "What exactly is it that you're doing?"

Bryke continued without pause as she said, "Training."

"Not real big on wasting time are we?"

As her smooth movements continued she spoke quietly, "Here on Earth you have mayflies. Do you know of them?"

He shrugged. "I've heard of them, that's about all."

"They are born, they live, they mate, and they die in only eighteen hours," Bryke said, intent upon her movements. "Mayflies see only one night. Only one moon. They use the gift of life for as long as they are allowed." Her pink eyes looked over at Nathan with a calm, masterful softness. "They are wise."

IN SMALL, URBAN GILMAN PARK SOME KIDS WERE PLAYING HALF-court basketball on the badly cracked surface. The hoop on the rusting backboard had no net. It banged and rattled when the ball hit it. The mayoral limousine had stopped on Griffith Street alongside the small park exactly as Emma had requested. Mark was standing beside it while the two motorcycle officers in his entourage patiently chatted with each other. Mark was feeling much less patience and also concern. Emma's voice had sounded extremely distressed but he hadn't been able to fathom what was concerning her. To the south, Mark could see the top of the stadium and he was frustrated, knowing that he should have already been there. He glanced at his watch, which indicated that the time was 12:02.

Emma's car was just reaching the entrance to the Candlestick parking lot. She was waved to a stop by the Patrollers at the gate. Seeing Diana's shuttle, Jeremy's silver one, the fighter craft, and the SFPD squad cars she realized how tight the security was.

The Patroller approached her window. "May I see your photo ID, miss?"

Emma was fumbling to retrieve it from her purse as the captain in her passenger seat leaned over and spoke to the Patroller, "I'll vouch for her, Sergeant."

"Oh, yes, sir. Sorry. I didn't see you."

"That's quite all right," the captain said, smiling.

The Patroller waved them forward and Emma drove toward where Martin was waiting anxiously by the two shuttles.

On the street outside the parking entrance Street-C drove past very slowly as he and Gary watched her car nearing Martin. Gary was trying to stay hopeful. "She might just make it."

Street-C shook his head nervously. "Ain't no way."

A thin film of perspiration had appeared on Emma's brow. She glanced at the clock and saw 12:03 become 12:04. She could literally taste fear in her mouth as she pulled the car to a stop near the shuttles. Martin rushed urgently toward her. "Emma! You've got to—" He cut himself off as he saw her Visitor passenger. Martin forced himself to slow down. "Ah, Captain. Good morning."

The captain acknowledged the greeting and climbed leisurely out of his side as Martin quickly opened Emma's door and spoke pointedly to her, "Running a tad *late*, Emma."

"Yes. I'm so sorry." She was frazzled, knowing there were only seconds to go.

"My fault." The captain waved chivalrously.

Martin took her arm quickly. "Well, let's just get on inside."

"Martin," she whispered, "what about the—?"

"No time to dilly dally," he interrupted with what she knew was patently false cheer, "come along."

Martin was hurrying her away from the deadly car. The captain had fallen into step with them and noticed something, "Emma, did you forget your purse?" She looked at him. Then at the car.

Martin felt that the moment was turning awkward. "I'll get it for you." He took a step but Emma caught his sleeve.

"Martin. No. I'll get it."

He wanted to protest, but she was already on the move. She hurried back toward the car.

From their position a block distant Street-C was dumbstruck. Gary also stared in disbelief. "Holy Christ, what is she doing!?"

Martin glanced at his watch. There were only eight seconds to go . . . then seven . . . six . . .

Emma opened the front door, glancing at the boom box as she grabbed her purse out and walked quickly back toward the men. She forced a little smile, inwardly praying that the timer might be running just a little slow.

It wasn't.

In the Candlestick meeting room, Diana's eyes snapped up sharply to meet Jeremy's when they heard the loud explosion.

On Griffith Street, Mark spun around and looked off toward the stadium. He saw the boiling fireball, thirty yards in diameter, mushrooming upward into the sky.

Though Street-C and Gary were a block away they were still close enough to feel the intense heat of it. They were trying desperately to see through the smoke what had happened.

Martin and the captain had been knocked down hard. The explosive force had also set Diana's shuttle afire, causing a secondary blast. A Visitor with his entire uniform in flames scrambled out screaming in hysteria. He stumbled over a woman who had been flattened by the concussive force of the primary explosion. The woman, wearing a red sweater and an ankle-length peasant dress, was not moving.

ONE OF THE DOORS AT THE CHEMICAL FACTORY THAT WAS MARKED *Restricted* opened as a big African-American worker emerged. Blue was very nervous but trying his best to act casual and professional as he slowly walked away. He was concealing a small vial of orange liquid in his large hand and anxious not to attract attention. His eyes were focused on a stand of vertical pipes about fifteen feet ahead of him. If he could just manage to get around them he could quickly disappear into the innards of the noisy industrial plant. He was about three steps away from the pipes when a Visitor technician in a white lab coat with a security badge dangling around his neck came out of the same restricted door and called to him, "Hey. What were you doing in here?"

Without looking back, Blue waved an apology and answered casually, "Nothing. Wrong door. Sorry."

The technician was insistent. "Just hang on. What have you got there?"

Blue knew there was no place to hide the chemical sample he'd stolen. "Nothing. Look, I'm gonna be late so—"

The technician slapped a button just inside the door and an alarm siren began to wail. Blue took off running. He saw two Teammate guards responding to the alarm and hurrying toward him blocking his route through the forest of pipes. He looked around quickly and dashed up an open metal stairway within the network of huge pipes. He knew that the Teammates would be right behind him. He ran across a grated platform, turned a corner, and collided with Charles Elgin who was understandably startled. Then Charles saw the look of panic in the big laborer's eyes. "Blue? What's wrong? What is it?"

"They're waiting at the south wall!" Blue urgently pressed the chemical sample into Charles's hand.

"What? Who's waiting?" Then Charles recognized the orange liquid in the vial. He tied to push it back at the big man. "Blue, no. What have you done?"

"Do it, Charlie!" Blue was vehement. "For your daughter. For my sister. For all of us!" He heard heavy footsteps coming quickly up the metal stairs beneath him. Looking down, Blue saw the Teammates clambering up, readying their weapons. He looked at Charles and shook him, trying to make it look as though Charles were trying to hold on to him. He shouted at Charles, "Let me go, dammit! *Let go!*"

He "struggled" for a second longer, then broke away and ran on up the steps. Charles instinctively hid the vial of chemical as the two guards dashed right past him after Blue, one of them shouting, "Take him alive! Alive! So we can get his connections!"

Blue heard that shout as he reached a catwalk on the next higher level. Stella Stein was working there and was completely bewildered as Blue ran past. He knew there was a nearby catwalk that bridged to the next section. If he could get to that one he might be able to make it to the north perimeter and escape. But his heart sank when he saw a helmeted Patroller coming toward him from exactly that last route to freedom. Blue realized there was no way out for him. He looked back fearfully at Stella, a woman he despised, but the only human being near. She had never seen such a look of terror in anyone's eyes, certainly not big, strapping Blue. He said quickly, with his voice trembling, "I couldn't handle torture. I couldn't." Stella was dumbfounded as she watched him swing his leg over the catwalk's safety rail. Blue looked down with tears in his brown eyes and said, "God save the Resistance."

Stella realized what he was about to do and screamed, "Blue! No! *Blue!*" But he had jumped.

She watched in horror as Blue fell forty feet down through the air among the pipes. From Charles's vantage point a level lower he also watched in shock and disbelief as Blue landed in the smoking vat of acid, disappearing beneath the surface. No one heard Blue's final, submerged shriek of searing agony. It was as though he had landed in the liquid fire of molten steel.

The others stared in terror at the surface of the violently churning acid for a long moment as Blue remained submerged. Then erupting up from it fleetingly appeared his bloodied, melting, half-eaten body, which burned a nightmarish imprint that Stella and Charles would ever after see in their mind's eyes.

Stella screamed again, "Blue! God Almighty!"

The Visitor Patroller had reached Stella's side, furious that Blue had escaped. "Fucking bastard! What'd he say to you?" Stella was so stunned and nauseous that she couldn't speak. The Patroller shook her and shouted in her face, "*What did he say to you!*"

Stella looked at the Patroller's glaring eyes that she could barely see through his dark visor. She was stammering, "He . . . he said . . ."

"What?" The Patroller shook her harder.

"He said, 'God . . . forgive me.'"

The Patroller angrily flung her aside with a huff and headed down. Stella continued to stare at the acid that was still smoking and boiling violently below. She was overwhelmed, not just by the horror of Blue's death, but by his astonishing dedication, his loyalty, and his ultimate sacrifice to the cause of the Resistance.

20

FLAMES ROILED OUT OF THE OPENINGS WHERE THE FRONT AND BACK windows of Emma's car had been. The two rear doors had been blown completely off along with part of the roof. The two front doors dangled open. The car's entire metal frame was glowing red-hot. Martin had finally recovered himself enough to get to his feet, but was still trying to clear his head as he stumbled to where Emma lay stunned but stirring. Her clothing and hair had been badly singed and she had been nearly deafened by the explosion. She had nasty scrapes on her hands and the left side of her face from landing on the pavement. She was trying to raise herself up, looking around dazedly confused. Her whole body suddenly started trembling violently.

Shawn had rushed out from the stadium office and raced toward them shouting, "What happened? Emma!"

The question shocked Emma back into awareness. Her panicked eyes met Martin's. She had no idea what to say as Shawn reached them and forcefully repeated, "What happened here?"

As she opened her mouth to speak Martin jumped in ahead of her. "Can't you see?" He shouted at Shawn. "Someone tried to kill her! They put a bomb in her car!"

"What!" Shawn stared at the flaming wreckage in amazement.

Martin continued on the offensive. "Help me get her up." Then he met Emma's eyes. "Are you okay? Can you walk?" He and Shawn lifted the battered young woman to her feet. She was dizzy, disoriented.

"Oh, Martin . . . I'm sorry that I—"

Again he cut her off. "I'm just glad the bastards didn't kill you." She looked into his strong eyes that were willing her to be silent and to follow his lead. Martin led her toward a nearby SFPD car as he called out to the Patrol captain. "Take this car! Get her out of here!"

As the captain hurried around to the driver's side Martin eased the shaken young woman into the passenger seat. Their faces were very close and she whispered tearfully to Martin, "I'm sorry. I'm so sorry."

He looked again into her fearful green eyes. He pressed his forehead firmly against hers for a long moment to honor her courage. Then he kissed her cheek and stepped back, closing her door. Her squad car window reflected the fiery scene behind him, but Martin looked through it to hold Emma's eyes until the captain pulled the car quickly away.

AS NATHAN WATCHED FROM BEHIND THE JUNK PILE JUST OUTSIDE THE chemical plant's perimeter, he was surprised and wary to see someone other than Blue hurriedly approaching on the other side of the Cyclone fence. It seemed clear, though, that the stoop-shouldered man in glasses was nervously searching for them. Nathan decided to stand up just enough to be seen. The man spotted him, looked back over his shoulder toward the plant, to be certain he wasn't being observed, then hurried to the fence.

Bryke kept a sharp lookout behind Nathan as he met Charles, who pulled the vial of chemical out from inside his shirt.

Nathan was scanning the area behind the scientist. "Where's Blue?"

"He's dead." Charles's eyes held Nathan's. Nathan saw profound respect in them as Charles said, "Blue died a hero." Then the scientist carefully slipped the vial through the fence and into Nathan's hands. "Here's your sample." Nathan saw there was a small slip of paper attached. "It's my name and contact number." Charles locked eyes with Nathan again, then turned and hurried back toward the factory.

KAYTA WAS MASSAGING MIKE'S KNEES AND LEGS AS HE LAY ON HIS cot. Mike had been struck by her extreme attentiveness to him since administering the first excruciating treatment. "Why are you bothering to do this?"

Her violet eyes met his for a tiny moment. "It's what healers do." She continued working a deep massage into his legs and he found himself flinching. She noticed his reaction. "It hurts?"

"Yeah, some."

"That you feel the hurt is good. When I first touched your legs was no feeling at all, you remember?"

"Yeah, I remember," he said grudgingly. Donovan hated to admit being wrong, even when it was about something that might be good for him. But he had felt as though his muscles and nerves were very slowly reawakening after a long, torturous nightmare. The last years had been an endless, swirling miasma of pain and darkness interspersed with seasons of glaring light designed to sear his eyes and dislocate his nervous system. The Visitors' treatment of him had been very effective. More successful, he privately feared, than he really wanted to know. Even so, since being rescued by the Resistance Mike had wracked his memory, straining every neuron and synapse of his brain trying to recall what he might have told his interrogators, what secrets he might have unwittingly passed along, whose names or locations he might have given up. But he felt as if he was looking down an impossibly long, shadowy hallway that was interspersed with dozens of gauzy drapes billowing one after the other, stretching nearly to infinity and obscuring the distance between himself and the truth.

The touch of Kayta's hands was healing. Her hands had a uniquely soothing quality, as if something more than mere physical therapy was being transferred to the tissues that she manipulated in his leg.

"You remind me of a guy I met once," Mike said.

"I do? A 'guy'?" She looked at him with a curious smile as her fingers continued to probe deeply and manipulate his popliteal nerve and its attendant artery just behind the femur on the back of his knee.

"A guy, yeah, a man." He saw she was still confused. "I mean, it's not that you look like him. It's something else."

"Who was he?"

"He was this strange old hermit priest I met in the Himalayas. People in the villages told me nobody could remember when he hadn't been there, which meant he was well over a hundred years old."

"Very old for a human," she knew.

"Yeah, particularly nowadays. But this old coot was as spry as a twenty-year-old. He'd go bounding up the steep cliff sides like a young billy goat."

"How did you meet him? Through your job as a news cameraman?"

"You know about that?"

"Some." She could tell by his occasional grimace that her massage of his crural muscle above the patella on his right knee still caused him discomfort. She hoped that talking might perhaps distract him. "Tell me."

"I was embedded—that means living among and traveling with—you understand?"

"Like we three Zedti are with you," she said with a nod.

Mike thought about the irony of that parallel for a moment before he continued. "Yeah. Anyway, I was in country embedded with a group of Tibetan freedom fighters who were struggling against the Chinese army that had occupied their nation. I was in some battles with them. And once I got injured pretty bad. Took a bullet in the side."

"Your left side, yes." He looked up at her, she smiled shyly. "I saw the scar. Please go on."

"And I also took a fun little tumble down a cliff. I was pretty thrashed. One of the villagers slung me over an ox and took me to the old man." Mike's eyes grew distant as he recalled, "It was a little mud and straw hut that smelled like spices and licorice. And from the first moment his hands touched me I knew there was something very special about him."

"I too have known that feeling," Kayta said. Mike looked into her violet eyes. Something about the tone of her voice suggested that she was speaking about the current circumstance. That she was referring to him. She returned his gaze steadily.

She certainly was lovely. Finally Mike said, "Yeah."

Then Kayta turned her attention back to his legs. "It sounds as though your old 'guy' was a healer."

"He must've been. There was this warmth that seemed to radiate from the palms of his hands—just like yours—and it spread right through me. It was amazing then and it is now."

"He got the bullet out?"

Mike laughed lightly. "Yeah. Suddenly he was holding it up to show me. I hadn't felt a thing. He was like a magician. He stopped the bleeding, saved my life."

"Well, I'm very glad he was successful," she said quietly, "I know that many others are glad as well."

Kayta changed her position to work on his other leg. In doing so she bent over him in a way that unintentionally allowed Mike to see a considerable amount of cleavage within her pale blue button-down shirt. Mike studied her a moment, then, "Kayta, forgive me but I can't help but be curious . . ."

She looked up. "About . . . ?"

"Why a race evolved from insects has breasts."

The lovely blonde smiled charmingly. "Evolution works in mysterious ways, doesn't it? Why do human males have nipples?"

Ysabel was passing and overheard the question. She peered saucily over her glasses. "So they have something else to pierce."

Mike looked back at Kayta. "Seriously . . ."

She continued kneading his legs. "There are so many variations in life-forms I've encountered during our travels across space, and even among the Zedti, that I've gotten used to curiosities."

"Such as?"

"The females of Ayden's species are different from mine. They excrete gelatinous eggs which the male carries to fruition in a pouch within his abdomen."

"Like sea horses here on Earth. Okay. Not so far-fetched," Mike agreed. "What about Bryke?"

"In Bryke's genus, the breasts are merely nonfunctioning remnants. Not unlike the nipples on a human male. Her species deposits larvae in a birthing colony."

"So she doesn't have parents in the sense that we do?"

"No."

He looked at her sideways. "And your species . . . ?"

"Obviously evolved more closely to Earth's mammals. We give birth to living young who require the nourishment of breast milk."

"So the Zedti species are very different from each other. But you all get along?"

"Our ancestors realized long ago that our most promising future lay in a cooperative society which welcomed and nurtured all."

"But among the Zedti, your particular species . . . is the most like mine?"

Her soft violet eyes looked again, and gently, into his. "It would seem so, yes."

EMMA WAS LEANING HER HEAD AGAINST THE COOL GLASS OF THE squad car's passenger window. Her eyes were fixed with a thousand-yard stare. She was still stunned by what had befallen her and amazed that she had survived it. Being only twenty-seven she had always felt that sense of immortality common to most young people. Only in the last few days had that begun to change. The feeling first originated with her eye-opening experience in the blimp hangar as she'd walked among the ill, dying, and dead. But today it had become much more personal and tangible in the extreme. The concussion that had flattened her to the pavement was a shocking blast of pure reality. The physical heat from the fiery explosion had scorched her badly. Had she been only a step or two closer she might not have survived. Death was a concept that had now become real to her for the first time in her life. It was something she could no longer ignore. And something she realized she was going to have to consider in all its aspects. In addition to that, or perhaps because of it, she was having grave second thoughts about her ability to function as a member of the Resistance.

"Here you go. How are you feeling?"

Emma looked up, slowly registering that the black Patrol captain had pulled the police car to a stop in front of her condominium on Clay Street.

"Oh," she said vacantly, "thanks. Sorry, Captain, but I'm still a little numb."

"Well, I guess so"—his deep voice was filled with genuine concern—"you've got to be. That was horrible." He glared out the windshield into the distance and gripped the wheel of the police car. "If I ever catch the bastard who planted that thing I'll personally take him apart piece by bloody piece."

She reached out and touched his sleeve. "You've been very kind, Captain. Thank you."

"It was my pleasure, may I see you in?"

"No, that's all right."

She was turning to open the car door when she heard him say quietly, "Excuse me, but . . ."

Emma looked back at him curiously, "Yes? What is it, Captain?"

"I've felt . . . sort of shy about asking, and this timing is certainly terrible, but I don't know when I'll have another opportunity."

"Yes?"

"Could I perhaps buy you a drink sometime?"

Emma gazed at him. She was exhausted, bruised, and battered. She wanted nothing more than to get away from the captain. She couldn't wait to go inside, take a hot shower, and nurse her wounds. Her chafed face was burning, her knees and wrists throbbed painfully. Her great distaste for any further involvement with the Visitor considerably outweighed the slight possibility of gathering any meaningful intelligence from him. She simply did not want to do it. So no one could have been more surprised than Emma herself was when she heard her own voice say, "You know, I could really use a drink right about now."

THAT EVENING, TED WAS WALKING ALONG POTRERO ON HIS WAY home. A shuttle craft cruised slowly past overhead on patrol. The usual good news about Visitors played on the large billboard vids, but Ted was unaware of them. He was ruminating on what a peculiar day it had been for him. Though he wore the Teammate uniform like the rest of his unit, it had been his only real connection to them. Like his partner, Debra Stein, the other four in his unit obviously felt demeaned by the half-breed's presence among them. He had gotten the distinct impression that rather than considering themselves in the forefront of some kind of positive affirmative action, they felt that the quality of their unit had been considerably diminished. The jokes and gibes that came from other Teammate units they encountered only served to further that impression.

For his part Ted had tried to quietly learn the ropes, to stay low-profile, and to not get in anyone's way. He ignored their racial slurs, sometimes even laughing along with their derision of him in an effort to prove he had a sense of humor and could take it. He had not expected to be welcomed with open arms, but the day had been very challenging. His years of subservience as a school custodian had prepared him well, however. He had long been required to perform menial, sometimes disgusting, tasks. He had cleaned hundreds of filthy toilets and mopped up stomach-turning puddles of vomit without ever complaining to anyone. Except endlessly to his parents, of course.

   Despite the ill treatment he'd received from his fellow Teammates thus far, his hope was that as the days passed he might be
more accepted into their ranks. Not ever as an equal—he knew
that would never happen—but at least as a reliable part of their
unit. He had also resolved to do the best job that he could. He
was ready to take advantage of every opportunity to win whatever amount of respect might be possible. He had already volunteered for extra duty even though it would be difficult to
balance it with his custodial responsibilities at Patrick Henry
Middle School. It would also mean that he'd sometimes have to
arrive at the school directly from patrol and so would still be
wearing his Teammate uniform. But that prospect made him
smile. The looks of astonishment and surprise on the faces of
the human students, and particularly Vice Principal Gabriel,
would be more than worth the long hours and hard work. They
would all be forced to think that for a scaly-faced half-breed to
be made a Teammate there must be something very special
about him.

   If it were true that clothes made the man, then a Teammate
uniform would certainly elevate a half-breed in the estimation of
all whom he encountered, particularly in the school. He had already noticed the reactions of those he passed on the street during the day, human and Visitor alike. And now as he walked
down Potrero toward his own neighborhood in the evening,
alone and unencumbered by the rest of his unit, he could strut
his stuff. He was feeling pride and a touch of arrogance as people or Visitor Patrollers who previously had never given him the
time of day suddenly turned their heads to watch him pass.

   Ted was cheered by that as he passed an alley just a few blocks
from his apartment. He heard a familiar voice call to him from
within the alley. Peering into the shadows he saw two people
beckoning to him. They were his parents, Willy and Harmy.

   Ted glanced around nervously to be certain he wasn't being

watched. Then, still with some trepidation, he entered the dank alley. Walking closer to them he saw his mother's arm was bandaged. He was afraid to ask, but knew he must. "What happened to your arm, Mom?"

Harmy smiled lightly and tried to brush off the question, "Nothing, honey. I just fell."

But Willy spoke up with the harsh truth. "She did not just fall. She was interrogated. They hurt her."

Ted was very uncomfortable. "When I heard they'd taken you in I went right down to the police station, but I couldn't get anybody to listen to me." Ted saw his father's intense, angry stare and continued rationalizing. "It must've been that nosy neighbor. The one who always smokes in the stairwell. She must've informed on you and—"

Willy suddenly grabbed his son and slammed him very hard against the brick wall. "Don't lie to us, you little good-for-nothing ingrate!"

Harmy put a hand on Willy's shoulder, "Willy, no! You promised you wouldn't!"

But Willy was right in Ted's face. The boy was shocked. Willy's nature was ever gentle. Even during moments of great difficulty he always approached a problem with calm. In Ted's entire life he had never seen his father angry like this.

"It's very clear to us what happened, Ted. Your mother gets informed on and arrested and suddenly our half-breed son is wearing a Teammate uniform! Something no other half-breed has ever done!" Willy's breath was hot. "Don't you lie to us!"

"Willy, please." Harmy was pulling at him.

"Look what they did to your mother! What *you* did to her!" Willy fumed into the boy's face. "She could've been *killed!*" He shook Ted hard to emphasize the point.

"Willy . . . No, Willy . . ." Harmy finally managed to pry them slightly apart.

But Willy still glowered furiously. "And so now you wear their *uniform!* Does that make you proud?"

"Yes!" Ted snapped back at him, his own rage suddenly gushing out. "You're damn right it does! At least now I'm *something!*"

Willy boiled over, grabbing Ted again. "Something? Really? What exactly? What are you? One of those fascists?"

"Stop it!" Harmy's voice was low, but insistent and urgent. "Both of you! Stop!"

The two men she loved stood glaring at each other.

Harmy was also distraught, but took a softer tack. "Teddy . . . Look, honey, I know you're in a terrible place. Caught between two worlds like you're always telling us. But I raised you. I *know* you. I know you have a good heart. A loyal one. I've seen it."

"Not for a long time," Willy was seething.

Ted shot right back at him with equal vehemence and sarcasm. "Oh, and just how loyal are you, Dad? You work for the Resistance while you pretend to be loyal to *your* uniform."

"That's very different," Willy countered.

Ted chortled derisively, "Oh, bullshit. It is not."

"Listen, Teddy." Harmy was determined to mediate, to explain. "When two sides are fighting and you don't fully support either one at first, life gets extremely complicated. It certainly did for us before you were born. But you know what I've taught you: that *all* life is sacred. Your father and I came to realize that the Visitors and the humans who collaborate with them don't believe that. But that the people who formed the Resistance do. They believe like we do."

"It's our only hope for the future," Willy added angrily.

"The future, Dad?" Again Ted laughed. "You want to see the fucking future?" He pointed upward toward the night sky to where the immense Mothership hovered monumentally overhead, above them and all of San Francisco. "*There's* the future. Right there."

"It doesn't have to be," Willy insisted.

"Oh, come on, Dad. Isn't twenty years enough to convince you of their superiority?"

"No," his mother said, "it's not, honey. Not twenty years, not twenty thousand years." With her uninjured hand she touched her son's arm. "Try to understand, Teddy, your father *is* loyal, and so am I, but to a *much higher cause*. And we want you with us. You're our family. We don't want to lose you to them." She reached up and touched his scaly cheek gently. "Teddy, listen"— she glanced upward referencing the enormous Flagship above them, then looked back into her son's mismatched eyes and spoke with simple eloquence—"I have never lied to you and I never will, so believe me when I tell you, Teddy: they are not good."

The teenager stared at her, his mixed adolescent emotions churning. Then he saw the shape of a Patrol shuttle passing above the far end of the alley cruising slowly and watching for any unusual circumstances to pounce upon. The boy grew anxious and took a step away from them.

"Teddy, please don't go," Harmy pleaded.

"I've got to." He took another step away.

"Teddy, no," his mother said, her heart aching.

The boy's eyes fluttered nervously. "You shouldn't be here." He moved on toward the street, not looking back as he reached it.

"Teddy . . ." Harmy said one final time, but her son had turned the corner and was gone. There were tears in Harmy's eyes. She wanted so badly to go after him, but Willy held her back. Willy was still angry, but he also was heartsick.

21

AFTER WITNESSING THE EXPLOSION AT CANDLESTICK PARK FROM HIS vantage point several blocks to the north, Mark had raced there with his mayoral escort, his motorcops' sirens wailing. He learned, to his great relief, that Emma had survived and had been driven away from the scene. He was unable to reach her by phone, but was assured by Martin that she hadn't been badly injured.

Diana insisted that their meeting go on as planned so Mark had attended it to help coordinate arrangements for the Visitor Leader's grand arrival. The session lasted for several hours, as Diana talked through every minute detail of the rally and the specific responsibilities of each individual.

From time to time throughout the meeting Mark realized his attention had wandered from the matters at hand to the questions that were disturbing him. His prime concern was to learn if Emma was really all right. At Mark's direction, his staff had continued trying to reach her but had not been successful. He wanted to understand how and why the attempt on her life had taken place. He was also puzzling over why Emma had asked to meet him but then had driven directly to the gathering.

The moment he left Candlestick Park he tried again to reach her from his limousine but was still unsuccessful. He had back-to-back meetings at City Hall into the early evening. After each of them he found a moment to try her private number, but got only her voice mail. When he was finally able to leave the office in the evening he drove his personal car up onto Nob Hill and was approaching her condominium on Clay Street when he slowed and pulled to the curb a half block away.

In the light of a streetlamp he saw Emma getting into a car with a redheaded woman. Mark was shocked. He thought he recognized the woman as being among the most wanted people in America. His suspicion was confirmed when Margarita drove right past his car. And Mark saw another female in the backseat, a blonde. He couldn't be certain because of the reflections of lights marring the window, but she might have been Juliet Parish. Mark drew a sharp breath and picked up his phone to call for a police unit. Then he found himself hesitating.

He dropped the phone and made a sharp U-turn to follow Margarita's car. He could see through its back window that Emma was frowning and talking to the other two with intensity.

Inside Margarita's car, Emma was very edgy and speaking hurriedly, anxious to get it over with as quickly as possible. "First off, I feel terrible about failing today. I want to apologize for that."

"We're just glad you weren't hurt," Julie consoled her, "Gary told us what happened. About that Patrol captain stopping you and then the traffic problem."

"It was a nightmare, I felt so helpless." Emma shook her head.

"None of the tie-ups would've mattered if they'd been able to rig the remote trigger properly," Margarita groused, then added, "We know you did the best you could, Emma."

"But it wasn't good enough and I'm sorry. I know it means their Leader won't hesitate to land now, to hold that war rally which has got to be bad news for all of us and—"

"Emma," Julie interrupted softly as she put her hand on Emma's shoulder, "we've all had our share of failures, believe me. I have, Margarita has, all of us. Nobody blames you, we're just relieved you're safe."

Emma searched Julie's eyes for a long moment, then touched her hand. "Thanks. You're very generous."

Julie looked closer at the long abrasion that mottled Emma's beautiful cheek. "How are you feeling?"

"I'm okay. A lot better than those people over on Treasure Island. And when the Patrol captain asked to buy me a drink I took advantage of it."

"Amazing, after what you'd been through," Julie said.

"What'd you learn?" Margarita glanced at Emma while she drove.

"He told me that the Visitor doctors have finally perfected eye coloration, skin sheen, and voice clarifiers to infiltrate the Zedti outposts on the way to the Zedti home planet."

Julie processed that. "So the clock is really ticking now." Then she squeezed Emma's hand. "Terrific work. Thanks."

Margarita spoke up, "The next thing we need to know is why the Secretary-General is always so carefully guarded. See what you can learn about that."

Emma looked at the two women, what she was about to say wasn't easy. "No. I can't."

Margarita frowned. "Why not?"

"Today was the last," Emma insisted. "I just can't do this anymore."

Julie saw that the young woman had begun to tremble. She spoke tenderly to her. "Emma, you had a terrible experience today. A near-death experience. It leaves you stunned. In shock. Believe me, I know. I've been there myself more than once."

"A lot of us have." Margarita tried to sound encouraging, to lighten the mood, "Unfortunately it's become part of our job description."

Emma was near tears. "But I don't have the strength you all have. I just wasn't cut out for this, Julie. To be some sort of revolutionary or freedom fighter or . . ."

"I've said those exact words myself, Emma." Julie nodded. "None of us were cut out for it." Then Julie had a thought and smiled. "Except maybe my daughter Ruby who's grown up in the middle of it." Julie pressed Emma's hand gently as she focused her blue eyes on the singer. "But you must believe me when I say that if it hadn't been for you, a lot of people would already be dead. Or being tortured. Including Ruby."

Margarita looked over at the tormented young woman. "You've got skills and access that no one else has. We need you, Emma."

Emma's head ached. She still wanted to protest but she felt the import of Margarita's weighty gaze.

Even from his car some distance behind them Mark could see

the connection and apparent camaraderie between the three women. His face had become a tight mask.

MIKE DONOVAN EASED THE WEIGHT FROM HIS RIGHT FOOT ONTO HIS left. It felt very strange to him, as though the hard, scarred concrete floor of the old warehouse were actually pushing up against him. The pain in his legs and particularly in his knees was intense, but he was amazed and pleased to see that at least they were trying to perform in the way he was asking them.

He had one arm on the shoulder of the small but sturdy Ruby and his other arm around Kayta. The graceful blonde was apparently stronger than she appeared and seemed to have no problem supporting the bulk of Mike's weight.

He was walking extremely slowly with shuffling, tentative steps but the half-breed girl was cheering him on, "Left, right, that's it, Mike, left, right." Then she began a chant: "'There's none of the enemy left, right? Left, right. We not only fought but we won, too. Won, too . . .'"

Mike grimaced at her puns. "And I thought *I* was lame."

"Fuggitaboutit"—Ruby grinned—"you're doing great!"

"You have improved, Mike." Kayta was watching his legs carefully. Though the steps were tiny and Kayta was bearing a good deal of his weight, Mike realized that there might be some hope after all. "You're doing very well," Kayta said encouragingly.

"Thanks to you"—he looked at her with grudging fondness, then at Ruby—"both of you."

Kayta accepted it lightly, as a matter of course. "On my world everyone helps everyone for the good of all." She looked into his eyes with a private softness that warmed him and definitely caught Ruby's attention. It was the way Ruby had found herself looking at Nathan more often than not.

"Ah," Ruby said after a moment, "like ants or bees, huh? So is your planet just one big hive? Or more like Earth?"

"It's mostly beautiful desert." Kayta's eyes grew distant, she seemed to be squinting slightly in her world's sunlight and looking at its surface as she described, "Constantly flowering with some plants you'd likely recognize, but others that are much larger and different from those here on Earth."

"Are there mountains, too, and oceans?" Ruby's curiosity was piqued.

"Our mountains are considerably taller than those of Earth. Many are younger than yours, more sharp and rugged."

"Because they haven't been weathered as much," Mike suggested.

"That's correct."

Ruby was intrigued. "What about oceans?"

"We have no oceans, however we do have many small seas and lakes."

"The climate?" Mike questioned.

"Is hotter than yours," Kayta said. "The air is very clear and clean, warmed by our great yellow sun and its small companion star."

Mike frowned curiously. "Really?" He was about to question her further when Nathan and Bryke entered. Gary and several others gathered quickly as Bryke held out the vial to Kayta.

"The chemical to analyze," said the dark-skinned Zedti.

"You got it! Fabulous." Gary's enthusiasm spoke for what all the others were feeling. Kayta eased Mike back down into his wheelchair, then very carefully took the vial of chemical.

"But there's also bad news," Nathan said solemnly as he looked around at all of them. "We lost Blue."

"Oh, no!" Ruby cried out. She stared at Nathan, then her tears overflowed. "Not Blue. Not Blue, dammit!" She turned away embarrassed, but she needn't have been. Everyone had felt the same crushing blow, the breath taken out of them. They stood silently, absorbing the enormous loss, mentally honoring yet another fallen hero. Blue had been such a big, physical presence among them, so strong and robust. He was a pillar of the movement. His sudden absence left a huge empty space. Each of those present reflected personally upon what their beloved companion had meant to them.

After an extended, respectful moment, Kayta eased quietly toward the biomedical truck to start her analysis of the deadly chemical. She was unaware that Mike was watching her very carefully. He was still frowning, deep in thought. Something she had said was troubling him.

EMMA WAS WEARING A PALE LAVENDER SILK ROBE AND PUTTING A cold wrap on her wrist, which had never stopped throbbing from the trauma it received when she fell during the explosion. In the perverse way that such things happen, it was the same wrist she had broken during a dance rehearsal for a music vid the year before. It had never quite regained its original strength. Landing hard on the Candlestick parking lot had stressed it anew, though she hadn't noticed it so much until the pain from her scrapes had eased.

When her door chime rang and she heard it was Mark, she had very mixed emotions. She knew she'd have to explain about her request to meet him before the planning session. She had formulated a bogus reason and when she let him in the door she jumped into it immediately to head off his questioning. She said she had wanted to tell him that she thought she was pregnant, but that by this evening she had discovered it was a false alarm. She said that she was prevented from reaching their rendezvous when the Patrol captain had stopped her and ridden on with her to the planning session, insisting that they be on time. She saw that he seemed to take her excuses on their face value. But while he was genuinely relieved that she hadn't been seriously harmed in the explosion, Emma sensed that he also seemed very distracted. She decided to continue treading lightly.

Mark poured himself a straight Scotch in one of her cut-crystal glasses and sat down on her overstuffed couch. But she saw that he wasn't relaxing back into it as he usually did. He sipped his drink with a frown as he watched her applying the cold pack to her wrist. She asked him about what had transpired at the planning session, what his office would be responsible for and such. He filled her in and also told her what Diana would expect of her, primarily to sing an opening song at the ceremony. Throughout their small talk she was aware that he had continued to study her carefully.

She finally eased onto the couch near him and asked who else had been at the meeting. After he had enumerated the various people, including the chief of San Francisco's police, the head of the California Highway Patrol, the Candlestick Park functionaries and several others, Emma casually asked if the U.N. Secretary-General had been included since he would likely be at the rally to welcome the Visitor Leader.

"Yes, he will definitely be there," Mark said as he looked steadily at Emma, "but he wasn't at the meeting."

Emma did her best to make it appear as though a thought had just occurred to her, "You know, Mark, every time I see Secretary Mendez it seems like he's being very closely guarded by Visitor Patrollers. Have you ever noticed that?"

"Yes," he said, watching her, "I suppose I have."

She scrunched her pretty face with curiosity. "I wonder why that is?"

"Well"—he tossed back the last of his Scotch and looked at her—"perhaps the Secretary-General's kept under close guard because he's a very important man . . ."

"Yeah, that's obvious," she acknowledged, "but still, it seems like—"

"Or perhaps," he interrupted sharply, "perhaps he's kept closely guarded to keep him away from spies. Like you."

"What?" Emma emitted a nervous laugh as though the idea

was outlandish. "Oh, yeah, I can just imagine that. I'd make a really great spy."

"Emma"—he sat his glass down onto her marble coffee table with careful emphasis—"I *saw* you tonight"—he was staring directly into her green eyes—"in their car."

She felt an unnerving chill but tried to lightly dodge his insinuation. "What? Whose car?" Then as she pretended to think back, "Oh, there were a couple of musician fans I was talking to, but . . ." Mark continued to stare silently at her. It was withering. She saw that there was no escape. She sat quietly for a full thirty seconds with him staring at her before she finally spoke quietly, "Mark, listen, it's not what you think."

"Oh"—he chuckled darkly, his sarcasm evident—"it's *not* you pretending to care about me just to milk me for information or—"

"I'm not pretending, I *do* care about you." She reached for his hand but he drew it back. "Why do you think I asked you to meet me away from Candlestick? It was to keep you away from that planning session."

"Because you knew a bomb was going to go off?"

She was aware that it would be a very dangerous admission, but she was compelled to tell him the truth. "Yes."

He stared at her. "That bomb was meant for Diana, Jeremy, and the others in that meeting. You were bringing it in."

Her eyes held on his. "Yes."

Despite the fact that he had already surmised the truth, hearing it aloud from her was like being kicked in the stomach. His throat tightened, his voice became barely audible. "Great God Almighty, Emma. What were you thinking?!"

"That I didn't want you anywhere near that place."

"Sure," he said dryly, "that way you'd have me left alive so you could keep pumping me for inside stuff."

Emma flared up, "That's not true! I care deeply about you, Mark!"

He laughed contemptuously. "Oh, please."

"I do, dammit!" She could feel tears burning behind her eyes. "And part of the reason I care is because *you've* helped them, too, Mark. That hospice out on Treasure Island—"

"Is hardly the same as *spying* for the Resistance!" he finally erupted. "Or carrying fucking *bombs* for them, for Christ's sake!"

She yelled back at him, "Would you have preferred me to say nothing and let you *die?*" He glared at her, angrily searching her eyes, trying to divine her true loyalty. She lowered her voice. "Look," she spoke slowly. She truly needed him to understand. "I didn't want to carry that device, okay?"

"Oh?" He cocked an eyebrow. "Did they put a gun to your head?"

"No. I agreed to it because, I don't know, because I understood if Diana and that other Commandant died it might delay their Leader's arrival and give humanity a chance to—"

Mark's hands were shaking as he threw them up and said, "I don't want to know about it, okay!?" He stood up abruptly. "I don't want to hear!" His voice quaked with angry, conflicted emotions. "I don't! You wanted to save my life. For . . . for whatever reason. Okay. Thank you. But even if you did save it, how can I know this about you and not turn you in! Jesus, Emma, how can you—"

He cut himself off, still glaring down. He genuinely cared for her, too. He had had hopes of a future entwined with hers. But he couldn't reconcile his personal emotions with this shattering revelation of her secret loyalty to the Resistance.

He tried to speak, but his jaw only worked silently. He turned sharply away and headed for the front door in angry confusion. Emma was on her feet and hurrying after him. "Mark! Wait, Mark, please listen . . ."

But he slammed the door in her face. Emma leaned her forehead against it, trembling, staring at nothing, left hanging. She knew she'd been in danger when the bomb was ticking in her backseat, but now she felt far more imperiled.

CHARLES ELGIN, AFTER SMUGGLING THE VIAL OF CHEMICAL TO Nathan and the strange dark-skinned woman with him, had hurried back into the metal forest of large pipes that comprised much of the chemical plant. He sought refuge in an alcove between two massive storage tanks. The constant high-decibel level of the factory around him provided a wash of white noise that actually gave him some solitude. Charles was trying to understand the surge of new feelings that had been coursing within him since he witnessed Blue's astonishing sacrificial death. Charles's highly rational mind that had always served him so well as a research scientist was trying to comprehend and carefully evaluate the strange elation he felt since he'd completed Blue's perilous mission.

The peculiar feeling of renewal and invigoration that Charles was experiencing persisted through the remainder of the afternoon. He carried it back to his home neighborhood that evening; somehow even the Sci ghetto didn't seem as gloomy as usual. Once he caught himself actually smiling.

Even the water being cut off in the midst of his washing some broccoli and carrots for his family's meager meal didn't diminish his spirits. He felt that his vision somehow seemed clearer. He had become aware that the persistent low-grade headache he'd had since the death of his daughter Charlotte had disappeared. As he prepared the food, he tried to explain himself to Mary and his father. "It's like some sort of new energy." He searched for evocative words, but came up short. "I don't know, maybe I'm just feeling like this because I finally took a big chance and took some positive action."

Mary was methodically going through the motions of setting the places at their small table. She seemed weighed down by excessive fatigue. Charles's words had been flooding out of him, but Mary's speech was like a trickle. "Taking care of us, holding this family together, that's a very positive action."

"I know, Mary"—he hugged her from behind—"but this was different. Seeing what Blue did . . ." He relived it in his mind's eye. In his memory, Blue fell in extreme slow motion so that Charles was able to study the big man's strong, ebony face. "There was this fire in his eyes," Charles said. "And perhaps regret. But not regret at taking his own life," Charles quickly amended. "It was more like regret that he would never see the results of the efforts he'd made." Charles was profoundly moved as he recalled the scene. "But there was a sort of serenity about him, too. A peacefulness. A calm satisfaction."

Mary was somewhat incredulous. "You saw all that while he was falling?"

"Yeah." Charles was gazing distantly, back into the early afternoon. He was equally amazed at the phenomenon; his voice came low. "Yeah. I did. I really did, Mary."

She glanced at him through tired eyes and slowly set out the napkins. Charles drew a breath, refocusing on the life-affirming feelings that had been kindled within him. "And then when I carried through his mission, sort of picked up the torch, it energized me in a way I haven't felt for a very long time."

His father had been listening to it all from the moth-eaten easy chair nearby. The older man was pleased. "You know, Charlie, I saw a difference the moment you walked in. Your shoulders weren't stooped over like usual."

Charles became aware of it and a little chuckle escaped. "By God, I think you're right, Pop."

"Damn right, I'm right"—his dad grinned—"I haven't seen you like this since your research days twenty years ago. Since before *they* came."

"Exactly, Pop"—Charles took a healthy bite of a carrot and then pointed it at his dad—"it's that feeling of accomplishment or pride or—"

"But of course Blue is dead." The two men looked over at Mary when she spoke. A curious smile was working on her face. "He's dead, isn't that right?"

Charles continued studying her as he said sadly, "Yes, he is."

"Well, then." Mary nodded smartly. Somehow that seemed to conclude the matter for her and made her remarkably more cheerful. She drew a breath and smiled brightly at Charles. "But I'm so glad you feel perked up." Charles and his father exchanged a private glance as Mary continued. "I think we all need to perk up a little. Me, particularly. I surely do." She looked down at the table and noticed she had set *four* places. "Oh. Good one, Mary." She looked up at her husband and father-in-law, shrugging lightly. "Force of habit."

The men watched as Mary removed one place setting. Then she inhaled deeply again and smiled expansively, more brightly than either of them had seen her do in years. "I really am glad you feel better, Charles. Really!" She noticed the cutting board. "Oh, and you did the veggies for me. Thanks, honey. I'll get the soup."

She turned away from them, looking very optimistic.

Charles and his father continued to watch her.

22

IT WAS MARGARITA'S FAVORITE PHOTOGRAPH OF BLUE. HE'D BEEN trying to work up a homemade pizza and the results had been a wonderfully funny culinary disaster that had occasioned many jokes over the years. Blue was grinning broadly, a smudge of flour on one cheek.

She looked for a place to fit his photo into the mosaic of others that comprised the memorial inside the vid truck's door. There were so many of them. So many that she had known personally. Then she saw Mike Donovan's picture and took it down since he had returned to the ranks of the living. She taped Blue's photo in its place with tender care and gazed at his face. She recalled the story he once told her about his ancestor being captured on a West African beach. Powerful alien creatures with frightening white skin had arrived in gigantic ships with fiery weapons unlike anything his people had ever seen. His ancestor was among hundreds who were entombed side by side aboard the monstrous vessels and transported to a fearful new world where they were forced on pain of death to do the bidding of their masters. Blue was very proud of a subsequent ancestor who escaped and worked alongside Harriet Tubman's Underground Railroaders to bring slaves to freedom. The history had been passed down in the oral tradition of his people. Margarita determined to continue the story, adding the latest chapter about brave Blue.

Strong sad emotions were working inside her, bringing to the surface a flash of memory of a moment in Seattle several years earlier.

A young woman, barely twenty, was lying in the middle of a city street, her face blistered. She had been severely burned. A Patrol shuttle was in flames behind her. Margarita was bent over her, urgently murmuring, "Pamela? Pamela?"

But the woman had already died. Margarita was heartbroken. Then a pair of strong, mahogany arms had lifted Margarita. It was Blue, sweating and bloodied from the skirmish he and Margarita had just survived. He raised her up and enfolded her tightly within the protection of his massive, solid embrace.

The sound of a match being struck brought Margarita back into the moment. She saw that Nathan was beside her, lighting a votive candle by the photos in honor of Blue. She forced herself not to look directly at him and quickly wiped away the one tear that had escaped. She nodded businesslike thanks for his thoughtfulness in lighting the candle, then she walked away.

Nathan's warm brown eyes followed her. He understood her

self-enforced isolation, her determination not to allow herself to become too emotionally involved with people she might lose. Having lost Sarah, Nathan was sympathetic to Margarita's conviction that caring deeply for someone could be hazardous and heartbreaking in these extremely uncertain times. But all the same he was drawn to Margarita, to her intelligence, her wit, and her strength of character. He wished that she would open her heart to him, even if it were ever so slightly.

STELLA STEIN HAD ALSO BEEN LOOKING AT A PHOTOGRAPH. ON THE bookshelf in her modest house sat the framed picture of her family, taken three years earlier on her husband's birthday. All four of the Steins were smiling: Stella, young Danny, teenage Debra, and the now-missing Sidney. Stella gazed at Sidney's face. In the last several hours she had given in to something she never before had allowed herself: introspection. It had begun that afternoon at the plant when Blue had leaped to his death before her astonished eyes.

Moments after his gruesome suicide Stella and two other workers were conscripted to put on the thick, acid-resistant hazardous material suits with hoods and fishbowl faceplates so that they might try to recover the remains of the big man from the fuming tank of acid.

Word had spread throughout the plant that Blue had died horrifically. More than twenty-five people, both white-collar from the offices and many of the factory's blue-collar workers, had hurried to the scene and were being held back behind a safety line by the Patrol guards and Teammates.

There was very little left of big Blue, only a few of the thicker bones: a femur and a portion of his pelvic bone. Then with her net Stella retrieved Blue's skull, which was pitted and cratered appallingly from the corrosive effects of the acid. She tipped it out onto the concrete beside the tank and doused it with an alkaline solution to neutralize the acid. And then she stared at it for a very long time. It was so difficult to comprehend that only a few minutes earlier it had held the face of a living, breathing human being who had looked fearfully into her eyes and spoken his last words to her. He was a man whom Stella had seen every day for fifteen years; she often had felt his silent censure of her clever political maneuvering and upward mobility, but she had respected his solidity and reliable work ethic.

Stella wondered about him now and how their relationship might have been different if she had allowed or encouraged it. But such had never been her nature. She had always been less concerned about the feelings of others than about getting what she wanted. Stella had convinced herself that her actions were for the good of her family. But Blue's shocking, selfless act had shaken her to the core of her being. She was also surprised and deeply uncertain about why she had instinctively lied to the Visitor Patroller about Blue's final words.

Stella looked up from the skull at the numerous men and women who had gathered nearby, and she saw that many of them were crying. She wondered if anyone would have mourned her passing as they did Blue's. She had many acquaintances there, but no one had ever allowed themselves to befriend her in a meaningful way.

Stella knew that whenever workers like Connie Leonetti had been denounced over the years, though the informant was always anonymous, suspicion fell upon her. She, more often than anyone else, had somehow seemed to benefit from their disappearance. She sensed that several of the people who came to the death scene to pay their respects to Blue privately wished it had instead been Stella who had fallen into the tank of acid. She felt that more than one of them might actually have pushed her.

As she stood in her house that evening staring at the family's picture, Stella wondered if even her husband Sidney would think of himself as her friend. They had lived together for nearly eighteen years. But Stella was a very headstrong, domineering, opinionated woman who ran the household exactly the way she wanted. In an earlier era it would have been said that she wore the pants in the family. She had always been pleased that her bullish, willful daughter Debra was following in her footsteps.

Debra passed by her at that moment. Her thick legs were bare but she still wore her Teammate uniform shirt as she talked enthusiastically into a cordless phone. "No, the one that shoots a shell that *explodes* the chemical is the coolest. Didn't you get to try that one?" She paused, listening to a question, then, "No, they haven't told us either who we're gonna be fighting. Maybe some Resistance scum. But whoever it is, we're gonna seriously kick their asses!" Watching her daughter go into her room, Stella found herself frowning for reasons she couldn't define, then she looked back at the photograph before she realized her son Danny had been watching her from his doorway.

"You've looked at that picture a lot, Mom," he said softly. "Thinking about Dad?"

"Yes, of course." Stella paused a moment, then with a slight nervousness she quietly asked, "You really saw them load him onto a shuttle?"

"Yes." Danny's eyes were clear and firm. "He wasn't 'killed by the Resistance.' They took him up to the Mothership." He stepped closer, speaking more confidentially to make sure Debra didn't hear. "Was that guy who died at your work today with the Resistance?"

"Yes, I guess he was." Stella was struggling with the concept. "I just don't understand how somebody can risk their whole future by helping them."

Her son had a ready answer. "Don't we risk our whole future by *not* helping?" The boy touched her arm. "Mom, the Visitors *took* Dad."

They both tightened up slightly as Debra came from her room and passed by them, still intent on her phone call. "And did I tell you I got like a major commendation for finding that icky husk thing and shooting that Arab brat?"

Stella and Danny watched the teenager walk off toward the kitchen. Stella felt a cautionary fear of her own daughter rise within her. She abruptly shook her head as she spoke sotto voce to Danny, "No. No. It's just too dangerous."

She turned away from her son. He watched her go into her room and close the door.

EMMA WAS IMMOBILE. SHE HAD BEEN SITTING ON ONE OF THE TALL stools by the wet bar in her pastel living room. Her legs stretched down out of her silk robe to the rosy carpet. There was a tension in them and an aspect that suggested she might bolt at any second, though she had essentially been frozen there since just after Mark left. She stared, her expression grave.

Her mind seemed both deadened and spinning at the same time. She had considered immediate flight. She possessed the much-coveted Visitor VIP pass that was only given to the most key Players such as herself. In an era when travel was carefully monitored by the Teammate and Visitor authorities, moving from state to state was extremely difficult without first obtaining the necessary visas. But Players such as herself were allowed considerably more freedom. And yet, she wondered, where could she go? To her pied-à-terre on Central Park West? To her parents' home in Portland? She thought also of her cabin at Lake Tahoe and that brought to mind the wonderful snowy weekend she had spent there with Mark the previous year.

It also brought a blurring to her vision, which she realized was caused by tears welling in her eyes. The emotions she felt for him were strong and true. But she feared that he was now lost to her. And yet, and yet, she wondered if there might perhaps still be some small spark for her in his heart.

She forced herself to quell that unlikely hope and face the harsher, more probable realities. Her thoughts swung back again to flight. She could call and alert the corporate jet that was always at her disposal at San Francisco International to be ready for a quick departure. Or were the Visitors already listening for her to make such a call? And even if she were able to depart safely, would they not be able to easily track her progress and be waiting to arrest her at whatever destination she chose? Anywhere on the planet? Certainly they would.

So she sat. The world, which yesterday she had owned, grew ever smaller and tighter around her. She realized now why so many people had disappeared into the Underground. She looked at the special cell phone Julie had given her and strongly considered calling her or Margarita, but then worried again about being overheard. She wondered how untraceable their numbers actually were. Emma feared she might have already endangered Mark's credibility with the Visitors. To also bring disaster down upon Julie and the others was something Emma could not do.

So she sat, barely breathing, on the stool in her elegant darkened living room. She thought of all she had gained since she began singing and dancing in her parents' double-wide when she was seven years old. She remembered their nurturing despite their trailer park poverty, how their support allowed her to develop her talents. Emma had worked very hard and spent long hours to improve herself, to train her natural abilities. She remembered finally catching the eye of the local Visitor supervisor who had suddenly opened all the doors for her. Or at least that was the way Emma's mother had described it happening. From the time she was a teen Emma had noted how her pretty mother invariably grew somewhat closemouthed whenever that particular Visitor's name came up. She recalled how her father would smile, acknowledge the Visitor's help, and then change the subject. Emma had always thought that perhaps her parents were jealous of the Visitor helping her.

But recently, especially since Emma's own close encounter with the press secretary, she had begun to wonder if perhaps her mother had some other, more personal reason for avoiding talk about that Visitor supervisor. Emma had intended to raise the question with her mother the next time they were together. It had become important for Emma to know just how her extraordinary good fortune had been initiated. And it disturbed her to contemplate what her mother's answer might be.

Her door chime sounded with the impact of a lightning bolt. She stared at the intercom and could hear her own heart pounding loudly. Her breath came in short, shallow puffs. The chime sounded again and she inadvertently emitted a frightened whimper. Her eyes flitted frantically around the lovely living room, searching one last time for an escape route. There was none. Even if she jumped from her second-floor window she knew the fall wouldn't be enough to kill her.

Then, suddenly, for reasons Emma couldn't fathom, she became totally calm. It completely surprised her. Her breathing became slow and measured. It was as though she had subconsciously drawn from some deep well of strength within her that she hadn't known existed. She sat for a moment longer, trying to understand it, but she couldn't. She decided to simply accept the strange phenomenon because it gave her the courage to at least face with dignity whatever was to come.

She touched the intercom and spoke evenly, "Yes?" She anticipated an authoritative, resonant alien voice demanding her to admit the Visitor Patrollers.

"It's me," Mark said quietly.

Emma's heart fluttered with joy, but as she reached for the button to open the downstairs front door, she paused as her heart quickly sank. Of course he wouldn't be alone. He would have returned with them. It would have been his duty. She paused, resigned herself, and then she pressed the button to admit them.

Emma thought again of her corporate jet, of her high-flying career above the rabble and the real world. Now she felt as though she had leaped from the plane, as though she had gone into free fall from a great height and was now spiraling downward at increasing velocity. The air was whipping past her, the ground rushing toward her at terrible speed. And she had no parachute.

With her head held high she opened the living-room door and was immediately confused. Mark was alone. He looked into her green eyes, then glanced downward, extremely pensive and conflicted. He finally said, "For whatever reason you saved my life, I'm appreciative." She gazed at him, as unsure of herself as he seemed to be of himself. All she could imagine was that he had come up alone to collect her and deliver her to the waiting troops below. She could tell that his mouth was very dry as he continued haltingly, "I won't say anything about what you're doing. I do love you, Emma."

"Oh, my God," came out of her in a great exhalation as she wrapped her arms around him and held on to him in a trembling, tight embrace. "Oh, my God," she murmured as she felt a parachute open and catch her mere inches above the unforgiving ground.

Neither said a word as they held each other like two drowning people might have clung to a life preserver in a storm-tossed sea.

Finally Emma broke the silence when she whispered, "I love you, too, Mark. And I won't jeopardize you, I promise . . . I promise . . ."

"I know you won't." They stood silently, clinging to one another amid the perilous times, each listening to the other breathing, feeling the other's beating heart.

WILLY WALKED THROUGH THE MURKY, STEAMY CORRIDORS DEEP within the bowels of the Flagship. His face reflected his troubled mood as he thought back to the confrontation he and Harmy had had with Ted. Willy and Harmy had tried so diligently over the years to bolster Ted's low opinion of himself, to help him understand that despite his being a half-breed he still had possibilities if he could only learn to perceive the glass as being half full. But when Willy saw the teenager proudly wearing the uniform of a Teammate, and realized that his son had informed on his own mother, it was a devastating blow, which left Willy very near despair. Their last confrontation in the alley had taken Willy the full distance.

Willy also knew that it was a good thing he had never shown his human face to their neighbors or he too would likely have been captured, tortured, and killed.

Even the miraculous rescue of Mike Donovan had failed to cheer him once he learned that Mike's great spirit had been so badly damaged and that his attitude had become defeatist.

So Willy had decided to give himself a small dose of positive energy from the one source aboard the Flagship that could encourage him. He turned the corner, passed a hissing vent in the dark corridor with its pipes that coursed with the Flagship's flowing fluids. He peered into Jon's janitorial hovel that was part living space and part piecemeal laboratory.

The young half-breed was bent over his latest project, which Willy couldn't see, though it was clear the youth was happily engaged in scientific pursuit. When he heard Willy approaching Jon turned and his misshapen, half-scaly mouth contorted into a grin. "William! So good to see you, sir."

They greeted each other not with the Visitor salute, but Willy gripped the boy's nearly human hand with a warm handshake. Then Willy winked and said, "Take a look," as he handed some data plugs to the boy who beamed broadly.

"*The Nasus Ganilppa Periodic Tables*!" Jon was beyond amazed. "Brilliant! Wherever did you find them, sir?"

Willy smiled, very pleased with the teenager's reaction. "Just did a little digging."

"You're too modest, sir, I have searched and searched and could never find them."

"Well, there you are," Willy said, smiling.

Jon looked at him carefully, sensing a sadness beneath. He asked tentatively, "Permission to speak freely, sir?"

Willy frowned curiously. "Of course, Jon, always."

"That was a very melancholy look you had, sir."

Willy sighed and sat on a container of custodial supplies. "I guess I was just wishing my son Ted were like you."

Jon chuckled with genuine modesty and said, "Oh, I'm certain he can do much better than me, sir. Just give him time."

Willy smiled sadly at Jon, appreciating his sensitivity. Then Willy's eyes drifted to the project the boy had been busy working on and Willy's expression became one of amazement. "Jon?"

"Sir?"

Willy stood up and moved to the makeshift lab table. Sitting on top of it was a foot-tall, jerry-built mini-capsule. It was a rough miniature of those in the Capsule Storage Chamber in which millions of humans were entombed.

Willy was astonished. "Did you make this?"

"Yes, sir," the boy said as though it were not much of an achievement. "It wasn't terribly difficult." Then he added with a touch of humor, "I've certainly had ample opportunity to study the technology."

Willy looked closer and was even more dumbfounded. "What is that inside? A mouse?"

Jon nodded. "My friend Dr. Eric let me have it from one of the food carts."

"And it's alive? In stages?"

"Uh, that's *stasis*, sir," Jon said shyly.

"*Stasis*, yes," Willy corrected himself. "It's alive in stasis? Like all the people in Capsule Storage?"

"Yes, sir."

"Jon, this is amazing!"

"Oh, no, sir. A very modest effort. Believe me."

"Modest!" Willy looked back at the homemade capsule, with its outer intestinelike tubes undulating. He examined all the various electrical and hydraulic connections that led from the capsule and were attached to the small-scale, makeshift life-support equipment that had obviously been fitted together by Jon from cast-off items. Willy studied the small living creature inside. "How long has it been in there?"

"Oh, not long," Jon said with a shrug, "only a month or so."

Willy looked with wonder at the self-effacing young genius.

THE BLACK AND WHITE VIDEO IMAGE FLICKERED ACROSS THE SMALL vid screen. In the expansive Visitor laboratory which, like Jon's hovel, was also deep within the bowels of the Flagship, the Hispanic-looking Visitor technician named Teresa was trying to coax a steady picture. But the image was extremely jumpy, in and out of focus with video static and much interference.

"Come on," she muttered, "you can do it." Through the static came a tantalizing, brief glimpse of what looked to her like the inside of an old warehouse. Then Teresa was rewarded by a tiny peek at a woman wearing a flower-print blouse as she passed the clandestine camera. Teresa thought she recognized her from all the vids of most-wanted Resistance fighters. The woman looked like the seventy-year-old Peruvian named Ysabel Encalada. If that proved to be the case, then Teresa knew she was getting a live image from a hidden camera within the Resistance headquarters.

She glanced around the large shadowy laboratory chamber at the various Visitors working within it. Eric, the research doctor, was at the far end and busy with several others. Teresa wanted to shout out her triumphant achievement to them, but decided to keep silent until she could refine the reception. She looked back at the black and white screen.

There was another brief clear moment where the camera

transmitting the image jostled one way and then another, as though it were being held in someone's hand. Teresa wasn't surprised about that characteristic because she knew that someone among the Resistance group was transmitting the image.

23

THE PICTURE ON THE HIGH RESOLUTION MONITOR OF THE SCANNING electron microscope was confounding to both Julie and Kayta. They stood in the truck parked inside the old warehouse and studied the strange image on the screen. The electron microscope was the size of an office desk with a large, complex appendage on top. All in all it stood almost six feet tall. Julie, Blue, and Robert had stolen it years ago. It had been cared for since then like the precious jewel it was. It was the first major diagnostic apparatus they had come by and was the cornerstone of their biochemical lab. Julie had the unit installed into its own small truck that was specially padded and armored for extra protection. Blue had rigged additional shock absorbers onto the truck to cushion the delicate rig during transportation. Julie also had the truck fitted with the appropriate 220-volt generator to keep the microscope functional whenever they were in a location where they couldn't steal city electricity.

Julie and Kayta were using the powerful instrument to investigate the chemical weapon sample that Blue had stolen. The image on the microscope's high-definition monitor showed a webbing of octagonal shapes.

"I've never seen a viral or bacteriological structure that looked remotely like that," Julie said as she studied the image closely. "Is it something you're familiar with?"

Kayta shook her head. "Unfortunately, no."

"Not the answer I was hoping for," Julie admitted, chewing her lip. "What's the resolution here?"

"It was at your maximum, but with this device I've improved it." Kayta indicated a small Zedti unit the size of a deck of cards that she had attached to the microscope's electronics.

"By how much?" Julie asked.

"About 250 percent."

Julie was impressed, but frustrated, "And that's still not enough for us to get an idea of how we can fight it."

"Their science is very advanced. In many areas it exceeds Zedti knowledge." Kayta sighed. "What about your spectrographic analysis?"

Julie turned to another unit within the truck where Robert and two others were intently engaged. The spectrographic analyzer was about two-thirds the size of the electron microscope, but was equally valuable and complex. Robert was also analyzing a few drops of the chemical weapon. Data was scrolling and building up on two monitors and three differently calibrated oscilloscopes that were part of the apparatus. "It's still cooking," Robert told them, "probably another hour or so."

Ayden leaned into the truck. "Have you determined anything?"

"Not yet," Kayta said. "Neither of us have ever seen a compound like it."

Julie looked at the Zedti leader. "You said your breathing was impaired?"

"Yes, extremely."

"Describe the symptoms for me as carefully and specifically as you can." She picked up a PDA to make notes.

Ayden thought back. "There was a coolness at first. I paid little attention to it, but then I began to experience lightheadedness."

"You were dizzy?"

"Yes. Disoriented. And then that coolness began to grow more painful, like placing one's hand on frozen carbon dioxide."

"Dry ice," Julie said with a smile, "that's what we call it. It can cause frostbite and severe burns very quickly."

Ayden nodded. "That's what it felt like within my lungs, extremely cold and yet fiery hot at the same time."

"And you weren't even directly in the line of fire," Kayta reminded him.

"No, Margarita and I were on the periphery some distance from their targeting range."

Julie's mind was working, thinking back over research she had done herself trying to discover an airborne biological or gaseous weapon that the Resistance might use against the Visitors. She was trying to imagine how some element of that research might help them now.

For their part, Kayta and Ayden exchanged a weighted glance. They both knew what a formidable weapon the Visitors had created with this chemical. Since Ayden had felt its effect personally, he particularly had a keen sense of the terrible impact it would have on the Zedti forces. He finally drew a breath and said, "Battlefield circumstances such as Margarita and I witnessed would be bad enough, but if they have delivery systems capable of breaching our warship defenses . . ." He let the lethal consequences hang unspoken.

But Kayta understood. "The results would be devastating to the entire fleet."

Ayden looked from Kayta to Julie. "I should say catastrophic."

"We have to find a method to neutralize this chemical," Kayta said quietly.

Across the warehouse, Mike had been sitting on his cot watching them inside the truck. He had been particularly studying Kayta, still troubled by something she'd said. As Gary walked past carrying a load of vids, Mike called to him, "Hey, uh . . ." Mike wasn't sure of his name.

"Rumplestiltskin." The smart-looking man grinned back. "But you can call me Gary."

"Thanks. You guys got any astronomical data here, Gary?"

"I'm sure. In our database. It'd be in the bookmobile"—he

indicated a nearby truck—"tell me what you're looking for and I'll check it for you after I dump these vids."

"That's okay, I'll go look for it."

Gary nodded and went on about his work with the vids. Mike sat up on the edge of his cot and reached for his wheelchair. He was about to slide into it when he paused, staring at it for a moment. He glanced over at the truck Gary had pointed out. It was only about ten steps away. Mike made a decision and spun the chair around so he could grasp the handles on the back of it.

He didn't notice that over in the kitchen area Harmy had touched Ruby's arm to get her attention. Harmy nodded toward Mike. They watched as Mike struggled up from his cot, clutching the back handles of the chair and leaning on it for support. He was very unsteady and they saw him flinch with pain. But Ruby felt a bubble of joy rise inside her as Mike slowly began to shuffle on his aching legs toward the truck, pushing the chair inch by inch ahead of him.

He was about halfway to his destination when his right leg suddenly buckled. The wheelchair scooted erratically to one side. Mike grabbed for a handhold on a rickety cabinet beside him, but it wouldn't support his weight and it toppled backward as he fell down on top of it.

Harmy immediately took a step to help, but Ruby caught her sleeve and whispered, "Wait, let him try."

Mike's cheek was against one of the cabinet's cold metal doors, his jaw clenched in frustration and anger. He saw that just inside the cabinet was a medical box containing several packets of morphalyne. He stared at the drugs right in front of him. Pleasant, warm, inviting oblivion was within easy reach. But then he finally pushed himself up from the cabinet and got painfully onto his knees.

Mike heard a man's voice say with a touch of humor, "Hey, while you're down there . . ." It was Nathan. He grinned, then offered a hand to help, encouraging Mike to grasp it. Mike did and Nathan pulled him up and into the wheelchair. Mike was scowling, obviously embarrassed. He merely nodded thanks.

"No biggie," Nathan said, then added, "You know when I was a Teammate we all wanted to see you on your knees. Funny how times change." The young man gave Mike a comradely pat on the shoulder and headed off.

Ruby had witnessed it all from the kitchen area. She traded a smile with Harmy. Ruby was very pleased by Mike's effort and also by her Hawaiian heartthrob being on the scene to help.

From the door of the electron microscope truck Julie had also been watching Mike. She knew that there was morphalyne inside the cabinet, which represented the easy way out for him. She was encouraged that he hadn't taken it. Then Margarita hurried toward her, enthused about something else. "Hey. Emma called about the Secretary-General. I think we're on to something."

ONE BLOCK NORTH OF LAFAYETTE SQUARE, NEXT TO THE CALIFORNIA Historical Society Museum on Jackson Street, stood an elegant, two-story Victorian brownstone. The east corner of the house bore a cylindrical appendage that suggested the tower of an old Norman castle with tall, curved windows. Inside the first-floor window sat an elderly woman of Spanish descent.

She was in her early seventies. Her gray hair was pulled back in a bun, like her mother's had been long before. The colorful, thickly knitted shawl that covered her shoulders also emphasized her Spanish heritage. Her kindly face had become very careworn, particularly over the last two decades. She was sitting in the good light inside the window trying to work on a small needlepoint Christmas ornament for one of her seven grandchildren, but she was having difficulty concentrating on it. Her mind frequently wandered to matters of graver importance. She glanced out through the window at the two Visitor Patroller guards stationed on her porch. They, or another pair just like them, were constant fixtures. The old woman sighed and looked down again at her needlework.

Under the portico, the two Patrollers sat on camp stools. One of them was snacking. He reached in his mess kit and withdrew a white mouse that squirmed out of his hand and tried to scurry across the Visitor's lap, but the guard grabbed it and chuckled. "Ha. 'Fast food.'" He held out the little rodent to his companion. "Hey, do you want it? The white ones give me heartburn."

Margarita suddenly popped up into view on the west side of the porch. "So will this."

They jumped to their feet, facing her, reaching for their weapons. But Ayden appeared behind them. The white sword-like bone flashed from his wrist. It zipped one way, then slashed back the other. And there were two less Visitors.

Ayden and Margarita quickly dragged the guards into a corner of the porch where they wouldn't attract notice, then Ayden turned to face the front door. It was locked. With one hand he easily bashed it open. Margarita smiled tightly at him, saying, "Where have you been all my life?" Then she brushed past him and ducked inside while Ayden kept careful watch.

Margarita passed a startled half-breed housekeeper. The scaly-faced teenage girl stood staring fearfully. The dustpan she held in her hand had wilted downward and a small trickle of dust was sliding from it. Margarita held up her palms to indicate she meant the girl no harm and then hurried on to the front room where she had seen the old woman through the window. The lady had dropped her needlework when she heard the entrance door crash open and she was standing. She stood tall and her proud eyes seemed almost regal to Margarita who entered and bowed respectfully to her.

"*Buenos tardes, señora.*" Margarita's Spanish was well accented and she continued in that language. "I've come to help you. To take you to your husband."

The old woman's eyes flashed at the striking redhead.

When they reached the porch Ayden also greeted the Spanish woman with a courteous nod. Then he and Margarita swept her down the steps and into the sedan that Street-C drove up at precisely the right moment.

A few seconds after their departure the very nervous white mouse peeked up from between the two dead Visitor Patrollers. Then it quickly scampered off to freedom.

GINA HAD FIRST CAUGHT JEREMY'S EYE ABOUT EIGHT YEARS EARLIER, just before she had left to join the Visitor Armada in its occupation of the Earth. He recognized in her a calculating, upwardly mobile drive that matched his own ambition. She had a whipsaw intelligence and caustic sense of humor that he found a refreshing tonic. While she managed to endure the boring necessities of protocol she was clearly unintimidated by superior officers. Jeremy understood how part of that bravery arose from her virtuoso skills as a fighter pilot. Like many top guns, Gina had long since developed a don't-fuck-with-me attitude because she knew of her extraordinary worth to Team Visitor. Above all, crack pilots like Gina knew that their Great Leader prized such aggressive and adroit combatants, and that the fighter pilots were the crème de la crème of all Patrollers. The Leader frequently rewarded them with elevated standing in the ranks and with personal wealth.

Gina had arrived at Earth in time to be a squadron commander during the Great Purge of 1999. Her talents as a fighter pilot inspired those under her command to attempt astonishing, sometimes foolhardy, maneuvers. Seven had been killed while trying to emulate her or merely to keep up with her. She had not been disciplined nor even castigated for leading them into precarious situations, because her superiors knew she was such a valuable and efficient killing machine.

Shortly before her departure for Earth Jeremy had become intrigued by the possibility of bedding her. Her initial, very definite resistance only whetted his appetite all the more. In a desire to enjoy at least her presence on a regular basis, Jeremy made her his advisor on all matters concerning flight operations. While his other aides were often cautious and hesitant around Jeremy, not wishing to ever offend the Commandant in any way, Gina, in stark contrast, was outspoken in offering her frank opinions. Because she understood her value to Team Visitor, she knew that with or without Jeremy's support she would rise, perhaps even into the Leader's inner circle.

The other aides were naturally put off by her brash attitude, and even Jeremy was sometimes ruffled by her abrasiveness. He recognized, however, the great value of having someone around him who was not only clearheaded and fearless in the extreme, but never a sycophant.

All of those qualities made her even more attractive to him. The value of her smart, unblinking counsel, added to the burning appeal of forbidden fruit, finally prompted him to recommend and secure for her an elevation in rank.

For her part, Gina had recognized in Jeremy the likelihood of his becoming even more powerful than he already was. She had watched his nimble play in palace intrigues and seen him constantly benefit from those skillful maneuvers. She also saw the simpering quality of his other aides and realized that she could be much more helpful to him than any of them if her approach was more forthright. She was quick to point out weaknesses in his plans and strategies. And she was generally right. She also enjoyed Jeremy's icy, scathingly dark sense of humor, feeling it was a match for her own. And she was not unmindful of his sexual possibilities.

A short time after her elevation in rank, Gina one day dropped a tiny hint that she might consider sampling him as a lover. Jeremy was very pleased at the possibility, but decided to reverse roles with her, temporarily putting her off in order to further whet *her* appetite. She was sharp enough to know exactly what he was doing and they fell into a tantalizing game of sexual cat and mouse with each other for several months. It amused and greatly frustrated each of them in turn, but it only ramped up their mutual desire.

Finally came a moment of synchronicity that took them both by surprise and swept them into their first sexual encounter. It was a carnal firestorm.

Neither had ever before experienced anything remotely similar. They were equally matched in both strength and libido, but Jeremy was particularly aroused by her aggressive nature. Gina had a no-holds-barred approach that was a direct parallel to her skills as a fighter pilot. She was able to make him fly sexually with the same heated passion she brought to her airborne combat adventures. Her subtlety in the handling of his control surfaces would excite him to the very razor edge of quaking consummation, then she would back off a mere hair's breadth to hold him trembling at that preclimactic level for astonishingly long hedonistic moments.

In spite of her tightly disciplined nature Gina allowed herself to enjoy him equally. Gina had sometimes taken her fighter up two hundred thousand feet into the stratosphere. There, looking out into the star-filled, black sky at the very edge of space she would cut the engines. The craft would begin to fall, spinning downward at increasing velocity, totally out of control. She allowed Jeremy to do the same with her. Both experiences were characterized by an extreme wildness. The ingenuity of Jeremy's stimulation was as unexpected as the unpredictable twisting and turning of her fighter as it plummeted and swerved dangerously downward. Jeremy was very experimental and sometimes momentarily painful, but always stimulating and invigorating.

Their sexuality was thrilling to both of them. But neither Gina nor Jeremy associated it with anything remotely like love or affection. It was strictly, intensely, and deliciously carnal, an intoxicating end in itself.

Gina was leaning against the hatch of Jeremy's quarters aboard the Flagship as they slowly took pleasure in a final, luxuriant kiss. Both of them were still fevered with the afterglow of their passions. Gina's dark Asian eyes focused sharply onto his as she said with a touch of her edgy humor, "I'll come again tonight."

Then she touched the hatch control, removing its privacy notice. It slid open behind her. She gave him a final saucy salute and exited. Jeremy turned back toward the desk at his workstation as the hatch began to close. But just before sealing shut it paused and reopened. Jeremy glanced around at it and saw wily Shawn lean his head in, subserviently, "Commandant? . . . May I?"

"Of course," Jeremy said as he began to look at the latest dispatches hovering in the air over his visualizer. Shawn stood waiting until Jeremy looked up again, "Well? What is it?"

Shawn seemed slightly distressed. He closed the hatch behind him and chose his words with even more care than usual. "I need some advice, sir." Then he hesitated again for a long moment.

Jeremy finally turned his chair fully to face Shawn. "All right, go on."

"Permission to speak freely, sir?"

Jeremy flicked his hand impatiently in the supervisor's direction. "Yes, yes, Shawn. Out with it."

"Well, sir, I'm very concerned about finding myself in an awkward position. As you may know there are certain, how shall I say"—he selected the word cautiously—"certain *rumors* about your personal relations with our Leader."

Jeremy's brow lowered slightly as he looked at his subordinate. "Go on."

"Well, sir, if our Leader ever questioned me directly about what I knew of your involvement with a certain Wing Commander and statements you might have made to her"—Shawn let the implication hang—"well, sir, I would naturally have to be truthful about—"

"And exactly what knowledge do you have?"

Shawn shifted uncomfortably, implying that he was very sorry about the situation. "Considerable, sir, I'm afraid." Then he added quickly, "Not that I've sought it, sir, but neither can I deny it."

Jeremy's voice became low as a serpentine smile grew. "Shawn, by any chance did Diana put you up to this?"

Shawn was startled and apparently taken very much aback. "Oh, no, sir! Quite to the contrary, sir . . . my desire is to serve at *your* pleasure."

Jeremy's antennae were up. He probed warily, "Is it really?"

"Indeed, sir. That's why I've come to you. Oh, my years with Diana have certainly been very fruitful and instructive." But then he added with a tilt of his head that indicated he was taking Jeremy into strictest confidence. "I haven't always agreed with her decisions, not unlike yourself, sir. But of course I was required to implement even those commands I disagreed with to the best of my limited ability."

Jeremy studied him, "Yet you wish to serve at *my* pleasure?"

"I can see the future clearly, sir," Shawn said admiringly of the Commandant, "and I'm certain that I could be a great asset to you."

"And perhaps be given responsibilities *greater* than those Diana affords you," Jeremy surmised.

"Well, sir"—Shawn bowed his narrow head slightly in a humble gesture of respect—"although that is obviously within your gift, it would certainly not be for me to presume nor to request."

Jeremy scrutinized Shawn with admiration for the supervisor's skillful and devious shrewdness even while he recognized the blackmail that it represented.

STREET-C WAS CHEWING NERVOUSLY ON A MATCHSTICK AS HE SAT ON the bench in the Civic Center Park on Grove Street. His keen eyes darted one way and then another, on the alert for trouble and for something else. He glanced at his watch. "Shit, man. Didn't Emma say ten?"

Nathan was next to him, still in his Teammate uniform. He was looking as casually as possible toward Larkin Street on the east perimeter of City Hall's park. "That's what she said."

"Well, the suckers are late, man."

"I'll be sure to speak to them about that."

Street-C twiddled his matchstick between his teeth and clenched his hands closed and open. "My palms are sweaty. Yours?"

"No." Then Nathan admitted the truth, "Yes." He glanced at Street-C. "This could definitely be a biggie."

"Got that right," Street-C said, twisting the knotted end of one of his cornrows.

Nathan gestured off toward something. "But have you checked out the ladybug?"

Street-C looked over to where Bryke was sitting in the sun on the nearby lawn. Her long black fingers were delicately touching the petals of a daisy.

Street-C marveled, "She's gotta be about the coolest character I've ever known."

Bryke was indeed completely calm and peaceful, seemingly oblivious of their conversation.

Nathan nodded and said, "The only one I ever saw with that kind of Zen was an old Buddhist priest on Kauai. I saw that old guy once in the middle of a hurricane, people running scared all around him and he was like the eye of the storm, totally calm and unfazed. He was just—"

Nathan cut himself off. He had seen Bryke's eyes flick up as she sensed something. Nathan and Street-C followed her line of vision and saw what they'd been waiting for.

Approaching from Larkin, headed west across the grassy park toward the looming, neoclassical dome of San Francisco

City Hall, was United Nations Secretary-General Alberto Mendez.
A light breeze was ruffling his fine white hair but seemed to
bring him no comfort. His dark eyes behind his horn-rimmed
glasses were downcast as he walked. He was in the company of
his usual Visitor Patroller entourage, two in front and two
behind.

As they passed Bryke she casually got to her feet and began to
trail them at a short distance. At the same time Street-C stood up
and walked across the park, crossing well ahead of the path the
Patrollers were taking. He made eye contact with Gary who had
been waiting in a sedan parked on Fulton with its front end aiming across Larkin toward the park. Gary had been the first to see
the Secretary-General heading into the park and had already
started the sedan's engine. Now he slipped it into gear while
keeping his foot firmly on the brake.

About ten seconds after Street-C headed toward his position
just north of the route the entourage was taking, Nathan stood
up, stretched in the sunlight, and turned casually to follow in the
same direction. He walked more slowly so as to remain on their
target's south side.

One of the Patrollers glanced over at the sandy-haired Teammate and nodded a greeting. Then the Patroller frowned and
took a second look. The Resistance team knew going in that it
was possible Nathan might be recognized as a wanted fugitive.
When they saw the lead Patroller take a closer look it was their
cue to launch their offensive.

Nathan and Street-C each pulled out pulse pistols and fired on
the two Patrollers leading the Secretary-General. Simultaneously
Bryke attacked the rear guards from behind. Her Zedti martial
artistry dispensed with one immediately, but the other was grap-
pling with her. Nathan grabbed for Secretary-General Mendez,
but the older man pulled back and struggled against him. "No!
No, please, you mustn't!"

"We're here to help you, sir," Nathan said urgently.

"No, please! You don't understand." The Secretary-General still tried to pull away. Then suddenly there were fiery bursts around them from other pulse weapons.

"Up there, man," Street-C shouted, pointing toward the two Airborne Patrollers who were flying in from over Fulton Street. They were firing their pulse rifles. Nathan was still struggling to hold on to Secretary-General Mendez and finally jabbed a tranquilizer dart into the old man's arm. The Secretary-General's eyes widened with shock, then glazed over as he went limp in Nathan's arms. Nathan pulled Mendez onto his shoulder in a fireman's carry as he saw that Gary's sedan was on the move toward them. It jumped the curb as Gary drove it right across the broad lawn toward them.

"There's more coming! From City Hall!" Street-C shouted as he aimed and fired toward a Teammate unit that was running from the building toward the fracas.

Bryke had finally taken down the second rear Patroller. She shouted to Nathan as she pulled her sonic pistol. "Go! Get him away!" She aimed up toward the incoming Air-Pats who had separated slightly to make a more difficult target. Bryke fired toward them. The shock wave from her sonic weapon caught one of them full on and slammed him hard into a tree, but the other Air-Pat got off a nearly simultaneous pulse burst. The ball of energy flashed through the air, blasted Bryke hard on her left arm, and spun her to the ground. She dropped her sonic weapon.

"Bryke!" Nathan cried out as he carried the dead weight of the Secretary-General toward Gary's oncoming car.

The Zedti was struggling onto her knees. "Get him *away!*" Then she grabbed her sonic pistol and turned back to exchange more fire with the inbound Air-Pat.

Gary's sedan had sped across the lawn and skidded to a stop beside Nathan who barely managed to open the back door while supporting Mendez. Then he trundled the unconscious old man onto the backseat and climbed in behind.

Street-C had been exchanging fire with the approaching Teammates. He had taken down two of them and gotten nicked himself in the side. Then he saw that two more Airborne Patrollers were coming from overtop the dome of City Hall. He ran for the car, which took a pulse hit on the front fender as he pulled open the passenger door, shouting to Nathan in the back, "We gotta blow, man!"

"But Bryke!"

"I'm telling you, we gotta *blow!*" He stomped his foot on top of Gary's and the car sprang forward, running right over one of the oncoming Teammates.

Nathan leaned out of the car window and fired staccato pulse bursts at the two new Air-Pats who were firing back at the escaping car. Nathan took down one of them as the sedan lurched across the sidewalk through scattering pedestrians and bounced onto Grove Street. Leaning out his passenger window Street-C got off four quick pulse bursts, one of which caught the pursuing Air-Pat in the leg and threw him out of control and into the side of Davis Symphony Hall.

Nathan looked back toward the park and was grieved to see that back in the park Bryke was being overwhelmed by Teammates.

The brave Zedti fought fiercely, until a nervous young Teammate put the muzzle of his pulse weapon right against her head and brought her to a stop. Bryke realized further struggle was futile.

The Teammate holding the gun to her head was a half-breed: Willy's son Ted.

24

THE VISITOR TECHNICIAN TERESA WAS VERY TIRED. SHE HAD BEEN working steadily in the Flagship laboratory for nearly seventy-two hours without sleep, driven by her intense desire to rise in the estimation of her Commandant. She had been experimenting with various combinations of the Flagship's numerous external high-gain antennae, trying to find the precise configuration that would bring in the most stable signal from the clandestine camera inside the Resistance headquarters.

It had been a slow and laborious process, but she had finally been rewarded with a fairly reliable image that she felt was worthy of showing to the Commandant at least as a work-in-progress. Teresa also thought of Diana as her colleague in the project. When Teresa initially showed the invention to her Commandant at its earliest stages several years ago Diana had immediately seen its possibilities and put Teresa to work on it full-time. Teresa was very pleased that Diana had given it such a high priority and that she had also classified it as secret.

An hour earlier Teresa had sent word to Diana, who had just come down into the lab. The other technicians and doctors, including Eric, immediately snapped to attention when Teresa announced, "Commandant on deck."

Diana waved them to be at ease. "Please continue your work." Then she turned to Teresa and spoke more quietly, "You've made progress, I take it."

"Yes, Commandant," Teresa said nervously. "But please understand that this is such a delicate process I've been concerned that something might go wrong with it just when I try to demonstrate it to you. It's not yet completely stable and as yet I'm unable to receive any audio; but I'm still experimenting to see if

I can find a better combination of antennas. I hope you'll have patience with me."

Diana stepped closer. "Let me have a look."

"Here's what I've managed so far." Teresa activated the small vid display on the electronic lab table. They were able to see a blurry, unsteady image from within the Resistance warehouse that jumped and jostled as though the transmitting camera was being held in someone's hand.

Despite that wobbliness and the overall grainy, vacillating quality of the transmission, Diana could make out a redheaded woman whom she instantly recognized. "Ah. Margarita Perry."

"Yes, Commandant," the technician agreed. "That's what I thought. And I've also caught glimpses of a few others I think I recognize from our most wanted list: that Peruvian woman Ysabel Encalada, and once I'm almost certain I saw Juliet Parish."

Diana's hand came to rest between Teresa's shoulder blades. Teresa was deeply gratified to feel it; she felt that Diana was literally giving her a pat on the back. "This is good work, Teresa," the Commandant said. "Excellent work." Teresa was surprised and then thrilled to feel Diana's hand slide slowly down to the small of her back and then feel Diana's fingertips gently massage her lower spine. "I'm very pleased with what you've accomplished so far. And I'm very pleased with you personally."

The technician turned slightly to look into Diana's large brown eyes as the Commandant smiled faintly and said, "Continue to refine the image and work on the audio. Take very careful notes about everything you observe." Then Diana leaned closer to Teresa, pressing her hand more firmly against the technician's back as she said confidentially, "Be certain that you report directly to me."

"Oh, yes, of course, Commandant," Teresa said, trying to conceal the flutter in her heart she felt at Diana's touch.

"And only to me," Diana concluded as she held her gaze a few seconds for more emphasis.

"Naturally, Commandant, only ever to you."

Diana gave her a final conspiratorial smile and turned toward the hatch. She paused to look at several small animals in their cages. She examined them a moment, then asked, "Are these only for experimentation?"

"No, Commandant"—Teresa indicated with a welcoming gesture—"please, help yourself."

Diana examined them all. There were several mice, a few rats, and other small mammals. But what caught her eye the most was a tiny black and white rabbit. She gently removed the trembling little creature from its cage. As she did, the technician felt emboldened to step slightly closer.

"If I may ask, Commandant," Teresa spoke very softly, excited by their new confidentiality. She gestured toward the vid screen on her worktable. "Since you have this inside track to their headquarters, why not just raid them?"

"Everything in its proper time, Teresa." The technician saw Diana's brown eyes glisten, hinting at a sexual innuendo. Then the Commandant turned and exited through the hatch. Teresa paused a moment. Her heart was pounding. She looked out the hatch after Diana. Just before Diana reached the aide who was waiting by a transport tube, Teresa saw Diana tilt her head back and swallow the rabbit alive.

AT THE RESISTANCE WAREHOUSE, THE STATELY GRAY-HAIRED WOMAN whom Margarita and Ayden had liberated was having a tearful reunion with her husband, U.N. Secretary-General Mendez. The pleased Resistance team watched from a discreet distance as the two embraced and conversed in Spanish.

"I've worried so much about you," Secretary-General Mendez said as he stroked his wife's smooth gray hair. "Did they hurt you, Juanita?"

"No, Alberto," she said, wiping her eyes and smiling at him. "I just felt so terrible. I could see you on the videos so I knew you were all right, but I knew you must be worried sick about me." She hugged him tightly again.

Across the room, Nathan approached Ayden. "Listen, I really feel awful about Bryke getting captured."

Ayden shrugged it off without the slightest emotion. "Bryke is a soldier. She knew that could happen."

"We're trying to locate her," Nathan said encouragingly, "we've gotten word to our spy in the Flagship Centcom. If there's any chance we can spring her, then I'll personally lead the charge."

"You needn't worry."

Nathan was confused. "What do you mean?"

"She won't betray your operation," Ayden said dryly.

"What?" Nathan was put off by the Zedti's assumption. "That's not why I want to rescue her. She's part of our team. And she saved my life twice."

"And mine at least six times over the years," Ayden said without looking at him, "but we have more important matters pressing." Ayden walked over toward the others. Nathan watched him, thrown by the Zedti's lack of emotion regarding Bryke.

Secretary Mendez was saying to Julie and Margarita, "I thank you all for bringing my wife out of harm's way."

"We're glad we could help," Margarita said.

Then Julie elaborated, "We learned that the Visitors were holding her and realized they must be threatening her in order to make you speak in their behalf."

"Yes," he said, his arm around his wife who stood close beside him. "And they kept me under close guard so I had no possibility of escape." Then he went on with great difficulty, "I also was prevented from taking my own life in order to no longer be their puppet." His wife clutched his hand tightly as he said, "I attempted it more than once. And would have again had they not threatened me with torture and death for Juanita if I succeeded. So obviously I was in no position to ever reveal the truths I had discovered about them."

"We'll be only too happy to give you that opportunity, Mr. Secretary-General," said Julie.

The Nobel laureate looked at her with eyes that now burned brightly with enthusiasm. "And I shall certainly take that opportunity, young lady."

AT THE ACCESS GATE IN THE LASER FENCE THAT SURROUNDED THE Mission District Sci ghetto, the Visitor Patroller on station was surprised. He had just looked up and discovered Emma standing before him. He had only ever seen her on the music vids and once in the distance when he had been assigned to one of her concerts. But he had never seen the star up-close. Her creamy, coffee-colored skin was perfect even from two feet away. And she certainly had a presence that people couldn't help but take notice of. He stumbled a bit with his words as he greeted her, "Uh, yes, miss? Can I help you?"

Emma smiled, but was very businesslike. "I'm sure you can, Sergeant, I just need to go inside there for a few minutes." She was indicating the Sci Section that lay beyond the gate.

"Are you certain, miss?" The Patroller was surprised. "I'm afraid you'll find it very unsavory."

"You're probably right, Sergeant"—Emma looked down the Sci street with distaste—"but I have to set something right."

"Can't one of us handle the matter for you, miss?" He indicated himself and the other two guards who had drifted closer to get a good look at the music star.

"No," Emma said with a tone that implied she had a nasty score to settle, "I need to do it personally."

"Very well, miss, I'll just tag along, if you don't mind."

He moved to escort her, but she caught his arm. "I'd rather

you didn't, Sergeant. It will have much more impact on the people involved if I confront them on my own."

The Patroller was reticent. "I'm afraid my superiors wouldn't be pleased with me if I let someone as important as yourself go in there alone."

"I'll take the responsibility, Sergeant," she said firmly.

He stared at her for a long moment during which Emma considered what reward she might offer him if he required more convincing, but the need didn't arise. "Very well, miss," he said, "but please come back out this same gate so I can be certain you've departed safely."

"Very thoughtful, Sergeant. You can be sure I will."

Emma pulled a baseball cap and dark glasses from the large purse she was carrying and moved through the gate into the ghetto as a Patrol craft glided by overhead. She saw another Visitor vehicle patrolling in the distance and felt the ominous weight of their presence. There were always shuttles and occasional fighters passing over the streets and buildings of San Francisco. They were a fact of life in every city and town across the planet. But here in the Sci Section they definitely passed by at lower altitude and with much greater frequency.

Emma had never gone into a Sci Section before. It was a far cry from the "charming, parklike communities" that appeared in her vid *The Visitor Way*. These streets were much more crowded. They smelled of inadequate sanitation.

Despite her sunglasses and baseball cap, many people recognized her as she passed among them. Most of those who did were startled and amazed to see her in their dismal ghetto. Though she tried to keep focused straight ahead, several people purposely got into her line of sight. She nodded politely to them as she walked. A few other people made bold to ask her for some money or other help. She said politely that she would try to come back but couldn't help on this particular day. She did, however, manage to slip a few dollars into the hands of three emaciated and particularly desperate-looking children who each approached her separately.

Mary Elgin was completely surprised when she answered the rapping at her thin wooden door and found it to be Emma. Mary didn't know exactly how to react, but Emma quickly resolved the problem by embracing Mary. Emma could feel that the frail woman was tremulous in her arms so Emma held her tightly for a long moment. At length Mary eased back and looked at her employer. They both had tears in their eyes, but Mary looked much more upbeat than Emma had expected. Mary was the first to speak, "Thank you for what you did for Charlotte."

Emma shook her head. "Unfortunately I didn't do very much, I'm afraid."

"No, no, that's not true," Mary said brightly. "You took our side. You tried to help. That meant everything, really!"

"Well, I wish I could've done more. I wish we could have saved her."

Mary tentatively took her arm. "Please, come on in. Not that there's much farther to come," Mary joked. Emma stepped into the center of the tiny living room and took it all in: the battered furniture, the stained sink in the ramshackle kitchen, the thread-bare carpet, the curtain on a rope that created a bedroom for the elder Mr. Elgin in one corner of the central kitchen-living room. Mary had turned enthusiastically to the stove. "I'll put on some tea!"

Emma watched her closely. She knew how emotionally fragile Mary had always been and something about her current behavior seemed off-key to Emma as Mary continued in an effusive vein, "Oh, that's my father-in-law, Charles Senior. Pop to us."

"Mr. Elgin, hi." Emma reached down to take his hand as he sat in the ratty easy chair.

"None of that, young lady, it's Pop to you, too"—he shook her hand with a grin, then pressed it sincerely—"and thanks for trying to help Charlotte. She was . . ." His throat tightened. Emma understood and kissed his forehead.

Mary was beaming. "Charles will be so sorry he missed you. But why did you come all the way down here?"

Emma set her purse on the scarred Formica table. "Because I should have come a long time before now, Mary. I brought you some stuff." She took from her purse an eclectic collection of quality food and wine.

Mary's eyes went wide. "Emma! You didn't need to do this."

"Oh, yes I did. Here, this is especially for you." Emma took out a gift basket of bath products she had carefully selected.

Mary was amazed; she sniffed the flowery fragrances. "I can't even remember the last time I had anything like these."

"And this is for you, Pop." Emma took out a bottle of prescription pills.

The old gentleman peered through his glasses at it as Mary also realized it was medication for his diabetes. She was so astonished that all she could say was, "How?"

Emma winked. "I've made some new friends." Then she grasped Mary's arm and looked at her with genuine concern. "Mostly I came just because I wanted to see how you were doing."

Having witnessed how Mary had been so ravaged on the horrible, heartrending evening when Charlotte died, Emma expected her to still be extremely grief-stricken. She was thus unprepared when Mary seemed to almost toss off her answer, "Me? Oh, I'm okay." Mary cheerfully turned toward the kitchen, opening a cabinet. "What do you take in your tea?" Then she laughed a bit too loudly. "I sure hope it's something we've got!"

Emma stared at her for a second, then looked at the elder

Mr. Elgin seeking some explanation for Mary's odd effervescence. But the old man just met Emma's eyes with equal concern.

Emma went gently to Mary and touched her sleeve. "Mary?"

The woman turned to Emma with a friendly grin. "Hmmm?"

"Are you sure you're okay? I really want to help if I can. If you need to talk, or—"

"You are so sweet," Mary said with a smile. She touched Emma's cheek and the singer felt the slightest vibration emanating from Mary's hand. "You really are a dear. Oh, it was hard, God knows, but I'm doing much, much better than I thought I would. Really I am. And look"—she held up a very small box as though it were diamonds—"sugar!"

Emma saw that Mary's eyes were twinkling very brightly.

YSABEL WAS PROVIDING A BIT OF MAKEUP TO RELIEVE THE PALLOR from the cheeks of the Secretary-General and his wife. As she touched them up, Ysabel spoke to them in Spanish to ease their tension and help prepare Mendez for the vid recording session.

There had been no word at all from the Flagship about the fate of Bryke. Neither Martin, nor Lee who worked in the Visitor Centcom, nor Willy, nor even Jon had been able to penetrate the cloak of security that had been tightly drawn around the imprisoned Zedti warrior. Ruby was worried for Bryke, not only because Bryke had helped to save the half-breed from torture at the Parnassas jail, but beyond that Ruby felt a unique bond to Bryke as a fellow twelve-year-old.

Kayta noted Ruby's worried look and also saw the tense expression on Nathan's face as he helped Margarita and Gary arrange the small vid recording setup in one corner of the Resistance warehouse. Kayta knew that Nathan also had concerns for Bryke; that he was very frustrated by being forced to leave her behind at City Hall and by not being able to effect a rescue of the noble female.

When Nathan and Margarita stepped to one side as Gary

checked the audio levels and camera positioning, Kayta came to stand nearby, speaking softly to Nathan, "You have sad feelings about Bryke."

Nathan glanced sharply at her. "You could say that, yeah."

"I, too, miss her presence. We have long been comrades," Kayta said matter-of-factly.

"I just can't understand how Ayden can be so cold about it." Nathan shook his head. "I know you people have less emotion than we do, but don't you feel anything?"

Margarita agreed. "It's almost like he just doesn't care at all about what happens to her."

"Ayden knows the great value of Bryke, believe me," Kayta confirmed. "But he also knows—as every loyal member of our race does—that any one of us must always be prepared to sacrifice our individual selves for the benefit of all Zedti."

Nathan was impatient. "Yeah, yeah I *understand* all that, but forgive me if I just don't *get* it."

"You approach the situation from human perspectives and emotions," Kayta tried to explain. "The mind-set of our race has evolved differently. If it had been Ayden who had been captured, Bryke would feel the same as Ayden does now. She would regret deeply the loss of him, but accept it without—without"—she searched for the proper phrase—"without anguish—I believe that is the word you would use."

"Yes, it certainly is," Margarita said sadly.

"Bryke would accept the loss of Ayden just as he accepts the loss of her. She would be focused instead on what actions must be taken to perpetuate the Zedti race."

The frustration that Margarita and particularly Nathan felt had not been assuaged by Kayta. But they quieted themselves, realizing that the Secretary-General had begun to record his message.

The entire Resistance team gathered to listen. Mike Donovan rolled closer to Nathan and Margarita in his wheelchair so that he, too, could hear. The Secretary-General's wife stood proudly at his side as Gary operated the vid camera. Mendez explained to the camera how his wife had been kept hostage by the Visitors to ensure his collaboration.

"And thanks to my good friends in the Resistance," Secretary-General Mendez was saying, "I am now able to speak out." He took a deep breath and focused on the millions of people whom he hoped would eventually see him and hear his words. "This is what I know for certain. The Visitors have been *lying* to keep our hopes up. They *will absolutely not* return our water. Just as the Resistance has long suspected, Earth's water will fuel their growing Armada and their weaponry. The millions of Earth's people who have disappeared will be used as slaves or soldiers or, most horrible of all, they will eventually be used as fresh-killed *food*. And those who have been taken thus far have indeed been cocooned within stasis capsules on the Motherships . . . *I have seen them*."

As the Secretary-General continued to describe the nightmare world of the Capsule Storage Chambers, Ayden stepped closer to where Margarita and Nathan stood and spoke quietly to them, "Prisoners we took in our last war told us that those kept inside the capsules are subjected to a barrage of information."

Mike and the others reacted to this surprising new information. Nathan spoke softly so as not to disturb the recording process as he framed the question for all of them, "Why?"

Margarita was more specific. "What kind of information? For what purpose?"

"To indoctrinate the prisoners and train them for tasks they'll perform for their captors. They are subconsciously instructed in operational duties as slaves or in the use of various weapons for combat so they can become good, obedient soldiers."

Nathan was sardonic. "And what kind of training do they get to be good sushi?"

Margarita's eyes flicked over to him, then back to where the Secretary-General was still being recorded.

"All of Earth's people will eventually be used for the sole benefit of the Visitors," Mendez said. "The Visitor Leader seeks to enlarge their empire. All of our human Teammate units are being readied as expendable foot soldiers to go on the ground against a Visitor enemy called the Zedti." The Secretary-General paused and drew himself proudly up to his full height. "But I now bring you the most stunning news of all. The Zedti are a powerful and honorable race of individuals who have come to our aid. Their scouts are already here on Earth doing reconnaissance in our behalf. One of their people sacrificed herself to aid in my escape. I have met with the Zedti commander. He has told me that behind these scouts stands their massive battle fleet. The Zedti leader has further assured me that his mighty force is poised to fight alongside humankind against our common enemy, the Visitors!" The Resistance team all shared hopeful glances with one another. They were unaware that the scene was also being observed by someone else.

Teresa, the Visitor technician in the Flagship laboratory, was still unable to receive intelligible audio, but the video image had improved. She was fine-tuning, trying to finesse a yet clearer image from the jostling, clandestine camera that someone was holding within the Resistance headquarters. Teresa was so intent on her work that she wasn't aware of the Visitor doctor Eric passing behind her. Eric chanced to look over her shoulder and he froze fearfully when he glimpsed on the hazy, black and white screen someone whom he instantly recognized: his lover, Gary.

ALSO DEEP WITHIN THE BOWELS OF THE GREAT FLAGSHIP, LESS THAN a half mile from the laboratory, was one of the medical chambers that had been generally reserved for autopsy work. It was windowless but there were vid screens on two walls for the display of various imaging. There was also a pair of long stainless metal tables that were slightly concave to contain any fluids escaping from the subject under investigation. They were slightly inclined so that such fluids would flow to the collector drain at one end.

Large surgical-style lights hung overhead on adjustable arms for advantageous positioning. The room was very clean and it smelled of chemicals used in the autopsy process or for cleanup.

Built into the walls were cabinets with glass fronts. They contained surgical equipment necessary for the work that transpired within the room. One cabinet, set somewhat apart from the others, contained unpleasant-looking surgical implements. That was because in addition to autopsies this particular chamber had been designed for another use.

Nearest the cabinet with the unusual instruments was a straight-backed metal chair affixed within a vertical circular rail that allowed the chair to be rotated completely upside down if necessary. The floor beneath it, like the autopsy tables, was slightly concave to collect and drain fluids. Several instruments hung from the ceiling near the chair. On Earth they might have been mistaken for something like small X-ray units or dentist drills. One of them was brightly labeled in the Visitor alphabet *Danger High Voltage*. Suspended from the low ceiling were three small, adjustable lights, which could be trained on the chair. One of them was on, illuminating the individual sitting there.

Bryke was alone in the shadowy room, her arms and legs clamped tightly to the chair. She was bruised from the battering she had taken in the Civic Center park, yet her face displayed the same calmness it had when she sat in the park a few hours earlier. She was meditating on the beauty of the daisy she had seen there. She did not register even the faintest reaction when the hatch in one wall hissed open.

Jeremy stood in the hatchway looking at her, surveying her blue-black skin that even in the dark of the chamber had the sheen he recognized so well from his previous encounters with Zedti. He studied Bryke for a long moment. She never acknowledged his arrival in any way. She was focused on the daisy.

At length Jeremy indicated for the female aide accompanying him to wait outside. Then he closed the hatch and approached Bryke, speaking with genuine appreciation of her talents. "I'm given to understand you're quite an artist at combat, yet you are also extremely soulful." He considered that prospect for a moment. "A most interesting combination for a warrior."

He rolled a tall metal lab stool closer to hers and sat, speaking in a friendly manner. "I have a true admiration for artists, having risen through the ranks because of some modest skills of my own." He leaned slightly closer, speaking with a shade of pride and in a more confidential tone. "I have something of a gift for being able to inspire conversation. To excite in my subjects sensations of such . . . such"—he pondered, then, like the connoisseur he was, proceeded to select the most appropriate description— "sensations of such *intensity* that my subjects never imagined they could experience them within their lifetime."

Bryke had continued to totally ignore his presence. Neither did she display the slightest belligerence or hatred or anger. She was as calm and quiet as a soft summer day.

Jeremy was intrigued. He continued speaking, with false humility. "And just when that extreme intensity seems to have reached its peak, I have schooled myself in the ability to *increase* it ever so slowly and subtly to a crescendo that becomes, I'm told, truly exquisite."

Still, Bryke was unmoving and focused on the daisy.

"And, do you know, I quite enjoy it," Jeremy confided, smiling. "I find it absolutely exhilarating to be able to take someone to the virtual brink of mortality, the very edge of sanity, yet keep them alive and alert," he leaned close and whispered into her ear, "so that we can talk."

25

MARGARITA ROLLED THE OLD DRY-ERASE BOARD OVER TO WHERE Julie was leaning on her cane facing the assembling Resistance team. They were pulling up boxes or chairs to sit on to listen as Julie wiped the board clean, preparing to outline and diagram their plans. All of the regulars were in attendance, as were about two dozen others who represented all the secondary cells from the San Francisco-Oakland area.

Margarita looked at the ragtag gathering. "This will be our most critical operation."

"Ever," Julie emphasized. "We intend to stage a carefully coordinated, two-pronged attack."

FOUR THOUSAND FEET ABOVE JULIE AT THAT MOMENT, JON WAS about to leave the Flagship laboratory where he had been doing his regular cleaning. He looked around for Eric to see if the doctor had any old equipment to discard, but Eric was not at his usual station in the lab near Teresa. So Jon started toward the hatch, passing Teresa's table where she was intent upon a small vid screen. Ever curious, Jon looked closer and his breathing went shallow as he realized what he was looking at. The inconsistent picture on the lab screen and the intermittent, faint sound was coming from a shaky camera spying within the Resistance headquarters.

Jon started to back out and away when Teresa noticed him and snapped, "Hey, where do you think you're going?"

Jon tried to stay calm but it was very difficult. "On to my next location, ma'am. I've finished my normal work here and—"

"You're going nowhere until you clean up that mess over there." She was pointing at a greasy hydraulic spill oozing from beneath a piece of chemical equipment.

"I'll have to get some special cleanser," Jon lied.

"It'll be all over the place by then. Clean it up as best you can with what you've got and do it now."

Jon had no choice but to comply. As Teresa turned back toward her screen and prepared to take careful notes, Jon also glanced fearfully at the flickering image of the Resistance cadre who had not the faintest idea that the security of their headquarters had been breached.

IN THE RESISTANCE WAREHOUSE THE BAND OF BROTHERS AND SISTERS continued their conference. Margarita had divided the board in half and was jotting down bullet points on one side of it. "The vid transmission from their big Candlestick Park rally will be sent to their main ground station in Marin County. From there it's beamed up to the Flagship."

"A dozen of us will hit that facility just as the broadcast starts," Julie said. "Then at the right moment we'll cut off their rally telecast and we'll transmit instead our own broadcast. Our Centcom spy will beam it on around the world."

There were murmurs of enthusiasm from all the others, including Harmy who said, "Oh, my God, what a perfect idea!"

"We're broadcasting the Secretary-General's thing, huh?" Street-C presumed.

"Yes"—Julie nodded—"what he recorded, including the news that the Zedti are here to help—"

"Plus the images from our vid—" Margarita interjected.

"That's right," Julie continued, "all of that could be the catalyst we've needed to finally make everyone rise up"—she looked specifically over at Mike—"and get humanity back on its feet."

IN THE FLAGSHIP LAB, JON HAD BEEN CLEANING AS QUICKLY AS possible while keeping an eye on Teresa. She was recording the transmission from the spy camera but also jotting down information that she could hear or read on the board in the Resistance headquarters. The sound was intermittent and she was straining to make out as many of the staticky words as possible. Jon was edging his way toward the hatch watching desperately for a chance to slip out.

IN THE WAREHOUSE, MARGARITA HAD TURNED HER ATTENTION TO the Zedti commander. "Ayden, now would be the time to call in your fleet."

Kayta quickly hedged, "No, we shouldn't endanger other Zedti if we can stop them ourselves."

Street-C wasn't the only one annoyed. "Hey, what're you guys, chicken?" Others among the humans grumbled agreement.

Ayden ignored the criticism, looking at Julie. "And what is the other half of your plan?"

Nathan spoke from where he sat in the front, half facing the group, "With Zedti help: a 'decapitation attack' on the Visitor High Command."

"Emma has told us that there'll be at least fifty Mothership captains on the dais at Candlestick," Julie said.

Margarita nodded. "It's the greatest opportunity we've ever had to hit so many at one time."

"Very well," said Ayden, "I have a tactical missile that can accomplish that task. It is very small but nuclear, easily enough to destroy the stadium."

"Whoa, wait a minute." Harmy wasn't the only one concerned. "*Nuclear?* No"—she looked toward Julie for support— "too many innocent people would die!"

Ayden shrugged. "You must sacrifice a few in order to save the majority."

"A few?" Ysabel peered sharply at him over her half-glasses. "There's a hundred thousand people gonna be there. Over half of 'em human."

"And Emma among them," Gary reminded everyone.

"Maybe we can get her clear," said Street-C, "but either way it's war, man. I'm with Ayden, I say we gotta slam the suckers."

The group voiced many arguments. There were compelling justifications on both sides of the issue. Harmy looked pleadingly toward her leader. "Julie?"

Julie's mouth went dry as she weighed all the options. Before she could respond Gary spoke up, "How about a vote? I'm against. Who else?"

A slim majority raised their hands along with Gary. Ayden and Kayta were among those in favor of the nuclear attack, along with Nathan and Street-C, but it was voted down.

"Okay," said Margarita. "Then the action will be confined to a specific sniper attack to take out just the leadership." She looked toward Nathan, inviting his opinion.

"No way we'll get all fifty," Nathan said, "but we'll try for the Visitor Leader, Diana, Jeremy, and as many of the captains as we can nail." He looked toward Ayden. "Right?"

The Zedti commander held Nathan's gaze for a moment, considering the situation, then he nodded and said, "Very well."

Margarita said, "Julie and I will lead the team that hits the comm link up in Marin." She looked at those representing other Resistance groups. "The rest of you should advise your individual cells around the city. Be prepared to hit the streets and rally our people." The representatives all vocalized their readiness.

Julie looked to Ysabel. "Ysie and Gary have begun alerting all the other American and international cells to be prepared for a big push when they see it go down."

Gary stood up. "We've already reached more than half."

Ysabel had started back toward their communications truck. She waved over her shoulder to Julie. "We'll stay on it, boss."

Margarita drew a breath and encouraged the others, "Okay, gang, let's do it."

As the group began to mobilize, Gary's cell rang. He waved for Ysabel to go on into the communications truck as he paused outside it to answer his phone. A short distance away, Robert took Nathan aside and handed him a small plastic card with a clip on its back. "Take this."

Nathan turned it over in his hand. "A radiation sensor?"

Robert looked sharply at Nathan, then glanced over toward Ayden. "Just to keep him honest, you understand?"

"So he doesn't try to do his own show. Yeah."

"It'll go red if he primes any kind of nuke."

Nathan nodded and slipped the card into his pocket.

Julie was preparing to leave when she saw Donovan in his wheelchair beckoning her to one side. She went to him, thinking she understood what was going through his mind. "I wish you could come, Mike."

"Yeah. Me, too. But . . ." He suddenly paused as he realized what she had called him. "'*Mike*'?" He looked at her, touched. During their entire relationship she had only ever called him Mr. Donovan. It had started as a little joke, but never changed. Until now. He chuckled. "That's a first."

Julie smiled wistfully. "Well, I just hope it's not a last."

"Yeah. Me, too." He was gazing at her and she at him. Their whole history flashed before his mind's eye: his first meeting with Julie when he'd been dragged into her original underground headquarters and his total disbelief that the shy, tiny young intern could possibly be leading the Resistance cell; the sparks that initially were struck between them because of their different approaches to fighting back against the Visitors; his slow realization of Julie's natural abilities to shape a disparate group of people into a unified, disciplined, and viable fighting force; his amazement as her organizational skills helped establish and interconnect other Resistance cells across the country and around the world; the astonishing bravery he witnessed from Julie when she had been under attack by Visitor fighters at that first mountain camp engagement. He remembered her undaunted courage in the midst of that fierce battle. He could still see Julie standing straight and tall over a wounded comrade as Diana's fighter strafed her with blistering pulse fire. He remembered the small, unblinking woman defending her fallen compatriot and firing back—the first time Julie had ever even fired a weapon—a mere pistol versus the devastating pulse cannons of the fighter. She was David impossibly challenging Goliath, hopelessly outgunned, yet determined to fight to the death. He had come to feel enormous respect for her. And fond affection.

And at the same time that Mike was looking into her eyes, Julie was having a similar rush of recollection: the tall, swaggering, cocky Donovan of their first encounter; the man wearing a stolen Visitor uniform that he'd used to effect a hair's-breadth escape from the Flagship after an aborted mission to discover the Visitors' secrets; the veteran news cameraman who had seen more good and particularly bad in the world than Julie could even imagine; the truth-seeker who had been embedded and embattled among freedom fighters from El Salvador to Tibet; the brave man who had lost his best friend and his son to the monsters from Sirius; the muscular, agile, athletic Mike Donovan who never turned away from even the most desperate challenge; the man who had saved her life more than once. A man whose supposed death in 1991 had totally stunned her and made her realize the depth of emotion she felt for him. A man whom she genuinely loved.

All of that passed between Julie and Mike in an eyeblink. And laced within the memories of what had been between them, there was also a thread of quiet hope and yearning for what they might yet share in the future.

Then Mike drew a breath. "Listen, Kayta was talking about the Zedti planet."

"And?"

"She said their two suns were yellow."

Julie frowned, confused. "Okay?"

"No"—Mike shook his head emphatically—"not okay. I'm pretty certain that Altair is a *green* star, and it's definitely *not* part of a binary system."

Julie felt her blood turn uncomfortably cool as she instantly processed the import of what Mike was saying. She glanced fearfully at the Zedti. Ayden and Kayta were standing to one side, conferring. Julie lowered her voice and leaned closer to Mike. "So where *are* they from?"

"Exactly my point."

"And why have they *lied* to us?"

"I'd say that's sort of the key question, huh?"

From across the warehouse, Margarita called out, "Julie? We've got to roll."

"I know, Margarita, I'll be right there." But she looked back at Donovan, struggling to evaluate the dangerous new information about the Zedti. She said urgently, "I don't see how we can possibly delay this mission."

"Neither do I," he responded tensely, as frustrated as she was.

But already Julie was rethinking her decision. "I mean the timing is so critical."

"Tell me about it," he acknowledged. "Look. You go ahead. I'll try to find out more and fill you in."

Though still having trepidation, she said, "Okay." Then she started to turn toward Margarita and the others.

Mike caught her sleeve. "And Doc"—he gazed deeply at her—"*Julie* . . ."

She drew a breath because in all the years they had known each other he had never once called her by her name either. Their eyes held. They had been comrades of many battles, yet in that moment they both felt their relationship rise to a new level of emotional connection. But Julie also saw a disturbing darkness in Mike's troubled eyes.

"There's something else . . ."

Sensing the personal turmoil stirring within him, Julie leaned closer, her voice almost a whisper. "What is it, Mike?"

His voice became equally low, and he looked downward toward the oil-stained concrete floor, unable to meet her eyes. It was obviously the most difficult thing he'd ever had to tell anyone. "The Purge of '99 . . ."

Julie stared at him and knew instinctively what he was about to say. His eyes remained downcast as if he were a supplicant.

"Because of all the drugs I'll never know for sure, but other than you, nobody had as much information about the Resistance as I did," he said, and drew a halting, emotional breath, "so I've got to believe it was probably me that—"

Julie put a finger to his lips. His eyes rose to meet hers. She saw his soul-deep remorse in them, his burning regret for the role he likely played in the capture or death of so many loyal freedom fighters and friends. She leaned closer and kissed his cheek, then pressed her own firmly against it.

Finally she drew back slightly and looked at him with an expression of the utmost respect. Then she squeezed his hand one last time and hurried off to lead her troops.

At the door a very pale and distressed Gary snagged Margarita, indicating his cell phone. "I just got a call. The doctor who saved my life said he needs me. He said it was life or death."

Margarita was frustrated, but as she saw Julie heading out, she nodded to Gary, "Look, do what you have to do."

"I'm sorry," Gary said. Then he rushed out as Nathan came to Margarita and extended his hand.

"Good luck, Red."

She took his hand in hers and held it firmly. "You, too, hotshot." They shared a last wistful smile and headed in different directions.

At the other end of the warehouse, Ayden was speaking to

Kayta beside the table that held her makeshift chemical laboratory. The willowy blonde told him that she hadn't yet been able
to complete!y decipher the molecular structure of the Visitors'
chemical weapon, nor had she begun to contemplate some way
to neutralize it.

"But from what you've already done . . . ?" He held out the
question.

"It seems to be as we first feared," she said. "It's lethal to us.
It would be catastrophic on a battlefield. And if they had delivery
systems capable of breaching the fleet's defenses . . ."

With a slight wave of his hand Ayden gave her to know that
he understood and she need not continue. He thought for a brief
moment, then looked at her. "All right. We know that as yet they
are still in the preparation stages. You remain here. If this present mission fails in any substantial way . . ."

Kayta nodded slowly. "I understand," she continued with
great reluctance to confirm his order, "I will call in our fleet to attack before they can distribute the chemical and mobilize their
Armada."

"Correct." Ayden gave her a look that each knew might be a
final farewell, then he departed. Kayta had extremely mixed feelings as she watched him leave. When she slowly turned back to
her worktable she realized that Mike was staring at her as
though he were trying to penetrate her thoughts.

THE YOUNG HALF-BREED JANITOR BURST OUT OF A TRANSPORT TUBE
into one of the dark, steamy inner corridors of the Flagship. Jon
had finally managed to get clear of Teresa's watchful eye. He had
run from the laboratory and was desperately seeking Willy who
should have been somewhere nearby on his maintenance rounds.
Jon looked both ways along the endless black passageway, then
dashed down a nearby stairway, all the while muttering nervously
to himself, "Where is he? Where is he?"

Breathing hard as he reached the level below, Jon's eyes

searched in one direction. He spotted a half-breed female janitor the top of whose head was completely reptilian but who had an almost fully human face except for yellow eyes and vertical pupils. Jon ran to where she was repairing a pipe leaking a viscous, foul-smelling fluid. "Willy," Jon said breathessly, "William. Maintenance. Have you seen him?"

The girl signed to Jon that she was mute, but tried to communicate where she thought Willy might be. Jon struggled to understand, "Level 207? No? 208?" The girl nodded. "What section?" She signed again and Jon said, "152? Right?" The other teen nodded and Jon took off running.

THE HATCH TO THE AUTOPSY ROOM OPENED AND JEREMY STEPPED slowly out to where one of his female aides and a Patroller stood at the ready in the damp, dimly lit corridor. They snapped to attention but Jeremy didn't even look at them. He was greatly annoyed. Within the chamber, on the side reserved for interrogation, Bryke was still securely restrained in the chair. But it had been rotated so that she was hanging upside down. Her head dangled limply. From the top of her head, as well as from one arm and her groin, droplets of her pale yellow blood were falling into the shallow concave section of the floor beneath her. That area was shiny with her yellow bodily fluid.

Jeremy was petulantly flicking a trace of yellow blood from his sleeve as Jon came racing around a corner and plowed into the Commandant at full speed. Jeremy was startled and the unexpected impact landed Jon on the floor.

"Oh. Sir!" The boy groveled at the feet of the Commandant. "I am so sorry, sir!"

Jeremy was angry and disgusted, he kicked the half-breed viciously. The Patroller jerked Jon roughly to his feet. "You stupid dreg! Get away!"

The Patroller shoved Jon hard. The youth scurried off as Diana approached from an intersecting corridor with Shawn and several aides trailing her. She glanced into the chamber toward the Zedti, then she caught the taut expression on Jeremy's face that reflected his frustration. It pleased her, so she gouged gently, "Successful, I presume? What have you learned?"

Jeremy's smile was acidic, "If I had a bit more time I would be successful."

"You know, while I don't pretend to be the master that you are," she said, enjoying his discomfort, "I've had a fair amount of experience at soliciting information from individuals. Perhaps *I* should, shall we say, have a stab at her?"

"Thank you, but no," Jeremy said politely, "I have other plans for her. Shawn, I want you to—"

"Shawn is with me," Diana interrupted with a piercing smile. Jeremy stared back at her while the aides around them all wished they were somewhere else.

Then Shawn stepped gingerly onto the tightrope between his two patrons. "But I'd be most happy, sir, to pass along whatever order you might wish to have implemented."

Jeremy brushed brusquely past them both, grabbing the arm of his female aide, who had been waiting outside the interrogation room. Diana carefully watched her fellow Commandant move partway down the shadowy hall, then she glanced sternly at Shawn, who shrugged innocently as if to privately say, *what's to be done with such a petulant person?*

Diana looked into the autopsy chamber where Bryke was still suspended upside down and bleeding.

"Excuse me, Commandant," Shawn said quietly, "it's time for us to be departing for the rally."

She looked at him and then nodded for him to lead the way.

Down the corridor the other way, Jeremy had paused with his female aide. "See to it that the Zedti is delivered and prepared exactly as I described."

The aide inclined her head subserviently. "Of course, Commandant. The arrangements have already been made."

"And the other element we spoke about?"

"I've taken care of that, too, sir. He will be at your disposal in Candlestick Park." Then she added more privately, "And if I may say, sir, our Great Leader will be most pleased."

"That is my intention," Jeremy said as he gave the aide a regal nod of dismissal. The female hastened back toward the interrogation chamber.

Jeremy stood alone in the dark corridor. A faint, somewhat austere expression of pleasure touched his face as he contemplated what he had prepared.

26

MARY ELGIN WAS SITTING ALONE ON THE EDGE OF THE THIN MATtress of Charlotte's bed. She had been there for some time, unaware that dusk had fallen. The photograph she held in her hands was now illuminated only by streetlights filtering in through the short, tattered drapes on the window.

The picture frame was brass and very cheaply made but the photo that it contained made it the most valuable treasure among Mary's few personal possessions. Charlotte looked out from the photograph with her unassuming, sweet smile. It had been taken a year earlier when she still had a flush of youth and promise. Her long raven hair framed her gentle face and hung down thickly in front of her shoulders.

Mary gazed at Charlotte's image, talking very quietly to her daughter. "I can't believe I didn't notice what you were doing." Mary shook her head slightly with a faded smile. "I mean, it was right there in front of me, wasn't it? From one day to the next." She stared at the photo. "I knew you weren't well, but I hoped. I didn't think it was as bad as . . ." Her voice trailed off for a moment, then resumed, "Why didn't I see?"

Her forefinger traced delicately across the glass covering the girl's picture. "And when you cut your beautiful hair I actually believed what you told me, you little bugger." She poked admonishingly at the photo, feeling very foolish. "What an idiot I was. Why would I ever . . . ?" Mary paused. She realized she knew the answer, "Because I was trying to delude myself? Because I knew there was nothing I could do? Oh, Christ, Charlotte . . . I should have done something more . . . there must have been *something* . . ." The photo grew blurry in her vision. "I'm so sorry, honey. I feel so empty . . . so—"

"Mary?" It was Charles Senior, speaking softly from the doorway.

Mary sat up straighter. "Oh, hi, Pop." She didn't look back at the old man because she knew her eyes were glimmering.

"Are you all right, honey?"

Mary swallowed her emotions and tried to sound much better than she felt. "Yeah, Pop. Just having a little moment, you know." She took a breath and turned toward him with a broad smile. "I'm fine. Really. See?"

The old gentleman was not convinced, but decided not to press. "Well, if you ever want to talk."

Mary smiled brightly. "You bet, thanks."

THE DOWNSTAIRS FRONT DOOR OF EMMA'S CONDO WAS OPEN AND the Visitor Press Secretary leaned back in for a final, delicious good-bye kiss. Emma was wearing a silky, pink low-cut slip that displayed her body in a very appealing manner.

"I'll see you at the rally," Paul said as he reluctantly separated from her.

"Mmmm"—Emma purred as she ran her hand down his chest—"and after." Then he took his leave as she waved and closed the door. He had lingered far longer than Emma had wanted. She knew Mark would be arriving soon to pick her up for the rally, but she'd been unable to ease Paul out any more quickly. The moment she shut the door she bolted to the phone in her foyer. She dialed it desperately with one hand while she rubbed the awful scent of Paul from her lips. She was muttering impatiently to the phone, "Come on, Julie, answer!"

The front door suddenly burst open behind her. It was Mark. He was furious. He slammed the door and crossed angrily toward her. "Sorry I'm a little early coming through your revolving door."

She was totally startled and confused. "Mark? What is it? Wait—wait," she spoke urgently into the phone, "hi, it's Emma . . . Listen—"

Mark grabbed the receiver from her and slammed it down as he pointed at the door, glowering at her with a frightening smile. "How many?"

"What!"

"How many of us suckers are there? And how many of 'em are *reptiles?*"

She was firm and brusque with him. "It's not what you think." She reached for the phone, but he kept his hand firmly on top of it. She looked at him with heated desperation in her green eyes. "Mark, I've got to warn them! Diana's got a spy inside their headquarters and—"

"You were so fucking convincing"—he laughed darkly—"and I am a prize fucking fool, huh!"

"Listen to me!" She looked fiercely at him. "I do love you!"

"Right"—he laughed bitterly—"funny way of showing it: by screwing Paul and God knows who else so you can pump all of them for information, too!"

She suddenly shrieked at him through angry, bitter tears. "*I hate what I've had to do! Okay! Do you hear me? I detest it!*" She leveled her gaze at him, speaking forcefully, "But my body is no more important than all the others who risk or lose theirs in this war! Now let me call to warn them before—"

"*Stop it!*" He bellowed so loudly the walls seemed to shake. He grabbed the phone from her, ripped it from the wall, and drew back his arm about to smash her face with the instrument. He paused at the last second, quivering with rage, and then he threw it past her, shattering the large, ornate mirror that had been reflecting them. He glared at her with an intensity she had never seen from him, then he turned resolutely and walked out.

IN THE FLAGSHIP'S BOWELS JON RUSHED OUT OF THE TRANSPORT tube onto the dark lower level where the half-breed girl told him she'd seen Willy. Jon ran flat-out down the inky passageway, startling other Visitor workers. He was finally rewarded with a brief glimpse of Willy passing a distant intersection ahead. Jon called out, but Willy didn't hear, so Jon ran even harder to intercept him.

At the same time on Nob Hill, Emma reached the phone in her living room and was dialing it hurriedly.

The Resistance warehouse was nearly empty because the teams had already left on their missions. Harmy was filling in for Gary and helping Ysabel contact the rest of the international Resistance cells to alert them of the forthcoming action. Mike was shuffling painfully behind his wheelchair, again using it as a walker. He was coming from the database truck where he had been doing further astronomical research. His suspicions about the Zedti's home planet had been confirmed. They had lied. Mike was heading to confront Kayta.

Ruby was also in the warehouse and feeling very frustrated. Julie had laid down the law to her to stay put this time. When the base cell phone rang, Ruby grabbed it. "This is Lexington Base, go ahead." Mike glanced over and saw the human aspects of the girl's scaly face go pale as she gasped, "What! Oh, my God! I'll try to catch them!" She rushed toward Mike and pressed the phone into his hand. "Emma says the Visitors know everything we've planned! We've got a spy!"

"What!"

Ruby was running for the door. "Right in the middle of us!"

"Who is it?"

"She didn't know. But we've got to tell Mom they're all in danger." She shouted back to him, "See if you can reach her! Speed dial one! I'll try to catch up with them!" The frightened girl dashed out the door. Mike dialed the cell and got a fast busy signal. Then he was surprised as the phone rang in his hand.

He was confused as he answered, "Yeah? Julie! Listen—"

He heard a Visitor voice on the other end speaking urgently, "No, it's me, William. Is that you, Mike?"

"Willy, yeah it's me, listen—"

"No, you listen first. I'm in a laboratory on the Flagship. Jon snuck me in here as soon as the others left for the rally."

Willy glanced around nervously to be certain the lab was indeed still empty. Young Jon had been keeping a careful watch. They were the only two in the chamber. Then Willy looked back at the black and white screen, which showed a blurry, unsteady view of Resistance headquarters. "Listen to me: there's a hidden camera down there in the warehouse."

"What!" Mike's eyes scanned the place quickly. "Where?"

"Jon thinks it's *inside someone*!"

Mike was appropriately startled by that concept. "*Inside someone*!"

"Yes, transmitting an image from their optic nerve! I'm looking right now at an image from the warehouse! There's faint audio as well. Who's there with you?"

He looked around quickly. "The Secretary-General, his wife, Ysabel, one of the Zedti named Kayta . . ."

Willy was watching the monitor and saw the people Mike was describing. "Who else?"

"Ruby was here, but she just took off"—then he saw—"Harmy?" Mike had a sudden flash. "Oh, my God. While she was interrogated! They must have—"

"No, no," Willy said, "I can *see* all of them. Harmy, too. So it has to be someone else."

Mike looked around again. "But everybody else is—Oh, my God . . ." He had chanced to look at a shiny teakettle nearby where he glimpsed his own reflection. In the Flagship lab Willy saw the same thing Mike was seeing. They both realized the awful truth simultaneously as Mike said, "It's in *me!*"

Outside, Ruby was rushing back across the junk-filled industrial complex toward the Resistance warehouse. She was grief-stricken because her attempt to catch Julie had been fruitless. Then she looked up to see a squad of Visitor Patrollers moving in to surround the building. She ducked behind a rusting forklift, her eyes quickly scanning for more of the enemy. She saw that four Airborne Patrollers, two Teammate units, and a pair of Patrol shuttles were all inbound. The twelve-year-old felt her world crumbling around her. She whimpered desperately to herself, "Oh, God. Please, no . . ."

Although Mike wasn't aware of the troops encircling the building, he had alerted the others within to the danger he himself posed to them. Secretary Mendez and his wife Juanita had climbed into the communications truck as Ysabel jumped into the driver's seat and started it up. Harmy closed the side doors of that truck, shouting, "Good luck!" Then she stepped up uncertainly into the truck housing the electron microscope. Julie had instructed her to endeavor to save the priceless equipment that truck contained in the event of an emergency. Harmy had never driven a truck, but was determined to do it.

Kayta had opened the wide doors of the warehouse and then hurriedly began collecting all of her Zedti medical equipment as Ysabel drove the communications truck out of the warehouse with Harmy's equipment truck stuttering out behind her. They were barely clear of the warehouse when they were suddenly and brilliantly illuminated by glaring searchlights from the incoming Patrol vehicles overhead.

Ysabel squinted into the bright lights and grabbed for a pulse rifle on the seat beside her, but then realized that they were hopelessly surrounded. She was furious, spitting the words angrily in Spanish, "God damn it to hell."

In the truck immediately behind Ysabel, panicky fear gripped Harmy as she also saw they were trapped.

Inside the old building, Kayta helped Mike get painfully to his feet, but didn't have much encouragement. "They're everywhere. I don't think there's a way out for us."

Then they heard a scraping of heavy metal and Mike saw a rusty drain grating in the concrete floor sliding open. Ruby's scaly knuckles were bloodied and she was smudged with filth. She called urgently to them, "This way, you guys! Hurry!"

AYDEN'S AIRBIKE WAS GLIDING THROUGH THE NIGHT SKY A THOU-sand feet over the rooftops of San Francisco. He was flying south toward Candlestick Park. Nathan was firmly on the seat behind the Zedti commander. He had just checked the radiation card Robert had given him and was pleased to see that it was green, indicating no radioactivity.

Ayden's piloting and attitude was as thoroughly commanding, businesslike, and focused as ever. Nathan had observed the en-tire process of flying the bike and noticed Ayden making slight adjustments to the airbike's trim just as Nathan had often made himself when flying a Visitor patrol craft or a fighter. He did not realize that the final adjustment Ayden casually made was to a control for the small nuclear missile mounted on the lower front of the bike. The Zedti surreptitiously switched its guidance sys-tem on and activated the primer for its nuclear triggering mech-anism. A tiny indicator on the bike's control panel began to blink a cautionary yellow.

RUBY, MIKE, AND KAYTA WERE HURRYING THROUGH THE STEAMY storm sewers that led away from the warehouse complex. Ruby was trying to contact Julie by radio while Kayta supported Mike who was angry on several counts. "Diana kept me alive to *use me*: she figured there was probably still a spy or two up on the Flagship, maybe she even suspected Martin, so she dangled that bait about her 'special prisoner' waiting for someone to bite."

Kayta understood and completed his thought, "Knowing you'd then be rescued and brought to the Resistance, yes. And that's why they let you escape from Harmy's. Ayden and I saw their troops arrive, then hold back."

"But why'd they arrest Harmy later?" He immediately realized, "For show. Of course. To throw us off the scent." Mike felt terribly responsible. "I can't believe I let it all happen."

"You were barely alive, Mike," Kayta counseled as she helped him limp along. "You didn't even know where you were." She saw that it was no comfort to him. She felt guilty herself. "I'm the one who should have realized it. I sensed something wrong the first time I met you."

"When I said it was just my bad vibes, yeah. We didn't know how bad they were."

Ruby pounded her radio in frustration. "I can't get a damned signal. I'm going up." She grabbed the slimy rung of an access ladder nearby but Mike pulled her back as a searchlight knifed through a grating over them casting sharp parallel shadows across their faces.

"I wonder if the bastards can still get a signal from me? Still see where we are?" He looked at Kayta. "Can you feel it in there? Shut it off somehow?"

Kayta touched Mike's left temple with her fingertips. She closed her violet eyes, trying to sense it. "I am not certain."

He was resolute. "You've got to try, otherwise I'll be no good to anybody but them."

Kayta reluctantly reached into her pack and withdrew one of her electric needles. "There will be pain, Mike."

He chuckled darkly. "What else is new? Go for it."

She felt his temple again with her ultrasensitive fingertips until she pinpointed the source of a ghostly faint electrical fluctuation. Then she pierced his temple with her needle. Mike gasped. Kayta glanced upward, having heard Visitor and Teammate voices drawing near overhead, searching for them.

"We must be quiet!" Kayta said, about to withdraw the needle.

"Don't stop," Mike hissed through his teeth, which were clenched against the pain. It was far worse than he'd expected.

Ruby had also flinched in sympathy with the agony Mike was undergoing. Her scaly little hand snapped out to him in support. Mike grasped it and held on tightly, choking down his pain as the voices continued almost directly over their heads.

"My left eye," Mike gasped, "I can't see out of it now."

Then Kayta withdrew the needle and Mike sagged, damp with sweat. Kayta checked a tiny indicator on her instrument and nodded, whispering, "I think I disabled it."

Mike swallowed hard, drawing deep breaths. Then he whispered back to her, "You better give my legs another dose." The blond Zedti looked at him, she feared putting him through additional pain, but his insistent gaze spurred her on.

She prepared the electric needle for the second operation and Ruby positioned herself behind Mike, whispering, "Lean back on me, Mike." He did and the girl reached around him from behind to hold his hands again.

As Kayta injected his right leg, Mike squirmed and pressed back against the supportive little half-breed girl. He was nearly fainting from the searing, stinging pain. Ruby held him tightly.

AFTER THE GIGANTIC, SIXTEEN-MILE-WIDE FLAGSHIP THAT FILLED the sky over the city, the second largest structure in San Francisco was Candlestick Park. It was massive. It had been built in a roughly oval shape, with the east side twisted slightly into a boomerang curve in a failed effort to diminish the winds that plagued the playing field. It was the height of a twelve-story building and the forty thousand seats of the upper level completely encircled the thirty-five thousand seats below them. On the evening of the Visitor rally, an additional twenty-five thousand seats had been set up on the field to accommodate the overflow crowd.

Located right on the water of San Francisco Bay, Candlestick Park had been infamous for being very cold and foggy even in the middle of summer. But since the waters of the bay had been taken away, the fog had all but vanished as well. It was said that the prevailing, chilly winds from left center field made Candlestick the most difficult American ballpark in which to hit a home run. But that was exactly what the Visitors intended to do on the night of the rally.

The enormous coliseum had been decked out like a grand opening ceremony for the Olympic Games. Huge Visitor and American flags wafted from its highest reaches. Of the hundred thousand people gathered, over half wore Teammate uniforms. There were also tens of thousands of uniformed Visitors present. Some were interspersed among the humans, others were marshaled proudly into individual rank-and-file contingents. Several companies of armed Patrollers with gleaming stainless-steel ceremonial helmets surrounded the raised dais in the center of the stadium field behind where second base would have been.

The dais, elevated some eight feet in the air, already that evening had been the stage for a number of performers in a program designed to invigorate the assembling crowd. A dozen huge vid screens had been erected around the stadium to show close-up images of those onstage. Two rock bands selected for their crossover appeal to numerous age groups had gotten the evening off to a rousing start. Then three tenors from the Metropolitan Opera in New York had dazzled the audience with their intricate vocal pyrotechnics accompanied by the San Francisco Symphony Orchestra and Chorus, who were on the field in front of the dais. Finally the orchestra had performed the concluding movement from Beethoven's Fifth Symphony during which the fifty Mothership captains took their seats along one side of the dais. Joining them on the other side of the stage were many of the human Players who worked most closely with the Visitors. The mayor and his key aides were among them, as were the owners or managers of the principal Earthside facilities that served the Visitors' needs, including Alexander Smithson, the weapons manufacturer, and J. D. Oliver.

Several secondary aides to the Visitor Commandants were sitting in a section reserved for them on the field next to the orchestra. Martin sat among them.

As the Fifth Symphony ended and the applause died down, a deep human voice echoed from the stadium's huge loudspeakers, "Distinguished guests, fellow Visitors and Teammates, ladies and gentlemen, please welcome Commandants Diana and Jeremy!"

The symphony played a slow, strong, and dignified work, reminiscent of Elgar's "Pomp and Circumstance," as the two powerful chieftains were escorted onto the stage by Shawn and several other aides. Diana and Jeremy graciously acknowledged the welcoming applause and the straight-armed palm-up salutes from the assembled multitude. Then they took their seats in the center of the dais. Shawn and the other key aides sat down behind them.

From the dizzying heights at the top of the stadium to those on the field closest the dais, there was an expectant enthusiasm among the buzzing crowd. Then their myriad conversations grew hushed as the orchestral work diminished to silence while the lights began to dim, revealing more of the stars twinkling in the black sky above.

Everyone focused on the dais where a lone African-American

female stepped into the powerful spotlights. In the darkness nearby, Diana was discreetly eyeing the beautiful singer who wore a floor-length, off-the-shoulder, ivory sheath dress. Emma began to sing an a cappella solo in her clean, clear voice. People recognized the familiar melody of "The Battle Hymn of the Republic," but the lyrics were new. Emma's singing was extremely slow and measured.

> *"Mine eyes have seen the Glory . . .*
> *Of the People from the Stars . . .*
> *They will bring a bright Tomorrow . . .*
> *To this troubled world of ours . . ."*

Because her face was being shown in close-up on the giant screens in the coliseum, everyone there and also around the world noticed that there seemed to be tears in Emma's eyes as she sang. Most of those watching assumed that her tears were occasioned by the emotional, poignant honor she felt at representing the Visitors and her devout dedication to them.

The new lyrics continued to glorify the Visitors and herald the arrival of their Great Leader.

Emma's image was also displayed in the Centcom aboard the Flagship where the Resistance spy, Lee, had secured a key position for herself near the transmission section. Numerous monitors in front of her were individually labeled *To Europe, Asia, Africa*, and other specific areas of Earth. Lee knew that billions of people in cities and villages across the world were being sent the images from Candlestick Park. From mansions in cities like New York, London, and Paris, to suburban homes on the outskirts of places like Indianapolis or Prague, to cheap walk-up tenements in the likes of Buenos Aires, Auckland, or Osaka, to scanty huts in Third World locales like Afghanistan, Chile, or Indonesia, the inhabitants of Earth were watching. All of those billions of people had felt the impact of the Visitors, both good and

bad, for over twenty years. Tonight they all felt anxious anticipation. They had been told that on this evening something very
new was going to begin; an exciting new chapter about to open.
The broadcast from San Francisco was the only transmission being allowed that evening and it was on every channel worldwide.

And among the vast audience that was watching were the
women and men who were secretly working against the Visitors.
They had received the communication from the Prime Resistance Cell in San Francisco to be prepared for what would tran-
spire this evening. The freedom fighters had been told by their
local leaders to arm themselves. And they had all done so in the
hopes that the Resistance would finally be able to achieve their
long-awaited breakthrough, to turn the tide against their hated
occupiers.

In the Centcom, Lee glanced at a slightly larger monitor that
was designated as the incoming on-air feed and was duly labeled
From Marin Comm Link.

The Marin Communications Center was situated on a rural
hilltop north of San Francisco. Its large dish antenna was fifty
feet in diameter and aimed at the distant Flagship. Margarita,
Street-C, Julie, and others of their team had stealthily made their
way up the thickly forested hillside. They were inching carefully
closer through the undergrowth toward the Cyclone fence
topped with razor wire that denoted the perimeter of the facility.
They made careful reconnaissance of the four guards who were
casually on duty. Two of them were watching small vid players
that carried the ceremony underway at Candlestick Park.

The Resistance team communicated to each other with hand
signals about the best approach, then Street-C began to quietly
use a heavy bolt cutter on a section of the fence closest to him.

IN THE MURKY, FOUL-SMELLING STORM SEWERS RUBY WAS AGGRA-
vated that she still couldn't get a signal to warn Julie. She shook
the radio in her hands. "Come on, dammit!"

Kayta was dressing the areas on Mike's knees where she had just operated on him. Blind in his left eye, he was still recovering from the excruciating medical treatments, but now that they were behind him he was focused on grilling her, "You're not from Altair, are you?" The way in which Kayta glanced away, ashamed, confirmed his thesis. "Right. You're from a binary star system much closer. My guess is that you got our distress call a long time ago, huh? You could've come to help us a lot sooner!" Kayta maintained a grim silence as Mike seethed, "You Zedti just watched us going to hell, but you didn't give a shit, until you thought the Visitors were threatening *you*."

Her violet eyes finally looked directly into his with surprising strength of purpose. "Yes, Mike. That is all true. Now try to stand. We must hurry if we're to save your friends."

AT CANDLESTICK PARK THE SYMPHONY ORCHESTRA HAD SOFTLY BE- gun accompanying Emma as she sang the stirring new "Battle Hymn" and as Emma began the next verse the hundred-strong voices of the chorus also softly joined with hers to create a feeling of deep, almost spiritual anticipation.

The people and Visitors gathered within the enormous bowl reacted with surprise as beams of high-intensity searchlights po- sitioned outside the stadium suddenly shot up into the dark sky and trained upon a startling object.

It was a spacecraft, approaching at a ceremonial, measured pace. Though clearly of Visitor design, it was unlike any that had ever been seen before. The sleek, beautiful craft was golden.

An audible gasp escaped from the entire assemblage. The symphony and chorus built steadily upon the triumphant song and then the lyrics appeared conveniently on all the screens of the stadium so that everyone present could join in. It was an as- tounding sound: a full symphony orchestra supporting the massed voices of one hundred thousand humans and Visitors.

The music was transformed stupendously into a glorious choral hymn of welcome.

The craft glided closer and lower, reaching an altitude of less than a thousand feet over the eager multitude. In the brilliance of the searchlights the surface of the ship looked like liquid gold. And as the thousands of Visitors within Candlestick Park saw the side hatch begin to open, they raised a mighty chant, *"All hail our Great Leader!"*

There was a moment's pause, then the Leader appeared in the hatch of the golden craft and stepped out into midair, causing the entire gathering to catch its breath. Flanked by four airborne honor guards like attending angels, the Visitor Leader floated downward.

She was a striking, mature beauty. By earthly standards she appeared to be about fifty years of age. Her hair was thick and dark with a few streaks of gray, drawn to the sides of her head and fastened so that it might fall to its full length midway down her back and in front of her well-shaped bosom. She wore the Visitor ivory blouse and dark pants, but with a magnificent, flowing, purple robe of state that caught the wind and billowed outward. Her face was strong with high cheekbones, her lips full and, some would have said, sensuous. Her eyes were large, expressive, and a very dark blue. There were smile lines radiating from the corners of them. She combined the warm, inviting, and assuring smile of the Madonna with the supremely confident bearing of an archangel. She seemed strong as forged steel, yet blessed with effortless benevolence. There was a primal force inherent in her, a magnetism, a gravity that was undeniable. She was every inch a charismatic.

The symphony orchestra continued the inspiring music that accompanied her arrival, each aspect and detail of which had been carefully designed by Diana to achieve the most potent and inspiring psychological impact on the hundred thousand gathered at

Candlestick Park and the billions of others watching across the entire planet.

Huge billboard screens on the walls of buildings worldwide displayed the Leader's strikingly august image to awestruck humans and Visitors. People everywhere watched intently as she slowly descended from the starry night sky like a veritable goddess, smiling and greeting the cheering throng below. She looked delighted as thousands of camera strobes flashed and sparkled like the facets of so many diamonds, capturing her image.

Her hand was extended, palm up, in peaceful greeting. The elated crowd, including Debra Stein among her fellow Teammates, saluted her in kind. Thousands of arms outstretched, palm upward in the direction of the Great Leader.

The humans, who had not known what to expect, beheld her imperial, portentous, otherworldly arrival with wonder. Some, like Emma and Mark, felt a tightening in their throats and recognized a faintly metallic taste in their mouths. It was fear.

27

THE PATROLLER GUARDS OUTSIDE THE MARIN COMM LINK WERE SO focused on their vid player showing the telecast from Candlestick that they never knew what hit them. Street-C, Margarita, and several of the militarily trained Resistance team silently and efficiently dispatched them from behind.

Street-C was jazzed, but as Julie came up the hill to join them he saw the concerned expression on her face. "What's up, Doc?"

Julie looked around worriedly. "This almost feels too easy." Her radio crackled and she reached for it. "Yes? Hello?" But there was only static.

Street-C pointed up at the big dish antenna looming over them. "Too much interference up this close."

* * *

KAYTA'S AIRBIKE WAS AIRBORNE AND FLYING NORTH TOWARD MARIN County in an effort to intercept and warn Julie, Margarita, and their team. As the airbike sailed out over the Golden Gate Bridge, lights of tiny cars glittered below. Ruby was on the seat directly behind Kayta, and Mike sat behind them both. Ruby frantically adjusted her radio. "Mom? Can you hear me? Mom!"

"I thought you had her for a second there," Mike said tensely. "Keep trying, Rube."

AT CANDLESTICK PARK, DIANA AND JEREMY WERE BOTH WATCHING with gleaming eyes as the Leader descended lower until she skimmed just overtop the people on the field. The symphonic music continued. She had already made a transit over the entire upper level of the stadium, acknowledging the up-reaching hands of the standing people. Now she drifted lower still so that a few lucky ones on the field might touch the hem of her flowing purple cape.

Diana and Jeremy had risen along with everyone else. Now they stepped forward to greet the Leader as she descended through the night sky punctuated by thousands of camera flashes. The brilliant, narrow spotlight beams cut through the dark air and followed her down to the dais. She alighted like a lovely feather. As the masses applauded, Shawn was pleased to see the Leader cast a very intimate glance at Jeremy. But to Shawn's surprise, Diana was gifted with an equally intimate look from the deep blue imperial eyes.

The Leader turned toward the eager masses, who again brought forth a grand ovation with whistles and shouts accompanied by the strong chant from her fellow Visitors, *"All hail our Great Leader!"* She accepted their cheers and applause graciously.

As the grand reception continued undiminished for many minutes, Diana glanced at the mammoth vid screens, which flashed close-ups of the Leader's compelling face. They showed her clear, soulful eyes and her kind, caring countenance. Diana had personally selected and approved each of the camera positions. Those capturing the closest shots were all somewhat below the Leader's eye line, which made her appear just slightly taller and above all of those whom she addressed. It also lent a subtly heroic stature to the Leader's image. It was a tried and true device long employed by classic filmmakers. John Ford and Orson Welles had used it. So had Leni Riefenstahl in her stunning, provocative works of Nazi propaganda. Like Riefenstahl and the skillful media wizards who orchestrated the coverage of giant American political conventions, Diana sought to convey all the persuasive aspects of the intense gathering by placing other cameras high and wide to illustrate the expansive grandeur of the adoring masses. Still other cameras were handheld down among the breathless multitude, capturing glimpses of the exuberant human faces in the Teammate units, the solidarity and brave confidence of Visitors in their neatly formed squads, the elation of earthly civilians and Players who were thrilled to be in the presence of, and an integral part of, such dazzling power and greatness. These were the images seen around the world.

With self-effacing modesty, the Leader graciously accepted the adulation of the people whose cheers might have continued for many more minutes. But finally by merely standing still, she slowly quieted them with the easy friendliness of a Great Communicator.

When she spoke, her voice, with its resonant alien quality, proved to be uniquely mellow. It projected a calm demeanor and infinite charm. She spoke in English, but as the scene was transmitted globally her words passed through an auto-translator in the Flagship Centcom so that her own confidence-inspiring voice was heard in every human language worldwide. The quality of her voice was consistent in every language: melodious, caring, like balm.

"My dear, dear friends," she began with a beguiling, humble smile, "how I have longed to be among you. For I consider myself to be thrice blessed." Her bright eyes twinkled with anticipation. "Firstly, I am privileged to lead"—her voice swelled with pride—"*the mighty race from my home planet.*"

The legions of Visitors instantly took their cue like sworn delegates at a political convention. They raised a mighty cheer that lasted for two full minutes and only quieted when the Leader slightly lifted a finger.

She spoke directly to her adoring troops. "You are a true hyper-power." She paused, knowing that they would again raise a cheer, which they did. Mark, a veteran of many political gatherings, recognized the Leader's tremendous natural skill at being able to play to, and with, an admiring audience. Her hand swept over her people as if in blessing. "You are destined to be masters of all that you survey." Again, an ovation affirmed her statement and that her faith in her legions was well placed.

In their cheap tenement in the Sci Section, the Elgins' old TV displayed the thrilled reaction of the Leader's troops, panning across their strong faces. Charles and his father were intent on the screen and were both frowning. Mary, wearing a thin chenille bathrobe, watched stoically, until Charles looked over at her. She instantly took a deep cleansing breath and smiled. "Fascinating, huh? But I think I'd rather take a bath." She stood and kissed both her father-in-law and her husband on the forehead. Then she looked into Charles's eyes lovingly, ran her fingers through his hair, and kissed him a second time.

The TV drew Charles's attention as Mary quietly exited. The smiling Leader had begun to speak further to her uniformed compatriots. "You are a race unique in the universe. But what wonderful helpmates you have found here . . ."

From the dais in the center of the stadium her voice boomed out, "*Among the wonderful people of Earth!*" The humans in the huge audience responded to their own cue and cheered loudly. The Leader spread her arms wide and turned in a complete circle as if to symbolically embrace those on all sides of her.

Some of the humans like J. D. Oliver and Teammate Debra Stein were intensely passionate and exuberant; others, like Mark, were polite but not swept away, and a few were entirely silent. Mark noted that Emma was one of the latter.

In the Steins' modest house Danny and Stella were watching the rally unfold on their TV. Danny sniped angrily, "At least among the people of Earth you haven't captured or killed." His mother glanced at him, but Danny wouldn't return her look.

At Candlestick Park, the Leader continued to draw everyone into her grand plan. "Let me be very clear about this: I want all humans to join our society and help us claim new worlds as part of our *mutual dominion*." Her eyes sought out the eyes of specific humans on the field nearest her. "I want you, and you, and you"—she then looked directly into the camera she knew to be carrying her close-up, speaking directly through it to the billions of humans watching around the world—"and *YOU*—to share in the vast riches to be found across space. By uniting with my own extraordinary race each one of you here on Earth has absolutely *everything to gain!*"

Mary Elgin stood in the small bathroom of their tenement. Cheers from the stadium echoed from the TV in her living room as well as from other TVs and radios in nearby apartments outside her window. Mary was looking at her drawn face in the bathroom mirror, which had a small crack on one side. She gazed searchingly into her own tired brown eyes, looking for something that she couldn't seem to find. Then she sighed and looked down at the stained, pitted sink. She sat down on the edge of the bathtub, which was equally as distressed as the sink. She turned the tub's squeaky, rusting faucet. It sputtered as always, then began to fill the tub. The basket of sweet-smelling bath soaps and gels that Emma had brought rested on the small, cracked octagonal tiles of the floor. Mary lifted the basket into her lap and began to unwrap one of the gels. But her eyes were not focused on it; she stared right past it, her breathing shallow, measured.

THE SMALL STAFF OF VISITORS AND HUMANS INSIDE THE MARIN communications Link was startled as Margarita and company suddenly swept in like professional soldiers, surprising them. Margarita was in the lead, pulse pistol held in both hands at arm's length in front of her as she commanded, "Everyone on the floor!"

Street-C shoved one recalcitrant Visitor down. "You heard the lady! Now!"

Julie's voice was more calming. "Just take it easy and no one will get hurt, I promise." Julie went to a bank of equipment. She sought out the unit she needed and inserted their Resistance vid disk that now included the Secretary-General's powerful revelations. She clicked the unit onto standby.

ON AYDEN'S AIRBIKE, NATHAN PEERED OVER THE ZEDTI'S SHOULDER. He saw they were already passing over the old Bethlehem Shipyards five hundred feet below them. He could also see the searchlights of Candlestick Park crisscrossing the night sky in the distance. "Shouldn't you be switching to stealth mode?"

"Soon," Ayden said, nodding.

Nathan saw Ayden reach down and subtly activate a small control. A tiny indicator light on the airbike control console switched from yellow to blinking red. Something about the indicator coupled with Ayden's secretive body language troubled Nathan. He pulled the radiation sensor card from his pocket and saw that it, too, had turned red, connoting that intense radioactivity had initiated nearby. Nathan realized that the Zedti had armed the missile. "Ayden! We agreed *no nuke!*"

"I'm sorry," Ayden said unemotionally, "but it's the best way."

"No, God damn it!" Nathan reached around for the missile

controller, but was no match for the Zedti's strength. Ayden grabbed Nathan's shoulder and leveraged him right off of the bike. Nathan yelped as he fell. He barely managed to grab a handhold on the side of the bike, but he was dangling five hundred feet above the ground. Ayden was trying to steady the flying bike that had been thrown out of balance by Nathan's predicament. Nathan realized his face was right beside the handle of the Zedti sonic weapon in its storage sheath by Ayden's leg. He whipped out the sonic pistol and fired it at Ayden.

The startled Zedti commander took the vortex concussion full against his side. The shock wave blew him off of his seat, away from the bike, and into free fall. The bike began to fishtail wildly, threatening to shake Nathan off.

As Ayden swiftly gathered velocity toward the ground a small device popped from his belt and snapped outward to form a triangular parasail. He swung down beneath it and grabbed the guidance straps that allowed him to maneuver it as he glided down toward a rooftop. He glared up into the distance and saw the airbike was out of control and spiraling downward quickly.

Nathan strained against his own dead weight and the powerful centrifugal force of the spinning airbike. Only with a mighty effort was he able to pull himself back up onto it. He grasped the controls and brought the nose of the bike up just yards above the shipyard's weathered concrete. Breathing hard, he gained altitude and saw Ayden drifting downward beneath his parasail. Nathan grumbled angrily, "Good idea: go fly a kite."

Then he deactivated the nuclear missile and switched the airbike into camouflaged stealth mode as he flew on quickly toward Candlestick Park.

WALL-SIZED VID SCREENS FROM AMSTERDAM TO PHILADELPHIA TO Tokyo were carrying the live image of the Leader, who had been speaking fondly of the Visitor connection to Earth's women, men, and children. As the applause to her latest words died down, she drew a breath and a particularly earnest expression appeared on her face. "But I said that I was *thrice* blessed. And so I am. I now address both those of my own race and of the human race about a subject that is very important and dear to me. Because in addition to embracing all of you into our grand new community, I also open my heart to the newest members of our two races"—her voice took on an earnest tenderness—"those of mixed heritage—our wonderful *half-breeds.*"

A murmur of surprise mixed with slight disenchantment rippled across the stadium. Lowest-caste half-breeds everywhere suddenly grew more attentive, including the mute girl Jon had encountered aboard the Flagship. She was watching in the steamy, overcrowded barrack that housed her and many others of her kind.

"These youth have been too long ignored. Too long disenfranchised and demeaned. But I ask you, my friends, was it their fault to have been born of mixed heritage?" She looked strongly into her audience's eyes, prompting them, "Well, *was* it their fault?"

The Leader paused and heard scores of shouts from across the expansive stadium crying, "No! No, it wasn't!"

"Did those mixed-race children *choose* to be born? Did they?"

"No!" came the heartier return cry from many more voices now. Mark noticed that Shawn had looked away, apparently uncomfortable with the subject. But the Leader pressed on.

"Of course they did not. Who would choose to be an outcast? Who would choose to be called a *dreg*?" She shook her head with consummate sadness and distaste. "I tell you, my friends, that word is anathema to me." She looked up, solemnly presenting a new concept. "Let us show what a great society we are by never speaking it again. I urge human and Visitor alike to join me in laying prejudice and intolerance aside. I urge you to embrace our half-breeds even as I do. They are a great resource, for these vigorous offspring physically *unite* our two magnificent races." A low groundswell of applause had begun to build within the coliseum. "They are blood of our blood and flesh of our flesh." The Leader's voice grew in passion, shepherding the audience's growing response. "And they deserve to be equal partners with us. So please, I beg you . . . *Will you let them be!*"

The crowd roared its approval. Half-breeds around the world looked at each other in wonder, feeling a powerful new allegiance to this remarkable and caring Leader.

On the dais, the Leader soaked up the generosity of the multitude. She responded with humility and an appreciative bow. "From the depths of my heart, I thank you all." Again the applause continued for a long time. People of all races were entranced by this incredible female. How could they not be? She had made them feel at one with her and with each other.

As the Leader rose back up from her bow her tone darkened, growing more portentous. "I thank you, my friends. Particularly because we need the help of *all* our people to defeat *a devious enemy*. They are a willful race of warmongers descended from horrid insects. They are called the *Zedti*."

The tight ranks of Visitor Patrollers in the stadium hissed angrily. The Leader nodded her agreement. "Yes. My people know them well. We have witnessed firsthand the Zedti cunning, the Zedti lies, their total lack of honor, and the horrendous Zedti brutality." Her eyes slowly scanned the huge stadium, her words came echoing from the loudspeakers, "And now they are threatening Mother Earth."

The Leader heard tense whispering stir through the crowd. She confirmed it and built upon it. "Yes. Their advance scouts are already among us. They have united with Earth's criminal scientists, determined to destroy us *all*." She felt the crowd's unease increase and she fanned the flames. "Oh, yes. It's true. Let me give you proof. Just look at some of their nightmarish handiwork . . ." She pointed toward the huge screens positioned high around the arena. On those screens and on television screens across the planet appeared grisly images of the grotesque chrysalic husks to which some photogenic blood and gore had been artistically added for effect. Everyone watching, both in Candlestick Park and in their homes everywhere, gasped in shock.

The Leader spoke reverently, "These were our comrades, humans and Visitors who fought alongside one another to preserve our future." Then her voice grew more intensely challenging, "Shall they have died *in vain?*"

From a hundred thousand throats came shouts of *"No! No!"*

"Or"—the Leader's voice grew stronger still—"shall their martyrdom *inspire and strengthen us?*"

The crowd before her and all the Mothership captains on the dais behind her shouted affirmation. And still the Leader's voice intensified. "Shall we avenge their deaths, *a thousand times over?*" The positive cheers of outrage and determination swelled throughout the arena, but the Leader's voice boomed the loudest, "Shall we *begin tonight?*"

The massive crowd roared, *"YES!"*

Then families across the world watched as a small circular cage with vertical laser bars slowly rose up from the stage floor near the Leader. Like many watching, Emma drew a sharp breath when she saw the prisoner within. It was Bryke. She sat cross-legged on the cage floor, very composed. But it was clear to Martin and to Emma that the Zedti female had been badly brutalized. Sections of her blue-black, shiny skin were blistered from burns. The close-cropped curly black hair on her head had many bare patches where it had been scraped off and raw skin showed through, some of it oozing her yellow blood.

Diana had not known about this demonstration and glanced sharply at a smugly smiling Jeremy, who had obviously orchestrated it.

The Leader pointed at Bryke in the cage. *"This* is the beast who did these foul deeds. *This* is one of the demons from the despicable race known as the Zedti." The Leader pointed again at the close-up, frighteningly gory images of the husks. "These are just their first acts of terrorism against us. The Zedti do not cherish life as we do. They are aggressive, vicious, deadly."

The Leader's sincere eyes looked out across the thousands of faces in the dark arena before her and the billions of others she knew to be watching. "Be assured, my dear friends, that I would never put any one of you into harm's way unless there was a clear and present danger. But that is precisely what we are facing." Her words became measured and specific. "We have solid, irrefutable intelligence that the Zedti are creating new weapons—chemical, biological, and nuclear—that can cause even more mass destruction than those they already possess. We know for certain that they pose an *imminent threat to all of us*. We cannot have true peace and security in our homelands until the Zedti are destroyed. We must join together to launch *a preemptive strike against them*. And since their planet is *heavy with water*, Earth's oceans can be restored *much sooner!*"

The masses roared their approval.

Nathan heard their cheers as he guided his nearly invisible airbike past two Visitor fighters, which were making slow patrolling circles around the half-mile-wide coliseum. He eased in for a landing on the roof of the stadium, choosing its southwest side that put him slightly behind and to the left of the dais. He slung over his shoulder the three pulse rifles that he had charged to their maximum potency before he'd left the warehouse. Then he climbed off the bike and out of its stealth shield. He moved carefully across the dark metal roof toward a firing position.

In the Flagship Centcom at that moment, the Resistance's female Visitor spy, Lee, ran her hand through her short black hair, trying to hide the tension that was tightening her face. She wanted to remain nonchalant and not attract any undue notice from the other technicians who worked at the various consoles near her. She was watching the vid screens sending the transmission out to the world while monitoring the up-link feed from Marin County. Right next to her there was a much smaller screen from a security camera mounted inside the Marin control room. She kept her fingers near that particular monitor so she could turn it off instantly if any other Visitor approached. On the little screen she could see Margarita, Julie, and the others holding the Marin staff at bay and awaiting the right moment to interrupt the rally telecast. Lee knew that they were waiting for the assassination attempt to begin at Candlestick.

Lee had secretly repatched the outgoing circuits making them redundant six times over so that other technicians would have great difficulty in finding and cutting off the Resistance telecast once she began transmitting it.

But then a worried Willy eased in beside Lee, whispering, "Big trouble." He pointed at Margarita and Julie on the small screen. "We need to warn them."

Lee snatched up a communicator and keyed a switch on her console. "There, see?" Lee was pointing at the image from the Marin security camera and to a phone line that was blinking in that distant control room. One of the Marin Visitor techs reached for it, but a wary Margarita stopped him.

Willy agonized, whispering, "No, no, Margarita. Pick it up. Please." But the critical call blinked, unanswered, as Willy and Lee watched helplessly and the rally continued on the Centcom screens.

"To defeat the Zedti and protect humans and Visitors alike," the Leader was saying, "Team Visitor has created a powerful new biochemical weapon. It is harmless to Visitors and humans, but it can and will exterminate these Zedti vermin. Another triumph for our wonderful *Team Visitor!*" The crowd responded with healthy and appreciative applause. Then the commanding female smiled proudly. "To demonstrate it, please help me greet a young person whose inspiring loyalty and dedication to our cause is unsurpassed. He is the youth who actually captured the brutal Zedti you see here. He is the first of our wonderful half-breeds to become a Teammate. Please welcome with me . . . *Teammate Ted!*"

Jeremy watched the great crowd applaud enthusiastically as the Leader went to the front of the dais and beckoned Ted up from the seat of honor Jeremy had arranged for him in front of the dais. The boy looked extremely nervous.

Ted had been excited at being a party to capturing the Zedti and pleased how his action had instantly elevated him among his fellow Teammates as he had always wanted. But the extraordinary attention of the crowd and the presence of the Leader had very much unsettled him. In spite of the Leader's eloquent words about half-breeds and about him personally, Ted felt that he had become something of a pawn in a grand drama, which was suddenly sweeping along so quickly that he didn't entirely comprehend where it might lead.

Sitting in the Centcom control room, Willy's stomach knotted painfully as he saw his son take the Leader's hand. Lee glanced at her friend sympathetically. She knew that Willy was feeling sickened by the sight, by Ted's betrayal of everything Willy and Harmy believed in so deeply.

In the midst of the Candlestick crowd, however, Debra Stein was elated and beaming. She shouted to all the Teammates around her, "He's *my* partner! Yeah! *Go Ted!*" Debra whistled and cheered along with the others.

The Leader, being an extremely keen student of psychology, discerned Ted's unease. She whispered to him, coaching fondly, "Wave to them, Ted, and watch what happens."

The teenager glanced into her deep blue eyes, then turned and raised his hand high in the Visitor salute. The crowd went wild, cheering madly for him. The Leader turned him in a slow circle, taking in the adoration of the entire audience. It was an

Earth-shaking experience for the scaly-faced half-breed with mismatched eyes who all his life had been spat upon. As the roar of the crowd filled his scaly ears, elation and exaltation of oceanic proportions such as Ted had never imagined stirred and nearly overwhelmed his young soul. But something deep within Ted seemed to prevent him from entirely embracing it. His brow, which normally clenched tightly during times of anxiety, was strangely numb. His father's words whispered faintly to him: beware what you wish for.

Images of the grotesque husks had again appeared on the screens and when the Leader completed the circle with Ted her voice grew solemn as she called her audience's attention to them. "Those lifeless husks could be your family. They were gentle, living, breathing creatures just like *you.*" Her voice rose powerfully again as she challenged the gathering, "Can we let this *continue to happen*?"

The crowd was roused, shouting, "*No! No!*"

The Leader grasped Ted's hand and pressed into it a small pistol. She spoke with a low but muscular voice that everyone could hear, "Teammate Ted, I am placing into your hand the means to render justice. Do you have the *will?*"

Ted looked uneasily at the spray weapon in his hand and then at Zen-like Bryke who was watching him from within the laser cage. He saw that her pink eyes were swollen from bludgeoning, but she was extremely calm.

On the top level of the stadium, Nathan had lain down into a firing position, his two additional weapons at the ready beside him. He brought the Leader's head into the crosshairs of his pulse weapon's vid sight as he murmured, "Say good-bye, bitch." He eased his finger onto the trigger, took a breath, and held it. He was squeezing the trigger as a fiery electrical pulse burst slammed into his side. It blew him onto his back and disabled his rifle. He looked up dazedly to see a Visitor fighter hovering silently a few yards behind him with its cannons aimed at him. The faint light of the fighter's control panel illuminated the pilot gazing at him with a cobra's smile. It was Gina.

On the dais, the Leader guided Ted closer to Bryke, who was completely at peace, until a Patroller unexpectedly prodded her sharply from behind with a laser spear. Bryke's head instinctively jerked around 180 degrees, the proboscis tubes lashed out from her nose, her arms hinged inhumanly backward to grasp at her assailant.

The assembled thousands gasped at her startling alienness and shouted angry encouragement to Ted. But he hesitated. The Leader felt his reluctance and smoothly placed her hand atop Ted's, aiming the weapon for him. Her finger pressed onto his, forcing him to spray the orange mist directly into the Zedti's face.

Bryke immediately seized up, unable to breathe. Her skin began to crack with thin, spiderwebbing fractures. Yellow blood oozed out from the hairline fissures. She turned and looked directly into Ted's wide, frightened eyes. Veins in her throat stood out under intense, mortal stress. He saw that her agony was extreme beyond measure, coursing through her in surges of splintered glass and icy fire, yet not the faintest sound emerged from the noble creature. Ted stared into her eyes as Bryke gazed back at him with consummate grace. Then her body shuddered horribly once, and remaining immovably upright, she died. Her sightless eyes remained open. They stared through Ted and into infinity.

Like millions of others, a huge wall screen on a San Francisco street had carried the image of Bryke's death. Among the many watching it was Ayden. He was on the rooftop nearby where he had landed after being blown from the airbike. His stoic, amber eyes stared at Bryke's lifeless body. Ayden brought his hands up in front of him and interlaced his fingers tightly.

On the dais, the Visitor Leader raised Ted's hand as though he were a champion, demanding an answer from the crowd, "And do *you* have the will?"

Her frenzied followers roared, *"YES!"*

Diana leaned close to Jeremy. "Nicely arranged." He nodded at her haughtily, then Diana continued. "It was a wonderful prologue for my part of the show."

In the control room in Marin County, Julie was glancing worriedly at Margarita. "Something's gone wrong with Ayden and Nathan."

Margarita nodded. "Let's broadcast now."

Julie sat at the console and readied the disk to play.

Ted had been guided to one side as the Leader rode the swelling wave of enthusiasm. "Now look at the screens, my friends, because history is being made at this moment: the worldwide leadership of the criminal conspiracy who called themselves the Resistance—*are being arrested!*"

On the stadium screens and on vid screens around the world Margarita, Julie, and their team at the Marin Communications link were seen being suddenly surrounded by Patrollers who sprang from hiding within the Marin control room. The Resistance vid disk that Julie was about to broadcast with the weight of the Secretary-General's revelations was pulled from the machine and destroyed.

Standing at the side of the dais, Ted saw his mother Harmy on one of the screens. She was with the others in custody outside the Resistance warehouse headquarters.

AMONG THE BILLIONS VIEWING THE ARRESTS ON HOME SCREENS Stella Stein watched with conflicted emotions while her son Danny was outright angry. In the Sci Section, Charles Elgin and his father were very worried. Charles glanced over and realized that Mary had never rejoined them. He called to her, "Mary?"

* * *

THE DOOR TO GARY LAVINE'S APARTMENT FLEW OPEN AS HE CAME running in, breathless and fearful of why his lover had summoned him so urgently, "Eric? Eric! What is it?"

The Visitor doctor appeared and embraced him, holding on tightly. Gary was confused, then he saw on their TV that his Resistance compatriots were being captured. "Oh, Jesus," he murmured, his heart fluttering. "You saved my life again."

But *not* the lives of his comrades, Gary painfully saw. Eric held him and Gary returned the embrace, but each of them was suffering gravely mixed emotions and confusion of loyalties.

IN THE DARK SKY NEAR THE MARIN COMMUNICATIONS LINK KAYTA had slowed her airbike to a hover. She had engaged the bike's stealth mode, but was concerned about being discovered because of possible microwave interference to her stealth shield from the fifty-foot dish antenna below. Along with Ruby and Mike, Kayta was looking down with great distress at the scene on the hilltop beneath them.

They could see Margarita, Julie, Street-C, and the others being herded into a Patrol shuttle with their hands on their heads. Ruby's bravado crumbled. She overflowed with tears of grief that trailed down her scaly cheeks as she whimpered, "Mom! No! Not Momma . . ." She wanted to shout out in anger, but Mike held her tightly as she sobbed.

WILLY AND LEE SAT DISTRAUGHT AND HELPLESS IN THE FLAGSHIP Centcom as they watched other images from around the world of international Resistance leaders and their compatriots being arrested. Young Jon had edged his custodial unit into the Centcom to be nearer to Willy and Lee. All the other Visitor technicians in the control center were cheering and clapping each other on the back, so Willy pasted on a false smile as he said to Lee, "It'll be much worse than '99."

Lee pretended to smile back at him and Jon, though she was so near tears she could hardly speak, "All of our best. All of our brightest. All of . . ." Her voice broke.

Gentle Willy completed her thought, "All of our friends."

CHARLES ELGIN STOOD OUTSIDE THE OLD FIBERBOARD DOOR TO their bathroom. He was knocking urgently on it. "Mary? Mary? You've got to see what's happened!" Getting no response he opened the door. "It's terrible it's—"

The bathroom was steamy and suffused with the fragrance of flowers. Charles saw that Mary was lying in the bathtub, unconscious. The water was bloodred.

THE THOUSANDS AT CANDLESTICK PARK HAD BEEN EXPRESSING THEIR approval boisterously. Martin, from his seat just in front of the Candlestick dais, had been watching and expecting at any moment to be arrested himself. But so far it had not happened. On the dais he saw Mark watching Emma and saw that she looked pale and stricken. Martin saw that Ted's mismatched eyes were riveted on the lifeless Bryke.

The Leader had been enjoying the crowd's enthusiasm. She flashed a glance of approval at a triumphant Diana, then she turned to the assemblage and began building toward her conclusion. "Tonight our first mission has been accomplished! The criminal Resistance has been finally and completely *crushed*! They have been swept aside because it is *our responsibility—our destiny—as the Chosen Hyper-power—*to make the cosmos safe and secure for all the generations to come!"

The crowd's cheers were swelling, but the Leader's amplified voice rang out loud and clear above them. "A New Era begins here tonight! And tomorrow we'll prepare to move against the Zedti! They shall hear a cry of revenge come from our throats that will make them turn pale and cower with fear at our combined power!—Rise up with me and unleash the storm!" The

crowd's roar grew deafening as her intensity rose to an unparalleled, climactic peak. "Let theirs be the first of many Brave New
Worlds *that we—shall—command—and—we—shall—share—
together*!"

The multitude was on their feet. They were jubilant. The very
concrete and steel of the great stadium shook with their collective, thunderous energy. Dazzling fireworks lit up the night sky
above and around the stadium adding more brilliance to the ex-
hilaration of the roaring crowd. One hundred thousand strong,
the people were swept up in the grandeur of their own superiority, the thrill of conquest and of unstoppable power!

IN THE SCI BATHROOM, CHARLES HAD PULLED MARY'S DEAD WEIGHT
out of the bloody tub and onto the old tile floor. He was administering frantic CPR to her and shouting, "Get Dr. Winslow, Pop!
Hurry, for God's sake!"

THE LIGHTS OF SAN FRANCISCO TWINKLED IN THE DISTANCE AS
Kayta settled the airbike to a landing on Pine Mountain several
miles south of the Marin uplink. She answered her communicator pin, "Yes, Ayden?"

Her commander still stood on the rooftop a few miles north of
Candlestick Park. "Signal the fleet to attack here and destroy the
Visitor Armada."

Ruby heard his command and glanced at Mike with new
hope. But Kayta frowned. "Very well, sir. I will transmit now."
Kayta's breathing was shallow as she tapped a code onto the pin.

Ruby was elated, finding new strength. She wiped away her
tears. "Yes! Now those damned bastards'll get what they deserve! We'll save Mom and all of 'em."

Mike was also very encouraged. "Thank you, Kayta. I'm sorry
if I—"

The blond Zedti interrupted them, "Mike . . . Ruby . . . It is
not what you think."

"What do you mean?" The feisty girl said, "Your fleet's coming to kick their butts, right?"

"Yes, Ruby, our thermobaric nuclear weaponry will hopefully destroy the Visitors." She drew a grieved breath.

Mike could see her deeply troubled expressions. "So how is that a problem?"

She looked at him. "The attack will also *vaporize your atmosphere and decimate the Earth.*"

Mike and Ruby stared, trying to comprehend her. "*What!*"

"I belong to a very pragmatic race," Kayta said quietly. "The Zedti are concerned only about our *own* world's survival. Earth is . . . unfortunately . . ."

"Expendable!" Mike was staring at her.

She nodded sadly. "It is acceptable collateral damage, yes."

He chortled with angry incredulity, "What? We're just a *disposable battleground*! To spare your planet from a nuclear holocaust!"

"Yes," Kayta was completely drained by the thought. She could barely form the words, "The Earth is doomed."

28

EVEN UTILIZING THEIR ZEDTI WORMHOLE TECHNOLOGY, WHICH ALlowed communication at faster than light speed, it took Kayta's signal over two minutes to travel the 821,190,000 miles necessary to reach the Zedti fleet marshaled behind Saturn.

Immediately upon receiving the message from her second-in-command, the Zedti Executive Officer keyed her communicator in the shadowy, organic, cavernlike control center, "This is Fleet Command. This is no drill. The Flagship is setting a course for Earth. Form with us immediately and activate stealth mode. Prepare for hostile contact. Repeat, this is no drill."

The stately, nude Zedti female clicked off the communicator.

She paused for a moment to feel the true weight of command that had been placed upon her shoulders. When she raised her amber eyes she realized that the other Zedti officers were looking at her from their various stations and crystalline view panels. They all realized the danger of the enemy they were facing but their expressions clearly gave the executive officer their unswerving allegiance. She knew that such loyalty was inherent in her race, but she appreciated their show of support.

She drew a breath, then spoke with a strong clear voice, "All ahead full. Flank speed."

Throughout the massive Zedti fleet rasping, gutteral alarms began to sound as their running lights changed from orange alert to battle red. The 177 enormous, strangely shaped warships began to move forward. As they engaged their stealth mode they became barely visible against the starry blackness of deep space. One of the billion pinpoints of light ahead of them was the embattled Earth.

BY THE TIME JON INCHED INTO THE CAPSULE STORAGE CHAMBER WITH his custodial module to observe the happenings, the Secretary-General and his wife, along with Ysabel, Harmy, Street-C, and dozens of others from the Resistance, who were under heavy guard, had already been made to step into open capsules. Patrollers were everywhere. Reptilian-faced capsule technicians were affixing a Medusa-like neurological unit onto each prisoner's head. Six Patrollers held Margarita and Nathan to one side as Julie was led into one of the forbidding containers.

Jeremy strolled past each of them one at a time along the edge of the semicircular Capsule Operations platform. Above, below, and around him stretched a million other capsules, each containing a previously entombed human. Jeremy spoke with a businesslike satisfaction, "You'll be in appropriate company. Your co-conspirators across the Earth are also being encapsulated at this very moment."

"Yes," said Diana, who stood by the curved control consoles. She sought to make the point to the prisoners and all the others present, including Martin and Shawn who stood slightly to one side of her, "We saw and traced your communications links to them and they have all been arrested, thanks to the optic implant and transmitter which *I* placed inside your dear Mr. Donovan."

Julie and the others were all startled to learn that truth. "He was unaware of it, of course," Diana continued, "but I found a certain poetic justice in having him lead us into your inner sanctum." Then Diana smiled at Martin, who stood near the Patrollers holding Nathan and a very angry Margarita. "And *your* help was invaluable, Martin. I had long suspected you were their spy. You'll continue to be with them."

The blond Visitor who had first come to Donovan's rescue over twenty years earlier was suddenly in the grasp of two Patrollers. Martin was led to a capsule near Julie and thrust into it. A female reptilian technician leered at the traitor as she clamped the neuro unit onto Martin's head.

Jeremy eyed the neuro unit on Street-C. "You'll all be trained to do exactly what we want. We look forward to your services and sacrifices on our behalf." Then he turned toward Margarita and Nathan. "And you two will get some very special treatment." He nodded for the Patrollers to take them away. They were led off, but a distraught Margarita looked back as the capsules began to close.

She saw Diana smile at Julie. "Your war is over, Juliet."

Julie shook her head, soft-spoken and undaunted. "Not so long as one person still fights for freedom."

As the intestinelike coils surrounding the capsules began to throb and surge to life and the plasticine containers slowly closed, some of the others screamed, but Julie's eyes were defiant even as the green gas swirled around her and she was entombed.

*   *   *

THE VISITOR LEADER WAS SELECTING A LARGE STRIP OF FRESH, PINK, veined mammalian flesh from a tray being offered her by an aide. The visualizers in the Flagship conference room were presenting three-dimensional images of various Motherships as Shawn described them to Diana, Jeremy, and the Leader, who were comfortably seated nearby along with several key aides. "With the exception of this Flagship, all 250 of our Motherships have now received Jeremy's plug-ins and are taking in water at a greatly accelerated rate."

The Leader gave Jeremy what Diana recognized as an intimate glance. "Yes, your plug-in is phenomenal, Jeremy." He smiled faintly and nodded appreciatively. Then the Leader opened her mouth and ingested the large piece of raw flesh.

Diana sought to subtly ingratiate herself. "Jeremy's contribution is indeed a wonderful *supplement* to the work we've already achieved. And since *I* have now quelled the Resistance—"

"Hmm." The Leader was licking some blood and membrane off of her fingers. She didn't even look toward Diana as she said very casually, "Oh, yes. Nicely done, Diana."

Diana paused, but only said flatly, "Thank you, Excellency."

Shawn was anxious to remain personally engaged with the Leader. "Excellency, you mentioned at the rally that the Zedti were developing *new* weaponry capable of even more mass destruction?"

"Did I?" The Leader said with offhanded innocence, "Well, then they must be, mustn't they?"

Shawn got the point and nodded immediately. "Of course."

"In any event"—the Leader dried her fingers—"we know this is a war that we are *determined* to wage so I wish to get on with it as soon as possible." She focused again on Jeremy. "Your suggestion of using that captured Zedti to inflame the masses was inspired. Truly inspired."

A haughty, satisfied smile crossed his aristocratic face. "They did rather like it, didn't they, Excellency?"

His mistress's eyes gleamed. "They certainly did."

"Well"—Jeremy inclined his head with studied humility—"I'm only too happy to be of service."

"And you will be," the Leader said with a promising smile as her eyes met his. And Diana saw it.

As the Leader stood up, all those in the room instantly followed suit. "Have the Armada begin preparations for our assault against the Zedti planet. And I want to know the status of readiness of our chemical weapon." As she exited, she spoke brusquely, without looking back, "Diana, attend me."

"Of course, Excellency." Diana followed, and though she tried to hide it, Jeremy noted her look of concern about the Leader's austere tone and earlier dismissive treatment. He and Shawn also picked up on the flavor of the Leader's command. The two exchanged a glance and Shawn eased his way past the other aides, discreetly following the two females at a distance.

The Leader moved ahead of Diana down the clean, gray corridor, passing several of her subjects who each paused and bowed to the Great Leader and the Commandant trailing her. "Diana, may we use your chamber?" Again the Leader had not looked back and her remark, though phrased as a question, was recognized by Diana as being a directive.

"Of course, Excellency."

The Leader paused before Diana's quarters. The Commandant touched the panel code to open the hatch, then followed her mistress inside. As the hatch closed behind them Shawn approached and casually assessed the corridor to see that he was unobserved long enough to deftly attach his tiny listening device. Then he stood by and pretended to study his PDA as other Visitors and Patrollers passed in the corridor.

Within the supposed privacy of Diana's quarters the Leader turned slowly toward the beautiful, stern Commandant and studied her for a long moment. If Diana was completely unsure what to expect, outwardly she was still maintaining a professional attitude. Finally the regal Leader allowed herself a slightly softer tone, "I've missed you."

Though Diana was unconvinced, her voice was strong and level, "I'm pleased to hear that, Excellency."

"It's been far too long." The Leader touched an errant lock of Diana's dark brown hair. Her movements had become more sinuous.

"I'm flattered," Diana said without emotion, then she decided to press the matter. "But I'm certain you had many important affairs of state to occupy your thoughts."

The Leader smiled at Diana's not-so-veiled reference to Jeremy. She touched Diana's cheek. "You don't imagine any such affairs could supersede my thoughts of you?"

"I wasn't certain what to imagine."

The Leader saw that Diana was holding her own without being insubordinate. It was one of the many shrewd qualities that the Leader found so appealing about her. "My relationship with Jeremy need not concern you."

"As your Excellency directs."

The Leader formed a knowing smile and spoke more personally still, female to female. "Oh, come now, have you had no minor dalliances during our separation? I would certainly not begrudge them, even now."

Diana's answer was again astute. "My thoughts have only ever been of you." Diana's keen brown eyes looked directly into the deep blue eyes of her Leader.

They both knew they were cut from the same dangerous cloth. They were both highly skilled in the darker arts. That was part of their mutual attraction. Like the Leader, Diana had also murdered her way upward to where she now had the power of life or death over everyone except Jeremy and the Leader herself. Diana was feared and respected by all her hundreds of thousands of troops. The Leader knew that those legions were exceedingly loyal to her own person, but after her their strongest allegiance was to their Commandant Diana. Jeremy was astute, clever, and ingenious. His inventive mastery of the new technology that would speed their conquests was unsurpassed, but it was ultimately not as vital as what Diana supplied. The Leader knew Jeremy could not muster the same personal support or enthusiasm from the soldiers and technicians of the Armada that Diana could.

At least he could not hope to do so while Diana was still alive.

And that was a consideration the Leader had pondered a good deal. Dispensing with Diana was an option about which the Leader had often weighed the pros and cons. Despite the Leader's abilities to provoke the masses to rise in support of her vision and her proven skills at maintaining power by Machiavellian maneuvers or murders of convenience, she occasionally remembered that she was still mortal. Even while enjoying absolute power she sometimes recalled that it could be a seductive trap to begin believing in one's infallibility and invulnerability. She knew that throughout the history of every known culture such hubris had been the ultimate downfall of many a great imperial conqueror.

The Leader knew that a powerful commanding general who gave her great victories could, with but a slight turn of fate, become an equally powerful adversary. She had certainly rid herself of many annoying or overly ambitious generals in the past. Whenever the Leader looked at Diana she saw enough of herself, of her own lethal capability and ambition, to be extremely wary. She knew that Diana must be relentlessly watched and always handled with significant care.

The Leader also had the wisdom to know that the brilliant Diana was equally aware of the delicate balance of power that existed between the two of them. The Leader knew that her undertakings would be strongly championed, supported, and well executed by Diana. But she also knew that the beautiful Commandant was an opportunist of the first order, equally as driven and determined to prevail personally as was the Leader herself. And the Leader knew that Diana also knew her Imperial Mistress was mortal.

Those same qualities that made them quite dangerous to each other also made them exceedingly attractive to one another. Though each knew she could never fully turn her back on the other, the feral, often incendiary sexuality they enjoyed together was not only intensely satisfying, it also served to strengthen their unique dance with one another. It solidified their dark bond.

As they stood facing each other alone in the dim chamber, the Leader suddenly pulled Diana close and kissed her, hard and forcefully, full on the mouth.

In the corridor outside Shawn had been listening carefully. He knew the dice were rolling. He drew a long breath, reconsidering yet again where to invest his loyalty, where among the shifting winds of palace intrigue might lay his safest harbor and his greatest advantage.

FAR BELOW THE CAPSULE STORAGE CHAMBER, IN THE DEEPEST BOWELS of the Flagship, the Patrollers guiding Nathan and Margarita shoved them roughly into a dank cell. Nathan landed hard on one hand and yelped with pain.

Margarita was picking herself up. "What is it?"

"Aw, nothing." Nathan was disgruntled as he rubbed his left wrist. "Scraped it when that bitch shot me on the roof. It's no biggie," he said, but stopped when he saw that her eyes suddenly brimmed with tears. He spoke comfortingly, "Hey . . . Red, really. I'm okay. There's no need to—"

"It's not about you. It's *me*." She was anguished. "I can't . . . *believe* I led them all into a trap. How could I have been so incredibly . . ." She couldn't find a word harsh enough to describe herself.

He was low-key, gently chiding, "Yeah. What were you thinking? Big-time Resistance general and you're not *omniscient*? What's up with *that?*" But his effort to assuage her guilt failed.

She turned away and planted her hands flat against the cold, black metal of the cell wall. Then she pressed her aching forehead against it. "Did you see their faces? Julie . . . all the others when those capsules were closing?" Her throat tightened with emotion. "Oh, God . . ."

"Hey. *I'm* the one who bungled it." Nathan leaned back against the wall beside her and slid down onto the floor by her feet, mentally replaying his lost chance. "If I'd pulled that trigger *five seconds sooner* . . ."

"And hadn't been shot by a pulse cannon," she said wryly, her turn to counsel him, "what's up with *that?*"

He looked up into her glistening eyes. They shared a melancholy smile. Then she slid down the wall to lean against it beside him. He touched her cheek with the back of his hand and was gratified when she actually let herself lean into it.

United in grief, they were finally connected.

IN THE TINY BEDROOM OF THE ELGIN FLAT CHARLES AND HIS FATHER looked on worriedly as a sixtyish black man with short white hair and mustache closed his medical bag and nodded to them. He rose up from where Mary lay on the bed. Her wrists were bandaged heavily.

Charles squeezed the doctor's arm with deep appreciation. "Thanks, Douglas . . ."

The doctor smiled sorrowfully. "Glad to help. Keep her warm. Lots of liquids. And get that iron into her. I'll check back tomorrow."

"Thanks again," Pop Elgin said as the doctor exited quietly and Charles eased himself down onto the edge of Mary's bed.

He touched her forehead. "You're going to be okay, Mary . . . The doc said you'll be okay."

Mary spoke without opening her frowning eyes. Her voice was thin and faint, but certain. "No. I won't."

She turned her head slightly away. Charles and his father watched her, not knowing what they could ever do to overcome the bleakness in her heart.

EMMA SAT ALONE IN HER LIVING ROOM STARING BEYOND THE WALLS of her home, trying to comprehend all that had happened and what fate might conceivably await her. She still wore her dress from the previous night's rally. The pale February sun did not warm her. When her phone rang she jumped slightly. She stared at it through three rings and decided to let her machine answer.

It was Mark's terse voice that she heard. "Thought you'd like to know we found a little nuclear missile that your friends were obviously planning to use on all of us at Candlestick. Including you. How does *that* make you feel about them?"

He hung up. And Emma continued to stare at nothing.

IN THE POTRERO SECTION, WILLY WALKED CAREFULLY PAST THE TEN- ement that had been his home with Harmy and Ted. His soft eyes looked up sadly at it and he breathed a long and plaintive sigh.

When he looked back down he came to an abrupt stop, star- tled to see, standing directly in front of him, a Teammate: Ted. The boy's expression was unreadable as he said, "I've been wait- ing for you."

ON THE OAKLAND SIDE OF THE ARID SAN FRANCISCO BAY VALLEY THE Resistance survivors had sought sanctuary in an abandoned fac- tory that bordered the former waterfront in Alameda. More claustrophobic than their San Francisco headquarters, it was depressing in the thin sunlight that filtered down through the dust in the chilly air from a row of grimy skylights on one side. Several panes were broken and pigeons fluttered in and out. Residue from them and other birds dotted the floor of scarred concrete. Several large and greasy lathes for the working of heavy mechanical parts were bolted to it. The building had an oily, musty smell.

It had been previously designated as a safe rendezvous point so Ruby guided Kayta and Mike there. Gary and a few others were already present. By the time Robert Maxwell arrived, Mike was in the midst of furiously confronting both Ayden and Kayta. "How do you *expect* us to feel when you lied to us about your true intentions! You've got to call off your fleet!"

Ayden was calm and resolute. "No. The Visitor Armada must be attacked and destroyed here."

"Along with our whole *planet*!" Gary couldn't believe it.

Kayta was sincere. "We are truly sorry."

"*Sorry*?!" Mike blurted with an incredulous laugh. "You get to just walk away while our whole fucking planet dies? And all you can say is you're '*sorry*'?!"

"Kayta and I will not be leaving," Ayden said. "We will remain here as forward observers."

All the humans stared at them. Robert finally spoke, "You mean to say that you've called in the fire *on top of yourselves*?"

"Of course"—Kayta nodded—"it was a natural course of action for the greater good of our race."

"So, wait a minute . . ." Ruby wanted to be sure she understood, "you're gonna stay and die here beside us?"

"Yes, Ruby," Ayden stoically confirmed. "We are as loyal to the Zedti cause as you are to yours."

For a long moment there was silence in the old factory as the Resistance team weighed Ayden's words. Then Mike dropped to a lower, less confrontational key. "Look, Ayden, God knows all of us here understand loyalty, but there's got to be some way we can—"

A door creaked open and the entire group spun onto the alert. Guns were raised and aimed. Then Willy appeared. "Don't shoot! It's me. It's . . . us."

The gentle Visitor opened the door wider to reveal his son, Ted. His former anger and belligerence were absent as he looked contritely at all of them who were staring at him. "If you don't want me to stay, I'll understand. But I came to tell you"—he paused as his mismatched eyes sought out the two who had the same sheen to their skin as had Bryke—"particularly to tell you two . . . that I didn't want to kill your friend. When the Leader put that weapon in my hand and I looked into your friend's eyes—" His voice choked off momentarily as he remembered it. Then he continued, "I suddenly understood everything my mother and father had tried to teach me. I realized my loyalty was to the wrong side. I know I can never make up for what I've done, for the mistakes I've made, and certainly not for your friend's life. But if you'd let me fight beside you, beside my father, it would be an honor."

There was a pause and finally Ayden nodded. Then the Zedti commander added, "But I'm afraid there is not much point now."

Mike found himself echoing Julie's words to him, "Ayden, we can't just lie down and die without a fight."

Little Ruby concurred, "Yeah. There's got to be a way."

The Zedti commander said, "I appreciate your sentiments, but look at the reality of the situation. To conquer the Visitors before the Zedti fleet arrives we'd have to *take control* of all the Motherships. To do that we'd need *a massive army* and a way to get that army *aboard all the Motherships simultaneously.*"

The group stood in frustrated silence. Victory had evaded the Resistance for over twenty years and they knew Ayden was right: now it seemed more impossible than ever.

But then Ruby saw Mike's frowning expression slowly change

as though a cloud was passing and the sun was brightening his face. He whispered, "Wait a minute." He was piecing something together. "Wait just a goddamn minute."

Robert also realized that Mike's eyes were focusing on a new possibility that was dawning on him. "Mike? What is it?"

Donovan's voice was low as he looked up at Ayden and the rest. "We've *got* that army! And they're already *aboard*!"

"Oh, my God!" Ruby understood immediately. *"The prisoners in storage up there!"*

"Yes!" Gary exclaimed. "Julie and our whole gang—!"

"Plus international leaders, military commanders!" Robert chimed in.

And Willy added, "Plus *regions* of others!"

"Legions," Ruby corrected enthusiastically.

"Legions, yes!" Willy nodded. "In capsules on *all* the Motherships!"

Kayta was slowly thinking it through. "They would be in a perfect position to lead an attack, *if* they could be alerted to the plan and set free."

"But they *can* be alerted! Don't you see?" Mike was on a roll now. "Ayden, you told us prisoners can be instructed *inside* their capsules! Right?"

"That's correct." The Zedti leader understood Mike's idea. "So if we could tap into the communications circuits . . ."

Willy jumped in, "Our friend Jon knows the capsule operations very well."

Kayta was shaking her head. "But wait: if any of their chemical weapon is transported to a Mothership that escapes, our people would still be in grave danger from it."

Gary had an answer, "So some of us hit the factory to destroy or neutralize that chemical."

"That scientist Charles Elgin will work with us." Robert's dark eyes were intense. "He's got access inside there and his scientist friends in the ghetto could help Kayta develop a neutralizing agent."

Ayden recognized the possible validity of the developing plan, but would not be rushed to a judgment. "We must prevent any export of the chemical weapon for duplication and mass production. I must be *certain* of that."

Donovan turned it back on him. "Okay, Ayden, then *you* handle that mission. Only your airbike has a prayer of dodging their fighters to do the job, anyway."

"May I go with you?" Ted asked of Ayden.

The Zedti looked into Ted's mismatched but sincere eyes, considering, "If you can learn to fly an airbike."

Then Mike turned to Ayden to press the key question. "And if we succeed, you'll call off your fleet?"

Ayden returned his potent gaze and spoke emphatically, *"If."*

29

DIANA GLANCED SIDEWAYS AT HER AIDE. "WHAT KIND OF 'PERSONAL information' are you talking about, Shawn?"

The lean, narrow-eyed Visitor stood subserviently before the desk in Diana's private chambers. "Information I felt you should be made aware of in case you felt it important for our Leader to know. About the relationship between a certain Wing Commander and Commandant Jeremy."

Diana studied Shawn with her sloe eyes. "Continue."

"Out of a desire to be useful to you I put myself at considerable risk to obtain the intelligence, because I thought it might prove helpful to you."

"And to yourself as well, no doubt," Diana chided.

"My first thought was of you, Commandant, as indeed my loyalty has always been to you." He clicked his heels and nodded respectfully.

Diana had risen and was slowly walking in a circle around him, her keen eyes upon him. "So you've always said, Shawn. But as you doubtless know, our Leader is a creature of many appetites herself. Why should she be concerned about some casual sexual tryst which is, I presume, what you are implying?"

"That is only part of it, Commandant." Shawn knew he was venturing out upon a minefield and he did so cautiously. "In addition, there have also been certain statements made."

Although Diana maintained her outward coolness, Shawn correctly sensed the slight amplification of her interest. "Statements about what, Shawn?"

"About our Leader's future fate. And your own."

MARGARITA WAS EXAMINING THE HATCH TO THE DAMP, FOUL-smelling cell where she and Nathan were imprisoned. She was running her hand along the seam where it joined the cell bulkhead. She glanced over at Nathan, who was investigating a small air vent. "What happened to Ayden, anyway?"

"Mr. Nuke-'Em? Now that's an interesting story." He was about to tell her when the hatch she was studying suddenly opened. Nathan was thoroughly amazed. "Hey! How'd you do that?" Then he saw that four Patrollers were in the corridor outside and had obviously opened it. "Oh."

One of the Patrollers stepped in and roughly grasped Nathan's arm. "Come along." As the trooper was pulling him out, Nathan daringly grabbed for the Visitor's weapon, but another immediately shot him in the chest, slamming him backward and down. Margarita rushed to him, fearful but insistent, "Nathan! Nathan! If you die I'll kill you!"

His eyes opened. He was severely dazed. His words slurred, "Die? Now that we've bonded? No way, José."

The Patrollers shoved her aside and dragged him out. Margarita could only watch as the heavy hatch sealed her in the cell alone.

* * *

IN THE FLAGSHIP CONFERENCE ROOM DIANA WAS MULLING THE secrets Shawn had told her about Jeremy, while he, Press Secretary Paul, along with Shawn, Gina, and several other aides, sat nearby. They were getting a progress report from smiling factory owner J. D. Oliver. "Our work has proceeded well ahead of schedule and the chemical essence is now ready for duplication aboard your Motherships, Commandants. The shipments can begin tomorrow."

"Excellent, Mr. Oliver," Diana said, "I will order—"

Jeremy interrupted, speaking to Gina as though Diana weren't even present. "Wing Commander, see to the dispersal of the new hand weapons to all of our Patrols and Teammates."

Gina nodded. As she started to leave, Jeremy turned to Diana and said innocently, "I beg your pardon, you were saying?"

Diana watched shapely Gina exit, then turned to Jeremy with a sly smile. "Unimportant. You're quite on top of everything. Shall we have lunch?"

WHAT HAD ONCE BEEN THE EDGE OF LAND BORDERING THE CHOPPY water at Fort Point in the Presidio was still a favorite place for joggers and bikers even though the bay had long since dried up. People were still drawn there because of the majestic Golden Gate Bridge, which stretched beautifully to Sausalito across the now-empty, 360-foot-deep chasm. The massive, foundational bases of the bridge support pillars had been entirely visible and dry for years. They were covered with sun-bleached barnacles and a few wispy fibers of long-dried-out seaweed.

Emma had been walking there and had paused to talk to a short, uniformed half-breed worker with chestnut-colored hair who was pretending to be cleaning up along the path. Ruby was explaining the truth to Emma, "The mayor doesn't know the whole story: we all voted *not* to use the nuke. When Ayden tried to anyway, Nathan risked his life to stop it."

Emma was still uncertain. "So will the Zedti fight on our side or not?"

"Until their fleet gets here, yeah. After that we're *all* toast and the clock's ticking. They're already smokin' in from Saturn." Ruby turned to pick up some trash as a Patroller walked past while Emma gazed out toward the bridge and watched two Visitor patrol shuttles pass each other over the top of it. Once the trooper was well away Ruby spoke again to Emma. "We've just got one last chance, but it's a goody." She wiggled her eyebrows. "Willy learned all about Capsule Operations from a half-breed janitor aboard the Flagship."

"A janitor!"

"Yeah, one who could give Einstein a run for his money. The kid's brilliant. Anyway, here's the deal: the training information fed through the capsule headgear into the prisoners' subconscious minds is transmitted directly from the Flagship. And a signal from the Flagship can also *open* the capsules throughout the fleet."

"So we've got to send *our* messages in to the prisoners and then get their capsules opened?"

"Bingo." The twelve-year-old winked. "To do that we've got to unlock the system. There are five code keys that have to be inserted directly into the Flagship's quantum computer mainframe which, incidentally, they keep at minus three hundred degrees for superconductivity. But Willy can take the chill."

"Okay"—Emma was getting the picture—"and those code keys are where?"

"Locked in a vault in good ol' Shawn's chamber. Kayta has a Zedti device that she thinks can unlock the vault, but we need you—"

"To get access to the vault?"

"Yeah." Ruby looked searchingly into Emma's green eyes as the young woman realized the daunting and dangerous challenge.

* * *

MARGARITA WAS PACING AGITATEDLY INSIDE THE DARK CELL. HER palms were sweating as she had flashes of the torture Nathan was likely being put through elsewhere on the Flagship. She drew a sharp, startled breath as the hatch suddenly hissed open and Nathan was thrown back in. He had obviously been badly beaten and was barely conscious. She knelt to comfort him, swallowing hard at his condition. "Too much partying, huh?"

His eyes wandered, trying to find her. His consciousness seemed beset by a leaden heaviness. His voice was hoarse, as though he'd been kicked in the throat. "No, they beat me. It was awful."

Margarita looked at him carefully and tenderly stroked his bloody brow. "I'm sure it was. But you're okay now. I've got you. You just rest." She cradled him lovingly in her arms.

In an autopsy room some distance away, Jeremy, Diana, and Shawn were conversing in front of a console that carried a vid image from a camera hidden in Margarita's cell. It showed her consoling Nathan.

"This will be a good field test of our new voice modifier," Shawn noted.

"Yes," Diana agreed, "if we can fool *her* to get information, we can infiltrate *anyone*."

Jeremy turned smugly to a prisoner who was secured in an interrogation chair. "Thanks for the use of your voice . . . and your face."

The battered prisoner whom Jeremy was addressing was the *real* Nathan. He was hanging tough and shook his head. "You fuckers won't fool Margarita."

"Really?" Diana was smiling. "She's already nursing *our* Nathan's wounds."

POP ELGIN CAME INTO THE TINY BEDROOM OF THEIR FAMILY'S TENE-ment with a tray holding a small bowl of chicken soup and a sandwich. "I managed to scrounge a little turkey from old Mrs. Kettenis."

Mary was sitting propped up in a threadbare chair. Her hair was disheveled. She was without any makeup at all and looked years older than she had before her daughter died. She was gazing listlessly out the window as she might have looked into an abyss. "I told you I don't want to eat, Pop."

He set the scratched plastic tray on the rickety end table beside her. "Well, maybe a little reading then."

Mary looked down and saw that also on the tray was a small brown book. "What is that?"

The old man shrugged. "Just something I found. I think it might have been Charlotte's." He gazed at his beleaguered daughter-in-law for a moment, then quietly left the room. Mary watched him close the door. Then she looked hesitantly down at the book.

IN THE SHABBY OAKLAND FACTORY KAYTA AND ROBERT MAXWELL were working at the rudimentary chemical lab she had established in one corner of the grungy place. Her entire facility sat on a couple of old doors set atop some shipping crates and had occasioned some healthy skepticism from Robert until he saw the advanced Zedti analytical instruments she had brought from her airbike. While they worked to create a neutralizing agent for the Visitors' chemical weapon, Kayta glanced over at Mike, who stood nearby on his painful, shaky legs. He was still getting used to having only one good eye, but that didn't keep him from taking stock of the weapons, which Gary had kept hidden in his apartment and now brought. Mike grinned. "Nicely done, Rumplestiltskin."

The handsome freedom fighter smiled back. "My grandmother was a big proponent of multi-basketing our eggs." But Gary saw the frown creasing Mike's troubled brow. "You think we've got a prayer of pulling this off?"

"Shit, Gary, I don't know"—Mike leaned against one of the rusting lathes—"and even if we do, I've been thinking about all our other people who were prisoners in the Motherships that have already left."

"Millions of 'em, yeah." Gary ran his hand through his smooth hair. His eyes went distant as he contemplated such a huge loss of humanity.

Kayta had drifted closer, bringing medicine for Mike. "I'm very proud of the effort you've made, Mike." She held out the liquid medication to him. "This will help to strengthen you." He took the glass and nodded thanks as she continued. "You speak of the Hive Mentality that we Zedti share, but your feelings for the Family of Man are really so very similar."

Mike looked into her soft violet eyes. "Yeah, I guess they are." They gazed at each other and it was clear to Gary that a strong bond had developed between the blond Zedti healer and her unruly patient.

A door burst open nearby and Ruby scampered in. She was smiling and two of her scaly fingers flipped up to form a "V" as she said cheerily, "Emma's in!"

RESISTANCE WORK HAD ALSO BEEN PROCEEDING SIMULTANEOUSLY on many other fronts. In one of the data storage areas of the Flagship, Jon was deftly stealing data plugs that held schematics of the Flagship and additional details about capsule operation. He slipped them into the trash in his floating custodial cart. Within the hour Jon emerged into Flagship Hangar Bay Thirty-two, where Willy received the stolen material, then boarded an outbound shuttle.

IN THE RURAL COUNTRYSIDE EAST OF OAKLAND, TED WAS BEING trained by Ayden in the proper operation of an airbike. The youth was not a natural pilot, but he was resolved to learn the techniques necessary to handle the vehicle. Ayden was gaining respect for Ted's sense of purpose.

WHILE THE RESISTANCE LABORED, MANY TEAMMATES WERE PREPAR-ing themselves for the assault on the Zedti outposts. At the Stein household, Debra was happily packing her gear for deployment while she chattered enthusiastically on the phone to a friend. In the hall, her mother Stella watched, brooding over her daughter and where the world was headed. Then Stella turned to see her son Danny focused intently upon *her*. His eyes calling for action.

ON A STREET JUST OUTSIDE THE SCI GHETTO, CHARLES ELGIN SAT down on a bus bench and lay a folded newspaper beside him. After a moment Gary sat down on the same bench, but didn't look at Charles. They continued to ignore each other, both star-ing straight ahead as Charles spoke quietly, "We made some progress on a neutralizer for the chemical. Tell me what Kayta thinks."

Charles stood and walked away, leaving his newspaper be-hind. Gary sat for a moment longer as a Patroller passed by, then he collected the newspaper and walked the other way. He could feel that inside the paper was a tiny vial.

THAT NIGHT, IN THE LARGE DARK PARKING LOT OF AN INDUSTRIAL area a small tank truck sat among several others, Dr. Robert Maxwell in the cab. He ducked low to hide from a Patrol shuttle that passed by overhead. Then he stuck his head down beneath the dashboard, holding a small flashlight in his teeth. He was amused that among his numerous skills as a Nobel laureate sci-entist his most important talent at the moment was knowing how to hot-wire an ignition. He got the engine started, then proudly drove the tank truck out into the nighttime streets of San Francisco.

* * *

IN THE OAKLAND FACTORY THAT SAME NIGHT MIKE AND RUBY WERE
poring over the stolen Flagship schematics while Willy pointed
out the details. Mike was still adjusting to his lack of depth per-
ception with only one eye, but under his leadership they formulated strategy and the tactics that the freed prisoners would have
to follow in order to commandeer the Motherships. Ruby was
typing the instructions quickly but carefully into a laptop computer.

Nearby, Kayta was using droplets from the vial Gary had gotten from Charles Elgin and the ghetto scientists to strengthen
her neutralizer for the Visitors' chemical weapon. Also within
the newspaper Gary had gotten from Charles was a ground plan
of Oliver's factory with the two chemical weapon storage tanks
highlighted. Robert was assessing the shortest route to them
from the front gate of the facility.

LATER THAT NIGHT, IN THE CONTROL BOOTH OF THE SMALL RECORD-
ing studio in the basement of Emma's condo, her long-haired
recording mixer, Westie, was busy. He was patching into the
twenty-four-track audio recorder a special computer module
that their Visitor spy Lee had stolen from the Flagship Centcom.
Then he rolled his chair over to the console and keyed the talk-
back switch. "Okay, girl, the auto-translator is good to go. You
ready to rock and roll?"

From behind the double-thick glass Emma gave him a
thumbs-up. Her voice came through the big studio speakers over
Westie's head, "Ready when you are, C.B."

Westie tapped a control and the twenty-four-track sprang to
life behind him. He keyed a cueing switch. "This is 'Lizards Go
Home' take one." He paused a moment, then pointed at Emma.

She read from Ruby's laptop that was set up on a music stand
before her. "This is the voice of the Resistance. You will disregard all previous indoctrination you have received. You will all

soon be freed from your storage capsules. Be prepared to fight. We are taking over all the Motherships. I will give you specific assignments to access arms and secure your specific targets. Any Visitors who are friendly to us will wear a small yellow sticker . . ."

As she continued, Westie checked her audio level as it was reflected by the bouncing light bars on his console. Then he clicked on each of the twenty-four tracks, one at a time. Each track still bore Emma's voice, but digitally modified by the auto-translator into one of two dozen different languages.

IN THE DARK CELL ABOARD THE FLAGSHIP, THE BOGUS NATHAN blinked awake as he lay against Margarita's shoulder. His voice was still weak. "Wow, have I been out of it very long?"

Margarita grinned tightly at him. "As long as I've known you."

"My head really hurts." He put a hand to it and seemed very dizzy.

"Easy . . . Take it easy . . . Just . . ." Their faces were very close. Their eyes held. Then Margarita leaned in and kissed him. The kiss lasted for a very long moment. When they separated her lips remained very close to his. "That was a lot better than I expected."

"I liked it, too." The counterfeit Nathan smiled. "Oh, look . . . I managed to steal this . . ." He pulled a peculiarly shaped tool from his sock. "Maybe it'll help us escape."

"You are definitely my hero." She smiled warmly and kissed him again.

When their lips parted he looked at her lovingly for a moment, then said, "But listen, we might get separated once we get out of here."

"I'd say that's a distinct possibility," she acknowledged.

"If we do, where should I go? Who should I contact?"

"There's an old factory in Oakland. At the corner of Park and

Piedmont, where everyone—" She cut herself off and glanced
around, whispering, "I better tell you the rest outside, this cell
might be bugged."

"Right, right." He nodded.

"Let me see that tool."

He handed it to her. She stood up to examine a small panel
near the top of the hatch to see if the tool might be of use.

In the Flagship conference room a visualizer displayed an image of Margarita and the bogus Nathan in the cell. Jeremy smiled
and glanced over at Shawn who was already getting to his feet.
"Park and Piedmont. I'll alert the Wing Commander and get
them on the way, sir."

MARY ELGIN SAT IN THE BEDROOM OF THEIR CHEAP TENEMENT. SHE
had finally summoned the courage to open the small book that
her father-in-law had brought to her. As she turned the pages
slowly she could hear her daughter Charlotte's voice as she read
some of the words that the gentle girl had written most recently.

"How I love this little book. Every blank page is like a new
day: so many possibilities . . . I worry about Mom and Dad . . . I
wish they'd know I'll always be with them no matter what . . ."
Mary turned another page and drew a sharp breath as she read,
"I felt that flutter thing in my heart again. It's so scary."

Charlotte had never mentioned anything about the symptom.
Mary continued reading her daughter's words.

"There must be some little valve or something really messed
up inside there and I know we've got no way to fix it . . ."

Mary rested her hand on the page for a moment as though she
were touching her departed daughter's cheek. She thought back
over all the wonderful Charlottes she had known: the newborn
with her startling profusion of dark hair; the infant at her breast;
Charlotte's first real smile that morning in her bath; how the
one-year-old would stand holding on to a chair and dance to the

ragtime music that Pop Elgin played on his guitar. Then the delicious three-year-old and the thoughtful seven-year-old who loved books and seemed to have such an old soul. Finally Mary pictured the sweet, selfless teenager who had written the words in the diary. Mary turned another page.

"Some people always think a glass is half empty. But the saddest part is when they don't appreciate what life they *do* have—while they live it every, every minute . . . In my heart I believe that somehow, someday everything will be right again . . . That Momma won't be sad anymore . . . That Daddy won't be so burdened . . . That Poppy will get stronger . . . I felt the sun on my face this morning. It was warm and peaceful. I was happy . . ."

Mary saw that there was no more writing. She slowly turned the blank, white pages one after another, aching for all of Charlotte's days that would go unlived. But then she looked again at the last words her indomitable daughter had written.

GARY WAS IN THE APARTMENT HE SHARED WITH THE VISITOR DOCTOR who had just arrived home from the Flagship for the evening. Eric looked at Gary curiously as the handsome young man gave him a yellow sticker and put his finger to Eric's lips. "Shhh. Don't ask . . . Don't tell."

MARK WAS AGAIN WORKING LATE IN HIS MAYORAL OFFICE AT CITY Hall. He looked up as Emma let herself in. He reacted coldly to her presence, but she held up her hand. "Just hear me out. I know you're angry because I was unfaithful. But the Zedti fleet is on the way and everyone—but *everyone*—is going to die if I don't get your help."

RUBY WAS THE FIRST TO HEAR THE APPROACHING RUMBLE. SHE RAN to look out one of the broken windows of the Oakland factory that had become their new headquarters. Her blue eyes went wide. "Holy shit! Kill the lights!"

The others responded immediately to her warning as Mike limped quickly toward her to see the trouble. "What is it?"

The little half-breed nodded urgently. "Looks like half their damn air force is coming right at us!"

Robert looked out and saw that the fighters were nearly on top of them. He went pale. "We'll never get clear in time!"

Mike shouted to Kayta who was in the midst of filling the tank truck with the neutralizer she and Charles's scientists had created, "Close it up, Kayta! We've got to save that truck!"

"Wait, Mike!" Ruby called out, "Look."

Donovan peered back out the window and saw that the fighters were directly overhead, but not stopping. They kept on going, moving several blocks to the north. "What the hell . . . ?"

"They're circling over Park and"—Robert squinted his dark eyes as he calculated—"looks like Piedmont. What's up there?"

Ruby pictured the place in her mind. "Just a bunch of sleazy used car lots." She traded a quizzical glance with Robert and Mike, who shrugged gratefully.

"We must have a guardian angel." Then Mike looked back at Kayta. "Finish it up quick, it's time to get this show on the road."

30

FLAGSHIP HANGAR BAY SEVEN WAS BUSY AS USUAL WITH SHUTTLES and fighters heading out on patrol or returning. A cargo shuttle glided in through the huge hangar door that was open to the sky. The fifty-foot craft eased upward through the hangar's open atrium and came to a landing on one of the balcony platforms eleven levels above the main flight deck. A number of Patrollers disembarked. Among them were several civilian Players including Mayor Mark Ohanian and Emma, wearing a killer dress.

They passed by the rear cargo hatch of the shuttle where some supplies were being off-loaded. Willy waited just within the hatch near a large biohazard container. When the coast was momentarily clear, he quickly broke the seal and opened it. Kayta and Mike had been crammed inside it, both wearing Patroller uniforms. Ruby was also with them, dressed in her usual ragtag, Artful Dodger clothes. Mike slipped handcuffs onto her scaly wrists, leaving them loose enough for her to slip out of in the event of an emergency. Then he and Kayta escorted their young "prisoner" toward a transport tube.

In one of the Flagship's upper passages a Visitor guard on duty saluted as the San Francisco mayor approached and opened the hatch to a small conference room. Emma slithered past the guard with a coy smile. The guard admired her cleavage and drank in the rosy fragrance of her perfume. Mark leaned confidentially close to the Visitor, handing him a mayoral business card, saying, "I could use someone like you down at City Hall. Come see me." Then he leaned closer and his voice became more hushed and confidential, "And listen, this place really turns her on . . . so I need a little 'alone time' with her, you understand?"

The guard glanced in at the sexy, cocoa-skinned beauty whose fingertips were sensuously grazing the shiny surface of the conference table. Then the guard gave Mark a knowing smile. "Yes, Mr. Mayor, you won't be disturbed."

"I knew I could count on you." Mark gave the guard's arm a comradely squeeze, then went in and closed the hatch. As he locked it from within Emma unlocked a rear entrance to admit Kayta, Ruby, and Mike. Still on weak legs, Mike pulled a corner table to a position beneath an electrical access panel on the ceiling and then climbed shakily onto the table. Ruby slipped loose from her handcuffs and handed Mike a small tool to loosen the panel.

Down the passageway outside and around the corner from

the conference room Willy was standing lookout, worried fo
everyone. Including himself.

In one of the low, dark, steamy corridors of the Flagship'
bowels, the hatch on Margarita's cell creaked open just enoug
for her to slip out, followed by the counterfeit Nathan. The
quickly scoped out their surroundings and the Nathan look-alik
pointed a direction. "There's a service shaft down there."

"Always looking to shaft me, huh?" Margarita grinned tightl

"Hurry . . . and stay close." Then he reacted to a sound be
hind them, whispering, "Wait!" They ducked into a dark alcove

A reptilian guard appeared. The imitation Nathan clubbe
him down, handed his pistol to Margarita, then dumped th
guard into the cell, careful not to let Margarita see his secre
conspiratorial eye contact with the guard. Then he rejoined Ma
garita and whispered, "We're in the clear! Go!" She heade
down the dim walkway and he smiled to himself at his successfu
subterfuge. A respected member of Diana's elite guard, he wa
pleased that she had entrusted him with this assignment: to worl
alone, gain Margarita's confidence and infiltrate the Resistance
He quickly followed her into the humid darkness.

———

ROBERT WAS DRIVING THE SMALL TANK TRUCK HE HAD HOT-WIREI
and stolen the previous night. Gary sat in the passenger seat a
they pulled to a stop at the main gate of J. D. Oliver's chemica
plant. The gate guard checked their invoice, didn't recogniz
that it was a forgery, and waved them on in. Once inside, Gar
picked up a small two-way radio as he surveyed the condition
on the factory's grounds.

Just outside the south perimeter of the facility Ayden and Te
were sequestered in the abandoned junkyard, waiting besid
their airbikes. They heard Gary's voice over their radios, "We'r
in with the neutralizer. But I can see two—no, make that *three*—
tanker craft already loading up the chemical weapon from th
first storage tank."

* * *

AFTER A BIT OF A STRUGGLE, MIKE HAD LOOSENED THE CEILING AC-
cess panel in the conference room on the Flagship. He pushed
a tiny fiber-optic camera up through it. Emma and Mark looked
at a small vid receiver showing the image from the camera. It
showed Shawn's chamber on the level above them, his feet large
in the foreground. Mark took his cue and dialed the communicator on the conference table. Shawn's voice came through it,
"This is Shawn."

"Hi, it's Mark Ohanian. Listen, I'm inbound. Could you meet
me down in Hangar Bay Thirty-seven?"

They heard Shawn say, "Of course, Mr. Mayor." Then they
watched their vid receiver and saw Shawn's feet leave the room
above. He locked the hatch.

"Let me go first," Ruby said, "then I can help Kayta."

Mike nodded agreement and boosted the girl up to the access
panel. He helped her through the ceiling and into Shawn's chamber. Emma and Mark helped steady Kayta on the table, then
Mike gave her a leg up to the panel, asking, "You really think you
can squeeze through there?"

"I'll manage." The blond Zedti smiled with determination. It
was a very tight fit but with Ruby's help from above and Mike's
below Kayta ascended.

The opening was too small for Mike's broad shoulders but he
stuck his head up through. He could see the security unit as
Kayta and Ruby approached it. It was not at all the way Mike expected a safe or a vault to look. It was merely a two-foot cube of
light atop a square pedestal. Its contents, including the vital code
keys, could clearly be seen within a pair of protective rotating
rings that seemed to defy gravity.

"Whoa. Not your average safecracking job," Mike said with
concern.

Kayta agreed, "No human device could open it."

"But a Zedti can, huh, Kayta?" Ruby was ever-optimistic.

Kayta glanced at the girl. "Hopefully, Ruby." The violet-eyed Zedti took out a complicated-looking, handheld unit and began calibrating. Ruby watched, then glanced back at the keys within the rotating rings, murmuring to herself, "We're coming, Mom."

In the conference room below, Emma and Mark looked at each other, knowing that discovery and death might be only moments away. She took his hand. "Thank you for doing this." She kissed his hand and pressed it to her cheek. He stared at her, not unmoved, but hoping to God that he had made the right decision.

IN THE CHEMICAL FACTORY STELLA STEIN WAS GAZING DOWN FROM A catwalk toward the acid tank where Blue had given the last full measure of his devotion to the Resistance. It was a place she could never just walk past any longer without pausing for a moment's contemplation. As she turned away she noticed a small tank truck backing toward the large storage tank by the security section. She knew the tank was one of two that contained the Visitors' new chemical weapon. What had specifically caught her eye was that Charles Elgin was guiding the truck driver. Stella knew that such work was out of keeping with Charles's job description. She realized that something untoward was going on. She looked around and saw a Visitor guard approaching. Stella called out loudly to him, "Hey, Nick. Come over here a second."

Charles heard her shout just as he signaled Robert to stop the truck. He pushed his glasses up onto his nose and looked more carefully. Seeing that it was Stella up on the catwalk he drew a sharp breath. "Oh, shit. I think we're in trouble." Then he saw Stella distract the guard, turning the Patroller away from the covert activity below. Charles was totally amazed. "I can't believe she did that on purpose."

But as Stella continued talking to the guard, she glanced down at Charles and nodded subtly. Charles was even more dumbfounded, but spoke urgently to Robert and Gary, "I guess miracles do happen. Let's get moving."

WILLY WAS DOING HIS BEST TO LOOK CASUAL IN THE PASSAGEWAY outside the small conference room, but he clutched as he saw Jeremy and an aide approaching. Willy hurriedly pressed a button on his watch to signal Emma and Mark, but inside the conference room Mark had finally given in to his feelings for the brave young woman and was kissing her deeply. Neither of them saw the warning that was blinking on his watch.

In the passageway, Willy sought to stall what he feared might be a catastrophic discovery. He pretended to be confused, "Um, excuse me, Commandant?"

The imperious Jeremy paused. "Yes? What's the matter?"

"I am . . . just . . ." Willy said with total perplexity.

Jeremy was completely bewildered. "You are . . . *just?*"

Willy beamed. "Yes, Commandant!"

Jeremy stared at him. ". . . Just *what?*"

In the conference room Emma emerged from the wonderful kiss and saw Mark's blinking watch. Her heart leaped. "Oh, my God! Someone's coming!"

Out in the passage Willy was still vamping, "I am just. I don't know where I am."

"You mean 'lost,' you idiot." Jeremy gestured impatiently down the hall. "Go that way, someone will direct you."

Jeremy pushed past Willy and rounded the corner toward the guard who went wide-eyed seeing the Commandant approaching the conference room hatch. He snapped to attention, nervously. "Uh, beg pardon, sir."

"Yes, what is it?" Jeremy's angry scowl was too much for the guard.

"Nothing, sir. Sorry." The guard flinched as Jeremy moved past him, opened the hatch, and came to an abrupt standstill.

Directly in front of him, Emma was lying on her back on top of the conference table. Her shapely right breast was exposed and her jersey dress was hiked up above her waist revealing all of her slender bronze legs and hips. The mayor was astride her with his pants half-down. They both looked toward the door and feigned utter shock, Mark shouting, "Oh, Jesus!"

But man-of-the-world Jeremy merely held up his hand for them not to be afraid. He enjoyed his eyeful of Emma for an extended moment, then nodded with polite humor and withdrew.

Mark looked back at Emma, astonished that they'd gotten away with it. They laughed quietly together, his forehead lowering to touch hers. Mark realized his love and loyalty to her had definitely been rekindled. Then Donovan peeked up over the wet bar where he had hidden. He shook his head at their virtuoso performance, and nodded congratulations. "Brilliant. How do I get to be mayor?"

In Shawn's chamber directly above, Ruby watched as Kayta used her device to slow the rotating rings of the security unit. "That's about the best I can do, Ruby, go ahead."

Ruby reached in and started slightly, feeling a mild electrical stinging on her leathery hand. But she persisted and gingerly lifted out the code keys. Then Ruby held up her hand to high-five Kayta, but the Zedti didn't understand. Ruby took Kayta's hand and showed her how. "Like this." The little girl lightly slapped Kayta's hand triumphantly.

AN OILY HATCH OPENED DEEP WITHIN THE BOWELS OF THE FLAGSHIP and the imitation Nathan peered through and into the thousand-foot-long vertical shaft containing pipes and cables. "This should get us to a hangar bay."

Margarita was right behind him, whispering urgently, "Hurry up! Somebody's coming!" The two of them climbed onto the precarious ladder inside and secured the hatch above them just before the people she'd heard came into view. Then they began to climb up through the dark, slick shaft.

THE REAR HATCH OF THE SMALL CONFERENCE ROOM OPENED AND Willy stuck his head in. "Quickly . . . while no one's here!" Kayta and Ruby headed for Willy's doorway, Mike was following them, but looked back at Emma and Mark.

They saw the appreciation on his face and responded in kind. "Good luck," Mark said. Mike nodded and limped away.

Emma was nervously stuffing the tiny spy camera and receiver back into her purse. "I'm just glad our part's over."

Mark put his hand lovingly on her shoulder. "I don't know, some of it was very nice."

Her green eyes shone and he kissed her gently. "Come on, let's get you off this goddamn ship."

AYDEN AND TED WERE MOUNTING THEIR AIRBIKES IN THE JUNKYARD beside the chemical factory. The young half-breed was nervous. "When will your fleet start firing?"

"In twenty-one minutes. That's all the time we have left." Ayden started his airbike. A long burst of ionized flame shot out the back, then Ayden idled it for a moment as he gave a final instruction. "You wait until I have brought down the first tanker."

"Right . . . right . . ." Ted knew the drill, but was very edgy.

Ayden saw Ted's scaly brow knitting and smoothing repeatedly. He recognized the boy's fear. "Ted"—the Zedti focused his strong, amber eyes sharply on the teenager—"you can do this."

Ted looked at the resolute warrior and tried to steel himself. He nodded firmly. Then Ayden activated the stealth mode and Ted watched Ayden and the airbike grow nearly invisible as the Zedti glided upward and away. Ted blew out a puff of anxiety, repeating his mantra, "I can do this."

* * *

MARK AND EMMA HURRIED TO A TRANSPORT TUBE, SIGNALED FOR IT, and waited restlessly by the hatch. When it opened they were surprised to see Diana with two of her aides. Upon seeing them, the Commandant's eyes lit up. "I didn't know you were aboard."

Mark stepped back to let Diana and her entourage emerge from the transporter. "Actually, we were just leaving."

"I asked Mark to show me some areas I might use in my next music vid," Emma said with a smile.

"Ah"—Diana was eyeing the lovely young woman—"so your business is concluded?"

"Yes," Mark said, nudging Emma toward the transporter.

But Diana caught her sleeve. "Then how about some pleasure? I've been wanting to talk with you, Emma."

Mark glanced at his watch. "Unfortunately today isn't great, we've got that appointment at—"

Diana spoke pleasantly, ignoring him, "Please excuse us, Mark."

Emma knew that it was not an invitation, but a command. She smiled humbly. "I'd be honored," then she looked at Mark. "They can get along without me, Mr. Mayor, but would you take this?" She handed him the vid receiver for the small spy camera, then looked at him pointedly. "And keep a very close eye on it, okay?" She held his eyes for an emphatic instant, then she turned cheerfully back to Diana, who smiled and led her away. Mark watched them go, worried for Emma. He looked down at the receiver she'd left in his hands and was a bit puzzled.

MORE THAN A MILE BELOW WHERE MARK STOOD, A YOUNG HALF-breed janitor was cleaning in the steamy, dark Flagship passage as Willy guided Kayta, Mike, and Ruby to him. Jon's crooked mouth smiled as he took out a special access card.

Mike was somewhat astounded. "A janitor can access the Flagship's mainframe?"

Jon's eyes twinkled. "If a janitor steals the card, sir."

Ruby had been checking out the teen and approved. "My kind of guy."

Jon opened the heavy hatch to a small chamber that contrasted sharply to the dark passageway. The chamber was white. Inside it was a control panel with numerous monitoring readouts and a second smaller hatch, the porthole of which was fogged from the intense cold on the other side of it. Jon showed them a diagram on one wall and described the operation. "You lie face up on a movable pallet and slide in, sir. The sockets for the five code keys are clearly marked." He glanced at Mike. "I'll go up and be waiting in Capsule Operations Control. As soon as William inserts the keys I will see five green lights indicating that the communications circuits into the capsules have been unlocked."

"And then you'll alert Lee up in Centcom to transmit our instructions in to the prisoners," Mike confirmed.

"Correct, sir. Once the prisoners have received them"—the boy's eyes flashed with enthusiastic pride—"I will activate the master control that *opens* the capsules throughout the entire fleet."

Kayta had been looking through the frosty porthole and was concerned. "Willy, you need no protective garment?"

The gentle Visitor shook his head. "No. My kind can withstand extreme cold."

The half-breed janitor reached out his hand to his dear friend Willy. "Good luck to you, sir"—then he looked from Kayta to Mike to Ruby—"to all of us."

Jon hurried off while Willy began opening the inner hatch. It unsealed with a hissing blast of arctic air. Ruby was startled by its frigidity. "Whoa! That's some serious cold."

They peered into the long tubular mainframe. Hundreds of glowing modules were inlaid into its circular wall and stretched into the cloudy distance. Willy was about to lie down on the sliding platform when the mayor rushed in behind them. "Wait!"

Mike looked at Mark and down the corridor behind him. "What's wrong? Where's Emma?"

"She's in with Diana! Look!" He held up the vid receiver that was showing a skewed image from the spy cam. It was peering out from Emma's purse on the back of a couch in Diana's inner sanctum. They could also hear the audio.

The sultry Commandant was saying, "I've been wanting some one-on-one time with you for quite a while . . ."

"I'm flattered," Emma said, "but a little nervous . . ."

"Whatever for?" Diana was utterly charming. "No need to be. Drink?"

Mike instantly understood. "My God, Emma's trying to set up a *sting!*"

"Yes," Mark agreed. He was very worried for her but knew they must take advantage of Emma's dangerous gambit. "So how do we use it?"

The two men stared at each other a moment, then Mike hit on it. "Willy, take this to Lee up in Centcom, get her to *broadcast it!*" He thrust the receiver into Willy's hands. "Everywhere but on this ship!" Mark cautioned.

Willy understood. "But then who'll insert the code keys?"

"Hello?" Ruby smirked. "I'm half Visitor, so I can do it."

Mike was adamant. "No way, Ruby."

Kayta spoke up, "I think I could endure the cold for just long enough. Go on, Willy."

Willy made final eye contact with all of them, then hurried away.

"Listen"—Mark was very agitated—"I'll go back near Diana's."

Mike understood. "In case Emma needs help. Good."

The mayor left quickly as Kayta crawled onto the movable plate and rolled onto her back. She took the five code keys that

Ruby handed her and glided into the supercold mainframe tube. She was startled. It was like diving into icy water.

In Capsule Operations Control, two bored reptilian technicians went about their normal routine. Five red lights were burning steadily on a far corner of a status board. They had not changed color in twenty years and thus never commanded any attention. From a catwalk among the thousands of nearby capsules entwined with their pulsing, intestinelike coils, Jon entered, guiding his floating custodial unit, and set about doing his chores—while he carefully watched those five red lights.

IN THE VERTICAL SERVICE SHAFT THE PHONY NATHAN LED MARGARITA up the ladder to a hatch. He carefully opened it and looked out into the dark horizontal passageway, cautiously checking around as he spoke to her, "So listen, who are your other contacts in case I get—" He turned back to find the muzzle of her gun at his forehead.

"Busted?" she said with a sardonic smile.

"Margarita?" he sputtered. "I don't understand."

"Well, let's see"—her eyes narrowed—"how 'bout you have no scrape on your wrist and the sense of humor of a tree stump. I made you the minute you opened your mouth. So take me to the *real* Nathan, you asshole, or I'll blow your lizard head off."

THE MYRIAD STARS IN THE BLACKNESS OF SPACE ABOVE THE NORTH pole of the magnificent planet Jupiter suddenly seemed to ripple, as though something massive but unseen was disturbing the light coming from them. It was the fleet of gigantic Zedti warships whipping past in stealth mode and heading toward the distant Earth.

The amber-eyed Executive Officer was in her view bubble on the bridge of the organic Zedti Flagship. Data was streaming in the air near her. Other operational Zedti were at their crystalline stations in the cavernlike chamber directly behind her. She called

back to her lieutenant who was at the helm, "Commence targeting
their Motherships . . . Detect and double-target their Flagship."

"Commence targeting, aye," the lieutenant said as he switched
to the intra-fleet channel and sent the directive to all the warships in the task force.

The Executive Officer looked back out into the darkness. She
knew they would be in Earth space and within firing range in less
than fifteen minutes.

31

WILLY TRIED TO APPEAR CASUAL AS HE SOUGHT OUT THE FEMALE
Visitor with short black hair on the second level of the Visitor
Flagship's huge, bustling Centcom. But when Lee saw him coming she could tell that the friendly expression on his face was a
tight mask. As he sat beside her she whispered, "What's wrong?"

He produced the small vid receiver from his pocket, "We need
to broadcast this. Through the auto-translator."

"To where?" Lee was confused.

"All channels, vid phones, everywhere—*except* this ship."

Lee looked curiously at the slightly skewed image of Emma in
her intimate session with Diana. As Lee realized what was happening her eyes snapped up to Willy, wide with amazement.

In the eighth-grade classroom at Patrick Henry Middle School
the ceiling-mounted flat screen was showing a biology vid about
the pistils and stamens of plants. The lesson provoked the standard scatological snickering among some of the boys. But not
Danny Stein. He was frowning about the situation within his
family. Thomas Murakami glanced guiltily at Danny from across
the classroom. They had not spoken since the day Thomas confirmed to Vice Principal Gabriel that Danny possessed an illegal
Resistance vid. He knew that Danny had been arrested and

heard that his father had been taken away. Thomas still felt terrible about what he had done, but like so many other thousands of informers, he had done it to protect his own family and himself. He missed being friends with Danny but couldn't imagine any way of repairing the damage.

Then Thomas was as startled as all the other students when the biology vid suddenly switched to the skewed image from Diana's chamber. The students didn't know that Diana had been privately emboldened by her renewed connection with the Leader, but most of them recognized that the gleam in Diana's eye was very sexual and predatory. She sinuously circled Emma, moving out of the camera's view. "Your singing at the rally was so stirring," she said as her hand came into the foreground on the classroom's vid screen, grazing Emma's shoulder and neck from behind, "I could positively feel your passion . . ."

"Thank you." Emma turned to look back toward Diana, which brought her own face into a big close-up. Emma glanced for a moment directly into the camera, hoping that others were observing the scene.

Mrs. Richmond, the dowdy classroom teacher, was confused and increasingly distressed. She instinctively sensed that this intimate, unfolding drama was something her students were not supposed to be watching. She headed to the front of the room to pick up the TV remote. But Danny had just as intuitively realized the telecast was something they all should definitely witness. He jumped up, snagged the remote before his teacher could, and he threw it out the window. The screen was too high for Mrs. Richmond to reach. She couldn't turn it off.

Emma was anxious to subtly steer the conversation in a particular direction. "Your Leader was certainly impassioned."

"Our Leader can be very fervent when she chooses to be," Diana said as she moved back into the view of the hidden camera, "and I'm most fortunate to be first in her favor. Which is a wonderful circumstance . . . for you as well."

"When she talked about that Zedti race she was particularly passionate," Emma prompted, "I heard that she'd been defeated by them once before. Is that true?" Diana nodded affirmatively. Emma pressed on, "She must be angry about that. She must want revenge."

Diana was eyeing Emma with a meaningful smile. "She desires to be dominant, yes."

One of the many police precincts where the live broadcast was being seen was the Parnassas Station. The black Patrol captain and everyone else present were also watching in stunned silence as Emma and Diana continued on the station's TV.

"God," Emma exhaled, "I'd sure be relieved to hear *that's* why she wants to go to war against the Zedti—*not* because they're planning to attack Earth."

Diana moved closer to the singer, speaking softly, "Then allow me to relieve you."

A Visitor Patroller grabbed for a phone to question what was happening, but a hefty Teammate caught his hand, stopping him in no uncertain terms. Similar actions were taking place in other locations across the Earth as people everywhere were glued to their televisions and vid phones while Diana continued. "The Leader is an individual who gets what she wants. By any means necessary."

IN THE CAPSULE OPERATIONS CONTROL ONE OF THE FIVE RED STATUS lights switched from red to green indicating one of the five critical communications channels had been unlocked. Jon continued cleaning, but watched the remaining four like a hawk.

Inside the icy, cloudy mainframe, one of the code keys was indeed in place, but Kayta found herself in serious trouble from the hyper-cold. The skin on her freezing hand was cracking as she shakily managed to push the second key into its appropriate slot, but then she dropped the other three keys and began convulsing. Mike had been watching vigilantly through the view port. He jerked open the hatch, shouting, "Kayta! *Kayta!*"

Little Ruby scurried past him into the long tubular passage. "I'll get her!"

"Ruby! No!" Mike grabbed for her but missed. "Ruby! Come back here!"

ON WALL SCREENS AND HOME SCREENS FROM LOS ANGELES TO Berlin to Beijing to Sydney, citizens and Teammates were watching a new type of reality TV as the live drama unfolded between Emma and Diana. The striking Commandant was saying, "I'm surprised you have such an interest in warfare, Emma."

"Moreso in understanding how the great Commandants think." Emma gave her a flattering look.

"Well, this Commandant thinks a great deal of you." Diana leaned even closer to Emma. "You have an eyelash . . . may I?"

"Of course, thank you." The singer tilted her face up inviting Diana's fingertips to touch her cheek gently.

IN THE OUTER CHAMBER OF THE MAINFRAME, MIKE HELPED RUBY pull the unconscious Kayta out of the supercooled inner area. The blond Zedti was covered with a layer of frost that Mike brushed away as he rubbed her hands and face, trying to revive her. Ruby climbed back onto the movable plate and slid back inside. Mike looked up, shouting furiously, "Ruby! Dammit!"

The girl shouted back, "Piece of cake, Mike!" Then she involuntarily shook from the outrageously low temperature and muttered to herself, "Ooo. Ice cream cake, maybe."

Ruby glided the movable pallet down to where Kayta had dropped the keys into a narrow slit alongside the pallet's track.

The girl stretched her scaly fingers down toward them. "Come on . . . Come on . . ."

With each breath, the freezing air stabbed like icicles deeper into her lungs. Ruby suddenly had the sobering thought that she might not survive within the icy mainframe. Yet she also knew the high stakes she was fighting for. Even as her fingers grew increasingly numb Ruby stretched them down toward the fallen keys, but she could just barely brush the frost on top of them.

THE HATCH TO THE AUTOPSY ROOM HISSED OPEN AND MARGARITA saw the real Nathan restrained in the interrogation chair. His head was slumped to one side and he looked very much the worse for his ordeal. He blinked heavily as he saw Margarita entering, "Hey, girl, thanks for dropping by . . ."

He noticed two Visitor guards lying unconscious in the corridor outside, having obviously been dispatched by Margarita. "Get him out of there. Now!" She shoved the bogus Nathan into the cell toward the real one.

For the first time Nathan got a good look at his double. "Whoa, what a handsome guy!"

The phony Nathan freed Nathan, then abruptly jumped him. They rolled onto the floor, struggling. Margarita lost track of who was who. One of them shouted, "Shoot him! Quick!"

"Not me!" yelled the other. "Him! *Him!*"

Margarita aimed her pistol, looking for the unscraped wrist but couldn't make it out in the dim light and the tussle.

Finally one Nathan yelled, "*Red!* I am the *hotshot!*"

Margarita grinned and immediately fired a pulse burst right into the face of the other. The counterfeit was spun backward by the impact and fell dead. His facial skin had peeled back revealing the reptile beneath.

Nathan rolled onto his side, breathing hard, as he looked up at her. "So . . . was he any good in bed?" She reached down and pulled his arm to help him up but he yelped loudly, "Ow ow ow! Watch it! Geez!"

She looked closer and saw blood leaking from his torn sleeve. She also saw something else that made her blanch, "Is that *bone*?"

Nathan was pale and sweating from pain, but he sloughed it off. "No biggie . . . Let's boogie."

SHAWN WALKED ACROSS THE LEVEL-FOUR PLATFORM OF HANGAR BAY Thirty-seven toward the shuttle that had just landed. It was off-loading passengers, but he didn't see the man he was looking for. He did, however, spot the Visitor press secretary and walked to him. "Paul, was the mayor on there with you?"

"No"—Paul shrugged—"I haven't seen him since the rally." Then, recognizing an opportunity to trumpet his worth, Paul warmed to the subject. "We certainly knocked them out at Candlestick, didn't we? My office has been swamped with congratulations from all over."

"Mmmm." Shawn's suspicious mind was definitely elsewhere. "Can I borrow your vid phone?"

"Of course"—he handed it to Shawn—"drop it off in my office." As Paul started walking away he mentioned, "Oh, it's not in the Flagship zone, it's a 415 area code."

"That's all right"—Shawn clicked it on—"I just need to—" He was startled by what he saw and heard on the vid phone. It was Diana's face, very close to Emma's. He heard them speaking.

Diana's face showed mild concern. "Emma, are you trembling?"

"I'm frightened," Emma was speaking more truth than Diana realized, "about the future. About you. You have so much power here—"

"Which can *protect you*, my dear, in the days to come." She toyed with Emma's ear and the image flashed instantaneously around the world to screens everywhere. They were being watched with rapt attention by Teammates and other humans, all of whom were reacting with deepening curiosity. The Visitors among them were growing increasingly edgy.

Emma spoke with concern, "I'll *need* protection?"

"I'm afraid it will soon get very unpleasant here. Only the humans who are very closest to our High Command will be guaranteed their safety . . . and our companionship."

"I hope I'll be among them," Emma said with as much lightness as she could muster.

"I'd certainly like for you to be . . ." Diana leaned even closer to Emma and thus unwittingly toward the tiny lens of the spy camera, creating a huge close-up of herself for all of the world to see. Emma coaxed her toward the key question.

"But when you say Earth will become 'unpleasant,' *why* exactly, Diana?"

The Commandant merely smiled coyly.

So Emma pressed, ". . . Is it the water?" Diana's lips touched Emma's cheek. ". . . Is it not coming back?"

Diana gently shook her head and said proudly, ". . . *No.*"

Several billion people, all around the planet Earth, stared at their screens, stunned to finally hear the truth.

Shawn was already on the run from the hangar bay toward Diana's chamber. He shouted to a pair of Patrollers, "Come with me! Hurry!"

RUBY'S SHAKY FINGERS HAD TURNED BLUE AS SHE STRETCHED HER arm nearly out of its socket and at last reached the three fallen code keys. She lifted them out and rolled painfully over onto her back in the freezing mainframe tube. The frigid air showed each of the very tiny breaths she was taking. She had realized that it didn't sting quite so terribly that way. The stinging she felt was the hyper-cold attacking the bronchioles and the tiny alveoli within her lungs that, like her blue eyes, were much more human than Visitor. In spite of Ruby's shallow breathing, the delicate tissues of the minuscule, grapelike alveoli in her lungs that were vital for oxygenating her blood were slowly being frozen solid. Ruby was pleased that at least her feet and legs no longer hurt. She took that as a good sign. She thought she must be getting used to the extreme cold. As she searched out the next socket to insert a key into, she began to sing very softly to help her keep focused. Of course she knew the appropriate song, *"Dai-sy . . . Dai-sy . . . "*

AT THE CHEMICAL FACTORY THREE VISITOR FIGHTERS FLEW IN OVER-head to act as cover for the tankers. It had been designated as such a critical mission that the Wing Commander herself was in the lead. Gina hovered her fighter overhead like a master horse-woman keeping a tight rein on an energetic thoroughbred. She keyed her communicator. "This is Red leader, we'll hang here un-til they're airborne."

From their individual hiding places on either side of the facil-ity both Ted and Ayden saw the fighters hovering in the air like menacing birds of prey and they both knew that their mission had just gotten a great deal more difficult.

JON SAW A THIRD STATUS LIGHT GO FROM RED TO GREEN ON THE control panel in the Capsule Operations Control. He knew that only two keys were left to be inserted and the communi-cations circuits would all be unlocked. His young heart was beating so loudly he was afraid one of the technicians would hear it.

In the vaporous mainframe tube Ruby's face had become as blue as her hands. She was quaking uncontrollably with the cold. Her frost-covered, quivering hands barely worked as she reached out toward the fourth socket. She was having great difficulty breathing. Had she been able to see the inside of her lungs she would have understood why. They were as frost-covered as her hands. Her fragile, critical lung tissue was almost entirely frozen and thus unable to absorb the oxygen that her young body was urgently crying out for. She was suffocating. Her straining body had already shut down her feet and legs. Her arms and hands were now failing. The extreme stress being placed on her entire little system would have long since stopped someone with less heart than Ruby.

She was still singing low to herself, now needing one shallow breath for each syllable, "... *I'm ... half ... cra ... zy ...*"

Her eardrums had frozen so Mike's hoarse, frantic shouts came to her as though through thick layers of cotton. "Ruby! You've got to come out *now!*" When she ignored him Mike gulped in what he knew might well be his final breath and began crawling toward her, unmindful that his own hands were being burned by the hyper-cold surfaces. But Ruby was at least thirty yards away from him, deep within the narrow glacial chamber.

Ruby pushed the fourth key into place. The ongoing effort was a desperate, mighty struggle for the brave little girl. Several tears had spilled from her eyes and instantly frozen on her scaly cheeks. She wasn't sure she had the strength or could even remain conscious long enough to insert the final one, but she reached the key toward its slot. Ruby knew she had to do it. She knew the only way for her dear Julie and all the millions of others to ever have a chance was if her fiery little spirit could somehow be a match for the nearly absolute-zero cold. Her song was barely audible now, even to her, but with grit that far exceeded her years, she persisted, "... *All ... for ... the ... love ... of ...*"

The fifth code key clicked into place as Ruby gasped, "... *Mom.*"

Then she slumped, unconscious.

* * *

IN THE CAPSULE OPERATIONS CONTROL, JON SAW THE RESULTS OF Ruby's magnificent effort. Five green status lights were now burning. The circuits were unlocked. Jon turned away from the technicians on duty and spoke quietly into his radio, "Go, Willy! Go! Go!"

Willy was sitting beside Lee in the Flagship's Centcom, appearing to be casually getting some information from her. When he heard Jon's voice in his earpiece, he nodded to Lee. She surreptitiously began transmitting Emma's recorded instructions into the neurological units that were fitted on the heads of the millions of entombed prisoners across the entire Visitor Armada.

Within every stasis capsule of every Mothership around the world, each prisoner, whether Asian, African, Latin-American, European, or North-American, suddenly heard Emma speaking in his or her own language, from Swedish to Swahili, Italian to Indonesian, Uzbek to English, they heard her saying, "This is the voice of the Resistance. You will disregard all previous indoctrination you have received. You will all soon be freed from your capsules. Be prepared to fight. We are taking over all the Motherships . . ."

Throughout the vast storage chambers of 250 Motherships, the multitudes of entombed humans all heard Emma's call to arms. Danny's father Sidney heard it. And Stella's coworker Connie. And Martin, Street-C, Ysabel, Julie. Though still deep within their comatose state, their eyes flashed with courage for the battle that was about to begin.

MARGARITA AND NATHAN MOVED QUICKLY THROUGH A LARGE MAchinery chamber within the murky bowels of the Flagship. Heavy chains hung from the darkness overhead. When they heard two technicians passing, they skittered into hiding amid the bulbous equipment. Moisture dripped down onto them as Margarita took advantage of their momentary pause to check

Nathan's bloody arm more closely. "We've got to get the bone back in to stop the bleeding."

He held his injured arm out to her. "Give it a yank. On three. One—"

She jerked it hard. He gasped as he saw stars and went white from the agony. She wiped his fevered brow and murmured "Sorry, sorry," to comfort him.

The room was swimming sickeningly around him. "Not big on arithmetic, are we?"

Her face was very near his. "I thought it'd be easier . . . Can you keep going?"

He glanced at her sideways with a painfully crazed expression. "Can I yank *your* arm later?" She laughed at his wherewithal and kissed his bruised cheek. Then she helped him to his feet.

MIKE'S SKIN WAS FROSTBITTEN, PATCHES OF IT TURNING BLACK, BUT Kayta had regained consciousness and with her help he pulled the nearly frozen twelve-year-old out of the mainframe. Mike saw the icy tears on Ruby's scaly cheeks.

"She's not breathing!" He was panting hard. "Help me!"

Kayta motioned Mike aside and then the Zedti bent toward Ruby. The wiry, defensive quills emerged from the back of Kayta's slender neck. She turned herself so that one of them pierced Ruby's neck. The child shuddered violently as though receiving an electrical jolt. She gasped in a breath. But her respiration was extremely shallow. Mike looked at Kayta who knew what his question would be. She shook her head. "Only once. Another would kill her."

They both looked back at the girl as Ruby's eyes lolled open. She struggled to focus and was barely able to ask, ". . . Did . . . we . . . do it?"

Mike clasped her hand, trying to transfer some of his strength into her, "*You* did it, kid. You saved us all, Ruby."

She managed a very faint smile. ". . . Give Nathan . . . a . . . kiss for me."

Kayta placed her comforting hand on the child. "You will give him one yourself."

Ruby smiled into Kayta's kind, violet eyes with a wisdom that belied her young age. Then she looked at Mike, whispering, ". . . Tell Momma . . . I . . ."

Her voice was barely audible. Mike had to lean his ear to her lips to hear the heroic girl's murmurs. Then he saw her small, frostbitten fingers form a V.

And with a proud, wistful smile at Mike, little Ruby grew still. Her courageous soul had slipped away.

IN THE UPPER PASSAGEWAY NEAR DIANA'S CHAMBER MARK WAS ANXiously standing by when he saw Shawn round a corner leading several Patrollers. Mark stepped in the way to block them. "Diana said she was not to be disturbed, so—"

The Patrollers paid him no mind and shoved him brutally aside. Mark then realized that Jeremy and the angry Visitor Leader were following immediately behind.

Shawn opened the hatch.

All of the billions of people around the world who were riveted to the images from Diana's chamber saw the Commandant kissing Emma with deep passion as Shawn and the Patrollers burst in, followed by Jeremy. Visitors, Teammates, and civilians everywhere saw Shawn take the stage grandly as he seized his moment and pointed at Diana in a posture of *J'accuse*, as he bellowed, *"There!"*

Jeremy stormed in toward Diana. "You fool! Don't you realize what she is *doing!*"

Two of the Patrollers grabbed Diana and Emma. Others had been searching for the hidden camera, which they found and smashed. Vid screens everywhere suddenly went black.

But the damage had been done. In the Parnassas Police Station and millions of other locations worldwide, human cops, Team-mates, and others, having finally seen and heard The Truth, turned slowly to stare at nearby Visitors.

In Diana's chamber the Leader entered seething and pulled Diana up close to her face. "You will learn the true meaning of pain." Her fiery eyes snapped to the Patrollers. "Imprison her."

As Diana was taken roughly away, Shawn, relishing his status as the hero of the moment, gestured toward Emma and Mark. "And these, Excellency?"

The Leader glared at the two. "Throw them overboard."

NEAR THE CHEMICAL FACTORY AYDEN HAD BEEN OBSERVING THE newly arrived fighter escort and devising his strategy. He keyed his communicator and said to Ted, "I will hit the first tanker, then distract the fighters. You must destroy the other two tankers. None of that chemical must be allowed to reach the Motherships for duplication."

On the opposite perimeter, still hidden in the abandoned junkyard, the teenage half-breed responded nervously, "Yes, sir. I understand." Ted was so focused forward that he did not realize a patrolling Visitor guard was easing up behind him, quietly drawing a pulse weapon.

32

OTHER ARMED PATROLLERS SWEPT ONTO THE LOWER LEVEL OF THE Flagship Centcom, searching for the source of the Diana-Emma transmission. Lee had anticipated such an investigation and had carefully patched the system in an intricate fashion that allowed her to control all of the switching remotely. She had also been monitoring the transmission to the entombed people and she whispered to Willy, "The instructions just finished. They've been received by all the prisoners."

"Good," Willy said urgently, "switch over, quickly!" Then he spoke into his radio, "Jon . . . you have a go!"

At the same moment that Lee lit up vid screens internationally with a view of the Flagship's vast Capsule Storage Chamber, Jon jumped bravely past a startled technician to the control console. The teenager grabbed and pulled the large handle to engage the Master Encapsulation Override.

A blaring alarm sounded. Throughout the vaulted reaches of the Flagship's cubic-mile-sized storage chamber—and simultaneously in all 250 other Motherships—the entombment capsules surged open.

The millions of liberated people let out a mighty roar. They ripped off their neuro headsets as they shouted enthusiastically in many languages, *"Vive la Revolution! Erin go bragh! Up the Rebels! Allah akbar! Bonzai! Hoo-ahh!"*

It was a cacophonous, earsplitting yell of pure joy, elation, and determination such as had never before been heard on the planet Earth.

Margarita and Nathan were in a nearby hallway when the mighty cheer echoed down the dark corridors to them. They glanced exuberantly at each other and dashed toward the sound, entering the storage chamber at a mid-level. Their jaws dropped as they saw the amazing spectacle before them: tens of thousands of prisoners were clambering quickly out of their captivity, climbing from the capsules that stretched a mile above, below, and away from where the two of them stood.

"Whoa!" Nathan was beaming. "Hey, Red, you got a date for the Revolution?"

Margarita's eyes flashed brightly back at him as the scene they were witnessing was transmitted by Lee to vid screens around the world.

People at Parnassas and hundreds of thousands of other police stations and city streets across the world also saw the multitude of prisoners excitedly exiting the capsules and helping each
other spill out onto the innumerable catwalks. The chambers
were so enormous and the swarming, liberated, elated individuals so plentiful as to stagger the imagination. People around the
Earth viewing the scenes realized that the dark rumors about the
stasis capsule storage chambers were true. They also knew that
the tide had turned against their captors.

Civilians and even formerly loyal Teammates went on the offensive, venting their outrage on the nearest Visitors, who were
now clearly seen as the foes and oppressors of all humankind.
The mass insurrection that Julie and the Resistance had dreamed
of and fought for over twenty years to inspire had finally begun.

In the Elgins' tenement, Mary was drawn to her window by
the noise in the streets outside. She opened it and heard the
alarms, sirens, and battle cries of a new day dawning.

In the Capsule Storage Chamber, Jon had been rescued from
the angry technicians, who were swiftly overrun by the hordes
of liberated people on their way to the assignments that Emma's
instructions had given them. Jon made his way through the eu-
phoric, energized people to reach the capsule of the woman he
had often paused to gaze at longingly. As he helped her out of
the capsule she looked at him in wonder and faint recognition.
The half-breed teen nodded happily to her. "Yes, Mother, it's
me." The woman was overwhelmed, and embraced her son tearfully.

Margarita and Nathan rushed past them and connected with
Julie, Ysabel, Street-C, Martin, and their Resistance team who
were in the forefront. Julie shouted to them over the multitude's
jubilation, "We're taking the ship!"

"Yeah," Margarita shouted back, laughing, "we sorta figured!"

Julie called out to the people massing behind her, "Level Eighteen people—*this way!*"

The freed people, young and old of every conceivable ethnicity, roared back their unanimous support. Farmers, soldiers, scholars, people of every diverse stripe imaginable, all followed Julie, Margarita, and Nathan.

As the burgeoning army flowed onto the catwalks and passages of the Flagship, some Visitor guards tried to stop them. A few of the humans were shot or injured, but they were a swelling tide that could not be held back. It swamped and overcame every Visitor obstacle as the freed people moved in a human tsunami sweeping through and out of their prison chamber, heading for the critical assignments they had been given.

DANNY, ALONG WITH MANY OTHER KIDS, RAN OUT OF HIS SCHOOL into the street where alarms and sirens were wailing. Danny saw a woman throw a Molotov cocktail into a Visitor shuttle that then exploded violently. He saw a squad of startled Visitor Patrollers being besieged by angry citizens including many in Teammate uniforms. The population of San Francisco had finally awakened and was striking out at the Visitors. Danny knew that the scenes he was witnessing were certainly being duplicated in city after city across the planet. He knew the Rebellion must be blossoming everywhere.

AT THE CHEMICAL FACTORY THE FIRST TWO-HUNDRED-FOOT-LONG tanker, heavily laden with the Visitor chemical weapon, was lifting off. It had barely cleared the ground when Ayden's airbike came swooping in at low altitude with its laser guns blazing. Ayden strafed the big transport, which took several glancing hits before it suddenly caught fire. It tilted precariously as its control surfaces failed to respond. Then it listed farther sideways and collided with one face of the five-story industrial facility. It exploded spectacularly, the flames vaporizing and consuming the deadly chemical.

On the opposite side of the factory at the secondary chemical weapon storage tank, Robert, Gary, and Charles heard the explosion and saw the mushrooming fireball. They were hurriedly uncoiling a hose from their small tank truck containing the neutralizer that Kayta and Charles's compatriots had created. Ayden's airbike flashed by over their heads. He was not in stealth mode, because of his desire to draw Visitor fire away from Ted, and he was succeeding. Gina's fighter was in hot pursuit.

In the junkyard at the south perimeter, the Visitor sentry had stealthily closed the distance behind Ted and took aim to shoot the unsuspecting boy in the back. The sentry was squeezing the trigger of his pulse pistol when Ted fired up his bike. The flaming ionic back blast from the bike literally blew the sentry away. But Ted had no idea of it as he banked his airbike skyward, heading on his mission.

IN THE BOWELS OF THE FLAGSHIP, NATHAN AND MANY OF THE FREED people fought through the lower passages. Some of those liberated, including Connie Leonetti, remained to tend the wounded or to secure locations as they'd been instructed while others swept onward as Nathan directed them, "Some of you, down that corridor! Take their barracks. Let's go!"

Two Visitors with yellow stickers appeared ahead of Margarita, who leveled her weapon at them until Ysabel shouted at her, "No! They're with us! See the yellow!"

"Gotcha"—the redhead nodded, then called back over her shoulder—"come on, gang!"

Shawn, who had been on a mission of his own and was hiding in an alcove, saw the hordes passing him and noted the significance of the yellow stickers.

In one of the clean, gray upper passageways, Diana was being led along by the stern Patroller guarding her. As they passed a female Patroller, Diana, in an eyeblink, pulled the pulse gun from the startled female and shot her in the throat. Before the other Patroller could react, Diana fired point-blank into his heart. Then she hurried on to find a means of escape.

J. D. OLIVER HAD HEARD THE EXPLOSION OUTSIDE HIS OFFICE AT HIS factory and ran out to investigate. Seeing the burning tanker he quickly ducked back into hiding.

Charles Elgin had glimpsed Oliver, but was busy helping Gary stretch the hose from the tank truck toward the main storage tank.

"More hose!" Gary shouted, "We need more!"

Robert was beside the tank truck and saw the spool was at its end. "There isn't any more!" Then he heard a woman's voice call out.

"Yes, there is!" Stella Stein was running toward them carrying an extra coil of hose. She knew that Danny would be proud of her. Charles was amazed.

Around the corner of the steel superstructure of the facility the second tanker transport full of the chemical weapon was lifting off.

On his airbike in stealth mode, Ted was crossing over the grounds of the plant and diving toward the tanker. The tense teenager whispered to himself, "This one's for Bryke." He pressed the firing button and a burst of laser fire flashed out. It caught the tanker amidships and pierced the hull, creating a stunning explosion.

But Ted had no time to celebrate because a pulse blast hit the back of his airbike, nearly unseating him. He looked back to see a Visitor fighter tight on his tail. Though he had fired while in stealth mode, the pursuing fighter pilot had seen the origin of his shot and correctly targeted Ted. The hit that Ted's bike had taken had damaged the bike's stealth generator and the boy realized he was now a visible target. Frightened, he looked quickly around for help but saw that Ayden was a half mile away on the other side of the facility doing his best to dodge the blistering fire from Gina's fighter. Ted realized that they were both in serious trouble as he glanced below and saw that the final tanker was beginning to lift off.

KAYTA AND MIKE HAD BEEN MAKING THEIR WAY OUTWARD THROUGH the long passages from the Flagship mainframe. They both were extremely weak from the debilitating cold they'd endured and Mike's legs were burning with pain. When they reached the Capsule Storage Chamber Mike remembered when he had been the first human ever to see it, over twenty years earlier. He was excited to realize that the capsules were now all open and the chamber was empty of captives.

"Look, Kayta! They did it!" He turned and grabbed her shoulders. "Call off your fleet!"

The Zedti was breathing with difficulty. "I must be . . . certain it is . . . worldwide."

Mike pulled out his radio. "Willy! Have we done it?"

The Flagship Centcom was in boisterous turmoil due not only to the Resistance's transmissions, but because of the messages flooding in about the revolutionary uprisings around the world. Willy and Lee were in the midst of the frantic chamber. He keyed his radio, "The reports are still very confused, Mike."

In the capsule area Kayta shook her head at Mike. "I'm truly sorry, but I have to be certain."

IN THE DEPTHS OF SPACE THE ZEDTI FLEET CONTINUED INBOUND WITH their mammoth warships in stealth mode. From her view port on their Flagship the Executive Officer questioned her second in command, "Target acquisition status?"

The lieutenant checked the crystalline display before him. "Acquisition at seventy percent, Commander."

*   *   *

THE HATCH OF ONE OF THE VISITOR FLAGSHIP'S ARMORIES OPENED.
Margarita shot the Visitor on duty and Julie hurried into the
large chamber where pulse rifles and pistols were at the ready on
charging racks. Julie addressed the crowd behind her, pointing
toward the weapons, "Grab those! The flashlights, too. Pass 'em
out! Follow us!"

Margarita handed out several of the weapons. "Harmy! You,
too. Here you go. Come on!" Harmy took the rifle, which was
heavy in her hands. She hated the idea of using it, but followed
Margarita and the others.

In a dark corridor several levels above, Shawn was hurrying
along, trying to find an escape route. He heard some of the liberated people approaching behind him and then saw Eric just
ahead, wearing the yellow sticker Gary had given him.

Shawn rushed up to Eric, saying, "Thank you," as he ripped
the sticker off of Eric and stuck it on himself. In that moment,
the freed people, now carrying pulse weapons, rounded the corner. Shawn dropped to the floor as though he'd been struck by
Eric and pointed at the doctor, shouting, "Get that bastard! Get
him!"

Eric was gunned down by multiple bursts of pulse fire and
trampled by the onrushing army while Shawn ducked safely
away.

GARY, CHARLES, AND STELLA WERE PUMPING THE LIQUID FROM THE
small truck into the huge storage tank, which had begun smoking and bubbling, an alkaline froth covering the surface. Stella
shouted to them over the blaring alarms, "It's a neutralizer?"

Charles nodded. "To make their weapon useless! Yes!"

Robert's dark eyes were intense, his black brow furrowed as
he tried to get through on his radio, "Willy? We've neutralized
the main tank. Willy? Did you get that?"

Ted's airbike skimmed past just over their heads, a Visitor
fighter directly behind him. The fighter pilot had a target lock on

the airbike and was about to fire when Ted suddenly dived his
airbike low through a narrow archway amid the massive factory
machinery. The pursuing fighter couldn't pull up in time nor fit
through. Its wings were sheared off as it crashed into the huge
pipes, sending fountains of water, steam, and flame rocketing
into the air.

Ted angled his airbike toward the third tanker, which was
slowly gaining altitude. Out of the corner of his eye he caught
sight of Gina's fighter as she scored a glancing hit on Ayden's
bike, which sparked badly and was going out of control. Ted
looked quickly again at the rising tanker, unsure what to do, then
he swerved sharply, flying to Ayden's assistance.

Gina was intent on the Zedti commander's airbike, which was
losing altitude directly in front of her. She was closing in for the
kill when Ted suddenly came diving at her right out of the sun,
his laser guns firing full tilt. Gina's fighter was hit hard. She was
furious and fought to maintain control of her damaged craft.
There was smoke in her cockpit. She had no choice but to angrily break off the attack.

Ted meantime had maneuvered directly over Ayden's failing
bike. The Zedti commander, realizing what the boy was attempt-
ing, reached up with his strong arms and grabbed on to Ted's
bike. Ayden was lifted up and away just before his own failing
airbike spun down into a confluence of pipes below, tearing itself
to pieces.

AN ECHOING LOUDSPEAKER VOICE IN THE FLAGSHIP CENTCOM AN-
nounced, "Warning. This ship has been targeted." The warning
repeated as new alarms sounded. From their position on the
upper Centcom platform Willy and Lee saw the Leader, Jeremy,
Paul, and a number of their elite guard rush onto the main deck
below.

The Leader was shouting, "Ready the pulse cannons! Alert
the Armada to prepare for attack."

Jeremy moved to a secondary command station. "Raise all defense shields!"

In one of the Flagship's upper passages a transporter tube hatch opened and Mike limped out on very painful legs with Kayta walking weakly beside him.

"Centcom's on this level," he encouraged her. "When you hear the reports firsthand then you can call off—" Mike saw Diana appear at an intersection ahead of them. The dark Commandant spotted him at the same moment. She fired her pulse weapon and Mike spun to shield Kayta, taking a partial hit in his side. He was knocked to the floor, carrying Kayta with him. As more bursts from Diana's weapon impacted beside him, Mike rolled around to exchange fire with Diana. One of his shots ricocheted electrically off the corridor bulkhead and struck her. It peeled off part of her human face to expose her angry, glaring reptilian visage beneath. She hissed fiercely at Donovan and darted away.

"Kayta, come on," Mike urged as he got to his feet. "We've got to get to—" Mike looked at the blond Zedti and realized Kayta had been hit by one of Diana's pulse bursts. She was limp and unconscious.

The Leader and Jeremy were trying to organize the growing tumult in the Centcom as they listened to a dozen incoming radio reports of the growing disaster. On the platform above them, Willy whispered urgently into his radio, "Mike! Listen! The chemical weapon's been neutralized. Rebellion is worldwide. I'm hearing it's overwhelming, unstoppable! Kayta can call off the Zedti fleet!"

Mike was bending over Kayta in the passageway as he shouted back into his radio, "Except that she's unconscious! Where the hell is Ayden?!"

THE ZEDTI COMMANDER WAS DANGLING BENEATH TED'S AIRBIKE AND had just managed to get a firm hold with both hands. Then, using his prodigious strength, Ayden pulled himself up and aboard the back of the bike. Ted meanwhile was focused on his pursuit of the third large tanker craft. He was dodging fierce rearward fire from the fighter that was protecting it.

Ted closed the distance, swerving right and left to avoid bursts from the fighter's aft-facing pulse cannons. Ayden reached around the boy, adjusted a targeting device, and fired an exceptionally large laser burst that struck and exploded both the fighter and the big tanker into a ball of flame and debris the size of an aircraft carrier. Ted screamed because he couldn't avoid flying them directly into the huge, broiling fireball.

THE SHIPBOARD REVOLUTION HAD NOT YET REACHED HANGAR BAY Twenty-two, though alarms were sounding. Visitor technicians and Patrollers were hurriedly arming themselves.

Emma and Mark were being manhandled across the main flight deck by their Patroller guards toward the hundred-foot-wide hatch that was open to the sky above and San Francisco nearly a mile below. It was from there that they would be thrown overboard.

Emma and Mark had been pulled almost to the brink of the huge open hatch when Nathan and Margarita appeared on the southern side of the expansive main flight deck and Nathan shouted, "Hey! Hold up!"

"Stop right there!" Margarita leveled her pulse rifle at them.

The guards holding Emma and Mark used them as human shields and opened fire on the two freedom fighters. Other Visitors in the hangar also began firing. Margarita and Nathan returned fire as they took cover behind some transport containers between a pair of shuttle craft. Julie's cavalry also began to arrive from the south. She led some of the freed people onto the flight deck level while other legions of them swept onto the dozens of platforms that hung like balconies above the main deck.

The Visitor combatants immediately in front of them along the south side were quickly overwhelmed. Some Visitors were blasted off of the higher platforms, falling to their death on the main deck. Visitor Patrollers and technicians on the north side of the hangar, however, had the benefit of better cover and the wide chasm of the hangar bay itself provided a natural no-man's-land between themselves and the Resistance fighters.

It became a furious firefight with both sides taking heavy casualties. Pulses of burning electricity flashed back and forth leaving their thin smoke trails across the hangar, triggering minor explosions. Flurries of sparks showered down from metal catwalks that were chipped away by the volatile pulse hits. The smell of charred flesh became pervasive.

When one freed person near Julie was hit and fell, she saw a balding, middle-aged man pick up the weapon to carry on the fight. Sidney Stein was focused on the mission. Julie saw from his determined expression he was proud to be part of it.

Julie shouted down to where Margarita and Nathan were on the front line still trying to liberate Emma and Mark, "We need to get to Centcom!"

Margarita yelled back through the gunfire and the shouts of the battle, "Go! We'll be right behind you!"

Julie beckoned to Street-C, Ysabel, and others of the liberated to follow her. They skirted along behind a tanker shuttle toward the nearest transport tube while Nathan and Margarita exchanged more pulse fire with the Patrollers holding the mayor and Emma.

THE RUSTY RED PLANET MARS, NAMED FOR THE ROMAN GOD OF WAR, stood as an imposing sentinel against the starry blackness and silence of space. Its two moons Deimos and Phobos, meaning Fear and Panic, had been named for the two children of Mars who drove his deadly chariot into battle. The smaller of the two gray moons was Phobos, only seventeen miles across. It zipped around its parent planet three times a day at a breakneck pace. But the Zedti fleet flashed past Mars at a far more astonishing speed, inbound toward the Earth.

On the bridge of the Zedti Flagship, the lieutenant spoke calmly to his Executive Officer, "Target acquisition at eighty percent. We are closing on the Earth."

The Executive Officer stared through her view port toward the tiny dot of blue and green amid the distant stars. She turned around toward her command staff on the bridge of the great warship. They all gave her their rapt attention. She knew that her image was also being seen throughout all the ships across the entire Zedti fleet. She raised her hands before her and interlaced her fingers tightly. All of her comrades joined the ritual and did likewise. Then with a tone of profound respect she said in a strong voice, "Long live Ayden, Kayta, and Bryke."

The other Zedti spoke as one, for indeed they knew they were, "*Long live Ayden, Kayta, and Bryke.*"

The Executive Officer looked into the eyes of her comrades, then finally at her lieutenant. "Commence firing."

She turned to look back out her view port. From her Flagship and several of the other massive warships in the fleet came huge, explosive bursts of Zedti weapons fire, which flared outward into the darkness toward the distant planet Earth.

33

MARY ELGIN EMERGED FROM HER RUN-DOWN TENEMENT BUILDING and joined the tumultuous crowd on the ghetto street. Scientist families were sweeping along like an unstoppable floodtide, overwhelming the Patroller guards by their sheer numbers, toppling the Visitor checkpoints, shutting down the laser fence that had enclosed their neighborhood. They were spilling out of internment into the open streets beyond their former confinement.

Mary moved along with them nervously. But hearing the triumphant shouts of so many others around her, she slowly gained strength as though awakening from a dark and distressing dream. She wasn't even aware that she was clutching something tightly in her hands.

IN HANGAR BAY TWENTY-TWO THE FIREFIGHT BETWEEN THE LIBERated people and the Visitors was still raging. Emma and Mark were lying on the floor, at the very edge of the massive hangar hatch, which was yawning open to the sky outside. They had taken what cover they could behind one of their fallen Patroller guards. Another Patroller still had one hand on Emma as he fired pulse after electrical pulse at Margarita and Nathan. Then Margarita took careful aim to avoid Emma and shot a pulse burst that caught the Patroller full in the chest, blasting him backward. But still he hung on to Emma, dragging her with him as he fell out of the open hatch. As they slid out, Emma's fingertips barely grasped the very lip of the flight deck, but the guard fell away screaming and flailing madly through the air toward the buildings of San Francisco four thousand feet below.

Emma was terrified, dangling in the void above the city. She cried out to Mark who had scrambled to the edge above her. He grabbed her free hand, but she was slipping.

Margarita leaped up from beside Nathan and ran toward them, unmindful of the gunfire tracing through the smoky air around her. Nathan gave her covering fire as Margarita slid in close beside Mark and grasped Emma's other hand. She and Mark struggled to pull Emma up. They had gotten her almost halfway when Mark was suddenly blown backward by a pulse burst that came unexpectedly from the sky outside. Margarita was left holding Emma's full weight, and now they both were slipping. The straining redhead saw that the shot had come from a wounded fighter craft that was slowly approaching the bay.

In the smoky cockpit of the fighter, Gina lined up Margarita and Emma in her sights and was about to deliver the coup de grâce when Nathan was suddenly beside Margarita, glaring and aiming his pulse rifle at Gina, "How 'bout *not*!"

He fired a burst that shattered Gina's windshield and literally took her face off. The bloodied reptile roared bestially as her fighter spun wildly out of control. It slammed against the outside of the Flagship and disintegrated, carrying the Wing Commander to a fiery death.

On the very edge of the hangar deck Nathan ignored the burning pain from his broken arm and helped Margarita pull Emma back aboard. Emma collapsed between them, gasping, "Thank you, thank you."

Nathan grinned at her. "Our pleasure," and he and Margarita shared a prideful glance. But they knew it wasn't over.

"Centcom," stated the redhead.

Nathan shrugged. "Why not, as long as we're here."

They got to their feet and dashed through the cross fire of the battlefield on the main deck while Emma crawled to help Mark who lay nearby, stunned but breathing. Margarita and Nathan were just reaching a transporter tube when they saw that more of the newly freed people were now swarming into the hangar in force. The battle was turning in their favor.

FROM THE DARKNESS OF SPACE IN THE DIRECTION OF MARS THE IN-coming Zedti fire was rocketing toward the Earth's surface.

In the confusion of transmissions and the tumult caused by

the swarming liberated people onboard, many of the Visitor Motherships had not processed the warnings of impending attack nor taken defensive action. The Mothership over the deep waters of the Japan Trench just east of Tokyo was one of them. It was still drawing up a half-mile-wide column of water when the first Zedti burst flashed down from the night sky and impacted on it. A chain reaction of explosions ruptured the huge curved hull as the Mothership blew apart, killing everyone aboard, Visitor and human alike.

It was also night over the Indian Ocean where a Mothership took a series of hits. Then a blinding thermonuclear blast momentarily whited out the scene, sending a gigantic tsunami shock wave rocketing out from Ground Zero across the ocean's surface. Armageddon was beginning.

Seen from space, several of the thermobaric explosions ignited thousand-square-mile sections of the Earth's atmosphere. And still more incoming Zedti fire was rocketing toward the Earth's surface.

One of the Motherships had moved inland and was over the ancient city of Athens when it received several smaller blasts, then a direct thermonuclear hit. The atomic shock wave tumbled the columns of the Parthenon.

A Zedti burst flashed down toward Northern California and ricocheted off the quavering defense shield bubble surrounding the Visitor Flagship. Immediately afterward, a second huge burst partially penetrated the weakened shield and collided with the sixteen-mile-wide hull.

In the Flagship Centcom Jeremy, the Leader, and her entourage felt the huge ship shudder under the mighty impact. Lights went out. Gases vented from ruptured pipes within the walls. Red emergency lights flickered on and off.

Jeremy grasped the Leader's arm and whispered, "I have an escape shuttle waiting, Excellency."

A moment later they rounded a corner in a darkened upper-level corridor to face Julie, Street-C, and their Resistance compatriots. Both groups stopped and trained guns on each other.

From behind the shoulders of her Patroller guards the Leader spoke imperiously to Julie, *"You will let us pass."*

Julie simply stared at her. "Oh, I don't think so."

Fingers tightened on triggers just as Margarita, Nathan, and Willy, weapons at the ready, silently arrived behind Jeremy's group and Nathan announced their presence, "Uh, guys?"

Harmy saw the Visitor Patrollers swinging their weapons to fire and she reacted instinctively to save Willy. She shot her pulse rifle, missing her targets but blasting the ceiling above the Leader's contingent. It collapsed in a whirlwind of dust, smoke, and sparks as return gunfire from a few Patrollers flashed through the hazy darkness.

But Julie's team leaped in along with Margarita and Nathan, taking down the disoriented, choking Visitors. The sharp beams of the Resistance teams' flashlights carved through the smoky, dusty dark. Willy rushed to Harmy who was lying facedown.

As they got their bearings Ysabel shined her light and looked around, "Jeremy and the Leader!"

Julie couldn't see them either. "Where'd they go?"

"We're on it!" Nathan shouted and headed one way through the darkness with some of the freedom fighters.

Margarita simultaneously said, "They're going nowhere!" as she and some compatriots hurried in the other direction.

"Julie, help!" Willy was fearfully supporting his wife's head. Harmy's strawberry blond hair had flowing blood in it.

ANOTHER POWERFUL ZEDTI BURST PIERCED THE DEFENSE SHIELD AND the Flagship took a second very severe hit. In the dark bowels of the ship Shawn was knocked down as a bulkhead near him exploded and flammable gases vented. A Visitor engulfed in flames staggered out screaming in hysteria.

The burning Visitor fell to the floor rolling and writhing in pain as the flames increased. Shawn ignored him, got to his feet, and turned, only to find Diana's pulse gun in his face. Her false human skin was hanging in hideous shreds. One of her eyes still looked human, but the other showed its yellow vertical pupil as she glared at him. "Traitor."

"Wait!" Shawn shouted. "I did it to *save* you! There was no other way! I was planning to kill your guard so we could escape together—but I lost you!"

"Yes," Diana said with a horrifying smile, "you certainly have." She rammed the gun under Shawn's chin. He knew that this was the end.

"Commandant!" He blurted, "I can save us both!"

Diana stared fiercely at him.

IN HANGAR BAY TWENTY-TWO, THE VISITOR PATROLLERS AND technicians had surrendered to the freed people who were now guarding them. Everyone felt the strong, fearful quake from another Zedti burst. Then into the smoky hangar bay flew a charred airbike with Ted at the controls. The clothes he and Ayden wore were torn and smoking. Their faces and hands were smudged, bloodied, and burned. Ted, utterly exhausted, landed the airbike in the dark hangar as they heard Donovan calling out hoarsely to them, "Ayden! Ayden!" Mike was struggling out onto the hangar deck, literally on his last legs, bearing the still-unconscious Kayta. "We've won!" Mike collapsed onto his knees in front of Ayden and held out Kayta's radio. "For God's sake, stop your fleet!"

Ayden's expression told Mike that it might be too late, but the Zedti commander grabbed Kayta's radio.

In the dark upper passages, the Visitor Patrollers and command level aides were being taken under guard by Julie's people. Willy and Julie were attending to Harmy's wounds. Willy had ripped material from the uniform of a dead Patroller and

Julie was wrapping Harmy's head tightly, while consoling Willy, "Head wounds always look awful, but I think she'll be okay." Then as Julie felt the great ship quake and creak from the massive stress of yet another impact of Zedti firepower, she added, "Hopefully."

The red emergency lights flickered and more chunks of ceiling fell as Nathan returned from his search for the Leader with only frustration. "Nada. Can't find the bitch."

They heard another voice, "Excuse me, ma'am?" Julie trained her flashlight in the direction from which it came and saw that Jon had joined them. The young half-breed pointed carefully toward a custodial closet. Margarita returned just as Street-C and Ysabel aimed their weapons and Julie slowly opened the hatch. Their flashlight beams played across fiery yellow eyes and reptilian scales showing through peeled away human skin.

It was Jeremy and the Leader. She drew herself up grandly and whispered, "Get me away. I'll give you whatever you want."

Julie stared gravely at the Leader for a very long moment. "All right," Julie finally said. "Give us back the last twenty years."

Margarita came to her mentor's side. "And give us back all of our dead friends."

THE ZEDTI FLEET WAS NEARING EARTH'S MOON AND ABOUT TO launch the final horrific blitz that would demolish the Visitor Armada and entirely desolate the Earth when Ayden's message reached them.

The Executive Officer cried out loudly, "Cease fire! Cease fire! Emergency stop!"

"Cease fire!" The lieutenant transmitted to the full fleet, "All stop! All stop!"

The fleet emerged from its stealth mode and came into full view against the starry blackness. The running lights on the strangely shaped warships flashed from red through orange to the standby color yellow.

Inside the dark, cavernous bridge of the Zedti Flagship the stately Executive Officer exchanged a long look of quiet relief with her lieutenant.

ON THE STREETS OF SAN FRANCISCO MARY ELGIN WAS STILL WALKING slowly, as if in a dream, amid the shouting and tumult around her. She turned a corner and saw several hundred people encircling the black Visitor captain, his Patrollers, and a few still-loyal Teammates including Danny Stein's sister Debra. But the oppressors realized that they were outnumbered by the citizens, by San Francisco police officers, and by hundreds of former Teammates no longer obligated to the Visitors. The Patrol captain held up his hands in surrender. Debra Stein was the last to throw down her weapon. She did so bitterly.

Standing up the street from them, Mary beheld the scene with silent wonder. Then she realized something was in her hand. She looked down at Charlotte's diary. She rubbed her thumb softly over its surface and drew a long, deep breath, thinking of her daughter's words, of all the blank pages yet to be written upon, of all the possibilities. Mary also became aware that the sun was shining brightly onto her face. She closed her eyes and in fond memory of her daughter she turned her face fully toward the sun, absorbing its comforting warmth.

IN THE FLAGSHIP CENTCOM SEVERAL HOURS LATER, JULIE AND MANY of the prime Resistance team listened with profound satisfaction as reports in many languages flooded in from everywhere. Lee had been doing her best to keep up with the bulletins and she distilled it for them, "The Rebellion has succeeded all around the world." A cheer came from those nearby. Then her voice grew more somber. "But the news is not all good, five Motherships crashed during the takeovers and thirteen were destroyed by the Zedti attack."

Julie and the others absorbed the difficult information with downcast eyes, internalizing their grief as they thought about all the innocent human souls who had been lost. Then Lee continued encouragingly, "But all the other vessels have been commandeered by human leaders, who have established communication with us. Pockets of Visitors along with die-hard Teammates are still fighting in some locations on the ground. Others have gone into hiding. Many fighter craft and shuttles are unaccounted for."

"So we may be facing insurgency for a while," Julie sighed.

Ysabel sloughed it off, "Small potatoes, boss. We've won the big one." She clapped Julie on the shoulder.

"Yes"—Lee smiled—"and many Visitors claim to welcome the overthrow of the Leader, Diana, and Jeremy." Lee looked at them all with thankful eyes. "I know I certainly do."

Margarita entered the Centcom and called to Julie, "We're ready down in the hangar bay."

On the main flight deck of Hangar Bay Twenty-two vid cameras scanned the Leader, Jeremy, Paul, their High Command, and a few hundred Visitor POWs who were under close guard, surrounded by several thousand liberated people. Mike Donovan was leaning on a maintenance console, rubbing his aching knees and looking over the Visitor prisoners. Kayta had recovered consciousness and was lying on a low transport container while Ayden checked her injury. Martin came up to Mike. "Still no Diana."

"Don't worry." Donovan was resolved. "I'll find her."

Julie and Margarita appeared from the transporter tube. They paused beside stretcher that held the San Francisco mayor. His chest was badly bloodied and burned from his pulse wound. Emma was beside him, holding his hand as medics from among the liberated people attended to him. When Emma saw the inquiring looks from Julie and Margarita she nodded with a positive expression that told them Mark would survive.

The Secretary-General, very weak from the ordeal, pressed his wife's hand and then walked with Margarita and Julie to the center of the hangar. The scene was being broadcast by Lee to televisions and wall screens worldwide. It was being witnessed by the great majority of the planet's people and being simultaneously auto-translated into multiple languages.

"My fellow citizens of Earth," Secretary Mendez began, "a great storm has passed. Unfortunately, it's taken much of my strength with it. So I have asked my Resistance compatriot Juliet Parish and her comrades to speak on my behalf."

Julie stepped to the microphones. "Thank you, Mr. Secretary-General . . . and also for the great personal courage you have displayed over so many years." There was spontaneous applause for Mendez from all the humans in the gathering as well as from Martin, Willy, Jon, and other Resistance allies. Then Julie continued. "I've been privileged to help lead the organized Resistance against the Visitors which has finally brought us all to this amazing day." People on one of the upper platforms began a cheer for Julie and her compatriots that quickly became a roar of approval from all corners of the great hangar. Julie accepted the accolade with humility, "Thank you. From all of us," then she continued with the business at hand. "We've been in contact with all of the Motherships. They are now under the control of our fellow humans who had formerly been imprisoned aboard them. We have requested those men and women who had been elected to local or national leadership prior to the Visitor occupation to please identify themselves. We naturally want their help and counsel in the days to come, but of course they will have to acclimate to the many changes that have taken place on Earth during their imprisonment. We urge that new democratic elections take place in individual countries as quickly and efficiently as possible. Obviously there is massive reorganization to be done. Our hope is that we, the people of Earth, having finally beaten back the alien

menace which threatened to destroy us all, can now work together for the good of our planet."

Margarita picked up the story, "All Visitors and their human
collaborators will be held under arrest until their loyalty can be
positively verified by members of the Resistance or reliable witnesses. Visitor prisoners will be placed inside the stasis capsules
and kept under close guard." She looked toward the shredded
faces of Jeremy and the Leader. "The Visitor Leader and her
High Command will face war crimes trials before the International Court in The Hague."

"Our most critical concerns," Julie continued, "are retrieving
our water—and most importantly—our *people* who've already
been taken away to the Visitor planet. Mike Donovan will supervise that effort." She looked fondly toward Mike and invited him
to explain.

"We'll hold all Visitor troops as hostages," Mike said. "Our
longtime ally Martin will monitor the return of Visitor POWs but
only *after* our people and our water have been brought safely
back to Earth."

Harmy was standing nearby. Her head wound had been bandaged. Her battle-scarred son Ted helped support her on one
side and her husband Willy on the other. Harmy was troubled
and privately whispered to Willy, "Will you be going home?"

Willy held her closer. "You two *are* my home."

Nathan addressed the gathering and the worldwide audience.
"We feel that good and loyal Visitor friends, like Willy there,
should be allowed to remain on Earth if they choose and become
part of our new society."

Street-C muttered to Ysabel, "Long as the suckers prove
themselves to me one at a time."

AT THE CHEMICAL FACTORY A WALL SCREEN WAS CARRYING THE
scene from the Flagship. J. D. Oliver, sporting a slight film of
nervous perspiration, stood among his employees who were

watching. He gestured toward the screen with his pulpy hand and boasted to some workers. "You know I was with the Resistance from the beginning. I've been working *secretly* with them the whole time." He smiled proudly until he noticed that Charles Elgin and Gary were striding purposefully toward him. Similar scenes were taking place from Paris to Buenos Aires to Osaka. Collaborators everywhere were finally being brought to justice.

IN THE HANGAR BAY, NATHAN CONTINUED. "WE'LL KEEP THE MAJORity of their Motherships as defense against the Visitors ever 'visiting' again."

"And," Margarita elaborated, "as operational platforms for restoring the Earth."

Mike brought forward the Zedti commander and the willowy blonde with the violet eyes. "Contrary to the Visitor propaganda you heard, the Zedti are not an enemy to us. They are our powerful allies. They were not preparing an assault against the Earth, but merely to defend their own race and their planet from attack by the Visitors." He put his hand on Kayta's shoulder. "This is Kayta, a wonderful new friend, and Ayden, the Zedti commander. They both risked their lives repeatedly to save us. It was Ayden who called off their fleet and prevented a nuclear holocaust from destroying the Earth."

There was extended applause and cheering for the two Zedti, who merely nodded and accepted the adulation stoically.

As the applause faded, Julie said, "We're pleased that Ayden, representing all the Zedti, agrees with our overall plan."

"Which I do," Ayden confirmed, "in principle."

Julie and many others glanced at him, wondering what exactly that meant.

He understood their unasked question and said, "We feel that the current situation won't be satisfactorily resolved until all Visitor holdouts are rounded up and all human prisoners have been returned. The Zedti fleet will gladly oversee peacekeeping here on Earth during this period of . . . untidiness."

That comment raised several eyebrows among the Resistance leaders. And they weren't alone. Many astute people around the world who were just coming out from beneath twenty years of oppressive occupation by a totalitarian regime were keenly sensitive to any phrases that portended anything of that sort in the future. They listened very carefully as Ayden presented his reasoning, "This oversight is of particular importance since I have learned that several of your countries—France, Russia, Iran, and North Korea—have already *nationalized* the Motherships over their territories."

Margarita sought to quell people's unease. "Which of course causes all of us concern as well, but we're determined to resolve any differences by peaceful, diplomatic means."

Ayden nodded agreement. "That would always be our first choice as well."

Julie recognized how his statement implied that a second choice existed, but she chose to skirt the issue. "We ask assistance from all our friends in the long-suppressed international scientific community. Please come forward immediately and help supervise the restoration of our water and the peaceful uses of Visitor technology."

Then Nathan concluded, "There will be another broadcast tomorrow at this time with further updates." Then he looked to Julie for any final words. As she stepped to the microphone, the serious expression on her careworn face brought absolute silence to the huge hangar bay.

"There is no one on Earth who hasn't been touched by what happened to us over the last twenty years," Julie said. "Many thousands have died, one at a time, in the cause that brought us to this day. And while it's certainly a day for celebration and will be every year from now on, I would hope that we'll always take time to remember the fallen victims and heroes, the loved ones and all those unknown to us who were killed or who sacrificed themselves so that humanity could survive." Julie looked out across the quiet faces and bowed her head. All the men and women in the hangar bay followed her example as did the billions who were watching. Around the entire planet there was a long moment of silent tribute.

Then Julie raised her head and took a breath. "Thank you very much."

Applause began and quickly grew into loud joyous cheers for Julie and the Resistance and Freedom. The happiness and ovations were not in the hangar bay alone, but came also from the billions of individuals watching in cities, towns, and villages across their reborn Earth.

Then came some jeers aimed at the reptilian Visitor Leader and Jeremy who were being led away, their faces and futures in tatters. The two of them were glaring at Julie, Nathan, Margarita, and the Resistance Team with harsh yellow eyes that vowed revenge. Julie turned away from them. Then she realized that Kayta and Mike were looking at her with great sadness. Julie immediately knew from their expressions that something was very wrong.

IN THE OUTER CHAMBER OF THE FLAGSHIP COMPUTER MAINFRAME, Ruby lay at peace. Her eyes were closed and her last wistful smile was still on her bright face. Julie was barely breathing, overcome with emotion, as she knelt slowly beside her adopted daughter. With the back of her fingers Julie touched Ruby's scaly cheek, then stroked her tousled chestnut hair. Kayta came to stand nearby as Mike knelt down beside Julie. He watched as she touched Ruby's little fingers, which still formed the letter that had always been the symbol of Resistance, determination, and ultimate victory. Mike's voice was very soft. "She told me you taught her how we all came from the stars . . . She said she'll be out there among them . . . waiting for you."

Tears dimmed Julie's eyes. She continued to gently stroke the hair of her treasured, incredibly brave, and irreplaceable little girl.

EPILOGUE

THE NEXT DAY WAS BRILLIANTLY SUNNY AS THE HUGE, GLEAMING Visitor Flagship glided out past the Golden Gate Bridge and over the Pacific Desert.

On the command deck in the Flagship Centcom stood the Prime Resistance Team including Mike, Robert Maxwell, Ysabel, and numerous others. Also present were the Secretary-General and his wife. Martin captained the great ship. His Executive Officer was the teenage half-breed genius, Jon. Beside Jon stood his proud human mother, whom he had freed from her tomb along with the grateful millions of others.

"All ahead one-third, Jon," Martin said.

"Ahead one-third, aye, sir." The boy's misshapen mouth twisted into a grand smile as he transmitted the order and glanced at his mother.

Lee was serving as communications officer. "Martin, all Motherships confirm they are ready to begin the operation."

Martin turned to look at Margarita, Julie, Mike, and Nathan, whose arm was in a cast. "Who wants to give the order?"

Margarita deferred to Julie, who thought a moment, then turned to look toward Charles Elgin.

The scientist was surprised and moved. His father stood to one side of him and his wife Mary was on the other. She squeezed Charles's arm with quiet pride and encouragement.

Charles stepped forward, his emotions running so high that he could barely find his voice as he spoke haltingly into the microphone, "On behalf of all my fellow scientists on Earth, and their families, I am exceedingly honored to say: Decompression and release to begin on my mark. Three . . . two . . . one . . . Mark."

On the bottom of the Flagship alarms sounded as an enormous panel slid open. And then the water began to emerge, more and more of it being decompressed within the Flagship and flowing out until it became a huge waterfall pouring down toward the dry scrub beneath.

Around the entire planet, in both the daytime and nighttime hemispheres, Motherships everywhere followed suit. Water cascaded forth into the vast, half-empty oceanic basins. Simultaneously all the church bells of Earth began to ring out.

From some Motherships the water became wind-whipped, quickly developing into massive storms bringing magnificently torrential rainfall. And rainbows. Rainbows were seen everywhere.

On the streets of the planet's cities from Bangladesh to Brooklyn people gloried in the downpour of water. They delighted in the transfusion of lifeblood that had been stolen and was now flowing back to a grateful Mother Earth.

Danny Stein's reunited mother and father, Stella and Sidney, were standing on their front steps in the showering rain with renewed appreciation for their unique world and for each other. Like children everywhere, Danny frolicked gleefully in the soaking rainfall, splashing in the puddles. Then Danny realized that someone was looking at him from down the street. It was Thomas Murakami, whose face was contrite and apologetic. He tentatively raised his hand and gave Danny a hopeful thumbs-up. Danny stared back at him through the falling rain and finally responded with a simple nod.

The water continued to flood forth from the Motherships, returning to churn and froth and replenish the oceans.

On the Embarcadero that evening, Margarita and Nathan stood in the rain among thousands of other celebrating San Franciscans. He and Margarita laughed together in the warm rainfall. Then they looked appreciatively into each other's eyes and finally enjoyed their first kiss.

SEVERAL DAYS LATER THE SKY WAS STILL OVERCAST AS THE KEY members of the Resistance gathered at a hilltop cemetery overlooking San Francisco to honor their fallen comrades.

Ayden and Kayta stood quietly to one side. Their hands were in front of them, their fingers interlaced. They saw Mike slowly approaching up the hill and saw the expression of sorrow clouding his face. Kayta noted particularly his unfocused, vacant, downcast gaze. Ayden inclined his head closer to Kayta, asking quietly, "Is there still no news of Donovan's son?" Kayta's eyes never left Mike as she sadly shook her head.

Willy and Harmy watched their son Ted step slowly forward. He knelt and reverently placed a wreath against a marble headstone upon which was engraved simply, *Bryke*. Ted remained there, his head bowed, his fingers touching the top of the stone.

A light rain began to fall again. Dr. Robert Maxwell and the others in the group looked skyward into it, welcoming the rain as being appropriate to bless the heartfelt memorial service.

Street-C stood beside his adopted mother Ysabel who took Gary's arm on which there was a black mourning band for the loss of his dear Eric. Gary smiled sadly at her. Her warmth comforted his melancholia.

Emma stood with her arm around Mark's waist.

Nathan had his good hand on Margarita's shoulder. She leaned against him as she looked toward Julie with heartache.

Julie stood alone beside another marble grave marker where the name *Ruby Parish* was carved in stone for generations yet unborn to visit and to honor.

Julie felt a man's hand slip gently into her own. Her eyes rose to meet Mike's and she held his poignant gaze. Their feelings of loss, of connection, of affection were beyond words. Mike saw that on a delicate gold chain around her neck Julie was wearing a small golden locket, which he had given her in recent days. Julie had determined it would always be there, close to her heart. Within it she had placed a lock of Ruby's chestnut hair.

As they stood on the hilltop, breathing the rain-freshened air, they slowly became aware of a low rumble that was gradually increasing in intensity. It sounded like thunder at first but it didn't diminish and pass. It grew steadily stronger.

The group looked up at the dark, billowing, cumulonimbus storm clouds that stretched from above them to the horizon and flashed with lightning. Then, slowly appearing through the clouds, came the mountainous Zedti Flagship, being seen by human eyes for the very first time. It was literally filling the sky.

Far larger than a Visitor Mothership, the asymmetrical, organic nature of the Zedti Flagship emphasized the impression that it had been somehow grown or daubed together rather than built. It had an inherently menacing aspect.

The gigantic, fearsome-looking interstellar warship was an overpowering spectacle. Even after all the truly remarkable sights and events humanity had witnessed over the last twenty years, none of the people looking up at it had ever been more awestruck.

After a long moment of astonishment and wonder, Nathan spoke, his voice very low, "Good thing they're on our side, huh?"

Margarita pondered the question as she stared up at it, also speaking quietly, "Yes . . . It certainly is . . ."

The gargantuan, extremely alien Flagship glided slowly toward them. Margarita, Nathan, Emma, Mike, Julie, and the others all studied it carefully.

They were trying to envision the future.

ABOUT THE AUTHOR

Kenneth Johnson is the award-winning writer, director, and producer of numerous television shows, TV movies, and feature films. He is the creator of the original *V* miniseries, and produced such TV series as *The Incredible Hulk, Alien Nation,* and *The Bionic Woman,* and has directed the feature films *Short Circuit 2* and *Steel*. He also cowrote a novel, *An Affair of State,* with David Welch. Johnson is the winner of the prestigious Viewers for Quality Television Award, multiple Saturn Awards, the Sci-Fi Universe Life Achievement Award, and has been nominated for Writers Guild and Mystery Writers of America Awards. He lives in Los Angeles with his wife, Susan.

A newly revised edition of the novel based
on the enormously popular miniseries *V*

V The Original Miniseries

Kenneth Johnson and A. C. Crispin

Kenneth Johnson's Warner Bros. television series
V swept the nation and drew in hundreds of millions
of viewers worldwide. Now, the novel *V* is finally
back in print, with an all-new, never-before-seen
ending, fast-paced action, political intrigue, and
memorable characters.

"Dazzling. *V* is a thought-provoking, sometimes
 shocking drama that keeps the viewer engaged."
    —*Daily News* (New York) on the television miniseries

"Nothing less than a retelling of history—the rise of
 the Nazis done as a cautionary science fiction fable....
 It is by politics and ideology that you will know *V*."
        —*The New York Times* on the television miniseries

In trade paperback November 2008
978-0-7653-2158-9 • 0-7653-2158-0
In hardcover November 2008
978-0-7653-2199-2 • 0-7653-2199-8

TOR®
tor-forge.com